BLOOD AND ORANGES

The Story of Los Angeles

A NOVEL BY

James Oliver Goldsborough

City Point Press

Published by:
City Point Press
P.O. Box 2063
Westport, CT 06880
www.citypointpress.com

Paperback ISBN 978-1-947951-30-3
eBook ISBN 978-1-947951-31-0

Book and cover design by Barbara Aronica-Buck
Map illustration by Georgana Winters
Beach Club photo, page 421, courtesy T. O. McCoye

Manufactured in Canada

To Miss Winters

Complacencies of the peignoir, and late
Coffee and oranges in a sunny chair,
And the green freedom of a cockatoo

—"Sunday Morning" by Wallace Stevens

Part One

CHAPTER 1

It began on an ordinary morning at the rancho, of which there'd been too many lately. Maria served him in the breakfast room before she took the buggy into Salinas. It was Sunday, and she attended church with her Mexican family before returning for work Monday. For Eddie, Sundays were no different. After breakfast he would saddle up and start his rounds. Eva, his mother, took breakfast in bed, though Maria set two places for lunch and dinner during the week. Sundays, Eva stayed upstairs in the sitting room off her bedroom to take tea when Father Ignacio came to pray with her and receive alms for the church. Eddie made the tea and set out the fruit and nut empanadas Maria made every Saturday. Eva didn't go to mass in Salinas anymore.

Eddie Mull was a creature of routine, a routine that started each day with coffee, eggs and toast in the breakfast room looking out on Tesoro's five thousand acres. Summer or winter, the room was filled with bright flowers gathered around the rancho. He was used to taking breakfast alone, which he'd done since his mother's descent into invalidity. He was a sociable person, but running a large rancho five miles from town didn't give him much time for society. His usual company at breakfast was his newspaper, the *Salinas Index*, delivered by bicycle each morning by one of Maria's nephews.

Eddie was twenty-seven years old and still living alone with his mother in the house where he was born. He'd been thinking a lot about that lately.

Normally, he skimmed the newspaper, looking for the usual things that interest farmers and ranchers: produce and animal prices; weather; the latest ships arriving in Monterey and San Francisco, where they were from and what they were carrying. Local miscellany didn't interest him. The *Index* didn't carry much news from the rest of the state, let alone the nation, but that morning an article about the aqueduct being built to Los Angeles caught his attention. The *Index* was not known for its prose, but the reporter held nothing back, gushing on about "an aqueduct to rival the Romans, the greatest engineering feat in California history, transforming the arid plain of Los Angeles into the new Jerusalem."

He read the story, drank some coffee and read it again. He'd heard of the aqueduct but never thought much about it. Water interests every rancher and farmer, but Los Angeles is a long way from Salinas. This time, for some reason, it stuck. He set the paper aside to take up with him that night. Sitting back, he stared out at the ranch for as long as he ever had at breakfast, maybe a full half hour, a long time for a busy man with a big ranch to look after. The aqueduct stayed with him all day, in the barns, in the sugar beet fields, on the range with the cattle, back at the house taking coffee with his Mexican foreman after Celestino returned with his family from church.

I think I should go and have a look, he thought.

After Father Ignacio left, Eddie brought the tea service and plates down and put them in the sink for Maria. Sometimes Eva took soup before retiring, but Father Ignacio remarked that she wasn't feeling good, and when Eddie looked in she said she wasn't hungry. He warmed the dinner of enchiladas and rice

Maria left for him, went over Tesoro accounts for a while, took the Sunday newspaper and headed upstairs, falling asleep reading about the aqueduct.

He was awakened by the clanking of the cow bell Eva kept by her bed, the signal to Maria, who slept at the end of the upstairs hallway. But Maria wasn't there. Eddie couldn't remember hearing the bell before on a Sunday night. He threw on his robe and headed down the hall. The grandfather clock on the landing said one o'clock. In her room, he picked the bell up and set it back on the night table. He didn't like going into her bedroom, never had.

His mother lay on her back, one arm dangling where she'd dropped the bell. Her eyes didn't see him. Like her mother and her mother before, Eva had a bad heart, but out on her horses when she was younger you'd never know a thing was wrong. She'd lived her life as she wanted, always had. Seeing her like this, sickly, frail, covers pulled up to her neck, was bad. Parchment skin and china bones. It was the women's damn Latin blood, not like the Mull men, tough stock bred on that desolate Scottish island. Hearts don't give out on Mull, just hope.

He picked up her arm and felt for a pulse, the faint throbs that tell us we're still alive. He looked closely into eyes that seemed more annoyed than scared. "*Mamá?*" He thought he'd try Spanish, but she didn't respond, just looked out with empty eyes, so maybe it wasn't the heart. If it was, he should get her coughing, so he sat her up and told her to cough, but she didn't. Or wouldn't. Her medicines were on the night table, and he gave her two aspirins, which she managed to get down with his help. He knew he should get her down to the car but waited to see that she didn't cough up the aspirins.

The room was stuffy, unhealthy, and he crossed to open a window, standing there a while looking out into the blackness, thinking what to do. Not a light anywhere. Critters asleep, except maybe coyotes on the prowl. He couldn't have said how long he stood there or why. The descent into frailty would only get worse, Doc Summers said. Eddie hated seeing her like this. She would go on having attacks until decrepitude was all that people remembered of her, not the woman she'd been.

She slipped down in bed, and he propped her up again, so she could see the crucifix. Carry her down or get Tin Lizzie out first? The ride to the hospital past one o'clock on a dark dirt road would not be easy. He'd done it before but never at night. He was vaguely aware he was wasting time, not consciously aware, but aware somewhere. That's what she always said about him: Eddie had six thoughts at once, all contradictory, not at all like Willie, his twin, focused on just one thing: Jesus. She'd always loved Willie more, everyone knew that, loved him almost as much as she loved Jesus.

For twins who shared the same egg, same sex, same genes, how could they be so different? That's what everyone said.

Strange that she couldn't talk. Eva was always talking. No panic, no fear, no pain, though he couldn't be sure of that. Frustration, yes, but also a kind of acceptance as though she'd passed through the pain stage or maybe just didn't give a damn anymore and wanted the whole thing over. He stood watching her, fighting against what he seemed to be doing. Doc Summers said to make sure she stayed awake if it was the heart. But was she? He'd have to call him before they left for the hospital. He would not be happy. First had to find the number.

Doc was waiting in the parking lot when they arrived. He looked in the car, felt for a pulse and shook his head. "You didn't tell me it was anything like this, Eddie." His hard voice cut through the cold night. "Your mother is dead. You didn't let her lie down, did you? Lying down's the worst thing for a heart attack. Get in there and get someone out here with a gurney. I'll take care of Eva. Why the hell did you let her stay out there anyway?"

Doc had known his mother forever, delivered her children. He knew she would never leave the ranch—unless it was this way.

The hospital sign said emergency, but he didn't see any lights and no one was coming out. He rang and rang again. Damn people were probably asleep. Why was he at the hospital anyway if she was dead? The morgue was the place, but wasn't the morgue part of the hospital? He looked back to Doc Summers, who'd laid his mother out in the seat. It had taken too long to phone him. Couldn't find the number at first. They hadn't had a phone out at the ranch that long. He hadn't said much, just that Eva had another attack and it looked different from the others. He was bringing her down.

Back up the hill close to four o'clock. Total silence. They'd been five in this huge house, six counting Maria. And now only him. Sleep impossible. Coffee, then saddle up and head into the hills, wear himself out, mind and body. Find Celestino. Get through the day. Through the week. Tesoro without Eva. Strange feeling, not sadness, more like emptiness. Go back to town to wire Willie in his sordid little church in San Francisco. Telling his sister in Monterey would be easy. Lola never was close to Eva. Willie would cry. Since returning from his church mission in China he'd been down to the rancho a few times— brought little Calvin down to meet his granny. Over sherry and a game of chess, Willie put on his preacher's smile and told his brother not to worry about *Mamá*. As children they'd spoken Spanish. He blessed her, prayed for her.

Eddie sipped his coffee, felt the hot blackness jet into his bloodstream and waited for some hint of the sun coming up over the Gabilans. He felt queer in the silence, his mind jumping from *Mamá* to Doc Summers to the aqueduct, which despite everything still lingered. A snort from the stables broke the silence. Horse having a bad dream. He didn't like riding in the dark. Fall out there in the hills and he'd be joining *Mamá* sooner than intended. Arrangements to be made, everything up to him. Of course.

He supposed they'd blame him, just like Doc Summers had. Maybe he'd been slow, but who's to say? Who's to know? And wasn't it better like this? Wasn't that the point? Wouldn't she say so herself? Better to go fast than sink into total senescence and orneriness. Eva Cullel Herzog Mull, *dueña* of Tesoro, the largest rancho in Monterey County, the woman with enough gold cups to fill the den, best damn horsewoman in Monterey County, maybe the state. She'd have beaten the men, too, if they'd have let her. He'd make damn sure he didn't go like that when his time came.

How could anyone reproach him with anything, anyway? He'd been there with her—the *only one*. The others had gone off to make their lives. Now it was his turn.

◆ ◆ ◆

The will was read the day after the funeral and couldn't have been simpler: Tesoro, the huge Salinas rancho that had been in the family since Grandpa Otto Herzog of Monterey married Isabel Concepción Cullel, daughter of Admiral Jose Maria Cullel, of Barcelona, in the days when California still belonged to Mexico, was left to the Mull twins, Eddie and Willie. Eddie had no problem with that. Despite their differences, the twins had always been close. How could they not be? Lola got the deed to the house in Monterey as well as all the family silver, gold and jewelry and anything she wanted to take from Tesoro except the Spanish walnut chess set that had been the admiral's gift to Grandpa Otto a century ago. Willie took that.

Beyond the physical property there was just the checking account. Wes Samuels at Salinas National long had urged Eddie to get into bonds, trusts, indemnities, the things bankers love, but Eddie was a land man. If there were no other assets, neither was there encumbrance. When Tesoro was sold it would give full return on value, and Eddie had every intention of selling. Willie would argue, but Willie never understood business. Born a few minutes earlier, Eddie had always been the boss. Together they would find something new. He couldn't let his brother go on preaching to bums in a former saloon on Turk Street. He'd been up to see it. Once was enough.

He already knew the buyer. Claus Spreckels was a German who like Grandpa Otto ended up in Monterey and did all right for himself thanks to sugar beets. Spreckels had been trying to buy Tesoro ever since the death of Robert Mull, who'd come west from Pittsburgh in the 1850s looking for gold and found another kind of gold in Eva Herzog and Tesoro. Spreckels pestered Eva for years after Robert was thrown from a horse and landed on his head. She put up with it because she liked the old codger, who might have struck up something more personal if he hadn't had a wife and thirteen children. When Spreckels heard Eva was gone, he sent condolences and came to the funeral, taking Eddie aside privately to commiserate.

He offered stock in his businesses, but Eddie wanted cash. Negotiations dragged on, for both men knew the value of things, but eventually Eddie received $107,650 for the rancho, a fortune. Willie agreed to the sale when Eddie told him Eva's last wish was that he should have a new church, which wasn't true.

They were drinking coffee at the kitchen table after packing up all day. Both men were exhausted. Little Cal, legs dangling, sat at one end of the table, staring from one to the other, still puzzled that two men could look so much alike.

Willie wore a funny look.

"Something bothering you?" asked Eddie.

"Something Doc Summers said at the funeral."

"What did Doc Summers say?"

"Didn't quite catch the meaning—something about you and *Mamá*."

"What did he say?"

"Didn't understand . . ."

Eddie glanced at the boy, whose stare bothered him. Cal had the blue eyes of his dead mother. "What didn't you understand?"

Willie shook his head. "Not important. I think he'd had a few."

They held each other's gaze for a moment.

Willie knew.

No one in the family was too nostalgic about any of it except, surprisingly, little Cal, Willie's motherless son born in China, named after John Calvin, a boy who'd visited Tesoro only twice but regarded it as the only permanent thing in his short and itinerant life. Cal was sent to live with Aunt Lola in Monterey while the brothers prepared to go forth and seek their fortunes. Eddie still thought it would be San Francisco, but the aqueduct was worth a look.

CHAPTER 2

Willie back on Turk, Cal in Monterey, the Spreckels' check deposited at Salinas National, Eddie caught the overnight train to Los Angeles. Arriving at Arcade Depot, he was bustled along the Southern Pacific platform, out across Alameda onto Fifth Street. He'd been to San Francisco, full of opportunities since the earthquake but risky. When would the next one hit? Los Angeles had no bay and half the population of San Francisco, but vacant land in every direction. Suitcase in hand, he set out walking. The crowd carried him down Fifth, people rushing in every direction, trolleys clanging, horses clopping, carriages and motorcars coming at him as he crossed the street.

Exhilarated, stiff from sitting up all night, he stopped a moment to rest. A large, able, self-confident man, rustically imposing, he felt foreign in this Mexican town of stucco and plazas about which he knew nothing except that an aqueduct was on the way. He set down his suitcase and leaned against a building, just one more newcomer, no one paying him any mind. They didn't know he had $107,650 in the bank. Thinking of the money, his mind flashed back to Salinas National Bank. Why, Willie had asked the manager, were they opening a joint account? Wes Samuels, who'd known the Mulls for decades but never before laid eyes on Willie, carefully explained, just as Eddie had told him to do.

Ready to move on and see the city, Eddie picked up his suitcase and suddenly froze. He wasn't sure at first, it was too strange. It wasn't fatigue, wasn't imagination. He wasn't religious like Willie, didn't believe in miracles, omens, things like that. Signs, now signs were another matter. Signs, if you knew how to read them, gave you an edge. Signs and water were a rancher's best friends. Crazy as it was—and he never told anyone—he heard a voice. Leaning against that building on Fifth Street, he heard a voice say, "think of the water, Eddie," heard it as clearly as the clang from the trolley down the street.

He'd come here for a look, yes, but why choose a Mexican town on an empty plain ten miles inland from where it should have been built instead of the beautiful Golden Gate?

"Think of the water, Eddie."

Eddie Mull knew about land and water. In Salinas, two plots of land not five miles apart could be fertile or barren depending on how the water came off the Gabilans. Gold made San Francisco, but the Sierra mines petered out. Water, clear cold water running off the Sierras into the Owens River and now on its way to Los Angeles would never run out. There would be water as long as there was snow, and there would be snow as long as there were mountains. All the mountains had to fear was fire.

He turned around to read the shiny brass plaque on the building chosen as the site for the message: Security Trust and Savings Bank.

Hungry, he crossed to the Alexandria Hotel, bought a newspaper at the cigar stand and eased onto a counter stool in the coffee shop. "Going to change things big-time around here," said the waitress when he asked about the aqueduct that was front-page news that morning in the *Times*. "What can I get you?" Her nametag said Agnes.

He was about to order his usual breakfast when he noticed a great pile of oranges in a basket behind her. Oranges, that's what he thought of when he thought of Los Angeles, orange groves and palm trees, neither of which you could find in Salinas.

"Orange juice, toast and coffee, please."

"Blood oranges."

"How's that?"

"From Pomona. Sweet and sour, just like L.A." Agnes smiled. He smiled back.

She squeezed and poured. The juice was red. "First time here?"

"How'd you know?"

She laughed. "Well, maybe the suitcase gave me a hint. And maybe that the train just came in. I expect you're in land like everyone else coming to town."

Afterward, he sat in the shade of Central Park and read the paper. Already, he felt the city's vitality flowing into him. That waitress thought I was in land, could see I knew land, he said to himself. The newspaper said the aqueduct had traversed Kern County, Antelope Valley and was at the San Gabriel Mountains, most of the two hundred miles to be covered. He bought more newspapers and maps and spent the night at the Alexandria, a fine hotel, they said, good as anything in San Francisco, maybe better since the earthquake. The next day he rented another Tin Lizzie and rattled his way up toward the Mojave Desert, following the maps, sweating through 100-degree temperatures.

He stood on a hill above the town called Mojave and observed what they'd built, followed the caravans south on roads that barely existed toward the place called Lancaster, moving south toward the mountains, standing on hills and watching the action below as a general might observe his divisions. He stopped when he came to towns to check the car and learn whatever people knew about the army of workers oozing its way southward, inch by inch, day by day, mixing concrete, digging trenches, building tunnels and reservoirs, laying pipe, approaching the end of five years of work.

Back in Los Angeles, he searched through records at the

county courthouse. If everyone coming to town was in land, he had to get a jump. Nothing, he noticed, was said about the aqueduct's final destination. Where would it enter Los Angeles? Over the mountains into Pasadena was the obvious route because it was the shortest, and Pasadena was where the people with big lawns lived. But the maps showed a second option, longer but requiring less tunneling. The aqueduct could turn west and skirt most of the San Gabriels at Saugus. That route led not into fertile Pasadena, but into the barren San Fernando Valley.

Why did county records not show where the water entered the city? Even the *Los Angeles Times*, which had bought up Kern County land all along the route of the aqueduct, said nothing about the project's final destination. But they had to know, someone had to know, and to know where the aqueduct entered was to know the future. Already a month in the city, he was hardly wiser than when he arrived. He'd met no one who could tell him what he needed to know. He had $107,650 in the bank and didn't know what to do with it.

Frustrated, tired of endless research, tired even of the grand Alexandria Hotel, he went down to breakfast one morning with no idea what to do next. Maybe it would be San Francisco after all. He bought his paper as usual and took breakfast as usual in the coffee shop, exchanging a few pleasantries with Agnes, who always made sure he got a juicy blood orange from Pomona to start. Afterward, he went out, crossed Fifth and stood where the voice had told him to think of the water.

Security Trust and Savings Bank.

He went in and asked to see the manager. The teller hesitated until he said the magic words: "I have a large deposit to make." An elevator took him to the sixth floor and a corridor took him to the front, overlooking the Alexandria. He'd never been in a bank this size, but was not the least bit intimidated. Something about a big bank account that gives a man confidence, especially in a big bank. He was impressed that a mere bank manager should have such splendid surroundings until he saw the name on the door:

J. F. Sartori, president, Security Trust and Savings

"Mr. Sartori will see you shortly, sir. Do you have a card?"

That's something I'll have to do, he thought.

"None made up yet, Miss, new in town."

"Just write your name and address on this card, please."

If some people are born to the stage, some are born to banking, and Mr. J. F. Sartori was one of them. If Eddie was put off by the name while waiting—Italians are mostly fishermen in the north—a glance at the man dispelled any doubt. Everything about him, from fine tailoring, to manicured hands, to penetrating eyes and a slow, measured way of speaking said: "I am a banker and a very good one." Ramrod straight, with a manly handshake, thinning gray hair, matching brush mustache and as sober a face as you will find on the chancel of any church, Joseph Francis Sartori was someone who made you want to give him your money.

"How can we be of service, Mr. Mull?"

Seated, Eddie explained—explained about Tesoro and Claus Spreckels and the $107,650, everything but the voice he'd heard outside the bank. He explained that he was deciding between San Francisco and Los Angeles as a new home for him and his brother, who was an ordained minister. He thought of saying an ordained *Presbyterian* minister, but it occurred to him that Joseph Francis Sartori probably was not Presbyterian.

"What is *your* line of work, Mr. Mull?"

"Land. I want to develop land."

Sartori pondered that for a moment. "There are certainly

opportunities for land development in San Francisco. Have you been up there since the earthquake?"

"Oh yes. Terrible devastation still."

"Of course, we have our own opportunities here. You've heard about the aqueduct, I'm sure. It's probably what brought you to our city."

Eddie liked the phrase "our city," liked the civic spirit, liked the way they were feeling each other out, liked that in a man. Never rush, take the other man's measure, weigh your comments carefully. It had been the same with Claus Spreckels.

"I sense there are opportunities here, yes sir, but it's hard for a newcomer to get the feel for how things will, you know— turn out. Big risks involved."

With canny, penetrating dark eyes, the banker stared at him for some time. "Certainly," he said at length, "we always want to minimize risk." Silence again, then: "Am I to understand that if you had a better understanding of the land opportunities here that you would be ready to transfer your Salinas bank account in its entirety to us?"

"I think that is very likely, yes, sir."

Sartori put his hands together in front, forming a steeple, looking down through them almost as if praying. It took some time for him to answer.

"I can't say that I have any inside information, Mr. Mull. But I think I can safely tell you that some of this bank's most prominent clients seem to think that great prospects for development are to be found in the San Fernando Valley. We, of course, are here to help them in any way we can."

It was the moment for a smile, but Joe Sartori was not a smiler.

◆ ◆ ◆

With twenty-five thousand others, Eddie Mull was there on the great day, November 5, 1913, the day the sluices were thrown. Watching the huge wave shoot down the mountain bringing its snow water from the peaks of the Sierra Nevadas three hundred miles away, he was dazzled. He saw himself tall on his skis, schussing down that water mountain, spreading out over the land, unstoppable, just like the water. Where there'd been nothing but dry and fallow land before, the city was ready to burst forth and prosper, just as he was. Willie still had his doubts, but Eddie had confidence enough for both of them.

The *Times* ran a front-page editorial the next day:

> Go to the whole length and breadth of the San Fernando Valley these dry days. Shut your eyes and picture this same scene after a big river of water has been spread over every acre, after the whole expanse has been cut up into five-acre, and in some cases one-acre, plots—plots with a pretty cottage on each and with luxuriant fruit trees, shrubs and flowers in all the glory of perfect growth.

The *Times* had always been in on it, part of the San Fernando Land and Water Syndicate that had been buying up huge swaths of the Valley, which back to the Spaniards had been empty and good for nothing. At statehood in 1850, the entire Valley—all two hundred square miles of it—had been given free of charge to a Spaniard, who went bankrupt over the years trying to raise sheep. A half century later, the land and water syndicate had taken over, buying up the best land, inviting others to join in the party.

Neither the *Times* nor the syndicate could ever have imagined how many millions of people would follow the aqueduct to the Valley and spread out over the city. Thanks to the timely death of Eva Mull and with a little help from J. F. Sartori at Security Trust and Savings, Eddie and Willie Mull were there at the beginning.

CHAPTER 3

Mull Gardens was a little farther west in the Valley than Eddie would have liked, but the city's growing trolley system, Pacific Electric, provided the link to downtown. People liked Mull Gardens because the homes were neat and modern and came fully furnished. You got off the train, found a job, maybe in the fledgling movie industry, bought a house and moved right in. Mull homes came with furniture, icebox, stove, everything down to linen and home delivery of milk and ice. Just make the down payment and bring your toothbrush.

Willie wasn't interested in the Valley, which had no churches because it had no people. He preferred to preach downtown, where the sinners were. While Eddie drove the Valley paths looking for the land that would become Mull Gardens, Willie explored the city, finally renting an ex-Baptist church off Wilshire, a former grocery store with a steeple. The owner would have sold, but Eddie refused to cosign for his brother. "A grocery on Wilshire is no better than a saloon on Turk Street," he said. "We can do better."

For Willie, returning from China after Millie's sad death had been traumatic. In San Francisco, he'd refused an assignment to the suburbs and left the Presbyterian Church, which had ordained him. He was an evangelist, a missionary, a healer, someone ready to hit the trails for Jesus, not a suburban preacher. He was also broke. He and little Calvin lived in the rear of a former saloon on Turk Street where the kegs were gone but not the smell. Beer cases covered in faded blue velvet made a preacher's stand for sermons to the street people who dropped by, mostly for coffee and rolls. Mornings he walked Cal up Turk Street to an old woman who ran a crèche. Eddie paid the rent for him.

Willie believed that Millie's death had made him stronger. It seemed a cruel thing to say, so he said it only in his prayers. His young wife had been trained as a nurse, was afraid of nothing and ready to go with him anywhere. When Calvin was born she carried him strapped on her back in the Shanghai fashion. For the Chinese, Willie used everything he knew to spread the word of Jesus, things they didn't teach at the seminary. He brought people to their feet shouting hallelujahs and hosannas, words they didn't understand. He baptized and practiced the laying on of hands and healing. Exotic in their robes and pigtails, baggy pants and hobbled feet, parishioners were able to forget war and misery for a few hours and come to Jesus.

In the fourth year, with xenophobia and revolution sweeping the country, his life fell apart. Calvin caught scarlet fever and nearly died. Millie died in his arms from the cholera. How could he bring Jesus to the Chinese when he was so wretched himself? He found a pretty young amah to care for Calvin. Chun hua moved in with them and into his bed. As civil war reached Shanghai, the church ordered him home. He obtained papers for Chun hua, and they were two days from embarking when her brothers came, pummeling the pastor and taking the sobbing girl. In those terrible days, father and son clung to each other as never before. Not until they were onboard ship and moving down the Whangpoo did Willie believe the nightmare was over.

At first, the former grocery off Wilshire didn't have many clients. Los Angeles was still a city of Protestant transplants used to granite and ivy, cassocks and scripture, things that weren't Willie's style. He called it the Church of the New Gospel and had a glass case built outside to advertise the name. People come to Los Angeles for a new life, so I'll give them a new church, he said. Who wants fire and brimstone in a sunny place like this? People need to be lifted by Jesus' message, not frightened by it.

Word got around. The Reverend Willie Mull had the dark good looks of a movie star, a beautiful, rich voice and was filled with the Holy Spirit. He replaced the Baptists' battered upright with an organ and the gray-haired piano teacher in chignon with a pretty young music student from USC. With doors thrown open Sunday mornings, hosannas and hallelujahs sounded from Beverly Hills downtown to Bunker Hill. Willie called his congregation Soldiers for God, and the first hymn sung before every service was "Onward Christian Soldiers."

He accepted his gift as God-given. In Shanghai he had baptized them, prayed with them, touched and consoled them. He healed them. By the time he reached Los Angeles he'd become an original, blending natural gifts with his own arduous personal journey. He knew what the people wanted before they knew it themselves. He was friendly and informal, though people understood his powers. He called himself Rev. Willie, never William, which was too stuffy, too Presbyterian.

It was the healing that first brought attention from the newspapers. Not all those coming to sunshine city were healthy young people looking to make a new start. Some were sick and some were old and some were lame and when they heard of the little church off Wilshire where you could be born again and healed by a vigorous young preacher whose little boy sat near the pretty pianist every Sunday, they came to see for themselves. When Willie stood over them, touching heads, calling out to Jesus and inviting them to throw away their crutches and walk down the aisle to embrace Jesus, some of them tried and some of them succeeded. The newspapers were skeptical.

So were the mainstream churches.

One of those who was reborn, though in truth he had never been christened, was a man of indeterminate age who showed up one Sunday and never stopped coming, always in the same suit, which needed pressing, the same boots, which needed polishing and the same hat, which needed brushing. When Willie stood on the porch afterward shaking hands, this congregant, bald as a stone and with a great drooping mustache, always said "fine sermon, Reverend," and moved on along. Willie, who sought to know all his Soldiers, found him a curiosity, someone who would have fit in better in his saloon-church on Turk Street than in the leafy suburbs off Wilshire. He would gladly have visited with him, but the man never lingered. Clearly of modest means, he never put anything in the plate.

Willie didn't even know the man's name. It was Eddie who told him: "You're talking about Henry Callender," he said one day, to his brother's great surprise.

◆ ◆ ◆

They said the aqueduct would bring water enough for a city of one million people, and it didn't take long. The trains from the East were full. Soon there was a Ford Model T plant, Goodyear and Firestone tire plants, even an aircraft company called Glenn T. Martin. The new movie industry liked the weather and moved out from New York to the place called Hollywood. Houses went up so fast companies bragged they could build a house, start to finish, in two weeks. The chamber of commerce sent out glitzy brochures around the country luring people to "life in sunshine city." Macadam was laid and a sign hung out reading: "Welcome to L.A.'s Newest Community."

Eddie met Number Seven at a beauty contest in Ocean Park.

A rising real estate figure thanks to Mull Gardens, he was asked to help pick Miss Ocean Park, a contest held each summer on Lick Pier, between Venice and Santa Monica. Fellow judges were men of similar prominence—a lawyer from a famous firm, a Crocker banker, a Pacific Electric executive, a Doheny oil man, a vice president of Coulter's Department Store.

He couldn't say for sure why he settled on Number Seven. She wasn't the prettiest, but was a bountiful girl with a sassy look that appealed to him. She had an easy way of talking to the mayor of Santa Monica, the host, that contrasted with the stylized method of girls trying too hard to be discovered. Incomprehensibly to him, Number Seven didn't even make the top three. The winners were whisked away to pose while the also-rans were left alone under the umbrellas by the lemonade and cotton candy stands.

It wasn't that Eddie had no experience with women. He'd gotten away from Tesoro sometimes and had his experiences. As a fishing town, Monterey was full of professionals who knew how to keep sailors happy, but they were not for Eddie. It also had its semipros, girls eking out livings working the shops and canneries and not averse to occasional evening activity. Eddie had liked one or two of them over the years, but it was his bad luck never to find a Monterey girl he wanted to marry.

At Ocean Park, the girls who weren't whisked away stood around drinking lemonade, putting on brave faces and looking slightly embarrassed in high heels and tight bathing suits. Slowly they drifted off—all but Number Seven, who stood alone, smoking a cigarette. Eddie stood off a while watching her, thinking she looked a little sad. She must have clothes somewhere, he thought. Not that she would necessarily want them in the heat, but she couldn't go far from the beach in heels and a bathing suit. Maybe she needed a lift.

"Sorry, I thought you were the best," he said, coming up and ordering two lemonades. "I voted for you." Her smooth skin glistened in the heat, and he was aroused.

"You're one of the judges," she said, putting out her cigarette on the boardwalk. "Should we be talking?"

"The contest is over. I'm Eddie Mull."

"Thank you for your vote. The others didn't seem to agree."

He laughed. "They wore sunglasses. Maybe they couldn't see well."

"Did you try to persuade them?"

"Well, it's not like a jury. We didn't consult. Frankly, I wondered what some of those girls were doing in a beauty contest."

She frowned. She was a wholesome-looking girl with thick brownish hair, feminine without glamor, the healthiest-looking girl in the contest he thought, something earthy that appealed to a Salinas ranch boy like him. The lemonades came.

"Say, how do you think that makes me feel?"

"Oh, I didn't mean it like that."

"How did you mean it?"

"I meant it as a compliment. That's why I voted for you. Say, don't you have clothes somewhere. Maybe I can give you a ride. What's your name, anyway, Number Seven?"

She didn't answer right away. She has something, Eddie thought, though clearly is wary. Maybe I shouldn't have mentioned clothes.

"Why do you want to know?"

"Shouldn't I know the name of the girl I voted for?"

"Okay, I'm Cornelia, Nelly for short. Nelly Sinclair. Now you know."

"Where you from?'

"Iowa, like I told the mayor. Couldn't stand the cold."

"You've come to the right place."

"Haven't we all."

"How'd you happen to get in the contest?"

"Just came down."

"You got a job?"

"Say, are all the judges this curious?"

"Is it a crime?"

"I'm at Woolworth's."

"What do you do at Woolworth's?"

"*What do I do*? What does everybody do at Woolworth's? I'm in sales, ladies' stockings to be specific."

"How would you like to work for me?"

CHAPTER 4

Water and sunshine weren't the only things bringing people to Los Angeles. The second California gold rush began in Los Angeles, and this time the gold was black. La Brea tar pits, oozing tar and dinosaur bones along the place one day to be called Wilshire Boulevard, were a clear sign oil was down there somewhere. A failed gold prospector named Ed Doheny who'd come to town before the water was not the first person to drive a stake in the ground near Rancho La Brea, but he was the first to get down past the tar to the less viscous stuff that shot a hundred feet into the air and got a few streets named after him.

Like Ed Doheny, H. H. Callender, a Scot, had worked his way west digging here and there for this and that, ending up as far west as he could go, planting his spade one more time and coming up dry. Eddie met him at another Ocean Park beauty contest on Lick Pier, on another hot summer Saturday. He was a married man by now with a second baby on the way and didn't hang around after the contests anymore chatting with contestants. Callender approached him as he left the pier, said he had a business proposition.

Eddie Mull had established a reputation, was often approached by people he didn't know and often listened. Some of the listening was a waste of time, someone claiming inside information on this or that, land or water or zoning, real estate specialties. Eddie learned to listen just long enough to get the gist and get away without being rude if there was nothing in it. This time, for some reason, he lingered, something in the way the man talked, something honest in the pale blue eyes and grizzled face that made an impression. And it didn't hurt that he had a good Scotch-Irish name like Callender. Eddie invited him for a cup of coffee.

They strolled the strand, pushing through the weekend crowd and settling in the shade of a shop that looked out on the beach. Eyeing a pyramid of oranges, Eddie ordered coffee and oranges for two. Callender looked like he could use some vitamins. In the distance, heads bobbed and surfers rode the breakers. Heatwaves wiggled up from sand that was mostly a blanket of towels and umbrellas. In front of them, along the strand, flâneurs passed, men in boaters, women in sunhats, children pulling on saltwater taffy and doughy pretzels. From next door came the sound of baseballs striking metal bottles and farther down sharp pings from a shooting gallery. Eddie was enjoying himself, pleased he'd not rushed back to the office, content to slow down for a few minutes and savor his very successful life. Lick Pier had been good to him before, why not give it another chance. He glanced at his odd-looking coffee companion and waited for the pitch. If he could have seen into the future he might not have waited, but that is not certain. In any case, no voice spoke to him.

"Yes sir, Mr. Mull," the man said when their order arrived, "I believe I'm on to something. Not for the first time either."

Eddie peeled his orange, sipped his coffee, which had almost no taste, and listened to Callender's stories of digging for silver in Nevada, copper in Arizona and gold in Mexico. For all his digging, he looked like a man who had washed out. Watching him lick his knife, Eddie figured he'd misjudged the man. He was ready to leave when Callender finally came to the point. It involved digging for oil in a place called Venice-by-the-Sea. He went on in some detail. Eddie didn't leave.

"It is guaranteed."

There wasn't much guaranteed in Los Angeles, but Eddie had sold some lots in Venice-by-the-Sea and knew something about the place, the brainchild of an easterner named Abbot Kinney who'd come west for his health and sought to do something with money he'd inherited, which came from tobacco, which was the cause of his health problems, though he didn't know it. He purchased a large tract south of Ocean Park and began building the New Venice, as he called it, complete with imitations right down to canals, arched footbridges, hanging palazzi and gondolas imported from Italy. For gondoliers, he used Mexicans.

Then he died.

"We buy Kinney's land, bring in the oil and we'll be rich as Doheny."

"How do you know about any of this?"

"Worked for Kinney."

"Who else knows?"

"No one for sure—only me. Now you."

On the pier the Ferris wheel turned and the roller-coaster swooshed. Callender had taken off his faded Stetson, and his bald head shone in the light. Droplets of sweat glistened in his luxurious black mustache. Eddie found himself pulled in opposing directions. The man was preposterous, his stories belied by his appearance. Yet who's to say?

"Why me?" Eddie asked.

"Your name's Mull, right? I go to the Reverend Willie's church. I am a Soldier for God. You're his brother."

That wasn't good enough. "Why not a bank?"

"No collateral but my good name."

"And you think there's oil down there?"

"Just like Long Beach," he said, blue eyes bright. "Signal

Hill—sand, clay, bitumen, oil, it all adds up. And Santa Fe Springs, you heard about that strike, I reckon."

"You know your stuff, eh?"

"Know oil soil when I see it."

"How come nobody else does?"

"Couldn't answer that."

"Land's for sale?"

"Kinney's estate."

"Asking?"

"Negotiable, not many people looking for mucky canals."

Eddie was sizing up his man. Was this another sign, another tip? He could never explain what had happened outside Joe Sartori's bank, didn't even try, but it had changed his life. He'd thought of telling Willie, but never did. Willie would have gotten biblical, and Eddie hated that. He'd gotten a sign and played it. The trick was always in deciding if the sign was any good. That's where instinct came in.

"You bring up oil there," he said, "and you turn the canals to goo. All those pretty houses will be sticky black in a week. That means lawsuits."

"Nope, creative destruction," said Callender. "Happens every day down here. Gold destroyed the Sierra Mountains, copper destroyed the Arizona desert, L.A. destroyed Owens Valley, automobiles destroying the streetcars. Think about it. At Armageddon everything down here gets destroyed."

"Down here?"

"You know what I mean. Make way for the Second Coming, the New Jerusalem. Don't you listen to your brother?"

One of Willie's Soldiers all right, Eddie thought—blunt, uneducated, mud on his boots (maybe oil), knows his Bible, ageless, probably younger than he looks, old hat, frayed suit probably the only one he owns. Strange eyes.

"You sure you haven't talked to anyone else?"

"You're the first. Seen those Mull real estate signs of yours all over town. Then, as I said, knowing you're your brother's brother, a holy man, means a lot to me. Had to find someone I could trust seeing as how I found the place but need the stake."

"What's to keep me from buying it on my own?"

"Like I said, your name's Mull. Like your brother. Trust you just like I trust him. Family thing, ain't it?

Eddie thought about that. He put a dollar down, watched the waiter take it and leave a few coins in change. He picked up the coins.

"We strike, we go fifty-fifty," said Callender.

Eddie chuckled, amused to be dividing up invisible profits. "Why not? Say, what do people call you?"

"I'm called Henry."

"Henry, let's take a drive."

"One other thing," said Callender, standing. "Let me tell you what I'm going to do with the money."

"Already spending it, eh?"

"I'm going to build your brother the biggest church this town ever saw—a temple rising so far into the sky you can see it in the next county. Willie Mull is the voice of God in this godless place, and I want his message to reach every sinner who breathes the glorious air of this great city."

Eddie had his man pegged from the start, though Callender didn't. He purchased five square miles of empty beaches and marshes from the Kinney estate just south of the canals, between Venice and the place called Playa del Rey, a large investment financed following a visit to Security Trust. Eddie sometimes sat next to Joe Sartori at L.A. Chamber of Commerce meetings. They were pals.

They brought in drillers to put down one test well after

another. They spent days watching the hammers bang deeper into the sand, one thousand feet, two thousand feet, nothing coming up but salty sand and tar. At two thousand feet, Eddie was ready to call it off. There was always a risk of an empty hole. The more you drill, the more you lose. Callender was always there, and the little man had begun to annoy him, marching around in his mucky boots like he owned the place, dowsing the land with his stick like a mystic with his wand. Eddie was sick of the whole thing, sore at himself for taking advice from a crackpot, sore at himself for having agreed to go fifty-fifty, though it looked like that wasn't going to matter.

"Give it a half mile," said Callender, catching the drift.

"Easy for you to say," said Eddie, "You don't pay the crews."

"Have to go a half mile—you don't, someone else will."

Why not? At two thousand, they were almost there.

When Venice #1 blew, oil shot ten stories into the sky, higher they said than Doheny's spout at La Brea, covering one square mile of Kinney's canals with gooey spray. It was the same with #2 and #3 and the subsequent wells. Venice wasn't Signal Hill and wasn't Santa Fe Springs, but there was oil a-plenty down there and before long they had fifty derricks pumping and had paid off all the homeowners who wanted to sue but knew that no judge was going to penalize someone for bringing in oil or water—not in Los Angeles. Having slept in a tent on the sand for three weeks, Eddie went home nearly as black as the oil. Up to the day of the blow, he'd been a successful real estate man, rising maybe faster than some others who'd arrived with the water, but not as fast as he wanted.

Oil changed everything for him. It took time to get rich on water: You had to find the land, borrow the money, develop the property and hope you sold enough houses to get back enough to pay the bank and start over again. Oil, on the other hand, was ready cash. It came up as fast as it went out. In the tarry sands of Venice Beach, with a little more help from the good fairy he'd found at Security Trust on Fifth Street, Eddie had what he wanted.

The problem was that Henry Callender wanted it, too.

CHAPTER 5

The Mull girls were born independent. Was it because Mother, who didn't nurse, was so uninspiring and Dad couldn't be bothered, or was it something innate, like the X factor, the genetic alleles that make us unique? Margaret, called Maggie, came first, followed by Elizabeth, called Lizzie, a year later. With two girls to look after, Nelly moved the family from Mull Gardens, which in her opinion was too common, to snappy Bel Air, an elegant new community in the hills above Westwood, built by a rancher, who, like Eddie, had struck oil—his in Santa Fe Springs. Willie moved into a rented bungalow in West Hollywood to be near his church, and Cal joined his aunt, uncle and little cousins in Bel Air rather than share another house with his father, who was rarely home.

Cal was the brother the girls didn't have and wouldn't have, for after Lizzie the doctor said there'd be no more babies. It was a shock, for Nelly thought of herself as the perfect physical specimen, which is why she hadn't nursed. Cal became the son she didn't have and Nelly the mother he didn't have. He was a pleasant and helpful boy, as if something in his unconscious had been touched by the misery he'd seen from his mother's backpack in the dingy alleyways of Shanghai. Willie said that Cal's good nature came from Chun hua, who nursed him (and Willie, too), teaching them something of Chinese endurance and stoicism. Cal was born "in the Tao," Chun hua used to say, an obscure Oriental idea Willie never fully understood.

For a while, Nelly tried to raise her daughters like other little rich girls in Bel Air, dressing them in cute pastel dresses for school and bows and pinafores for dance lessons at the Wilshire Ebell. The girls wouldn't have it. They were aided by Cal, their chief babysitter and confederate. He was in the eighth grade his first year in Bel Air, Maggie and Lizzie starting kindergarten and nursery school. Sometimes he caught the school bus down the hill, but often Nelly drove the three of them down together.

On her own, Lizzie, the younger, might have bent to her mother's schemes, but Maggie pulled her along in her draft. She was a gritty, outdoorsy kind of girl who preferred boys to girls and loved competition. When she was seven they got her a horse, named Dynamite, which they boarded at stables at Playa del Rey. A year later Lizzie got her horse, too. Nelly hated everything about horses—the dust, the smells, the flies, the shit—and soon was employing Cal to chaperone the girls on the trolleys that stopped in Playa del Rey on their way down the coast to Redondo beach. At fifteen, Cal got a driver's permit and new responsibilities as the girls' chauffeur. Nelly was more than happy to turn her car over to him. Riding days conflicted with her bridge days.

For Cal, a nature boy, Playa del Rey was love at first sight. A beachy village at the foot of a long sandy hill overlooking a vast area of marshes and dunes, it was home to every species of waterfowl known to Southern California. He'd take his bicycle along, and while the girls rode horses peddled the twisty hill streets with their view from Point Dume to Catalina Island. On foot he prowled the marshes of Ballona Creek. If he lifted his sights over the wetlands toward Venice, he could see the dozens of derricks Uncle Eddie had sunk into the marshy lands that once were part of Abbot Kinney's dream. He hated the sight and so didn't look.

For his sixteenth birthday, Eddie bought him a red Ford roadster. Twice a week he'd load his bike in the back, the girls in the front and head down Roscomare Road across Sunset to Wilshire and Sepulveda and on west to the stables, on the road soon to be named Culver. He graduated from high school that June and would start at USC in the fall but had two months to explore the city in his new car. It was a summer the cousins would never forget, the summer they spent every day together, free of adults, who were just as happy to be free of them.

The girls loved the roadster. Top down, they would shout over the wind as they motored along the open roads. Maggie was the daredevil, loving speed and urging Cal to go faster, faster, always faster, while Lizzie sat taking everything in and shouting questions to the chauffeur. You could already see the adult in both girls. Maggie could not resist a challenge or a dare. Lizzie would laugh at her sister and go back to making the mental notes she would later write in her diary. She started a diary at age six, and the time would come years later when they were auctioned off. She was as competitive as her sister, but in a different way. Maggie needed to test herself against others and dominate. Lizzie's competition was with herself. The goal was to get down in writing the precise words that represented her precise thoughts, get them down before they flew away forever.

One day Cal decided to head home from the stables through Venice. Normally, he returned the way he'd come—east toward Culver City, north on Centinela, east again on Wilshire or Sunset to Bel Air, sometimes taking detours into the Santa Monica Mountains for excursions through the canyons. He knew about Venice because Eddie never stopped talking about it, explaining how he'd turned the canals built by Abbot Kinney into oil fields because that's the price of progress, creative destruction he called it. Lawsuits brought against Mull Oil had been thrown out by every judge because oil was making everyone in Los Angeles rich, including the judges, including the people whose canal houses now looked out on muck and derricks, people happy to be sharing in the oil bonanza.

He took the bridge northward across Ballona Creek and turned off Pacific Avenue, the main north-south road through Venice to Santa Monica, onto a parallel access road running along the ocean, called, strangely enough, "Speedway." Quickly the bright sunlight was gone, obscured by a forest of gigantic steel trees. They bounced along the potted, tar-splattered asphalt, listening for the crash of breakers but hearing only the sucking of pumps. There were no other cars, no other people. A mile or so along, he stopped by a "no trespassing" sign and glanced at the girls, both strangely quiet. Maggie was squirming. Lizzie had come up on her knees and was turning her head like a camera on a pivot. They got out to walk.

Deep in the spidering shadows as the sun fell to the ocean, they headed through the mucky fields. He tried to keep the car in view—so easy to get lost when everything looked the same. The derricks, some with little cabins attached, were densely packed, almost rubbing against each other. Underfoot, the earth was black, as was what little sand they could see, which once must have been white but now was dark and coated with gobs of tar. Cal felt Lizzie's hand squeeze into his. The sound of pumping drowned out all else, and the smell of oil overpowered any scent of the sea. It puzzled him that each pump, each hole in the ground, would require its own giant steel framework; that the oil lagoon hiding beneath the sand could not be tapped by a single derrick or maybe a few rather than the dozens he saw. Only greed could explain it, the lust to get richer faster.

Why would Uncle Eddie, who already had everything, want more? Yes, oil to keep motors running was necessary, but why here? Why destroy miles of natural beauty, turning the sand black, rendering foul and useless white beach and blue ocean, not to mention the languid lagoons built by Abbot Kinney? Surely there were places to find oil without so much destruction. He felt Lizzie squeeze tighter.

"Hey, you kids!" shouted a man emerging from one of the cabins. "What the hell are you doing in here? Can't you read the signs? Get out!"

Startled, Cal turned to see a hardhat closing in on them. Stifling a desire to shout, "these girls own this land," he pulled Lizzie and turned back toward the car. Suddenly Maggie, quick as a cat, bolted away toward the nearest derrick. She was five rungs up the steel ladder before he reacted, and the hardhat, who'd stopped, began screaming. Maggie was like a spider flying up on its web. The Hardhat clumped toward the derrick but already knew he could never catch her.

"Get her down from there, boy!" he called. Other hardhats emerged from the cabin.

"Maggie, come down," Cal shouted, knowing it was futile. She'd already reached the first metal platform.

The man grabbed him hard by the shoulder. *"Get her down from there!"*

"I'm trying." He pushed the hand away. "Maggie, you know you can do it," he shouted. "It's not worth it! Come back down!"

"Mag . . . gie!" Lizzie was shouting, *"Mag . . . gie!"*

She'd already clamored halfway to the first catwalk, nimble despite her riding boots. The derrick looked to be five stories. Cal knew she would not stop. She never did.

"Better go after her, Bobby," one of the men said.

"I wouldn't do that," said Cal. "She'll come down when she's ready."

"Let's hope she don't come down head first," said a worker.

"Don't worry."

"Call the fire department," said someone.

"The hell with that—I'll call the police," said Bobby, turning back.

He didn't want to do it; didn't want to tell the men that the girls were Eddie Mull's daughters, heiresses of the land they were supposedly trespassing. The girls would hate it and so would he. But the police were a worse option.

"Hold on there," Cal called to Bobby, who seemed in charge. "Let's talk."

With Lizzie leaning in making her mental notes, Cal explained who they were, all of them Mulls. "You go back inside, and I'll get her down. We won't come back. I promise you that. Better that way. Better for everyone."

They listened. They would be blamed as much as the children and had more to lose.

◆ ◆ ◆

"How was riding today?" Nelly asked at dinner.

"Good," said Maggie. "We came home through Venice." She was smiling, and Cal wondered if she was going to blab.

Eddie had mixed Old Fashioneds instead of Manhattans because Nelly liked the sweeter taste, and they'd brought them to the table. "Wanted to see the wells, huh? Might as well get to know them. All that oil will be yours someday."

"If there's any left," said Cal.

Frowning, Eddie stared at the boy. "Long time before those wells run dry."

"I'd like the beach better without them," said Lizzie. "They're ugly."

"Maybe so, little one," said Eddie, "but that car you run around in wouldn't go far without them. And don't forget Uncle Willie's new church. That's going to cost a bundle." He looked at Lizzie. "See all the good things we can do with oil."

"You hadn't mentioned building a church for Willie," said Nelly.

"You're the first to know."

"Can we afford it?"

Eddie laughed. "Not much we can't afford anymore."

The Roscomare Road house was close to the apex of the Bel Air hills, a sprawling single level rancho that looked west over hills and canyons toward the ocean between Santa Monica and Malibu. Eddie owned five acres, which reached to the bottom of the canyon, and he'd fenced it off to keep the critters away. When wire fencing didn't work he replaced it with chain link, which was better but not by much. The critters had been there before the place called Bel Air and had no intention of relocating. Raccoons and skunks were a nuisance but not as much as coyotes, which came up looking for any cats foolish enough to go prowling.

"Dad said Henry Callender was going to pay for the new church, calls it a temple," said Cal, digging into a beef enchilada.

They were five at table for enchiladas and side dishes ordered from Castillo's on Wilshire by Lupe, the housekeeper/cook. They all liked Mexican food, which was growing more popular as newcomers from the East overcame their prejudices. Willie sometimes joined them Thursdays, but phoned earlier to say he had too much to do. The success of the Church of the New Gospel had enabled him to move from the former grocery off Wilshire into a larger, former Lutheran church, on Beverly Boulevard.

"Who is Henry Callender?" asked Nelly.

Cal shot a look at his uncle, surprised he'd never mentioned Callender. "The man who found the oil, who showed Uncle Eddie where to drill."

"That's not the way it was," snapped Eddie.

"Dad said you two are going fifty-fifty, that Callender was going to use his money to finance the temple."

Annoyed, Eddie went to the sideboard to refresh his drink. "Henry Callender doesn't have enough money to buy himself a new suit of clothes."

"Eddie," said Nelly, "who is he? I've never heard that name before."

"One of Willie's crazy Soldiers, that's all. Said there might be oil on the Abbot Kinney land. I drilled and hit. End of story."

Cal was staring at his uncle, trying to square the two stories. "He tells Dad he's going to build a temple with his oil profits and you say he's broke. I don't get it."

"He's goofy," said Eddie, louder now. "Obviously you never met him. A goofy old miner tetched from being out in the sun too long." He glanced at his wife. "Damn good enchiladas, Nell. You need your drink freshened while I'm up?"

"Don't mind if I do."

"Speaking of the oil business," said Eddie, trying to change the subject, "Cal—you decided yet what you're going to study at USC?"

Cal gazed past his uncle, out the window and down toward the canyon. "Not sure yet."

"Business administration, that's the thing. They've opened a new business school down there. Asked me to give a few lectures."

"I didn't know that, honey," said Nelly.

"What they really want is money. I told them to ask at the chamber. They'll have someone. What do you think, Cal—about business school, I mean."

"Maybe."

"There's a place for you in the company when you're ready.

But you gotta know numbers to run a business. I was running your grandma's ranch long before she died. Learned everything I needed to set up down here."

"A place for me in *which* company?"

Eddie laughed. "Any one you want."

Cal knew of at least four: real estate, oil, construction, and bootlegging. He wasn't supposed to know about the fourth, but knew from Nelly, who told him everything. The cases in the garage that said "toxic," were toxic all right. Every kind of liquor, mostly from Canada, was being landed at Tijuana and Rosarito and smuggled up the coast on what was called the "Bootleg Highway." Tecate, east of Tijuana, had built a distillery turning out 175 proof gin, with little of it going to the Mexicans, who preferred tequila.

"Uncle Eddie," said Cal, uncomfortable, "do you owe Henry Callender money?"

Eddie stared hard at his nephew, a boy who wedded the dark good looks of the Mull men to the sandy hair and sunny disposition of his dead mother. Of course, he'd welcomed him into the family: Nelly and the girls loved him, and Willie wasn't much of a father. But he'd begun to annoy his uncle, spending too much time with the girls, influencing them in ways he shouldn't. The sooner he went off to college, the better. Why had he taken them to Venice without a word to anyone, brought Lizzie home criticizing the oil fields? Something strange about the boy. Scarlet fever? He still wore signs of it on his face. Once at dinner they'd heard a scratching at the screen and looked up to see four eyes staring in. Nelly screamed, and Eddie was ready to go for his .22. Cal stood up, strode out through the kitchen and they saw him pick up two raccoons as if they were puppies, not wild critters with teeth and claws and maybe rabies. Dropped them back in the canyon and came back with a story about how the poor things were lost. Crazy.

"Of course, he's entitled to something, and I'm taking care of it. Now can we drop it?"

"I hope it's not fifty-fifty," said Nelly.

"Of course not!"

He finished off his second Old Fashioned. "Look, anyone can walk around saying, I bet there's oil down there. Let's drill. But it takes money to drill and risk coming up dry and going broke. Somebody told Ed Doheny to start digging on Alvarado because stuff was oozing up, but Doheny was the guy who got the loans and took the risks and when the oil came up got rich, not the guy who told him to start digging. That's just the way it is."

"Something not right about that," said Cal.

"The real world, winners and losers."

"Why do there have to be losers?" asked Cal.

"Dammit, Cal, it's the way it is, accept it."

"Eddie," said Nelly, reproach in her voice.

"No, dammit. Creative destruction, it's the way of the world. Winners and losers. Look at this city, look at Los Angeles, entirely built on water that was taken—call a spade a spade— *stolen* from the Owens Valley. They had to die so we could live. Even Willie will tell you there's nothing wrong with that. It's called the lesser evil. Right, Cal?"

"He could sue, couldn't he?" said Cal.

"For God's sake, Cal, drop it!"

CHAPTER 6

For months he'd stewed. Fifty-fifty, that was the deal. He'd been robbed, held up just as surely as if bandits had stopped the stage and walked off with his gold dust. He'd seen a lawyer, who asked to see the contract. Contract, what contract? He'd trusted Eddie because he trusted his brother. He'd gone to Mull Enterprises in Santa Monica and been turned away. He'd phoned and been hung up on. He'd written letters (unpublished) to the newspapers. Eventually, Eddie sent a check for five hundred dollars, finder's fee he called it. As if he could be dismissed like someone who finds your dog. He needed to talk to Willie. Willie would help him.

He'd gone through that five hundred dollars in a month, always lived like that, hardtack and water while prospecting and steak and whiskey when he hit. He'd misjudged his man, and the first time was always the last. He was broke, moved to a fleabag on Vermont Avenue and even went up to Bel Air when he found out where Eddie lived. He took the Pacific Electric trolley out Wilshire and trudged up through Westwood to the gates on Sunset and kept climbing like he used to do in the mountains only in hills of Bel Air the gold wasn't in lodes but in houses and swimming pools and three expensive cars in the garage. He'd stood out like a crow in a dovecote and wasn't a mile up the hill when a cruising guard spotted him and ran him out with the warning that next time he'd run him in for trespassing.

He'd gone to Willie soon after the oil strike, explained that he'd become a rich man and intended to give it away. "The church I will build for you will be the most glorious house of

God west of the Great Salt Lake, and must be superior to the Mormons for they are heretics. Find the site, Reverend. I will provide the money for the Temple of the Angels."

Willie loved the name but was surprised by the offer. Eddie had said nothing about a partner, and when Willie phoned, told him to forget Callender, that he was taking care of things himself. Willie forgot about it and set himself to finding a property to build on. The Church of the New Gospel needed a permanent home, one grand enough for the congregation, which just went on growing. They'd begun Sunday evening services—called "shows"—to compete with the growing audience for Sunday night dramatic radio.

He found an empty square block in Echo Park, next to a pretty little lake with geese and swans ten minutes from downtown on the Pacific Electric's Big Red cars, another ten minutes from growing Glendale. Conveniently, the sign on the property said: "Mull Real Estate." Eddie not only was agent for the land but owned it. *Mirabile dictu.* Everything was coming together.

Callender finally got his man alone on a busy Sunday following morning services. Willie had finished preaching, baptisms, blessings and healing, made his goodbyes, dismissed the elders and staff and closed the front doors, believing the church was empty. Overworked, exhausted, he'd turned down lunch with the elders and retreated to his office for a nap on the couch before the staff returned to open the kitchen and begin preparations for the evening show. They were feeding people now. Sundays were nonstop.

He'd just closed his eyes when he heard the door creak.

"You gotta help me, Reverend."

Startled, Willie sat up. "Oh, it's you, Henry."

"It's about your brother."

"Oh, dear."

As always, he was dressed in the suit that needed pressing, the boots that needed polishing and carrying the hat that needed brushing. His mustache was longer, drooping more and giving his long, weathered face an even more lugubrious look. He wore his jacket over what looked like an undershirt and had knotted a red handkerchief around his neck. Willie had not seen him leave with rest of the congregation. He came in, shut the door and crossed to the chairs facing the pastor's desk, moving a chair to the couch. The couch stood against a side wall behind a coffee table on which was posed the Spanish walnut chess set from Tesoro, the set once belonging to Grandpa Otto. A game was underway. Willie's custom was to keep a running game going with himself.

Willie laid back down. He would let the man have his say. It was his job.

But Callender wasn't talking. He was examining the board. Willie saw an intelligence in the man's face he hadn't noticed before. Despite the old clothes, there was something neat, almost prim about him, meticulous. His blue eyes and black mustache shone out from a closely shaven, weathered face. He liked Callender, liked him even before he'd struck oil. He was obviously a man of God, though he never put anything in the plate. Curious.

"Black's move, I'd say. Knight to queen's knight five."

Willie sat up and looked from the man to the board. He had contemplated that move himself. Who would the old sourdough have played with out there in the hills? Or did he, too, play by himself? Some players could play the game in their head.

He looked back to Callender. "I'd gladly let you make that move, my friend, if I weren't too tired to play right now." He lay back down. He didn't need to ask what his problem was. The *Times* had printed an article about a new evangelical church, the Temple of the Angels, to be built in Echo Park for the Rev.

Mull and the Church of the New Gospel. To be built by the reverend's brother, entrepreneur Eddie Mull. Willie had pinned it on the vestry bulletin board.

How did Eddie know about the name he'd wondered?

Callender was a good Soldier, as loyal to the Church of the New Gospel as anyone in the congregation. Despite the oil strike he still dressed and acted the same, diffidently, shyly, though Willie sensed the steel inside. God bless him, he thought. His heart was good and he was always ready to lend a hand—help in the commissary, help the infirm to their seats and afterward to buses and trolleys, sometimes even accompanying them home again. But why had Callender come to him? Cal had mentioned something about a quarrel with Eddie over oil profits. That certainly was not something Willie intended to get into.

He stared at the chessboard, wondering if black knight to queen's knight five was the right move. Probably not, but it was intriguing.

"It just ain't right, Reverend."

"What isn't right, Henry."

"*I* was going to build the temple for you, Reverend. I reckon you remember I told you about that after I met your brother. I knew there was oil down there. I think I told you all about it at the time, didn't I, Reverend? First time. Do you remember that?"

"I believe I do, Henry."

"I also told your brother the first time I met him. I told him that when we hit I was going to build you the biggest church this town ever saw. Did he tell you that? We had a fifty-fifty agreement. Did he tell you that?"

"I'm afraid not."

"You remember how I used that very name—Temple of the Angels. You do remember that, don't you?

"I do, I do."

"So you know how I feel about things. How is it that article on the bulletin board says your brother's going to build the Temple of the Angels when I was going to build it? Something not right about that, wouldn't you say?"

Something about Eddie owing him money, wasn't that what Cal said? Willie didn't get into things like that: Matthew 6:24: "You cannot serve God and mammon."

"My brother can be a hard man to move."

Callender shifted in the chair, leaning back and looking from the chessboard to Willie and back to the board.

"And I as well, Reverend."

Willie heard the edge in the voice. Delicate business.

"After all, what does it matter, Henry? The important thing is that the temple is built, isn't it? Built thanks to Venice oil, God's gift to all of us. What does it matter if the money comes from you or my brother? Seems to me the same thing. It is to be seed money only, for the temple should be built by the Soldiers, by God's little people.

Callender didn't answer right away. He'd had the same thought and rejected it.

"It ain't the same thing, Reverend. You'd think it was, wouldn't you? Same oil, same money, same temple. But it ain't the same. In my mind it ain't the same thing at all. Your brother has robbed me of what is rightfully mine and what I was rightfully going to do for you, and I have to find a way to set things right."

A threat? No, certainly not.

An idea came. "Henry, I can't give you back something I don't have, surely you can see that. But maybe I can give you something I do have. You are a good man, Henry, a good Soldier. One of the best, I would say. I like the way you help people, look after them. I don't know where you got the gift of compassion, but you have it. It is God-given and it is genuine."

"Thank you, Reverend."

"Will you join us? We're bigger now, have more to do. In a year or two we'll be moving into something far bigger still. I don't know what it will be yet, but I know this: It is God's will. We can use you, Henry, use your God-given talents. And of course, we will compensate you generously. Think of it as a start, Henry, however small, toward restitution."

CHAPTER 7

Willie studied the drawings for some time without reacting, without a single gesture or twitch of a facial muscle. The men were scrutinizing him, but he stood still as a statue, giving nothing away. Eddie had called the night before to say the drawings were ready, and he should come by to meet with the architects. "You're going to be bowled over," he said, and now Willie was staring dumbfounded at the thing expected to bowl him over. He'd not been asked about it. "After all, what do *we* know about architecture," Eddie had said. "I've hired the best firm in town, showed them the land, told them what I could afford. Don't forget *Mamá's* last words. This is the church she wanted you to have: the Temple of the Angels."

And so here they were: two brothers and three architects, Wynken, Blynken and Nod, for all Willie knew of these people, and what they were showing him was monstrous.

They never argued. As children they'd had their snits, but not often because identical twins, sharing the same sperm and egg, are mirrors of each other. They are Siamese twins lucky enough to be physically, if not psychologically, unstuck. From the beginning Eddie had known how to prevail without being aggressive, and Willie, blessed with an equanimity that was lost or suppressed in his brother, didn't mind. They'd learned when to leave each other alone. Their genes may have been the same, but their interests and values, things learned from experience, never were. Eddie learned the ranch business from his father: how to buy and sell crops and animals, how to make money. Willie went into the fields with the workers, visited their cabins, spoke Spanish to them, came to know them as people. Closer to his father, Eddie warmed to money and to business. Closer to his mother, Willie warmed to compassion and to Jesus.

Eva saw the changes in her boys as they grew into young adults, how temperamental and experiential differences intruded on genetic identities. She didn't mind that they were different, one taking after the father, one after the mother. Very Catholic herself, she thrilled at Willie's early love for the one true church. Later, when he chose the Presbyterian Seminary in San Francisco, not the Jesuits, she accepted his argument that the Presbyterians offered more freedom and hid her disappointment. She understood that Jesus prepared different paths to heaven. As for Eddie, she was happy when he took over the ranch when Robert was dead. She knew he wouldn't stay long, just long enough to see after his interests. There wasn't much more to it than that.

"Spectacular" was the only guidance Eddie had given the architects. The new Los Angeles Memorial Coliseum was going to cost a million dollars, and Eddie wanted something just as grand if not quite so expensive. In his mind the Temple of the Angels would be a monument to both of them, to their success in Los Angeles, something to stand forever as a celebration of the name Mull. He didn't need to consult Willie, just ask himself what he wanted, and if Willie demurred, persuade him. As for the cost, Joe Sartori hadn't turned him down yet. He took the church's accounts to the bank. Joe saw that Willie was doing all right.

Willie tried to concentrate on the drawings, which were like nothing he'd ever seen. He watched the lead architect move his pointer—up, down, front view, side view, cutaway, overhead, quick switch to blueprints alongside, the voice monotonous, hypnotic. Willie was tuning out, entering into a private monologue with himself. This was his moment of truth. He knew it was coming and here it was. Was this his destiny, this gaudy thing in front of him, this granite opera house? Is this what God's little people wanted? He was an evangelical, a pastor who'd left the Catholics and their catechisms and the Presbyterians and their stuffy traditionalism to work in the back alleys of Shanghai and San Francisco, a preacher without pretensions. His inspiration was Augustine, that tortured, splendid man steeped in sin. "Renounce, renounce!" Augustine adjured himself, "Give up this divided self, liberate yourself from torment."

He wondered when the architects would stop chattering, so proud were they of their hideous creation. Eddie hovered over them like an orchestra conductor, looking down, looking up following every word, smiling at this, frowning at that, clearly delighted. Eddie had organized everything. Willie was no part of this show. But if he walked away, where would they be? A palace without a prince. Renounce, renounce! But It was too late. Things had come too far. Here he was. A golden dome? But was it really so bad? A new church for new lives was what he'd promised the Soldiers. His eyes focused on the antennas above the dome, antennas to carry his message cross-country in the new age of radio.

"Willie?"

"Yes, yes," he said, returning.

"Magnificent, no?"

"I don't know quite what to say."

"You didn't expect anything like this, did you?"

"No, I did not."

They were meeting at Mull Enterprises on Colorado Avenue in Santa Monica, the hub of Eddie's business interests, which stretched across the county. It had taken months for the project to be ready to show to Willie.

"Where's the steeple?"

"It is a temple."

"Temples don't have steeples?"

"Not necessarily," said Wynken, or perhaps it was Nod. Willie had already forgotten their names. "Believe me, Reverend, we researched this. Some temples have steeples, some don't. In any case, your brother told us you should have something new, something grand, something never done before. And remember this: you don't put antennas on steeples."

"I knew you'd like it," said Eddie, wrapping his arm around him. "I'll tell you this: it doesn't come cheap. This little baby you're looking at comes at exactly half the price of the coliseum they're building out by USC. Only the best for you, little brother."

◆ ◆ ◆

Not a penny of it was Eddie's money. Joe Sartori was neither evangelical nor Pentecostal; he belonged to the one true church, and didn't mix money and religion. Eddie made the point to him that the Church of the New Gospel was as much business as religion, filling up twice on Sunday just like Grauman's Chinese showing a new DeMille movie. What finally sold Joe Sartori was the broadcasting. Hundreds of local stations were springing up across the nation, and the first national network, the National Broadcasting System, was about to be launched. Willie's Sunday evening shows would compete with Hollywood radio dramas, Eddie told the banker, and bring in far more money. Willie was a Hollywood star.

Sartori signed the loan that allowed construction to begin.

They called it the new religion, but it was really a mix of new and old: The new was the radio and Sunday night shows scripted like Hollywood scenarios and using Hollywood actors, who had no complaints about being broadcast into millions of homes. The old was down-home preaching about baptism and sin and the return of Jesus Christ. Raised as a Catholic inspired by Augustine, ordained as a Presbyterian steeped in the piety of John Knox and John Calvin, Rev. Willie Mull abandoned Augustine, Knox, and Calvin when he took the stage at the Temple of the Angels. He understood, but he rationalized: each thing in its time. The Church of the New Gospel became something never before seen anywhere: a little bit Pentecostal, a little bit evangelical, a little bit revivalist and a great deal Hollywood.

Circular rather than traditionally rectangular, with a mammoth stage and amphitheater, the Temple of the Angels took two years to build and when completed was topped by a 100-foot-high golden dome in place of a steeple. The interior was cloaked in heavy burgundy curtains, with three tiers reaching to the base of the dome. Soldiers seated on the higher tiers looked down on the stream feeding the baptismal pool as if viewing from heaven itself. The exterior was made of white stone speckled with crushed seashells to provide sparkle, visible for miles around. Parishioners climbed into the foothills of the San Gabriel Mountains to look down on their temple, glittering like thousands of diamonds in the sunlight.

Five thousand Soldiers came for the opening Sunday service and five thousand more for the first evening show. Willie was preaching not just to them but to tens of thousands listening on his own radio station, KWEM, beaming its signal from two tall antennas on the roof below the golden dome. It was the evening show, not the morning services, he'd chosen to broadcast, for radio, still in its infancy, had discovered that broadcast waves at night, unlike during the day, bounced off the ionosphere and traveled to far distant points. From there, relay stations were beaming them in every direction, soon turning tens of thousands of Los Angeles listeners into millions across the nation.

"Radio," Willie proclaimed that first night on the air, "used in the right way, is a beautiful priceless gift from the loving hand of our Father God."

At home that night, ashamed of his hypocrisy, sobbing by his bed in his West Hollywood bungalow, he confessed and prayed for penance. He turned to Augustine, opening the *Confessions* at random as Augustine had opened Paul's Epistles. His eyes fell on the immortal words: "If not now, lord, when?"

CHAPTER 8

Angie l'Amoureux was from Beaumont, Texas, a Baptist girl who'd come to Los Angeles with her husband Gil, a derrick roughneck from the Louisiana swamps. There is plenty of oil around Beaumont, but Angie's father, a Baptist preacher named Smallwood who'd married a Mexican dancer to save her from the saloons, didn't approve of Gil and so the couple ran off where he couldn't find them. Gil found a job in the gushing new wells of Santa Fe Springs, southeast of Los Angeles, where oil replaced the clear spring water citizens hoped would turn their little town into a world-famous spa. Oil paid better than water so no one complained, least of all Alphonzo Bell, the man who brought up the oil and got so rich he bought the place that would become Bel Air. Angie and Gil rented a three-room house in nearby Whittier, and Gil went off to work on the wells each day while Angie wondered what to do with herself.

She was twenty and pretty enough for Hollywood's new film industry but so were a few hundred other girls. The successful ones were the lucky ones and sometimes they even had talent. The talent part didn't matter a great deal because they stayed mostly in the background in the silent movies, usually as dancers or maybe just pretty faces in the crowd, but it was a better way to make a living than for the girls who weren't "discovered." The others looked for more conventional work, and in the days of telephone and elevator operators, typists, drug store counters, and Woolworth dime stores, they didn't have to look far.

Gil didn't take to marriage. A good-looking, hard-living,

tough-talking Cajun, he was irresistible to women and so didn't resist. He was twice Angie's size, beat her up as a going-away present, and she threw her wedding ring at him on his way out the door. When she'd saved enough money for a lawyer she would file for divorce, which took time in California. Gil found a better job in Bakersfield, where the women in Oil City were more to his taste. It worked out for everyone. Angie moved to Glendale where she was more likely to be discovered than in Whittier and took a job at a soda fountain called Tony's. Glendale advertised itself as the "Fastest Growing City in America"— fastest growing because, as a chamber of commerce brochure spelled out: "We have a strictly white population. There are not a half dozen [sic] other than Caucasians in the city." It was the soda fountain's proximity to her apartment house on Glendale Boulevard, not the city's racial preferences that attracted Angie to the job.

Glendale was close enough to Echo Park that the Rev. Willie Mull could go there or to Pasadena or Burbank for lunch or a soda without wasting too much time or attracting too big a crowd. Broadcasts from the temple had made him famous, as famous, some said, as Douglas Fairbanks or Will Rogers. He enjoyed moving around the city on his own. Dressed in street clothes, hat and sunglasses, he could pass incognito. The temple had a Cadillac for official events and Willie had his own sporty Chevy Roadster, but he liked to slip out without a word, hop on a Pacific Electric Big Red Car and take it wherever it was headed, which from Echo Park was normally Glendale, Pasadena, or Burbank.

He met Angie on one of those hot, downtown summer days when the air comes off the desert instead of the ocean and you have trouble breathing from the moment you step outside. He went out looking for an ice cream sundae, and since there were no drugstores or soda parlors in Echo Park, he caught the first Big Red Car that came along, which happened to say Glendale. It might have said Burbank or Pasadena or been headed south to Long Beach and the story would be different. But this car said Glendale.

Leaving the car at Silver Lake just past Van de Kamp's bakery and the Ford dealership, he could have entered any number of places along Glendale Boulevard. The one he chose, Tony's, had a window poster showing exactly what he wanted, a three-scoop vanilla sundae with whipped cream and strawberry sauce topped with a cherry in a tulip-shaped glass vase, and so in he went. He perched on a stool under the overhead fan, made his order and watched as the pretty girl whose figure was nicely displayed in a crisp brown uniform with the top buttons undone and a white apron cinched tightly at the waist put three scoops in the dish and slowly poured the strawberry syrup, which oozed down the sides of the white mounds like fiery lava.

"Whipped cream?"

"Oh, yes, please." He knew he shouldn't, that he was beginning to show a little extra at the waist and recently had to have his trousers let out, but on a hot day like this he could make an exception. The young woman held up the walnuts and he nodded. Walnuts are good for you. He noticed the nametag on the apron. He also noticed that she wore no ring.

"Cherry?"

"Oh yes, please. Just like the picture in the window."

He took off his hat and sunglasses. "I'd like a cup of coffee to go with that, Angie," he said in his well-modulated preacher's voice. "What a lovely name you have. Where are you from, Angie?"

"Texas," she said, setting the sundae down with a spoon in front of him and pouring the coffee. She hadn't paid much attention before, but now looked at him closely. Something in the voice. "Beaumont."

"Ahh," he said. "Texas. Never been there myself."

"Not worth the bother."

Willie was an impressive man, and he knew it. Though nearly twice the age of the young lady, he was not shy in showing off his skills. Communication, after all, was his business. He was the intermediary between Jesus and a world of sinners, a world whose salvation depended on his skills, a fearsome responsibility. He noted her brown hair, thick and tossed and down over the forehead. Her skin was creamy tan or gently olive, not unlike his own. Her eyes were deep brown and her mouth small but perfectly formed, as red and luscious as the cherry before him. It showed a sadness, and he wondered about that. Sadness was a big part of Willie's life. What could there be in this pretty young girl's life that brought sadness.

"What got you in the ice cream business?" he asked, hoping no one would walk in to disturb their tête-à-tête.

She leaned back against the rear counter, arms folded under her breasts, scrutinizing him. "You're kidding."

"Of course, I am. I wanted to see you smile."

She smiled. The sadness went away.

"You could be in pictures, you know."

"Ah . . . one of those. You've got a contract for me?"

He laughed. She was saucy. He loved it. Before he could answer he saw a change in her face. She was uncertain about something.

"*Are* you in pictures?"

"Well, not exactly."

She turned away, but quickly back again. "Oh my God, I *thought* I recognized your voice." Realizing what she'd said, she quickly added: "Oh, I'm so sorry."

Willie dug into his sundae. Sometimes he didn't mind being recognized. "Don't worry about it, my dear."

"I've been to the temple," she said. "I am a Soldier. It's just that I never saw you up close before. I'm up in the rafters."

Willie put down his spoon. His smile lit up the ice cream parlor. "Hallelujah! Put your sins behind you."

"Whosoever abideth in Him sinneth not."

"My goodness. John 3:6. The Lord be praised. You know your scripture. Tell me, Angie, what brought you to our glorious city?"

◆ ◆ ◆

Eddie's advice to come to Los Angeles was the best his brother ever received. So he firmly believed. Without Eddie, he would still be with the bums on Turk Street. They arrived with the water that irrigated the land that brought the people who bought Eddie's homes and oil and hooch and filled Willie's temple. Willie wasn't the only evangelist in Los Angeles, but he was ordained and a former missionary and in a profession of charlatans—some of whom he knew weren't even Christians—Willie's skills stood out. Rabble-rousers like the Rev. Bob Shoemaker preyed on God's little people—the poor, the unfortunate, the colored—and Willie denounced them regularly. "There is no darkness nor shadow of death where the workers of iniquity may hide themselves," he preached.

Encouraged by Shoemaker and others jealous of Willie's success, the workers of iniquity had begun digging into his past, combing through what was known of his career but finding nothing to attack him with. His personal life was spotless (how could they have known of Chun hua?) and his professional life exemplary, but that hardly slowed down the inquiry of those

whose self-appointed task was to find corruption and charla-
tanry where none existed. Newspapers assigned star reporters
to the temple in an attempt to expose him as one more fraud
in a city full of them. One by one they came back shaking their
heads.

Finally, the *Times* had to admit it:

> Did the Rev. Mull's prayers, his shouts of "heal,
> heal, heal" and his laying on of hands, produce what
> he said it would? The answer must be an emphatic yes.
> Our reporter approached the healed over a series of
> weeks, and their testimony left no doubt. Call it what
> you will, hypnotic power, positive thinking, subliminal
> suggestion or faith in Jesus Christ, it worked for these
> people, and that is enough for us.

He courted Angie warily.

If the Bible is full of admonitions against fornication, so is
it full of fornication. With reporters stalking him and the Rev.
Bob Shoemaker and other apostates hounding him, one bitter
woman was all it would take. He could not preach against the
temptations of a godless society if he did not lead a spotless
life. Like Augustine, he was tormented, one whose spirit was
ready to renounce but whose body was not. He prayed to find
the right woman, the new Millie, the woman to return him to
the safety and sanctity of marriage, end the torture of a divided
self. He read from Corinthians: "To avoid fornication let every
man have his own wife and every woman her own husband."
Exactly so, he thought. I am looking for a loving wife—and yes,
a new mother for Calvin.

And then came Angie, who was hardly what he expected.
She was young and (so he thought) single. There was something

of Chun hua in her—small but brave, less exotic but more alluring. He could not get Angie's bounteous figure from his mind.
He wanted to renounce, but could not. He fought, fought as
Augustine had fought, but was not ready. The spirit was strong,
but the flesh was stronger. A gentle man, like Augustine, he was
in the grip of something violent. "And up to the very moment
in which I was to become another man, the nearer the moment
approached, the greater horror did it strike in me."

On his knees in the bungalow, his mind seeking Augustine
but finding only Angie, he nodded and repeated the words: "I
all but did it, lord, but not quite."

◆ ◆ ◆

With the success of the temple, Willie moved to the top
floor of the new Sunset Tower, the tallest and most luxurious
apartment building in Los Angeles, a city whose earthquake
building codes did not like tall buildings. He rode the trolleys
down Sunset to the temple during the week, saving his Chevy
roadster for Sundays. Sunset also was more convenient for Cal,
who was at USC and worked part-time at the temple, sometimes staying overnight with his father.

Willie began dropping into Tony's regularly, sometimes
driving, sometimes taking the Big Red cars. She'd see him coming and already start making the strawberry sundae he always
ordered. The shop was not always empty. Sometimes Tony was
there and once he found two teenage boys at the counter eating
sundaes and flirting. It was harmless prattle about where she
lived and what time she got off and did she like the pictures,
but he found himself annoyed. He was about to say something
when she shut them off with a—"I don't think my boyfriend
Tony would like you talking to me like this."

When the boys left, she smiled for him. "Tony isn't really my boyfriend." He knew she said it for him.

Angie was anything but naïve. She knew the Rev. Willie's interest was not just in her soul and her sundaes, but she liked the idea of being courted by a famous evangelist. Her father was a preacher; her family was steeped in Texas Baptism and she'd been churchgoing until Gil came along. As a girl, she'd mounted the chancel with her father to recite scripture. One local newspaper named her "Sister Angie Smallwood, Beaumont's child preacher." Angie knew her Bible and she had her standards. She'd been seduced by Gil but had no regrets because she'd got him to the altar and he'd brought her to Los Angeles. Abandoned, she'd grown to miss her church but not her man, and had gone to the Temple of the Angels to be born again.

When Willie learned she'd done some preaching and knew scripture he invited her to temple rehearsals and soon cast her in minor roles in the Sunday shows—as an angel, as a member of the chorus, twice with minor speaking roles in shows based on the Beatitudes. Clad in long robes, she looked little different from the other girls, but Willie always knew where she was. For the first time since Millie he felt his heart engaged again. He'd not expected it, not from a girl he'd been drawn to, he confessed, by lust alone. On his knees in the temple chapel he prayed, and the Lord replied, "Love her, love her," and he did love her. It is what made everything possible. He knew there were risks: To love is to be vulnerable, to face loss, to face pain worse than anything physical. The heartsickness he'd felt after Millie's death crept back at the edges of his mind, the shudders of pain. He could not go through that again.

As for Angie, she loved it. Raised by a Bible-thumping father and a born-again mother, she missed all the church hooptedoodle. Saturday night in Beaumont had potluck and bingo, and Sunday the children dressed up and off to church for a morning of hallelujahs followed by cake and coffee and fruit juice and the families socializing while the children went outside to play with fruitless warnings not to get their Sunday best dirty. When she was seven she'd mounted the chancel for the first time and her father helped her onto a chair so she could recite the 23rd Psalm and the 91st, and the 103rd, and when she was nine she read from scripture, John 4 and 1 Corinthians and the Sermon on the Mount from Matthew, and when she was eleven she didn't have to read anymore because she knew it all by heart.

She still knew it. Maybe she'd forgotten it with Gil when she'd lost her way, but she still had it and sometimes lay in bed before work at the ice cream shop and sought it in her memory, and if there was a lapse she went back to her Bible, the same worn leather Bible given to her by her daddy. It was never far away. It was all coming back.

CHAPTER 9

The Depression slowed Los Angeles down but not by much. The city lacked the heavy industry of the East and big farms of the Midwest that doomed those regions. The main industry in Southern California was sun and entertainment, precisely what people needed to lift sunken spirits in hard times. Hollywood had begun with the water and became a billion-dollar industry in the twenties. The city reeled in 1928 with the collapse of the St. Francis Dam, the largest of the dams built to hold Owens River water. The disaster took five hundred lives and destroyed William Mulholland, the man who'd built the aqueduct, provoking many in the Owens Valley to claim it was God's revenge, but life in the city went on. With the Depression deepening, more people were heading west than ever, escaping eastern unemployment, misery, and ruin. When so many people with the same idea head for the same place, unemployment, misery, and ruin inevitably accompany them, but that was still a few years away.

Bel Air hurt a little. Some overleveraged residents along Roscomare and Stone Canyon and Beverly Glen suffered foreclosures just like ordinary people. Even Eddie Mull felt a pinch, for fewer people bought his homes, lots, and gasoline. He still made money, just made it slower. It cost him briefly when Prohibition was repealed and the Bootleg Highway to Tecate dried up, but he took his profits and sank them into a gambling ship to operate in Santa Monica Bay, just beyond the three-mile state limit. His bank account took a hit while the ship was being refurbished and refitted and brought through the Panama Canal, but not so much that he had to ask Nelly to stop shopping or even slow it down.

When Maggie turned fourteen Eddie bought her a snazzy red Ford coupé for the weekly runs to the Playa del Rey stables where the girls still kept their horses. Nelly thought her daughter too young to be driving, but by then Cal had finished at USC, was working at the temple for his father and could no longer play chauffeur. Nelly had no intention of returning to the stables herself, and so Maggie got her car. Nelly took her for her first driver's test and learner's permit, which required someone over sixteen to be in the car at the same time.

With Nelly and Cal unavailable, Maggie swallowed her pride and decided to ask Billy Todd, an old enemy, to accompany her to the stables. Billy was sixteen and had a license. He lived just up Roscomare, and during long years in grade school and University High School had come to hate Maggie with a passion. He regarded her as a bully, a boy-hater and probably a lesbian. At school bus stops, they stood as far from each other as they could. At sixteen, Billy got his own car, a beat-up old Ford Model A that could barely make it up the hill. Going down was easier, and Billy sometimes stopped to give friends at the bus stop—not Maggie– rides down the hill. She remembered.

Lately when Billy rattled down Roscomare, he saw the sweet red coupé parked in the driveway. He began cruising by slowly, once almost stopping when he saw Maggie outside dusting the car. He saw she was filling out her sweater in a way he'd never noticed, and it aroused him. She wasn't old enough to drive; why would she be dusting the car? One day Maggie saw him cruising, and the next time he passed she waved him into the driveway.

"That yours?"

"Like it?"

"You bet."

"Want a ride?"

He knew her better than that. "What's the deal?" he said, suspiciously.

The deal was that she'd pay him five dollars each Thursday to accompany her to the stables.

Younger, Maggie beat the boys in everything. She didn't even bother with girls. Cousin Cal had never beat her in anything and Cal was six years older, though Cal, she knew, didn't really try. At fourteen, with the changes in bodies, she couldn't beat all the boys all the time anymore but never refused a challenge. At the stables, on Dynamite, she was the best rider they had. Eddie said it came from Grandma Eva, who was a state riding champion, but Maggie figured she could do anything she set her mind to—like the day in Venice when she'd scaled the derrick and stood looking down on the men, daring them to come after her.

The deal started the following Thursday after school, and didn't go as intended. Billy hadn't understood that Maggie didn't need a driver, just a presence, and a silent one at that. After the third trip, he called it off. "Don't need the money that badly," he grumped.

It hadn't escaped her that Billy, like other males, had begun looking at her differently, turning around to watch her walk and not looking in her eyes but focused lower. She dressed as she always had for riding lessons, in Levi's and a checkered shirt, but the shirt didn't hang straight down anymore. She wore the same shirts she'd been wearing for years, which was part of the problem for they were tight on her now. It was a little uncomfortable under the arms, but she saw the effect on boys and so she stayed with the old shirts.

She needed Billy, so she negotiated, telling him he could

drive, but not all the time for the whole purpose of the deal was for her to learn how to drive. The following Thursday, after riding, they headed up into the Playa del Rey hills so she could practice starting and stopping. She drove south on Rindge Avenue to where it dead-ended in the sand dunes at Kilgore, about a mile beyond the last houses. They'd built streets for the houses, but the houses hadn't come yet. Kilgore had a steep twenty-five-degree slope down to the cliffs, as much as any car could handle.

"Whoa," shouted Billy as she turned down the hill, "are you crazy?"

Halfway down, she made a sharp U-turn and stopped in the middle, pointing up, cutting the engine. She left the gears engaged and pulled on the hand brake so the car wouldn't slip back. Billy turned around to peer straight down the hill. "Nuts to this," he said, opening the door. Death was not part of the deal. "You miss and we go over the cliffs."

"So get out and walk if you're scared."

"I am not scared. I am responsible. Get me out of here! No, move over. Let me do it."

He closed the door, she pushed him away and started the motor. It was tricky, jumping your foot from the brake to the gas pedal and coordinating with the clutch and the hand brake so the car didn't slip back or stall, but if she could do it on Kilgore she could do it anywhere. She missed her timing, losing control as they started rolling backward down the hill with Billy screaming. After a few yards she was fortunately able to stop.

He grabbed for the hand brake. "You'll kill us!"

She slapped his hand away. He was a twerp. His father was a Beverly Hills dentist, and she figured Billy for the same.

On the second try, she aced it, coordinating perfectly

between clutch, accelerator and hand brake and jolting quickly up the hill. She parked, angled the front wheels into the curb as you're supposed to do and cut the motor.

She smiled. "Not bad, huh?"

He was breathing fast, hyperventilating. "Last time. Give me my five bucks."

"Don't you want to drive home?"

"Pay me!"

He was mad—mad and humiliated, a bad male combination. She needed tact.

"Come on, Billy, I need you."   .

"Like hell you do."

"I do need you." She patted his knee.

He grabbed her hand, holding it on his knee. "So why don't you ever show it?"

She stared at him, trying to catch the meaning.

"Okay, you can take over. Let's switch places."

"That's not what I mean."

"What?"

"Can I touch them?"

"What . . .?"

It happened a few Thursdays after that. Lizzie didn't come again (Lizzie never did like horses), and they'd gone back on the hill after the stables. By now, Maggie knew what it took to keep Billy happy and wore a tight blouse with the top buttons already undone. She took Rindge to the sand dunes at Kilgore, turned down and cut the motor. She turned to him.

Suddenly he did something so unexpected that she slapped his face. He slapped her back and they would have gone at it right there except that she threw the car in gear, started up the hill to Rindge with a jerk, raced back to Culver heading east as fast as she'd ever driven with Billy screaming bloody murder.

She forgot about the ESS turn over Ballona, somehow made it around but coming out on the far side near the train tracks by the shed where they picked up the produce from the lettuce fields south of Ballona lost control and rolled. The passenger door sprang and Billy came out head first, landing on his head in a field of lettuce.

Dazed, she crawled out but had no idea where she was or what had happened. She went to Billy and looked down, but nothing registered and so she sat down and didn't remember anything until she was strapped down and heard someone say that the good news was that the boy was dead because his neck was broken.

When she awoke, the doctor—gray hair, white coat, horn rims, stethoscope, nametag, everything a doctor should be— was smiling down on her. He introduced himself as Dr. Lambert and told her she was in Santa Monica Hospital. She'd had a concussion, and they'd had to sedate her to make some stitches, including on her face, but everything would heal just fine. Nothing was broken. He asked if she could answer a few simple questions. She nodded. He asked her name and age, what year it was, who was president? She answered. He asked if she remembered the accident? Again, she nodded. People were waiting to see her, he said. She might still feel some effects from sedation, but did she feel up to seeing them?

"What people?"

"Your family, mostly."

She sat up quickly, too quickly for she felt suddenly faint. "I want to get up."

"Why not stay as you are until everyone is gone? Easier that way. Your parents are here, your sister, parents of the dead boy and—oh yes, the police want to see you first."

The dead boy . . . the police?

He saw her stunned look. "It's routine in something like this, Maggie, but only if you're up to it. You do remember everything, don't you?" Something inside her had stopped working, not her heart for she felt it thump, but something was off. She nodded.

"I ought to warn you." He frowned. "Some questions might be awkward."

Billy, oh, God!

He walked to the door, and Maggie saw that two people already were in the room, two men in dark suits and hats, unmistakably police, partially hidden behind a screen. One had a notebook and was writing. The door to outside was open and she heard voices.

"Hi Maggie. Just a few questions before the parents come in," the older one said, approaching. Neither man removed his hat. "We need a little information about the accident."

She sat up straighter, thankful the smock was tied in back. For the first time she was aware of the bandages, including one on her cheekbone. She knew her hair was a mess and would love to have washed her face, which felt icky.

"Just tell us what happened. Take your time. Tell us what you remember."

The younger officer kept writing as she talked and after a while she thought they were done because they stopped asking questions. Strangely, they didn't turn to leave. The older officer looked to the younger one, who shook his head. The older officer sighed.

"We found sperm in the car and on the young man's pants," he said, softly. "Can you tell us anything about that?"

Sperm?

"He tried to kiss me," she said, gathering herself.

"He tried to kiss you as you were driving—is that why you lost control?"

"No, before that. We were just sitting in the car. After the riding lesson."

"He tried to kiss you and had an orgasm, is that what you mean?"

They were practically whispering. "An orgasm?"

"You don't know what an orgasm is?"

"When the sperm comes, you mean?"

The two officers looked at each other, expressionless, professional, keeping it in. "Yes, Maggie," said the older one, "when the sperm comes. Did you see it?"

She wondered if they could hear outside. "I did not."

"Did he molest you?"

"He did not."

"Did you have intercourse with him?"

"*I did not!*"

"Is that why you were speeding? Because you were mad at him for what he did to you—or tried to do?" The voices were louder now.

"He didn't do anything to me—and who said I was speeding?"

"Why did you lose control of the car?"

Of course, she was speeding, going at least sixty coming out of the Culver ESS but they didn't need to know that. But lose control? Even at fourteen, she was a good driver. She was ready to race that car. She had no idea why it happened. Had Billy done something as they drove? She couldn't remember. And her pretty red Ford: she knew it was a total wreck.

Her head dropped: "I don't know. A tire maybe?"

"No," said the younger man. "It wasn't a tire."

The older man nodded. "That's all for now, Maggie. Thank you for your cooperation." They walked to the screen to join Dr. Lambert but did not leave the room.

Why did they have to let the Todds come? Nelly came over and took her hand, followed by Lizzie, who then moved to the window and took out her notebook. Eddie hung back, but Mrs. Todd, who looked a wreck, came right up to her and blurted, "what were you doing driving a car? You are a child." Mrs. Todd knew about the deal because she and Nelly had discussed it. Mr. Todd stood nearby, haggard and quiet, but Mrs. Todd seemed close to hysterics.

"Just tell us what happened, Maggie," said Mr. Todd. "As best you remember. It is important to us."

She couldn't do that, could she? She couldn't tell them that they went up into the hills so Billy could feel her breasts and that the last time he'd brought out his penis and she'd seen it spurting. At least they hadn't overheard the detectives. "I can't remember," she said. "He tried to kiss me and I pushed him away. That's all I remember."

"*YOU ARE LYING!*" shouted Mrs. Todd, so loudly that Dr. Lambert took a step forward.

Through all this Maggie was aware that her father stood off away from the others, sometimes watching her, sometimes looking around the room. She could tell he wanted to check his watch but didn't want to be seen doing it. For some reason she found that funny. Did he even care what had happened? She could not read him. She could read her mother, in control as always, letting others take charge in every situation because she hated dramas, but her father, finally peeking at his watch, showed nothing. How he wanted out of there! Where was Cal, she wondered. Why wasn't he here? They hadn't told him, that's why. She could have used a hug and a kiss at that moment, from anyone, even on the stitches, but everyone hung back. Cal wouldn't have.

"Kitty, Kitty, please," Nelly, finally said, stepping forward to put an arm around Mrs. Todd and having it shoved away.

"This is your fault!" she shouted at Nelly. "You arranged this because you were too lazy to drive her yourself—*so you could play bridge!*"

Kitty was not in Nelly's bridge group.

At that, the police slipped out. Good, Maggie thought. She wanted to get up, but not with a crowd around and the loose strings on the smock and hysterical Mrs. Todd standing over her. She needed to say something and felt she should probably be crying, but her eyes were too sore to produce tears.

"Mrs. Todd, I've told you all I can," she said, without lying. "What Billy did upset me and I was driving home and lost control of the car. It could have been me instead of him, and I'm sure you wish it was . . ."

"*What Billy did . . ?*"

"Come, Kitty," said Mr. Todd. "You know we have things to do." He turned to Eddie. "Terrible for all of us." His voice trailed off. "Our only son, you know. He would have come into practice with me."

Eddie nodded, the two men shook hands and Mr. Todd left with his arm around his wife.

During all this Lizzie sat on the windowsill, quietly writing.

"So what happened, Mag?" said Eddie. "What did he try to do to you?"

"Just get me out of here, will you, Dad? Mother, find where they put my clothes."

"Those clothes are gone dear, the blouse was ripped, you know. We've brought you some fresh ones."

CHAPTER 10

Eddie was in a hurry to leave because he had important things to do. Maggie was beat up, but he knew his kid; she'd be on her feet before the day was out. Too bad about the other kid, but he had his own problems. He left the hospital in his black Buick and headed down Colorado Avenue past Mull Enterprises to the Santa Monica pier. He walked halfway out the pier to a large heavy-lettered sign: PROVIDENCE WATER TAXIS. He showed his pass and descended the gangway to a canvas-covered launch belonging to a fleet making half-hourly runs to the ship *Providence,* anchored three miles out in Santa Monica Bay.

The *Providence* never closed, and the launch, a forty-footer seating fifty, was already near full at 11 a.m. The boat swayed gently in a calm sea. Eddie nodded to the boatman who shoved off. He had the night's proceeds to collect, deposit at the Santa Monica branch of Security Trust and Savings and arrive for an appointment with his brother at Mull Enterprises at noon.

The end of Prohibition had been painful. For a few golden years, Eddie Mull had done as well as anyone in Los Angeles, maybe not grossing as much as he once did, but still flush with cash. His core businesses, oil and real estate, were off, but bootlegging made up for it with the added bonus of no taxes to pay. Neither did he have payoffs because protection was part of his own operation. Never had there been more drinking in Los Angeles than when it was illegal to drink. It took a year for Prohibition to end across the nation, a year that gave Eddie and his associates time to make the transition from bootlegging to gambling, or "gaming" as they preferred to call it. They bought an old Ohio River collier, chugged down the Mississippi to Mobile for repairs and refurbishing and on through the Panama Canal. She was reincarnated in Santa Monica Bay as the *Providence*.

The ship was top-of-the-line stem to stern, two-decks appointed in the latest teak furnishings and salons equipped with the best gaming equipment—elegant craps and roulette tables and one hundred Mills slots from Chicago. There was a waiting list for slots: Nevada had legalized gambling as it, too, prepared for the end of Prohibition, but Eddie paid over list and got his slots before anyone. Because gambling was illegal in California, the ship was anchored three miles out, just beyond the reach of state law enforcement. The feds didn't care.

Eddie had a full day ahead of him. Willie had turned his preacherly indignation against sin squarely on the *Providence*—never mind that the ship was outside city limits. Eddie learned of Willie's campaign not from Willie's radio broadcasts—he never listened—but from an editorial in the Santa Monica *Evening Outlook*, which Henry Callender showed him. "If we have offshore gambling, what will be next?" the newspaper asked. "Floating houses of prostitution?" The *Outlook* was insignificant, but Eddie didn't want Willie launching a crusade that brought in the *Times* and *Examiner*. He'd have to reveal his ownership to his brother, but he would take that chance. Willie had his own reasons for keeping his brother's name out of the headlines.

Willie turned down an invitation to visit the ship. Eddie wanted to show his brother that the *Providence* was not out to squeeze people, but to lift them up. The ship was fairer than any other games anywhere. They took a smaller house cut—1.4 percent—than any house in Las Vegas. The keno payoffs were higher and the faro table faster. They had dining and dancing on the lower deck, and the *Evening Outlook's* food critic, apparently out of touch with the editorial page, had given the restaurant three stars. Eddie wanted to show him that the operation was exactly as the ship's name implied: providential, providing a little honest entertainment in a world of Depression hardship.

But Willie wouldn't come. One photo of him on that ship was all his enemies needed. Eddie told him he had a business proposition, and they agreed to meet at Mull Enterprises.

Willie brought Henry Callender with him. In hindsight, he shouldn't have done it, but he believed that time and prayer had brought Henry to the point if not of forgiveness of Eddie at least of acceptance. The relationship between these two devout Christians was delicate, for how could Willie fully embrace a man who hated his brother? Clever with his hands, Henry had worked his way up to become the temple's chief set-builder. The two men were friendly, and on Grandpa Otto's Spanish chessboard kept a running game going, games that sometimes lasted for weeks. Each man kept a chessboard at home to duplicate the game, pondering his moves and likely counters of his opponent. They were roughly equal in ability—skilled but not expert players, men who shared a deep love for the game.

At home, Callender did not always play alone. He lived on Lemon Grove Avenue, one of those leafy lanes of neat little stucco bungalows spread out around Hollywood Cemetery just south of Santa Monica Boulevard. Since most of the people in the neighborhood were studio workers who didn't earn that much, most of the bungalows were duplexes. Anyone who has ever lived in Hollywood or worked at the studios knows the kind of bungalow in which Henry lived. If it were a single house it would be two bedrooms and sixteen hundred square feet. As a duplex it was half that and suitable for one person or two at most, but no children.

The last thing you wanted if you were trying to get ahead at the studios was children. If you got a raise and got married and wanted children you could move into something larger in West or East Hollywood, but where Henry lived was just Hollywood, and Hollywood was duplexes and no children. In distance, Lemon Grove wasn't that far from Willie on the top floor of the Sunset Tower, a mile at most, but in status it was a different world. Henry lived with his cat, a smart Siamese named Nyx, which in Greek means night. Nyx got the name because he was more black than tan, rare in a Siamese. Henry found him in a Hollywood pet store, the black sheep of the litter, and since Henry was also a black sheep, they were well suited. Henry liked cats and tried to have one whenever he had a fixed address, which wasn't often. Gainfully employed, he'd found the cat, named him, neutered him and together they shared the duplex.

One reason Henry liked cats was that he talked to himself. Sourdoughs, prospectors, diggers, drifters, loners of every type accustomed to the solitude of the trail, often talk to themselves. In civilization, soliloquizing is viewed as unsocial, perhaps even pathological behavior except in cases where the soliloquist addresses an animal. As animals go, most people prefer dogs because they believe dogs listen, but Henry preferred cats. And Nyx listened.

The cat's routine was to seat himself in the chair across from Henry's coffee table to watch the game. His eyes followed the moves. Henry, seated on the sofa, would look into those deep blue cat eyes and know that the cat understood. He believed Nyx made him a better chess player, gave him an edge on Willie. Nyx respected the game. Whatever foul cat mood he might be in—hot, cold, hungry, lonely, brooding over his crushed testicles—he never took it out on the game. Left alone as he was most days, it would have been the easiest thing in the world for him to jump on the board and knock the pieces to kingdom come, but he never did.

Willie and Henry were the first to arrive at Mull Enterprises that day. If Henry did not know where they were headed when they left the temple, by the time the driver turned the Cadillac off Olympic in Santa Monica into the 19th Street Mull parking lot (the depot for heavy construction and drilling equipment had a separate entrance on Michigan Avenue), he understood. He'd been there before, of course, to see Eddie, only to be sent away. True to his nature, he didn't say a word. The car was parked, and the two men walked inside to be informed that Eddie was on the way. They were shown to his office and sat down under a Yosemite painting by Bierstadt, facing the door.

Entering middle age, the twins still looked alike. They didn't dress alike or talk alike and their lives and interests had taken different directions, but physically the resemblance was still strong. Eddie was heavier, for he had a less ascetic past, but Willie, consuming strawberry sundaes, was catching up. With their solid builds, slightly olive skin, dark wavy hair, deep brown eyes, easy smiles, they could have played any role in Hollywood, from producers to leading men to extras. Without knowing them, people still tended to look twice as if they'd seen them somewhere or someone very much like them. Some couldn't tell them apart, though for Henry Callender they were as different as Jesus and the Devil. They traveled in different circles and were rarely seen together, having decided it was best for both of them that way.

Eddie paused momentarily as he entered his office, surprised to see two visitors when he'd expected only one, still more surprised when he recognized the second one. He came quickly forward as his visitors stood, throwing his arms around his brother and embracing him.

"I believe you know Henry Callender," Willie said.

It was more than awkward. Henry moved mechanically, taking the proffered hand though immediately bringing his hand back as if bitten. Here was the man he'd tried so long to forget. If at times he erased him from his conscious mind, he still bubbled up in his unconscious. Henry was not known as a man of violence, though no man could live the life he'd led without his share of showdowns. It's like that on the trail. Even if you don't start quarrels, it's hard to stay out of them. You pack a gun for a reason. He still had his gun, a Remington Derringer.

His body quivered to the tips of his mustaches, and he struggled to conceal it. How many times had he gone over it with Nyx, telling the story as he made his moves? And now here not five feet away was the man who owed him so much—how much would it be, how many millions? Let it go, let it go, the cat would say. It's ancient history. But Henry's mind would wander and wonder what it was like to be a millionaire and live in Bel Air, live like Eddie Mull. "Why isn't it us up there?" he'd say to Nyx, who understood.

"Henry is my righthand man," said Willie, enjoying his brother's discomfort more than he should. Eddie had no desire to see Callender under any circumstances, but certainly could not discuss the *Providence* with him in the room. "I'm sorry, Henry," he said quickly, "a family matter has come up. Would you mind leaving us alone for a while?"

Henry looked to Willie, who vexed, nonetheless nodded.

"A family matter?" said Willie when he had left.

Eddie sat down at his desk and told him of Maggie's accident, leaving out the more lurid parts. Willie was shocked—he was the girls' godfather in addition to being their uncle and loved them both dearly. He promised to visit the hospital and to say prayers for Maggie. He was also annoyed, wanting to bring Henry back into the room for that was the whole point in bringing him, to reconcile with Eddie, who, Willie saw, had more than Maggie's accident on his mind.

Eddie turned to gaze a moment into the courtyard. A fountain burbled. He needed a moment to push Callender out of his mind. He had no idea why Willie brought him and would not ask. "There's something else," he said, turning back. "It involves the *Providence*, the gaming ship I believe you've mentioned in your broadcasts."

Ah, thought Willie: *He does listen.*

"You should know that I have an interest in that ship. I am a silent partner, so to speak."

Willie's expression never changed.

"It is legitimate, Willie. You should come out and have a look. People come to the ship for a good time and because they just might go home a little richer. Many do. Don't think of what we do as any different from the hundreds of games of chance played on Venice Pier, Ocean Park Pier, Santa Monica Pier." He chuckled. "Though we reward our winners with more than kewpie dolls. It's the Depression, Willie. People need a little sunshine in their lives. Why begrudge them that?"

"I begrudge no one sunshine. Eddie, what do you want from me?"

The tone annoyed Eddie. They were never brusque with each other.

"*Want from you?* Whatever gave you that idea? Just understand that we're in different businesses, that's all. We take care of people in different ways."

"I don't think of God's work as a business, as you put it, though I agree that we take care of people in different ways. I hope you're not asking me to condone illegal gambling just because you're involved in it."

"How can you call it illegal? What law are we breaking? Who is arresting us? We are law-abiding citizens, just as you are."

Willie raised his hand. "No sophistry, please. Gambling is gambling whether on shore, three miles out or in the middle of the ocean. It is a nonproductive enterprise, a biblical evil that preys on the little man who has better things to do. I shall continue to denounce it—without mentioning you, of course. I respect your wish to remain a silent partner."

Rising, Eddie walked to the front window and looked out on the parking lot. Callender was leaning against the Cadillac having a smoke. Spying Eddie, he quickly turned away. Eddie's skin prickled. "Which is exactly why you must keep this discussion private—even from your righthand man." He turned on Willie, anger in his voice. "Why did you bring him here?"

"I thought it might do you both some good."

"Salt in the wounds, Willie, salt in the wounds."

Willie thought of Lot's wife, turned into a pillar of salt. "I have no intention of discussing this with anyone, including Henry. Why did you invite me here, Eddie? Something about a business proposition, wasn't it?"

"Yes, yes." he cried, crossing to a cabinet behind his desk and extracting a large mahogany box. He set the box on the desk facing his brother.

"Have a look."

A brass plaque was inlaid above a large slot in the box, large enough for an envelope:

JUST A FEW DOLLARS OF YOUR WINNINGS WILL
FEED AND HOUSE A POOR FAMILY FOR A WEEK

"Alms boxes, Willie, placed throughout the ship, along with envelopes. That's why I want you to come out and meet people, talk to them, have a look around. Our clients will be invited to share their winnings with the less fortunate, and I have no doubt that they will be generous. Money from these boxes will be distributed to churches across the city. As much of it as you need will be sent to the temple. Just let me know."

Willie stared at the box as though a snake might crawl from the slot. "Surely you don't think you can . . ."

"*Stop*! I know what you're going to say, and you couldn't be more off base. I hold the temple's mortgage, remember. I'd like to pay it off some day. A little more money in the coffers is not such a bad idea."

"Pay off the mortgage with alms from gamblers? Surely you're joking."

"You know me better than that, Willie. When money's involved, I never joke."

CHAPTER 11

Willie knew little about Angie, which was just as well. She never told him more than that she was from Texas, and that her father, like Willie, was a preacher. They'd had coffee a few times after rehearsals, but with other cast members. He knew she lived somewhere in Glendale, somewhere near Tony's soda shop because she said she could walk to work. Though thinking about it constantly, he'd not dared invite her on a date, much less to Sunset Towers. The girl was cautious, but also a flirt, and he was powerfully tempted. At times he thought himself a fool for having feelings for her and, worse, imputing feelings to her for him. He admonished himself that if he did not act the fool no one would know. It was a dilemma, one he was helped out of, once again, by Henry Callender.

Callender brought him a clipping from the *Times,* an item about an unmarried girl who'd sought an abortion and died under the scalpel, murdered really, along with the fetus. The Los Angeles police caught the man, who was no doctor, and were looking for women to testify against him. The clipping had been sent in along with an unsigned note, short and to the point:

"*Rev. Mull. How can you tolerate such activities?*"

"A natural for you, Reverend," Callender said, " and for the young lady."

"Angie?"

"I could write the script myself."

"You can write?"

"I could give it a try."

They had to knock down a door and a wall to get Willie's Chevy roadster on stage for the show. All week long, a banner announcing "Taking a Ride" flapped from poles on the roof of the temple, visible from Echo Lake to downtown and to the thousands who passed each day on the trolleys running along the boulevards, Sunset and Glendale. Willie usually wrote the Sunday scripts himself, but this was a collaborative effort. He was impressed by what Callender had done, but needed to touch up the ending, give it the drama he wanted.

A few days before the show, Willie spoke of it on his KWEM radio broadcast:

> I'm speaking to all women who might be listening, but especially to young women who have left families in the East and Midwest to come to our fine city but still don't feel quite at home. "Taking a Ride" is a story for you, a story that can change your life. Don't be disappointed. Come to the temple early to be sure you find a seat. If you can't make it in person, be sure to tune into KWEM, 1020 on the dial, 7:00 p.m., this Sunday.

By five o'clock, thousands were swarming the temple, slowing trolleys on Glendale and Sunset to a crawl. At 5:30, the temple doors opened and ushers began helping five thousand fortunate people to their seats while hymns from the choir rolled through the building. At 6 p.m., the Rev. Marcus Wynetski, associate pastor, led the congregation in hymns and prayer, and at 6:45 deacons passed with the gilded plates. At 7 p.m. sharp, lights dimmed and the red stage light went on. A portly, silver-haired network announcer entered from the wings, embracing a large, diaphanous circle microphone:

"From the Temple of the Angels in the City of the Angels,"

he intoned in his liquid bass, "welcome to Sunday evening with the Reverend Willie Mull—proudly sponsored by Lux soap flakes, which won't turn silks yellow."

Willie, wearing his black clergy stole, stepped to the microphone. "Wherever you may be around this great nation of ours, I welcome you to the Temple of the Angels. Buckle up: Tonight we're going to be—'TAKING A RIDE!'"

◆ ◆ ◆

The curtain goes up on a stage plunged into darkness. A spotlight snaps on. On center stage sits Willie's Chevy roadster, top down, white sidewalls shining, waxed and buffed blue metal gleaming under the spotlight. Dressed in a pleated white flapper skirt trimmed in cardinal and a white sweater with a large gold "C" across her handsome chest, Angie l'Amoureux runs on stage followed by a young man in slacks and sweater of identical colors.

"Jenny and Pete are going to a football game at the new Los Angeles Memorial Coliseum," Willie narrates from side stage. "They're admiring Pete's new Chevy roadster, and talking about the glorious day ahead. No classes, no studies, no homework. It's Saturday, the day of THE BIG GAME! They climb in, Pete starts it up and they begin their drive across the city, top down, heading for the coliseum and the big game. Look there! Pete has produced a flask and passed it to Jenny. I wonder what's in it."

Nervous laughter peals through the building. A movie rolls in the background as Willie describes the scene. The audience sees familiar city landmarks as the car crosses town—Westwood Tower, May Company, *Daily News* building, city hall, Washington Park where the Los Angeles Angels play baseball, USC campus.

"And suddenly, there it is," cries Willie, "Los Angeles's own coliseum, the city's new pride and glory, seating seventy-six thousand. The largest stadium west of the Mississippi!"

Willie paints the scene: cars, buses and trolleys arriving from everywhere; people streaming down Figueroa and across Exposition Park from the USC campus carrying bags, hampers, blankets. Bands play as people climb to their seats, cheerleaders bark instructions, the crowd cheers, the teams enter the field from under the stadium. Henry Callender has made a recording of all the sounds, which boom out over the radio waves.

The curtain falls so the stage crew can change the scenery. The announcer comes out during the changeover, this time bearing the blue Lux box with the big red dot. He holds the box high so the congregation can see it: "Lux soap flakes," he cries into the microphone. "Keep undies lovely up to three times as long."

The curtain rises and sounds of the game fill the temple from a dozen loudspeakers. Jenny and Pete are in the stands with their friends. Flasks are passed. Willie describes the game, the crowd, the drinking, the action. The temple remains hushed, no one knowing where he is going with the theme, taking a ride. Surely he has in mind more than another sermon against alcohol. Or does he? "These young people are drinking in public," he says. "What do we read in Proverbs 23:21? 'The drunkard and the glutton shall come to poverty.'"

Suddenly, he stops. The sounds of the game fade away. Silence.

"When the game is over," he intones, his resonant preacher's voice dropped to a lower pitch, "Pete wants to take a drive. With night falling, he decides to head up into the foothills that surround our beautiful city. He wants Jenny to have a good view of the city at night." The film background starts rolling again.

"And that's not all Pete wants."

Deathly silence in the temple. A single spotlight illuminates the parked roadster, lights twinkling in the background.

"And now, my friends," whispers Willie, "what does Jenny do? She's a little tight, maybe even a little drunk. She's not a big girl. It doesn't take much." He pauses, thinking of Angie, his mind drifting. "Like so many of us, Jenny is new to Los Angeles. She is a good girl. She is a church-going girl. She is a Christian girl. JENNY IS A VIRGIN! She knows that sex outside marriage is a sin. She's come to Los Angeles from Pennsylvania or Kansas or Texas, and she knows—at least knows when she is sober, that one mistake can put her life in danger, physically, morally, that one mistake can ruin her, that one mistake can KILL her!

"WHAT DOES JENNY DO?" he shouts.

Not a sound is heard. The vast building, every seat filled, is as if empty.

"Look at the car—think of that car, my friends. The car has three forward gears. Jenny and Pete are in first gear. They are kissing. Now ask yourself this: What about Pete? Is Pete a low-life, a louse who would willingly take advantage of this tipsy girl? Of course, he isn't. Pete is a good boy, a college boy, a decent fellow who would never set out to ruin a girl's life."

Willie's voice falls lower. "But Pete is tipsy, too. Pete wants to go faster, to put the car in second gear."

From the rear of the temple comes a loud shout of "NO!" called out by a member of the staff. Quickly it echoes around the temple—"NO! NO! NO!"

"But, YES! YES! YES! my friends," shouts Willie back at them. "Pete wants to shift gears. Look, he is moving his hands onto Jenny's body, moving them places they shouldn't be, to private places under her clothes, warm places. Pete knows about cars. After first gear comes second. He is shifting gears, giving in to—TEMPTATION!"

This time the shouts from the audience are spontaneous. "NO! NO! NO!"

"What does Jenny do? She pushes his hands away, but they come back. She pushes again, and they come back again. The third time, she doesn't push. She's a little tipsy, a little tired—and yes, a little aroused. Clothes are unbuttoned and removed. Pete will say later that he's not responsible for Jenny's death. The gears in the car became automatic."

"Strike him dead, Lord," someone shouts.

"RUINATION!" answers Willie.

The curtain falls.

More than five hundred people declare themselves for Christ that night and $11,473 is offered to the church in gilded plates. The show has touched a chord with God's little people, people who have come from across the country to make Los Angeles their new home, people escaping the sin and corruption of the East, people determined to build new and better lives in the new and better place called Los Angeles.

Letters, many with offerings, pour in praising the Rev. Mull, praising the show and praising Angie l'Amoureux.

"A lesson for every girl in the country," the letters say.

Willie shows Angie the letters.

"It won't be long now," he says.

♦ ♦ ♦

The next day, at Oildale, outside Bakersfield, a roughneck named Johnny Perkins pauses while driving rivets into a derrick and shouts across the steel framework to a colleague:

"Hey Gil, I picked up this church broadcast last night. Girl in the cast's got your same weird last name . . . any relation?"

Part Two

CHAPTER 12

Cal wasn't supposed to be there. Sometimes when he was working late at the temple he would spend the night with his father at Sunset Tower, but he always let him know. This time, he hadn't had the chance. Maggie called to borrow his apartment at the last minute, and when he couldn't reach Willie he just headed for Sunset. He had his own key. Maggie was engaged to an Army Air Force pilot transferred to Honolulu, and Cal had no trouble vacating his apartment for a day or two when he came back unexpectedly. He didn't like Harold, though it was nothing personal. Harold had encouraged Maggie to take up flying. She was dangerous enough on the ground, quite frankly, lucky to be alive.

He was lounging on the couch with a book and a beer when he heard a click in the lock, then voices, one of them female.

No . . .

From a distance, he'd seen her before. Sometimes he would walk from the second-floor business office into the upper tiers at the temple to munch a sandwich and watch the noon rehearsals. Full-dress rehearsals meant choir and organist and for a really big show the orchestra would come in. Even from the high tiers, Angie's shapely, lithe body, even cloaked head-to-toe in immaculate white, stood out. They called her Sister Angie now, and she was doing some preaching. She was the new star.

He was on his feet in a second, stupidly smiling, wishing he could instantly evanesce.

"Oh," said Willie, flustered, "Cal, I had no idea. You didn't call . . . "

As his father blathered away, Cal observed the young woman he'd seen only from on high. Pretty, petite, not much make-up, short brown hair fluffed, dressed in a red and blue checkered cotton blouse and swishy dark skirt. Bare legs. Nothing white to be seen. She was nubile and girlish and devilishly sexy, and Cal did not know what to make of it. His father's flustering could not erase the hint of a smile on her lips. She is younger than I am, Cal thought. She held his gaze until he looked away. In all his years with his father, he'd never found himself in such a situation.

"Sorry, Dad," he said. "Maggie called at the last minute, Harold came in. You'd already left so I figured I'd just come over and—well, I think I'll be leaving."

"Don't even think of it," Willie said, improvising. "We've got scripts to go over. The guest room is yours. Everything is fine."

The guest room was his? Did the girl know that? Scripts? Everything was not fine. With Angie wearing not much in the way of clothes, they'd surely not come home to go over scripts. They could have done that at the temple and in any case, it was nearly eleven and they'd likely already been to dinner. His father's color suggested wine, but maybe it was embarrassment. Or anticipation. He looked to Angie, who was still watching him. The image of her naked in his father's bed passed his mind.

"You two excuse me a minute while I take off my coat and tie. Get to know each other."

"Can I get you a beer?" Cal asked.

She shook her head, moved his book from the couch and sat down. She'd not yet said a word. Was she his father's girlfriend? Was it possible? He'd had no idea. Chun hua, his Shanghai amah, passed his mind. He seemed to remember them in bed together, though how could he since he was a baby? He'd never thought of that aspect of his father before. He would gladly have sat down next to this fetching girl but couldn't because she'd come home with his father. He had to get out of there.

"You sign the checks," she said, finally breaking her silence, scrutinizing him. "How come we've never met?"

His brain was sending messages to leave, but his body was not reacting. He detected the smell of lilacs. Plumeria? Enchanting.

"I'm a bookkeeper. I rarely get off the second floor. Sometimes I sit up in the tiers to watch rehearsals. I've seen you."

"Why don't you sit down?" She was studying him, noticing the marks on his face. "You don't look like Willie."

He sat in a chair. "They say I look more like my mother. She was blonde, I'm told."

"A sad story. You caught the fever."

"He's told you?"

"Of course."

She'd kicked off her shoes and pulled her legs up under her. She was completely composed, not a trace of embarrassment. "Of course," she'd said. How much had Willie told her? How many times had they been here? Her skin was creamy, not olive like Willie's, but not light like his own. He wrote Angie l'Amoureux on her checks, but she was *Sister* Angie in the glass cases outside. French Canadian, maybe. He doubted that she was much over twenty-one.

"Angie, what can I get you?" Willie said, on his way to the kitchen. In the bedroom he'd fallen to his knees, prayed to

Augustine, who alone understood. He desperately wanted to make love to this woman, but why was Cal there? What did it mean?

"Dad—I'm off."

"No, you don't have . . ."

He caught himself, nodding, stopping in mid-sentence, as if to say, yes, we both know you have to leave. He'd changed into moccasins and cardigan, feeling better after his prayers. Why shouldn't Cal know he was in love? He'd think it was a regular affair, though in fact it was the first time Angie had come home with him. He'd been nervous as a debutante about it, and now was calm. Augustine understood that he wasn't ready. He hadn't been ready either.

Angie knew it was coming from the first day in the soda shop. Preacher or not, he'd seduced her with his eyes just like the others did. She'd been wary, tested him and he'd made good. What's more, she'd grown fond of him, even come to like the idea of being seduced by a preacher like her daddy, older even than her daddy, she imagined. The problem was not Willie; it was Gil. He'd disappeared, but she'd have to see him again if only to divorce him. If he found out she was with another man, he would kill her, she had no doubt about that. Kill her and the man, too, if they were together. Maybe she would get lucky and he would fall off a derrick, but she knew he wouldn't. He could dance up there like a ballerina.

"Where will you go?" asked Willie.

"Bel Air."

"It's late."

"It's not even eleven."

◆ ◆ ◆

He did not go to Bel Air. He stopped at the front desk and called Lizzie. Lizzie and Maggie lived together in Westwood, just down from the UCLA campus. Maggie was a fifth-year senior in engineering, and Lizzie a senior majoring in English literature. With Maggie at his place, he could sleep in her room until Harold was gone. Lizzie was up writing when he called, as he knew she would be.

She was not physically fearless like her sister, but she was a talented writer and she was tenacious. By all rights she should have been editor of the *Daily Bruin*, the student newspaper, except that the boys who voted for editor didn't think a girl should get the job. She was the only one on the staff who'd published anything outside the *Bruin* itself—including a piece in the *Times* on the Ku Klux Klan in Los Angeles. She also had the most story ideas, was the best editor and best rewriter for breaking stories on deadline. But she was a girl. She knew she had no chance but ran anyway to embarrass them, and when they offered to make her number two said no thanks and went back to writing.

She met him at the door of the apartment, upstairs in a long two-story stucco affair on a leafy Westwood street named Tiverton.

"Uncle Willie has a *guest*? What do you mean a guest? What kind of guest?"

"Don't ask."

"But he's a preacher," she said. "Aren't preachers supposed to be better than the rest of us?"

He didn't answer. "Can I get a beer?"

"Get two—I'm done for the night."

The sisters were as different as ever but had never been closer. The major change was that Lizzie no longer copied Maggie. If anything, it was the other way around, Maggie coming to appreciate her sister's composure. Lizzie had decided early on that if she copied Maggie she would die for she lacked her physical skills and fearlessness. She'd never been an equestrian, never climbed an oil derrick or into the cockpit of an airplane. She didn't drive fast or challenge men to physical contests. She was not as striking as her sister, but she was attractive. She was also talented, focused and gritty. You could not bully Lizzie Mull.

He opened two Eastsides and returned to the living room where she'd moved from desk to couch. She wore shorts and a T-shirt, and her bangs looked more like a boy's cut than a girl's.

"Who is she?"

He sighed. He hated gossip. "Sister Angie. Do you know who that is?"

"With that name I suppose some old bag in black high-buttons and chignon singing contralto in Uncle Willie's choir."

He laughed. "Not quite. Your age but sexier."

Her eyes doubled in size. "No! And they are . . ?"

"Reading scripts."

"At midnight?"

"I suppose they've finished reading scripts by now."

Now she laughed. "I never saw Uncle Willie as the type."

"What type?"

"As someone who fooled around."

"You haven't seen Sister Angie."

"My goodness. What is that I hear—envy, jealousy, desire?"

"Moving on. So, tell me, are Maggie and Harold finally going to tie the knot?"

"He wants her to go back to Honolulu with him."

"And?"

"No way she'll quit school ahead of finals."

"Tough choice."

"Not really. Maggie has her priorities—though I know she wants to try marriage someday, try children."

"Has to try everything, right?"

"If not Harold with someone else."

"I imagine she can have her pick."

"And do better than Harold." She smiled nicely. "So here we are, dear cousin, thrown together once again while everyone else out there is making love. *Uh oh.*"

They heard the key and saw Maggie at the door.

"Don't tell me."

"Cal, you might as well go home."

"What happened, Mag?" said Lizzie.

"Just who does that guy think he is?"

"You mind if I stay?" said Cal. "I imagine my place is a mess."

She laughed. "Broken plates everywhere."

"There's always the couch," said Lizzie

"First I'm going to get one of those," said Maggie, slipping into the kitchen for a beer. "Why exactly *are* you here, Cal?" she called out. "I thought you were staying with Uncle Willie."

"It seems Uncle Willie has a girlfriend," said Lizzie.

"*No!*" she cried, coming back.

"I knew I shouldn't have said anything."

"Who is she?"

"Look, I don't even know if she is a girlfriend. She works at the temple. They brought scripts home to work on."

"At eleven at night," said Lizzie. "Cal wasn't supposed to be there."

Maggie sat down next to her sister, Cal in an easy chair. He looked from one to the other. Though they didn't look alike, a keen eye could pick up similarities—shape of the head, line of the mouth, little mannerisms with the hands. Maggie was taller and more athletic, generally more spectacular. Her hair was darker and her skin more olive—more genes from her father's side, Nelly liked to say. She turned heads wherever she went. In UCLA's engineering department, no one had ever seen anything like her. Lizzie had a softer appearance, lighter, less commanding, eyes more hazel than her sister's almond, more of her mother's farm girl solidity. More introspective, less spontaneous, she'd always been more popular because she didn't have to beat everyone at everything. The sisters didn't have the same friends or interests, didn't talk alike or dress alike. Maggie wore Levi's to school at a time when girls were never seen in anything but skirts; Lizzie dressed like the other girls. Maggie was a talker and Lizzie a listener.

"Shouldn't the question be," said Cal to Maggie, "why are *you* here?"

"It is over."

"*Over* over?" said Lizzie.

"Over, over, over. He gave me an ultimatum."

"Ah, big mistake."

"You're taking it well," said Cal.

Maggie leveled her dark eyes on him. "I got what I wanted. I know how to fly. He got what he wanted. We're even."

"Didn't you both want to get married or something?"

"So, we'll marry someone else."

Hair still mussed, she drank her bottle half down with a few large swigs. "Now, back to Uncle Willie: Who is this script reader?"

"Sister Angie," said Lizzie. "Cal says she's sexier than I am."

"*What*? How old is she?"

He laughed. If Maggie could laugh about breaking off with Harold, he ought to be able to laugh about Willie and Angie. He was still thinking about Angie. "How would I know?"

"Don't be coy." Said Maggie. "How old is she?"

"If I had to guess I'd say she's about your age—maybe a little younger."

"Oh my God!" said Maggie. "Poor Uncle Willie. Who is she?"

"She's a preacher—quite good, too, I must say."

"Since when did you start attending services?"

"Sometimes I watch rehearsals."

"Uncle Willie wouldn't do anything stupid, would he?" said Lizzie.

"Like . . . ?"

"Like 'Taking a Ride,' remember that show?"

"I don't," said Maggie.

"Girl got drunk and got pregnant," said Lizzie. "Mother and I listened."

"That was Sister Angie before she was Sister Angie. Anyway, what do I know about anything," he said, feeling suddenly disloyal. "Maybe they *are* reading scripts."

"Come on, Cal. Who are we going to tell?" said Maggie.

"*Whom*," said Lizzie.

"Nelly for one," said Cal, "who would tell everyone, starting with Eddie."

"Cal," said Lizzie, annoyance in her voice, "haven't we trusted each other just about forever? When has any one of us ever blabbed—name one time."

She was right, of course. A hundred times one of them might have said something that could have hurt the others. No one ever did. Trust was their bond.

"If you want my uninformed opinion," he said, "I think Dad is in love. First time since my mother died."

"Their generation still believes in love," Lizzie said. "And marriage. Imagine."

"The trouble with love and marriage," said Maggie, "is that the men are in control. They get you pregnant to stay in control."

"So, don't get pregnant," he said.

"That's what was wrong with that program of Uncle Willie's" said Lizzie. "We talked about it at the *Bruin*—at least the guys talked about it. The girl was stupid, they said—should have brought her diaphragm."

"Why would she have a diaphragm?" said Cal. "She was a virgin."

"Exactly my point: that's the male mind for you."

He turned to Maggie. "So, what do you do now that marriage is out? What do you both do after graduation, which if I'm not mistaken, is around the corner."

"The *Times* asked me in for an interview," said Lizzie. "They're looking for women reporters."

"Well, hallelujah! Why didn't you say something to somebody?"

"Let's see first if it comes through—and they don't put me on the society page."

"And you, Mag?"

"I'm going to fly. Where and what, I don't know yet."

"Breaking barriers."

"Of all kinds," said Lizzie. "And you, Cousin Cal. What barriers will you be breaking—or are you going to be your father's bookkeeper forever?"

"As a matter of fact, I'm working on something."

"Which is?" they said in unison.

"To quote Lizzie: 'Let's see first if it comes through.'"

CHAPTER 13

Both men wore dark suits and fedoras, the common dress code for downtown businessmen in Depression-era Los Angeles, summer or winter. Willie stood at the door of his second-floor office to greet them, smiling as Miss Shields led them across the reception room, greeting them as he greeted benefactors every Tuesday, which was their day. He didn't know these men, just as he didn't know most people who phoned seeking an appointment following a particularly uplifting Sunday evening show. Tuesday mornings were for benefactors, Tuesday afternoons for Soldiers. The hungry and destitute, alms-seekers of all kinds, were always welcome, routed to the first-floor commissary at the rear of the building.

Miss Shields, his secretary, was good at screening people with legitimate interests from cranks and frauds, for the temple attracted all kinds. When she wasn't sure, she referred the petitioner to the Rev. Marcus Wynetski, the robust associate pastor in the adjoining office, a man who could see through any fake. Most of Willie's Tuesday morning visitors ended up contributing something to the temple. Jesus was served.

He led them into his office and invited them to be seated. From their chairs they could look over the pastor's head through large picture windows to the blessed San Gabriel Mountains in the distance, a view, in Willie's opinion, that inspired visitors to greater generosity. He turned a business card over in his hand: "John C. Porter, Used Auto Parts."

Was there something familiar about him? A clump of silver

hair rose in a pompadour over a large head resting on shoulders too narrow for the bulky body. The tailoring was first class if the body was not. Both men were businesslike, to the point, crisp.

"There are poisons, here," said John C. Porter, whose suit, unlike his friend's, was pinstriped. It was one of the stranger opening statements Willie had heard, but his expression never changed. He was there to listen to whatever his petitioners had on their minds. Confrontation was not the path to contribution.

"This is not the Los Angeles we have in mind, Reverend Mull. Since no one in our community has greater moral influence than you, we wanted to bring the issue to you directly."

His voice was wheezy, sign of a heavy smoker. Porter had reached into his pocket for what was surely a pack of cigarettes, stopping when he noticed the absence of ashtrays.

"Toxics," said the second man.

Leaning back in his swivel chair, Willie glanced at the second card: "Fred W. Gilmore, Real Estate."

Willie, too, wore a dark suit, as he always did during the week. They could have been three businessmen discussing insurance rates or stock prices or the real estate market rather than two men calling on a preacher on an unspecified matter involving something toxic.

Miss Shields intervened with coffee, and for a moment the visitors were diverted from poisons and toxics to take sugar and a little milk with their coffee and bite into biscuits up fresh from the commissary. No doubt they were craving to light up, Willie thought, but abstinence would do them some good. Gilmore commented on the beautiful view of the mountains, bringing a smile to the pastor's face. They returned to business.

"Los Angeles," said John C. Porter, his heavy face straining to look benign against its natural tendency, "is the only Anglo-Saxon city left in America." He paused. "Did you know that,

Reverend? I want you to think about that. We are the only ones left, the last bastion, the last pure city in America."

"And why is that?" added Fred W. Gilmore quickly. They've rehearsed this, Willie thought, rehearsed it or done it before. "It's because the people who come to our fair city, who come as a result of what they hear about it—hear about because of the work we do, we, the promoters of this city—are our kind of people: family people, God-fearing people, educated people, working people . . ."

". . . *white* people," said John C. Porter.

Ah, thought Willie.

"Ours is the only city in America not dominated by foreigners," continued John C. Porter, shifting his portly body in the chair. "The only city where American values—Protestant, white, moral values—still reign. Think of that, Reverend."

"And we aim to keep it that way," said Fred W. Gilmore. He was a lean man, knife-faced, with a healthier but meaner look than his partner. "You can help us."

"I'll need your help when I'm elected mayor," said John C. Porter. "I am running and there is no doubt in my mind but that I will win. I have the support."

It's coming back, thought Willie: article in the *Times* about Porter—Midwesterner, Republican, Methodist, if he remembered. There'd been something else in that article, too . . . something about . . . his mind jammed and it wouldn't come. Typical immigrant to Los Angeles: opinionated, self-educated, intolerant, ready to remake the city into his Chicago or Kansas City image. Probably listens to Bob Shoemaker, not KWEM. No chance to be elected, he thought. Porter's hat had slipped to the floor as he talked, and he left it lying there, upside down, annoying Willie.

They kept at it for a while, Willie listening, nodding, occasionally glancing at the hat trying to suggest telepathically to

Porter to pick it up or at least turn it over. He rarely said anything during these sessions unless asked directly. For him they
were confessionals where citizens came to unburden themselves. He could have objected or disagreed for he'd heard
some strange things in his time, but that would interfere with
the process. They came with a need of some kind. His job was
to listen and understand. Open the spigot and see what came
gushing out. See if there was room in there for Jesus.

There was never a quid pro quo. The Temple of the Angels
and Church of the New Gospel were supported by those who
understood the value to the community of the Rev. Mull's message of love, faith, and salvation in Jesus Christ. Willie listened
to all his visitors, not just for their support, but for the ideas
they brought. Sermons, even Sunday evening shows, had grown
from these meetings. It was not uncommon for him to usher
someone out on Tuesday morning and sit down immediately
to comb through scripture preparing his Sunday sermon. A
seed had been planted and was growing before his visitors even
reached the street.

The check written by Fred W. Gilmore was for two hundred
dollars, drawn on the Farmers and Merchants National Bank
of Los Angeles, Fourth and Main. Willie accepted it humbly as
he accepted all donations, as the due of his church. He would
endorse it, route it to the business office whence Cal at some
point would carry it to Security Trust at Spring and Fifth. It was
a modest first-time offering, but its value was enhanced by the
words spoken by Gilmore as he placed it in Willie's hand:

"Reverend, let this be just the beginning of our association.
I have to tell you: my whole family gathers around the radio
every Sunday evening to hear your splendid broadcasts. You,
sir, are God's gift to our community."

Willie smiled modestly and shook hands with his visitors.

He stared into John C. Porter's broad Midwestern face one last time, searching. It came to him, finally, as he bid them goodbye at the door: How could he have forgotten?

Porter and Gilmore were the Klan.

♦ ♦ ♦

This would not be one of the days when Willie was at work on his sermon before his visitors left the building. For this, he needed time and reflection. He'd heard of the Klan's growing presence in Los Angeles, which it made little effort to conceal. Honest citizens like John C. Porter and Fred W. Gilmore never announced they were from the Klan—any more than another visitor would announce he was a Republican or Freemason or Odd Fellow. People came to him as individuals, on personal business. But the Klan expected you to know who they were, and their message didn't leave much doubt.

It was not the lynching message of the South, for the target wasn't the handful of Negroes who'd come to Los Angeles during the Depression. No, the Klan in Los Angeles had its sights on Mexicans, Jews, and Catholics, all arriving in large numbers (though the Mexicans had been there first). When the Klan said white, it meant Protestant, Anglo-Saxon white. The Klan was behind the brochures sent out by cities like Glendale. Unwritten covenants were being established, and if the law kept racial and religious codes from being officially imposed, there were other ways. Unofficial ethnic enclaves were being established (no one dared call them ghettos) across the city. New residents had to pass interviews. It was no accident that Fred W. Gilmore was in real estate. Real estate agents know how to enforce covenants. If Willie had asked his brother about it, Eddie would have said, "What's the problem? People have the right to live with their own, don't they?"

He walked to the window and stood looking out over the panorama that brought him so much inspiration, over the city he loved more than any other, the only city he had ever loved. Could he ever repay Eddie for bringing him here? His eyes followed the mountains to the crest, the blessed green San Gabriels, his gaze slowly coming back down to the foothills and the mission, Mission San Gabriel, founded by the Franciscans, the fourth of the string of missions founded as the friars came up from Mexico.

"Protestant white values, Anglo-Saxon values," the Klansmen said. Los Angeles was the last Anglo-Saxon city in America, the last pure city. Was there a sermon in there somewhere?

But *who* in Los Angeles was Anglo-Saxon? Who was pure? Yes, they'd taken him for Anglo-Saxon—how could they not with a name like Mull, taken from that windswept island off the coast of Scotland? The reality was that he was Anglo-Saxon mixed with German and Spanish and yes, Mexican, blood, the very people the Klan sought to drive from the city. Nothing pure about any of that. Grandpa Otto Herzog married *Abuela* Isabel who was the daughter of Adm. Jose Maria Cullel of Barcelona and Doña Isabel de los Santos, born in Mexico, of Spanish Catholic parents. Willie and Eddie never talked about it, but they were part Hispanic—the dark eyes, the slightly olive skin, the wavy dark hair, the knowledge of the Spanish language.

His eyes crawled over the mountains seeking inspiration. For once he thought not of Saint Augustine, but of Saint Gabriel, the angel who appeared to Christ at Gethsemane, who comforted Him, offered Him succor before He was taken, helped Him see that this earthly life was but a prelude to eternal heaven. Saint Gabriel, who gave his name to the mountains and to the city, Los Angeles, city of the angels. He turned to look at his painting of Christ at Gethsemane, not the original Hofmann, he'd not yet been able to pry it away from the Riverside Church, but he kept trying. Such a beautiful story! Yes, there was a sermon in that, a sermon about sacrifice and courage and fate—yes, fate, predestination above all. He never forgot his Presbyterian training.

The Klansmen had hit on something, something about preserving what the rest of the country had lost with their sordid ghettos and tenements. Congress had banned Asians a few years before and maybe Mexicans should be next. Why not? They were Catholics who never set foot in the temple. If there was a Mexican Soldier, Willie had never met him. And what of the Jews? Chandler at the *Times* had been railing against Jewish influence for years, especially in Hollywood. And Negroes? No, not many had come yet, but who could foresee the future? Maybe the Klan was right: Maybe the *Times* was right. Maybe it was time to stand up for the city before it was too late. Los Angeles must not become another New York, another Chicago.

Beautiful sight, the San Gabriels, beautiful pure city, God's creation. He always let his ideas simmer. He closed his eyes, letting thoughts swirl, curious to see what would come. How long did he stand there? Five minutes, ten, maybe longer, but the only thought that came to him was Angie. He tried to push her away and concentrate on the message, but she would not go. The angel Gabriel had brought to mind his own angel, Angie l'Amoureux. Was that not the translation of her name—the angel of love? He felt a stirring in his loins. Everything else was wiped away. He could not work. He had to see her.

In middle age, the Rev. Willie Mull had discovered sexual ecstasy. It happens. "Renounce, renounce," he read in Saint Augustine. "Let it be done." But If it was to be now, Lord, he asked, why did you send Angie to me? It could hardly be coincidence.

And should not a beautiful woman be admired? And cannot admiration lead to passion and love. And marriage. Yes, marriage. Is that not the point of earthly beauty? Can we not see a beautiful woman as we hear beautiful music or admire beautiful mountains, letting their purity and perfection lift our spirits, inspire our soul, resuscitate us, rejuvenate us? What would life be without beauty?

He went to the chapel, fell to his knees and prayed to Jesus: I could have entered any shop that day, he said. She was a lonely girl, I a lonely man. My body was stuffed up, bloated, deadening my work. You sent me to Angie, and with her I found catharsis. My sermons move people like never before. In her arms, I was reborn and passed the feeling of rejuvenation on to the Soldiers, who love her as I do. If not divine will, what is it that brings hundreds down the aisles each week to be healed and reborn as I have been; that brings contributions that enrich the church in the name of Jesus Christ? Sister Angie lit up my body and soul, and I transferred that light to my flock.

"Love her, love her!" You said.

And I did.

CHAPTER 14

The distance from Cal's office at the rear of the temple to Willie's in the front was forty-seven paces, at the opposite end of the second-floor roundabout. He knew the precise distance, though rarely made the trip. He had no interest in religion and Willie no interest in accounting. He wasn't the first son reluctantly to work for his father during the Depression, when jobs were hard to find, even in Los Angeles. He'd worked his way up from part time bookkeeper while still at USC to fulltime business manager. The Depression had not hit Los Angeles as hard as some cities, but that was the problem: Armies of the unemployed trooped westward looking for work. The West did not have enough jobs for them all.

"Haven't seen you in a month of Sundays," said Miss Shields with a big smile as he stepped into the reception room. He liked the lady, briskly cheery and efficient, someone who kept him informed on the phone and took good care of his father. He never failed to ask about her cats, and she never failed to give the same answer: that she couldn't let them outside for fear of coyotes. She lived up somewhere in the Hollywood Hills where the critters had been used to living alone and took out their resentment on human intrusion by dining on their pets. Cal wondered if Miss Shields knew of Willie and Angie.

"He's working on a Sunday script," she said. "Go right in."

"Morning, Dad."

Jacket off, dressed in a starched white shirt with silver cufflinks and dark tie, Willie looked up and smiled. There'd been some awkwardness following the unexpected meeting at Sunset

Tower, but it had passed. Father and son had been through too much together to stop being friends. Cal still had his key for Sunset, though hadn't been back since That Night, as he thought of it. Even when he worked late, he drove home, taking no chances. Maggie had not used his apartment again. Harold was history, and as far as Cal knew, had not been replaced.

He surveyed the room, looking for changes. His eye ran over the bookshelves, old oaken desk, leather chairs and soft couch for afternoon naps. He saw the fresh flowers—brought by Miss Shields every morning, even in winter. Church people always know where to find flowers. He glanced out the picture windows with their view of the mountains, a view he did not have at the rear. He spied the chessboard from Tesoro. As usual, a game was in progress, most likely with Henry Callender. His eyes came to rest on the 1536 first edition Tyndale Bible on the reading stand by the desk. The bible and the chessboard were his father's two most prized possessions. It was a tidy, scholarly, preacherly room with a beautiful painting of Christ at Gethsemane, and he felt a rush of affection for his father.

Willie watched him examining the bible. "Never too late, you know."

Cal smiled. "Got some news for you," he said, sitting down.

Willie took off his reading glasses, laid down his pencil, waiting.

"I'm going to take a sabbatical, go off to Europe a while. Do the grand tour."

Willie frowned. "*Europe*? This is hardly the time to be visiting Europe."

"Calm before the storm."

"This is calm?"

"There's more: Maggie is coming with me."

"Maggie, heavens—does Eddie know?'

"Would he care?"

"Of course, he would," said Willie, annoyed. "I don't like it. People talking about war before the year is out and you're dragging Maggie off to Europe?"

"Just for the summer. I haven't seen anything about war. The Austrians didn't fight. They welcomed the Germans."

"The Czechs don't seem so enthusiastic."

"It's a chance to see things while we still can."

"Hitler's not done."

They were talking past each other.

"Do you know I haven't been out of the country since we came back from China? How old was I—four?"

Willie thought for a moment. "Yes, you were four. Where would you go in Europe?"

"We're working on the itinerary. So far it's London, Berlin, Prague and Paris."

"*Berlin*?"

"Why not?"

His father swung around in the swivel chair to look out at his favorite sight. "Because you might get stuck there."

"America isn't involved in those quarrels. I don't see a problem."

"Why Prague?"

"Because of *you*, Dad," he said with a huge smile. "Prague is where you went as a seminarian—at least that's what you've told me enough times. Prague, Jan Hus, where the Reformation began."

Pleased, Willie turned back from the mountains. "And what about the temple?"

"The department's in good hands. Don't worry."

"I always worry. It is my nature."

"Pray to overcome it."

"I do pray, Cal, I do. Seriously, does Uncle Eddie know about Maggie?"

"Maggie does what she wants. Right now she wants to fly European planes."

Willie nodded. "Impulsive girl—not one to let loose in Europe. Look a little odd, won't it—I mean the two of you together like that? You'll have to have separate rooms."

Cal smiled. "We'll manage."

"You're going to watch over her, right? Make sure she comes home again."

"Do my best. No one really watches over Maggie."

"What about Lizzie—she's not going?"

"Lizzie has been hired by the *Times*."

"I hadn't heard. No one tells me anything. Is that what she wanted?"

"You bet."

"Good for her. So when would you leave?"

"We're aiming for a month. Lots of preparations."

"You'll stay in touch?"

"At every stop."

"Say, I wonder if you'd do me a little favor before you go off."

"Name it."

"Take Angie to lunch."

He didn't answer. Didn't like it. Saw there was more in it than lunch.

"Cal, trust me on this."

"Are you trying to tell me something?"

"Take the Cadillac. Take her to the Brown Derby. She said you two kind of clicked that night at my place. Get to know her, that's all I ask. You never know."

"You never know what?"

Willie laughed. "Look, we preachers have certain gifts, but I've never known one yet who could see into the future."

Against his inclinations, Cal took Angie to lunch at the Brown Derby, the first time he'd seen her since That Night. As business manager he kept the keys to the Cadillac and thought he might as well use it for once. They parked on Wilshire and walked in unnoticed. They were seated at a booth by the window, ordered chicken salad sandwiches and iced tea. He was slightly surprised that no one came up for an autograph, for Angie was well known, though not yet quite well enough known to have her picture up on the wall with Willie's and the other Hollywood stars. That would come.

Reflecting on it later, it occurred to him that no one approached because she was unrecognizable. The woman on stage at the temple, the woman in the display cases outside, the woman dressed in white and posing under a halo with her hands behind her head so that the long sleeves billowed down and resembled wings, was neither the girl at Sunset Tower nor the girl next to him at the Brown Derby in tight yellow sweater and swishy skirt.

There were two Angies, and at lunch he decided that the Brown Derby Angie was the real one. The other one, Sister Angie, who preached and saved and healed on the stage at the temple and was adored by millions nearly as much as Willie himself, for him was no more than a plastic personage borrowed from a Hollywood stage set. For two hours they exchanged not one word about God or Jesus or the temple or Willie. It was as if they were on a real date, the kind he used to have at USC when he'd take a pretty sorority girl to a lunch counter on Jefferson. He was fascinated and he was aroused. Angie was deadly. He feared for his father. He feared for himself. He was glad to be leaving town.

◆ ◆ ◆

As war approached, the *Los Angeles Times* was a newspaper in search of an identity. Newspapers take on the characters of their founders even more than their cities and keep that character long after the founders are gone, especially when it is a family newspaper. It took four generations of Otises and Chandlers for the *Times* to transform itself from conservative to liberal, and when Elizabeth Mull went to work at First and Spring Streets in the summer of 1938 it had not yet begun the transformation. Harrison Gray Otis, the founder, was an antediluvian scoundrel. Harry Chandler, his son-in-law, a key figure in the San Fernando Land and Water Syndicate flimflammery, was only marginally an improvement. They pretended to run their newspaper in the community interest, but did so only when the community interest happened to coincide with their personal interest. The *Times*'s focus was always local. It had no national or international aspirations, but insofar as Southern California was concerned, it was the kingfish. Mayors, supervisors, councilmen, district attorneys, judges and police chiefs all came to pay obeisance at First and Spring.

Women weren't entirely unknown on the third floor. Journalism has been a comparatively good profession for women because it is a literary profession where girls, as any boy who ever sat with them in an English class knows, tend to excel. "Comparatively" is the operative word. For most of the twentieth century and all centuries previous, women were largely restricted to two respectable professions: teaching and nursing. If writers they were, they labored anonymously at home or, for the more daring, under a pseudonym. It was during the first half of the twentieth century that women came to be found here and there in newsrooms, generally working on the "woman's page," which in time became the "society pages."

The *Times* was the stodgiest of newspapers. Its city editor, a man named Larry McManus who'd come out from Detroit in the twenties and been hired by Harry Chandler himself, saw this as an anomaly in the entertainment capital of the world. With support from Norman Chandler, Harry's son and heir, he set out to change things, if for no other reason than to keep pace with Hearst's *Examiner*, which was not stodgy. Lizzie Mull was good enough to have gone if she'd wanted to New York, where newspapers were more enlightened, but since she had no desire to leave home, she accepted McManus's offer. She let Nelly think it was her pleading that persuaded her to stay home, especially with Maggie off in Europe, but the truth was Lizzie never intended to leave. Los Angeles was what she knew and loved. It was where she would make her mark.

Because of her name, she almost wasn't hired. If there was a better-known name than Mull in Los Angeles it would have been Fairbanks or Pickford or the new fellow in town named Howard Hughes, but McManus had wanted to hire her since he'd read her article on the Klan and invited her in. He didn't like that she came from a prominent local family and knew the males would complain about a female in the newsroom, but he wasn't about to turn down someone he wanted because of her name or her sex. His solution was to send her provisionally to the society pages, where there were no males to complain.

The society editor was a prickly matron named Miss Adelaide Nevin, and no one in the city, not even the publisher's wife, had more power in Los Angeles society than Miss Adelaide, as she was known. She could make or break anyone in the Blue Book or Junior League by the simple expedient of not covering—or not covering very well—her charity ball, cotillion or coming-out party. The publisher's wife had long ago stopped passing on complaints to her husband from her friends in Bel Air, Hancock Park and San Marino about Miss Adelaide's slights. The publisher refused to lock horns with his society editor for the simple reason that Miss Adelaide knew Los Angeles society better than anyone else, including his wife.

Lizzie was miffed. She'd been slighted and passed over on the *Daily Bruin* because of her sex, and the society pages seemed more of the same. McManus promised it would not be for long. "No one ever regrets working for Miss Adelaide," he said. She never did.

Society pages are all about names—the more, the better—and the names must be spelled right and their gowns precisely described, and of course the gown's designer must be identified, and the photos must be taken straight on—no profiles or at least not from the bad side, which is usually the left for some reason. And quotes. You get quotes wrong at the risk of lawsuits from people with more money even than the Chandlers. Society pages are good for training eyes and memories. Unlike newsroom reporters, the one thing a society reporter never has to do is ask for ages. Society pages don't run ages because they would all be lies.

Miss Adelaide's department occupied one corner of the *Times*'s huge third-floor newsroom and tended to be left to itself. Technically, Miss Adelaide reported to McManus, but in reality, she was autonomous. In her time with Miss Adelaide, Lizzy rarely ventured into the main newsroom. She had no business there. The males, though, sensing that she would soon be out of her cage, were curious. Most of the females working society were of a certain age and tended to the homely side. Lizzie was neither.

It started with Max Untermeyer, star reporter, who walked over one day, plumped his ample behind on a corner of her desk and said: "Doing anything tonight, hon?"

"I have to go straight home, Mr. Untermeyer."

"Call me Max."

"I have to go straight home, Max."

"Got a sweetie?"

"I don't like sweets."

After three months, McManus kept his promise and transferred her, not to the newsroom but to the hall of justice. He hesitated at first, for Eddie Mull's name had been popping up here and there lately and Willie was always in the news. But he stuck to his view not to make decisions about Lizzie based on her name. He talked with Miss Adelaide, who confirmed everything he thought. She was a thorough and relentless reporter, just what the hall of justice needed, a place that had become an old boys' network of reporters and cops bowling together and hoisting together and sitting on more stories than they produced.

It wasn't a popular decision. The hall of justice is a huge beat that includes everything that touches on law and order in Los Angeles City and County—namely police, sheriff, courts, jails, district attorney, public defender, tax collector and coroner. The *Times* had had dozens of people at the hall since it was opened in 1925, old and young, cronies and cubs, fast and slow, cynics and optimists, but they had one thing in common: They were all males. Lizzie was the first female. Pat Murphy, the bureau chief, visited McManus and asked him not to do it. The guys, he said, meaning the cops, reporters, and assistant DAs who ran the place, wouldn't understand. "Are we so hard up that you have to take girls off the society pages?"

"Don't get your prejudices up, Murph. She's a good reporter. She'll do a good job."

"What about her name?"

"If they ask, just say the *Times* never asks reporters about their parents."

"That's a lie."

"Say it anyway."

"There's something else."

"What would that be?"

"She'll be a distraction."

"She won't. Lizzie has learned the fine art of being inconspicuous. The boys in the newsroom found that out and now it's the turn of the boys at the hall. Take her around to all the departments. Don't delegate. *You* make the introductions."

The district attorney, Barton Pitts, was out the day Murphy took Lizzie to his office. He'd already taken her to the offices of the sheriff, police chief, and judges, and was saving the coroner, appropriately, for last. He'd arranged the DA's visit for when Pitts was out because Murphy regarded Pitts, a Texan twice elected on the basis of not interfering in the city's business interests, legitimate or otherwise, as his own exclusive property. Nobody on the *Times* was allowed to see Pitts without Murphy's express approval, which never was given and therefore never sought. Lizzie would have to be satisfied with the assistant DA.

Pat Murphy had been at the hall of justice from the beginning and knew everyone in the building, some as corrupt as Pitts and some as virtuous as Murphy's own daughter Mary, who was a nun. His dossier on Pitts was as thick as a Tolstoy novel and went on growing. He kept it hidden at home in a place known only to himself—and to Mary, just in case. Until Murphy was ready, no other *Times* reporter was allowed close.

"Corrupt as they come," Murphy wrote in his notebooks, cataloguing such crimes as protecting bootleggers, taking payoffs from gambling ships and protection rackets, kickbacks from contractors and shielding movie studio bosses from various crimes in return for being supplied with starlets. Murder was not included in the notebooks for the simple reason that time would run out for Murphy. Pitts's style of living far exceeded his district attorney's salary, and he was not shy about displaying it. His tentacles reached into every corner of the city, including the *Times* itself, which had endorsed his election—twice. His knowledge and his connections were his protection. He was protected from everyone but Pat Murphy.

CHAPTER 15

They began meeting at Angie's place. Sometimes Willie drove his blue Chevy Roadster, parking in different spots around the neighborhood so it would not be recognized. Sometimes he arrived on the Red Cars from the temple, sometimes on the Yellow Cars which came up Sunset to Glendale. They were discreet, Willie always arriving and departing alone, incognito.

Deprived of affection for so long, he hungered for her. "Girls are so far ahead of boys," she said. "It takes an older man to make us even." They spent hours awake in bed, fighting off sleep to rest in each other's arms. She'd never learned to make love before, just did what Gil told her. If Willie awakened first he would place his hand gently on her thigh and move it slowly upward. The smoothness of her body was astonishing and his hand moved along the curve of her hip and over skin as smooth as the silk sheets he'd bought for her bed.

Afterward, they liked to lie in bed reading scripture. He was amazed at her knowledge and gift of communication. She could take a snippet from either testament and turn it into a sermon. She had the gift. She was Sister Angie now, an authentic Pentecostal revivalist who, astonishingly, proved to have healing powers comparable to his. Her father, the Rev. Jimmy Smallwood, a Beaumont Baptist, had infused his daughter with Pentecostalist urgency before she was a teenager. ("Christ could return any minute, and we must be prepared.") The Soldiers loved her, and the ranks were soaring, coast to coast. She delivered the sermons every other Sunday, giving Willie more time to work on his Sunday night shows.

She demanded nothing of him, so that having found her, he began to fear losing her, as he'd lost Millie. He could not go through that again. The more they loved, the more addicted to her he became, the more he was afraid. She gave him no reason to fear, but he feared anyway. What had he done to deserve this gift, he asked himself, knowing it could not last, knowing it must not last if he was true to Saint Augustine. He sought to fortify himself:

"Let it end," he said, "and I will look back on this time as a new man, a better man, a stronger preacher. I am gaining strength." His body was performing as the Lord meant it to. He read from Corinthians: "The body is not for fornication but for the Lord."

He saw the change in Angie as well. When first they met, she was silent, suspicious, repressing her piety. Now she was vibrant, radiating love and energy and inspiring others. She'd become the temple's virginal star. Letters poured in from mothers testifying how Sister Angie had changed their daughters' lives and from men bearing witness to their new respect for women. Hundreds of new people joined the regiments of Soldiers for God every week. In the city, crime was down, the newspapers attributing it to the Church of the New Gospel.

The newspapers had rallied to him—or was it to Sister Angie?

"They offer not the torments of hell, but the joy of salvation," a Chandler editorial proclaimed following a long investigation by *Times'*s reporters. "They never fail to keep their eyes on the ultimate goal: *rebirth of the congregation.*"

Henry Callender brought him the editorial under the headline. "Rebirth of the Congregation." The words jolted him. Recently he'd gone to a theater off Sunset to see *Birth of a Nation,* a silent movie so strange and powerful that he'd sat through it twice. The theme, "a mighty cleansing must be wrought," was etched in his mind. What providential urge had sent him to see a movie about the Ku Klux Klan saving the nation from former slaves? He began to see his task clearly: rebirth of Los Angeles would be the basis of his sermon on race, the sermon he'd pondered since meeting with John C. Porter and Fred W. Gilmore.

He began writing on the lined pad he used for drafting sermons, his neat, small script fine and clear so Miss Shields could easily correct and transcribe. On the top he wrote: "Rebirth of the City Through a Mighty Cleansing."

The words flowed from his pen:

Sacred city hewn from the desiccated plains by the toil of our forefathers; city of sunshine, virtue and health eschewing forever darkness and vice. But beware of poisons: poisons from abroad eating away at the fiber of our community and the purity of our life; toxins that would destroy our homes, besmirch the purity of our womanhood and sully our social intercourse. The Lord has delivered us to this blessed place, the City of Angels, guarded by the Archangel Gabriel. We have brought forth the water that nourishes the orchards and sustains our life. We are flourishing. We will not be contaminated; we will not be overrun; we will not be defiled. We will be reborn through a mighty cleansing.

"What do you think?"

The sun was just showing through the curtains, and he had read it aloud to her in bed. They'd slipped out to a little Valley restaurant the night before and come home to make love. She was on her back, naked and propped up against the pillows, semi-dozing, sheets just covering her breasts. He found it hard to concentrate.

"Poisons?" she said. "Toxins—what are you talking about, Willie?"

"Well, you know . . ."

"What do I know?"

"What do you think?"

"I have no idea what you're talking about."

"Foreigners . . . Jews . . . Mexicans."

She was silent so long he suspected she'd fallen back asleep. He looked over, saw her eyes wide and staring at him.

"Jews . . . Mexicans?"

"Yes."

"*Mexicans?*"

"Yes, Mexicans."

She'd turned, the sheet slipping. His gaze passed to her body, and he was aroused.

"What do you mean, Mexicans?"

"What do I mean? I mean Mexicans, people from Mexico."

"Willie . . ."

"Dearest . . ." He moved toward her. She felt his erection poking against her thigh.

"You can't say that."

"I can't say what?"

"You can't give that sermon."

"What do you mean I can't give it?"

"You can't give it, Willie," she repeated, louder this time, pushing him away.

"But why?" He had begun to wilt.

She closed her eyes and laid back against the pillows.

"*Don't give it!*"

"But why?"

"*Because I am Mexican!*"

He was stunned, limp instantly, uncomprehending, nothing Mexican about her name. Why was he suddenly afraid? "*You?*"

"Me."

He fell back onto his pillow, the sermon slipping to the floor. Now it was he who lay on his back, eyes wide, staring at the ceiling.

She was mystified. "Being Mexican's not that bad, you know. I'm really only half Mexican."

He said nothing. Outside a Big Red Car clanged down Glendale Boulevard.

"Willie, for heaven's sake. Why should it matter?"

"No, no," he said, sitting up, urgency in his voice, "it's not that, not that at all."

"What is it then?"

"*It is that I am Mexican, too!*"

"You?"

"*Me, me.* I am *Mexican! Mexican!*"

He was crying.

"*You?*"

"*Me.*"

"*No!*"

"*Yes! Mexican!*"

"*Hallelujah!*"

"*Hallelujah!*" he repeated, and they fell into each other's arms.

◆ ◆ ◆

Fred W. Gilmore telephoned, and this time when the men returned to his office they were not bearing gifts.

"It's just that the time is not right," Willie said, adopting his most righteous tone. "That's all I can say."

It's not what they had come to hear. "When we are in charge," said John C. Porter ominously, "we will remember those who fought with us, like the Rev. Bob Shoemaker, and those who stood on the sidelines. We want you on our side, Reverend. We need you."

"It is a delicate matter," said Willie.

"It is an urgent matter," said Porter.

"I need more time."

"We're out of time. The situation grows worse with every passing day."

Willie shook his head and stood up.

"You will regret this, Reverend," said Gilmore, standing in the doorway on the way out and ignoring Willie's proffered hand.

Miss Shields looked on.

"You will regret this more than you know," he repeated.

Miss Shields wrote it down.

Distressed and needing solace, he caught a Big Red Car to Angie's that evening. A gentle man, he did not like to have enemies, powerful and threatening enemies. No sooner was the trolley in sight of her building, the familiar façade with its tall palms lighted from below and friendly green awning, than his spirits began to lift.

He found her pacing the floor.

Something was badly wrong.

"Tell me."

He tried to hug her, but she pulled away.

"Tell me."

She walked to the window and looked out. The silence frightened him. Was this it, the break he'd feared but expected,

the terrible swift sword of retribution. He was a sinning for-
nicator who had no right to the happiness this woman had
brought into his life. Had the time finally come?

"Angie, please. Some terrible thing has happened. I must
know."

Silence.

"What is it, dearest?"

She spun around suddenly to face him. "My husband . . ."

Willie's face drained of all color. Of all the things he
expected, all the things he deserved, to hear of a husband was
the last. Fornication could be forgiven, but adultery?

"Your husband?"

"He called from Bakersfield—says he's coming."

Sinking down onto the couch, closing his eyes, he listened
as she told him of the past she'd never talked about and he'd
never asked about; never asked about because something told
him not to ask about it, because he feared something exactly
like this, something that put everything at risk, not only their
relationship, but everything he had built, his very existence.
He knew the reckoning would come, it always does; he knew
the Lord's ways. She was his drug, his habit, his secret love. He
knew.

"Let's go away, Willie."

He was astonished. "*Go away*?"

"Just for a little while—why not? I told him not to come,
that I wouldn't see him, that I was divorcing him. Listen, I know
Gil. If I'm not here, he'll lose interest and go away."

"He knows where you live?" he said, shocked.

"He has a key."

"*He has a key?*"

"It was a mistake. He wanted to—oh, never mind. I should

have had the lock changed. Everything was going so well. Why does this have to happen?"

She stared at him, her dark eyes pleading.

"But run away? You're not serious."

"No, no, not run away, Willie—go away until he's gone, that's all."

He would not panic, could not allow himself panic. Too much was at stake. He stood up, his mind turning, churning, a kaleidoscope, seeking an answer. He came close to her, and this time she did not back away. Taking her in his arms calmed them both. He kissed her hair and forehead. And suddenly he heard the voice, just as Augustine had heard the voice in the garden so long ago. It said: "If not now, when?"

"Pour me a little scotch, will you dear. Let's talk about this."

CHAPTER 16

They arrived in Southampton after an easy crossing on the *Normandie,* stayed two nights at Portsmouth, crossed to the Isle of Wight for a day of hiking, rented a car and motored to Bath and Bristol, coming back to London through Oxford. Maggie struck out on her own each day, disappearing after breakfast to the local flying field, leaving Cal to see the sights and study the newspapers, which grew direr by the day. She was a flying phenomenon in a nation where women had not yet taken to the air. In London, Cal had to drag her away from her flying friends at Penshurst Airfield to keep to their itinerary.

Britain was in frenzy over Hitler, divided between those who would accommodate and those who would resist. Germany had annexed Austria in the spring, and even as the cousins motored across England was preparing for Czechoslovakia. The fear was that if France and Britain did not stand firm, Poland would be next on Hitler's menu, which meant all-out war. Every London pub was thick with men nursing pints, flicking darts, and arguing over the best means of dealing with the Huns, as they oddly called them.

They ferried to Holland and caught the Berlin train, crossing into Germany at Aix-la-Chappelle and getting their first taste of goose-stepping and Nazi salutes. Unlike London, steeped in dread, Berlin was bubbling with energy and excitement. Staying at the Adlon, Maggie met a young Prussian pilot who kept a Fieseler F5 at Tegel and hated Hitler. Lt. Joachim von Falkenberg was outspoken to the point of recklessness and perfectly suited for flying with Maggie. They flew three days running, leaving

Cal to dine alone. The second night, seeing she was not returning, he introduced himself to a young lady at the hotel bar and
invited her to dine with him. Afterward, they retired to his room
where she showed him how things had been done in the happier
Weimar days. Cal had no idea what Maggie was up to, at least
not until the third night when a phone call from Falkenberg told
him to come quickly to the Virchow Clinic. There'd been an "air
incident," he said, leaving Cal to ponder during the short taxi
ride to Wedding what that might mean.

She was lying in bed with her foot in a sling surrounded by
noisy people dressed in white. A table with bottles and glasses
suggested the air incident had not been too severe. "Joachim
didn't want to bother you, but I told him that since you didn't
come to see me in Santa Monica Hospital after my car wreck
that this would be your penance."

"I didn't *know* you were in Santa Monica Hospital," he
shouted over the din.

The foot was sprained, not broken, but Joachim had
insisted that she be admitted. He had one arm in a sling and
the other wrapped in bandages, but at least was on his feet. The
injuries had not prevented them from ordering a few bottles of
Henkell Sekt and inviting other inmates to join in the party.
No one seemed to be a doctor, but no one seemed to need a
doctor. "The accident was entirely my fault," said the young
pilot, sheepishly, generously. "I'm afraid I interfered with her
landing, and this is what we got. Fortunately, nothing serious—
except of course my poor plane." He asked someone to pour Cal
a glass of wine. "Sir, your cousin is a pilot par excellence. She
insisted on making the landing, herself. It's just that, you know,
a woman. I'd never seen that before. I'm afraid I lost my nerve."
Everyone laughed.

With Maggie limping but ambulatory, it was on to Dresden

and Prague two days later. Something had clearly sparked between Maggie and the young Prussian, for she wrote him at every stop until Paris, when everything changed. Crisis in Europe was everywhere. As Americans, they were mere spectators at the show, but the actors all seemed determined to win their approval. It was as if Americans, distant and unaffected, were the only objective arbiters in this deadliest European drama.

Wherever they were, Maggie made a beeline for the airfield. Flying was almost unknown to European women, nothing like in America where Amelia Earhart had been racing with the men and inspiring a generation of female pilots before her crash the year before. Showing up at the flying clubs with her long dark hair falling down her smart red flying suit, flashing her pilot's license and asking who would take her up and in what, Maggie made friends instantly. She was dying to race but had no plane. In England, she'd flown a Miles Falcon out of Penshurst, in Berlin the Fieseler and in Dresden a Klemm 32. In America, flying was still a sporting activity like yachting, but European men were fanatics. Even as their nations stumbled toward war, the clubs held cups and competitions. The pilots were mostly military and took fierce pride in their planes, certain they were superior and ready to prove it.

While in Munich, the crisis over Czechoslovakia came to a head. The Bavarian capital, bustling and beautiful in the September sunshine, was inundated with reporters and diplomats, and the cousins were fortunate to keep their reservation at a Goethestrasse pension, though it was reduced to a single room. Under a giant red and black swastika, Cal argued with a crisp, young Nazi, showing him the reservation for two rooms. Eyeing Maggie, the man seemed surprised Cal would need two rooms. Both Prague and Munich were under strict military control, and Maggie could not find a plane in either city.

And suddenly the threat was gone. Toasts were offered, pacts signed, the page turned and on to a new chapter. Reporters and diplomats decamped and statesmen flew home trumpeting peace in our time. Hitler had foxed them again. The cousins caught the train for Paris. Like Berlin, Paris was simultaneously in the grip of war fever and a sport-flying craze. Two days after arriving, Maggie met a French airman named Arnaud Ricot de Scitivaux in the bar of the Hotel Crillon and a day later was flying over the Channel in his Morane-Saulnier 341. The letters to Lt. Joachim von Falkenberg stopped.

◆ ◆ ◆

"I've booked the *Normandie* for Dec. 2," Cal announced into the hotel phone. "Think you can make it?"

His room was just down the hall on the second floor of the Crillon, but he'd learned on this trip always to call first. It was not his first call, but the first time she'd answered.

"Oh, Cal, *no*."

He knew what was happening and was helpless against it. Maggie was a person of spontaneity and inspiration; he one of planning and organization. They'd survived six months on the road by not interfering too much with each other. While he visited museums and read newspapers, she hung out at the airfields and flew planes. At night they occasionally met for dinner. If she'd been a spy she would return home with a full report on the performance of each country's latest aircraft. In France she'd even managed a side trip to le Mans for a few tours around the track with Jean Bugatti in his new test car. She'd become as fanatical about racing as the Europeans.

"I'm dressed," she said. "Why don't you pop around and we'll talk."

"I'm on my way."

Arnaud Ricot de Scitivaux, was exactly what his ancient name suggested: dashing, elegant, accomplished, and wealthy. He was also devilishly handsome. They'd met him in the Crillon bar when he'd sent a bottle of Veuve Clicquot around with his card as they were ready to dine. He was a captain in the French Air Force and had slipped the concierge a hundred francs to inquire about the young couple he'd seen in the dining room. Brother and sister, the concierge believed, staying in separate rooms. It was all Arnaud needed, but the concierge helpfully added that he believed the young lady was an aviatrix.

Cal walked down the hall, knocked and Maggie let him in.

Europe had changed her, sophisticated her. Months of touring lands living on the edge was putting things into perspective. The cities were lively, the people friendly, the men beautiful, the countryside lovely, exactly as they'd hoped except that over everything hung a great black cloud of doom. People covered up their anxieties with wine and dancing and making love, but the next morning the dread came seeping back. They were adrift in leaky boats in violent seas, reprieved occasionally by lulls of false hope, as at Munich.

She was dressed in white silk. Her luminous dress and gold bangles and dangles in stark contrast with her dark hair and bronzed skin. In Paris, where fashion demands the palest skin, where women invest in the costliest creams and salves to erase the slightest blemish and would never dare go outdoors uncovered, the vibrant Maggie Mull was as rare a sight as an Amazon princess on the Rhine.

"My goodness," he said.

"May I take that as a compliment?"

He smiled. "You look wonderful."

"Come sit down, Cal. I have some news."

They were at the front of the hotel in rooms looking out on Place de la Concorde. The noise from that turbulent racetrack of cars was diminished but not eliminated by two sets of thick double windows. He sat down in a meticulously stitched Voltaire chair with shiny brass-tipped upholstery pins that likely went back to the great man himself. He watched his cousin sit down on the settee across from him and light a cigarette.

He knew without being told. It was the largest diamond he'd ever seen.

Arnaud was waiting at the bar, and Cal immediately congratulated him. They shook hands and ordered champagne. "Before we sit to dinner," said Cal, as their flutes were filled, "may I toast you both. It is of course wonderful news."

It was not exactly how he'd received the news in Maggie's room. It had bothered him, alarmed him, and good soldier that he was, he still couldn't hide it. Nelly had fiercely resisted sending her daughter off with him, even knowing that no amount of resistance would change a thing. She'd taken Cal aside and made him promise to watch over her day and night, making clear that he was responsible for her, knowing it was an impossible demand.

They'd talked in Maggie's room until they were more than just fashionably late for the dinner with Arnaud. The diamond said he had no chance, but he had to try.

"Another Harold, no?"

"Nothing like that. Harold was flying lessons."

"Another Falkenberg."

"Stop it, Cal."

"And Arnaud?"

"I'd say we were made for each other. He would say the same thing."

"Excuse me for being practical, but at least Harold didn't

live in a place about to go to war. What do you do when it breaks out—and it will, you know."

"He wants to come to America."

"Everyone over here wants to come to America. The ships would be bursting if we gave them all visas."

"So, I stay here."

"Why is he any different from the German?"

"You bastard!"

"Well . . .?"

"Arnaud is on our side."

"Oh, you're taking sides?"

"I am now."

"He's in the French Air Force. No way they let him leave."

"Just for our honeymoon. He wants to meet everyone in Los Angeles."

"And when the honeymoon is over?"

"You're too far out there, Cal, as always."

"Someone has to think ahead."

She showed a flash of anger. "Why? Why does anyone have to think ahead? Why not take life as it comes?"

"Sure—unless what's coming is a war, a really nasty war, just like the last one, where just about everyone in uniform is killed and whole nations are destroyed and afterward everyone runs around asking themselves, goodness, how could this have happened?"

Her dark eyes closed down on him, and he had to look away.

"Cal, have you ever been in love?"

He stared at her without answering. She understood.

"Then how can you have an opinion? Love is not something you walk away from. You walk away and you hate yourself the rest of your life, wondering, always wondering."

"You make a mistake and you pay for it the rest of your life."

"God, you're cynical."

"No, I am not cynical," he said, with feeling. "And no, I have never been in love—at least not to the point of signing up for the rest of my life, if that's what you mean."

At dinner with Arnaud, over more champagne, his opposition softened, as things tend to do. There was nothing to dislike about Arnaud except that he didn't have long to live. He'd been raised in the best of Parisian families, gone to the best of schools, including in England and Germany. He was cultivated, curious, courteous and madly in love with Maggie.

"I was in love with her from the first," he said, laughing, "even *after* finding out she was a flier. As for flying, she is *magnifique!* I let her fly my MS, you know, all the way to Dover. She wanted to fly over London but we didn't have enough petrol. Anyway, we didn't have clearance." He laughed again and reached for her hand. "You never know about the English. They're never sure who the enemy is. Maybe everybody. They might have shot us down."

The wedding was set for March 4 in the Basilique Sainte Clotilde, just around the corner from the Ministry of Defense, where Arnaud worked. Cal stayed for it, though no one came from the States. Nelly wanted to come, but not alone, and Eddie and Lizzie were too busy. Lizzie wrote a long letter saying she felt awful but it would take a month and the *Times* wouldn't give it to her. In Eddie's absence, Cal gave away the bride. Everyone at home, he learned from Lizzie, was upset but not surprised. If Maggie hadn't shocked them this way, she would have found some other way. They peppered him in letters with questions he couldn't answer. Arnaud was first rate, he said, just that the timing was bad.

With no one else from the Mull side, there were plenty of Scitivaux to fill the pews at Sainte Clotilde. It was a military family from centuries back with roots all across France. Arnaud's immediate family lived in a nineteenth century *hôtel particulier* on the rue las Cases just behind the church, where the reception was held. Cal could not have known, but the bridegroom's family was as upset as the bride's, though civilized enough not to show it. The Scitivaux were not provincials and would have been just as annoyed at Arnaud's marriage to a French girl. It was not a good time for weddings. Not all the bridesmaids were as upset as the family, and Cal ended up on a couch in the library with one of them, entangled in the poor girl's crepe chiffons.

Three times in three years Europe had dodged war with Hitler, though at the cost of considerable self-respect. The sentiment was that Hitler would continue advancing until someone stopped him, and that someone would have to be, as it always was, France, perhaps with help from England, though you never knew with the English. The French and British hoped Hitler's next target after Czechoslovakia would be Soviet Russia, but he had other ideas. In a few months he would sign a peace treaty with Moscow.

Cal spent April Fool's Day, 1939, on the Santa Fe Chief rolling west through Kansas and Colorado. In Albuquerque, he got off long enough to buy a newspaper. He sensed it would be a terrible year but could not have guessed how terrible. He'd stopped worrying about Maggie. When they said goodbye at the Gare St. Lazare she'd never looked so happy or so beautiful. His thoughts had rolled back over the years, back to Bel Air, back to the stables at Playa del Rey, to poor Billy Todd, to the night she walked away from Harold and never looked back. Maggie could take care of herself. He was proud to have her for a cousin.

As the train traversed the Mojave, his thoughts turned back to his own life, knowing he'd been changed as much as Maggie by Europe, knowing he could not go back to being an accountant, at least not for long. If a new cataclysm swept across Europe, would America be next? We'd tried to escape the first time, ultimately dragged in, suspecting it would have been better to be in from the beginning. Roosevelt had made clear he did not intend to stand by and let Hitler conquer Europe. Congress wasn't with him, but where did the people stand?

Where did he himself stand? He was about to turn thirty. He sensed big changes coming.

CHAPTER 17

Hands on the sink, Angie gazed out over the ocean. Behind her the smell of coffee spread from the kitchen through the little *sala* toward the bedroom. It was the best way to awaken him. From where she stood she had a clear view as far as the jagged island on the horizon. "*Cómo se llama?*" she'd asked at the little store where they'd done some shopping. Isla San Martín, they said. Very good fishing at the isla just in case *la señora* and her *marido* wanted to rent a fishing boat. They had come for the fishing, *verdad*? Angie had turned a ring over to resemble a wedding band.

She spoke Spanish whenever she went to the store, spoke it with Willie, too, Memo, as she called him, short for Guillermo— and they took her for one of them, which she was, though her mother was from the other side of Mexico, near Vera Cruz. I could stay in this place forever, she thought. Well, maybe not forever. Too many years of a strict father, bossy brothers, nasty husband, men always telling her what to do. She needed someone gentle like Willie. During the day she wore a little shift, and her feet already were so hard and black she didn't need shoes. Willie admired her feet because his pink ones couldn't take two steps on the hot sand.

Hers was a loving family, but more than anything it loved Jesus. All that talk about sin must have worked because we turned out well enough, she thought. They hated me for running away with Gil but when they find out I've returned to the church all that will change. I'll see them again. I know I will. You don't just walk away from your family, not forever you don't. Children run off all the time, but families come back together. Jesus brings them back.

She took off the percolator and poured a cup. Mexican coffee, from Chiapas, strong and black. She went back to look out at the island again. We're not running away, she'd told him; we're leaving until Gil is gone. What would be better, Willie, tell me, tell me. I saw he was scared, scared but listening, something at work, his lips moving, and I knew he was praying. He lets Jesus make up his mind for him. The whiskey helped. *Where, where,* he kept repeating? I said anywhere, up the coast, Carmel, San Francisco. Anywhere. Then I said Mexico.

Mexico! That's what did it. He wanted to see where *Abuela* Isabel was born, "I never have, you know." He said *abuela,* the Spanish word, and we started speaking Spanish and laughing. As children we spoke Spanish with *Mamá* at the rancho, he said. After a little more whiskey I knew he was ready. We talked about Mexico all the way down. I slept some and missed the border but he woke me coming into Rosarito. We saw horses on the sand and fishermen shoving off in their little boats. He'd been up all night and was starving. The sun was just up when we pulled into the Rosarito Beach Hotel, walking through the lobby hand in hand, Willie in rumpled clothes and me in a skirt and blouse. People might have wondered, but maybe not. They say that if you posted the names of all the Hollywood couples that have shacked up at the Rosarito over the years, the gossip columnists could fill books.

In Ensenada, I inquired at *Propriedades* Gomez while he went for a beer and I found our little house. A half hour south of the city, Sr. Gomez said, nothing down there, just a village with a little *tienda* and some fishermen. You're surely not alone, he said as I paid the deposit and rent, and I said I was with my husband who was doing some shopping. The house is by itself, he said, but it's okay. Never had a complaint. He gave me the key and here we are.

"You bastards don't have a thing on me," he kept shouting from his cell, and after three days of no sleep they let him go. Didn't even take him to court.

He'd lose his job but so what? This was better. He laid in some food at Angie's, bought a bottle of rum and waited. Each day he read the papers: mystery unsolved, search continues, Klan questioned, husband held, candlelight vigils and evening prayer, reporters and police fanning out over the state, brother's reward money up to five thousand dollars. It was the chance for the reward that kept him. Sister Angie was worth five thousand dollars and the price was rising. He knew Angie's habits. Who better to find her than her husband?

Each day he roamed the city searching for clues. He joined the vigils at the temple, talked to people, stopped by police headquarters to complain about the tail they put on him. Each night he returned to Angie's to drink rum, fix some canned hash and beans, lie on the sofa listening to the radio and get mad as hell. He found men's clothes in the closet. The son-of-a-bitch is shacking up with my wife, he repeated to himself. One day he'll walk into this room and find out what happens.

He hadn't missed her in Bakersfield. Girls were crawling the bars in Oildale, or not so much girls as women. Angie was a girl and he preferred women. He also preferred variety. He was going through the Oildale women one by one and was far from done. Only now he was done because he was moving on. Suddenly he wanted Angie again. Not permanently, permanently she bored him, but for a little while. She did some good things. He went into her room, pulled out her underwear, sniffed it and masturbated into it. He felt better but didn't get it all. He went out and caught the trolley to Chinatown. He needed a woman, and Asians were always good. His tail caught the trolley with him. Maybe he would get laid, too.

McManus had thought it over. Reporters arriving from everywhere, everyone looking for the missing preacher and the girl—was she his girlfriend?— who had left no trace. Disappeared into thin air and that was very hard to do. Car missing, but what did it mean? What burned him most was that this was a local story, an L.A. story, a *Times* story and his job was to find them and make sure the others didn't find them first—especially Hearst! He had six reporters on it: Klan, love nest, mob, suicide, angry husband, and the *Times* had printed it all. Dozens of tips, mainly from another of the Rev. Willie's Soldiers having had another vision.

He had his own vision and summoned Lizzie from the hall of justice.

"What are you hearing over there?"

"Nothing everyone isn't hearing."

"Even from Aldridge?"

Lizzie was shocked, genuinely shocked, for she thought she knew McManus, knew him to be a gentleman. But he'd just asked about the man she was dating, Asa Aldridge, assistant district attorney, one of a dozen working for DA Pitts. She didn't answer.

"Look, Lizzie. Everything about this story is different. I'm asking you about Aldridge and in a minute I'm going to ask you about your father, because, honey, I am a desperate man. Aldridge is on the frontline over there. If he's told you anything I want to know."

She sat quietly, legs crossed, watching McManus light up another cigarette, looking out the window, trying to compose herself. She was as surprised as she was shocked for she and Asa had been almost paranoically discreet. He believed that no one in the DA's office knew a thing about them, and she believed the same about the *Times*. Yet here was the city editor knowing and asking.

"The truth is, Larry, that we don't talk about it."

He blew out a huge mass of smoke. "Okay, I believe you. Now, on to the next question: isn't Willie Mull your uncle?"

"He is."

"He is your father's twin brother."

"He is."

"Have you talked to your father about it?"

"Larry . . ."

"I know, I know—I told myself I'd never do it, but we have to find them, don't we? Your father won't talk to reporters. Has he told you anything that could help us?"

She answered honestly. "He has not. I think something came up between them. I don't think they'd been talking."

"What do *you* think—where did they go?"

She felt the conflict, understood why she hadn't been asked or volunteered information. Of course, she knew about it. She'd known ever since the night Willie and Angie walked in on Cal at Sunset Tower. They all knew and hadn't said a thing. It was nobody's business. Only now it was. The city editor was asking his reporter what she knew.

She took a deep breath and dodged. "I have my ideas."

"Which are . . ."

She was buying time, making up her mind. She studied his face—honest, tough, tired, creased from smoking, booze, not enough sleep, younger than he looks but newspapers do that to you. Get out in time they say, but no one does. You're either in or out.

"They speak Spanish, you know."

"Who speaks Spanish?"

"My father and uncle."

"What's that got to do with it?"

"My hunch says Mexico."

"Nah, we've combed Tijuana top to bottom. Talked to everyone, Customs, Border Patrol, cops, hotels, nothing. Mexicali, too. They know there's a reward."

"What about below the border?"

"Mexico's a big place."

She picked the morning paper from his desk, turning to the entertainment section, passing it to him. "Look at the ad at the top."

A photo showed a hotel's long arching veranda rising up amid palm trees and white sands stretching to the ocean. Tanned couples sunning themselves.

ROSARITO BEACH HOTEL

SO CLOSE AND YET SO FAR

ROSARITO: OUR NAME IS DISCRETION

"That's my hunch."

"Why?"

"Now look at the bottom, at the ad for the Temple of the Angels. Those ads run every day. Hard to see one without the other . . . the word 'discretion.'"

His eyes moved between the ads, up and down, up and down. "You might have something." Reaching in his desk, he pulled out some forms. "Get five hundred dollars from the cashier—take fifties and twenties. Discretion can be expensive but try to bring some of it back. Take Luis Ortega with you, good photog. He speaks Spanish."

"I speak some Spanish."

"Perfect. You can practice all the way down."

With a stop, they made the border in three hours and turned south onto the coast road, direction Rosarito. She liked Luis, a cheerful man whose family had been in Los Angeles for a century, before California was a state. They took fishing trips deep into Baja. "No Rosarito Beach Hotel in those days," Luis said. "Just adobes. Hotel went up in the twenties."

A twenty at the reception desk bought them a supercilious smile and lecture from an assistant manager that the hotel never showed its register, never gave out information on guests to anyone, including the *Los Angeles Times*.

She asked for the twenty back.

"What twenty?"

The dining room was empty, too late for lunch and too early for dinner. Drinks were being delivered to the pool. They chose a table by windows, overlooking beach and ocean. They ordered sandwiches and beer.

"I still have a feeling Uncle Willie saw that ad. How could he have missed it?"

"You really think he would do that—a preacher?"

She trusted Luis. Anyway, photographers don't blab. "Have you ever been to the Temple of the Angels, Luis?"

"I'm Catholic."

"I went one time—curiosity. A Sunday show."

"And?"

"Angie was playing Mary Magdalene. I kept thinking—poor Uncle Willie."

"That bad, eh. Look, they left L.A. late, probably hit the border at dawn. That puts them at Rosarito at six or seven. Maybe they just stop for breakfast. Gringos—they wouldn't take a chance with a street café. A place like this, chance to clean up. Say, I have an idea. Peel me a couple of twenties from your wad."

He motioned to the waiter lingering by the kitchen door. They whispered in Spanish, a bill was passed and the waiter disappeared. "Now, we'll see."

After a while a different waiter came over. Another bill was passed. He might have seen them he said, thought they were Mexican, spoke Spanish, didn't think a thing of it, why would he—just a man and a girl on their way somewhere. He remembered because they came in early, had to wait for the kitchen to open. Never saw them again.

Luis finished his beer. "You know, if they stopped for breakfast but didn't stay, then they were heading south, which means Ensenada. Not much south of that. I've been down there."

CHAPTER 18

"Buenos dias."

Wearing Levi's he'd bought in Ensenada and an old shirt, Willie shuffled into the kitchen, waking her from her reverie. With the beard and his Spanish she could put him on any fishing boat and he'd be a native. Here I am, she thought, just like my poor mother, living with a middle-aged preacher. The thought stopped her. Did this have something to do with Papa? She looked at Willie, smiling, barefoot in their little house, sweet man, so different from Papa. Willie was good at making love and she could not imagine her father with her mother at all. He would have been like Gil—short, ouch, bang-bang.

"We should go to the isla today," she said, "catch some fish."

"I mean to read my Bible today, my sweet. Sit with coffee and oranges in a sunny chair—like Jesus in Jerusalem."

"Where does the Bible say that?"

"You have to imagine it."

"You read your Bible and ate oranges yesterday."

"Yes. I've been doing some thinking."

The house was on a bluff, and to reach the ocean they had to climb down a steep cliff. They had no electricity, only gas lamps and butane for the stovetop. Water and groceries came from the *tienda* three miles away around a headland. Beyond the headland, the hills fell down to a small bay, home to a dozen adobe houses and the *tienda*. Below them, a rock promontory shielded the beach and formed a small cove. To the south, Isla San Martín was partially blocked by the promontory. To the north they saw fishing boats far out to sea off Ensenada. Exploring the cove, they found tidepools where water was warmed by the sun. She would slip in naked and bask like a water nymph until Willie could stand it no longer and go in after her. Then back to the house for fish, tortillas, wine, sex, and naps. And every day it grew closer to the end.

He'd escaped into the wilderness and now, like Moses, purified, must find his way back again. Renunciation. Had not Augustine made it clear? It is through the sexual act that original sin is passed. "If not now, lord, when?" To be a missionary— *that* was to be his life again, as in China, as in the San Francisco slums, before money poured over him, befouling him, money from his poor mother's death. *Ah, Mamá!* He knew now. The temple was not built by God's little people but by Eddie who had let their mother die and stolen from Henry Callender. He, Rev. Willie, was the accomplice. He had agreed to everything along the way.

"We will turn in the keys and drive to Tijuana," he said at breakfast the next morning. "We will leave the car, cross the border and catch the bus to Los Angeles. We are returning to the path of the Lord. If He chooses to punish us for having loved, we will do our penance. I will walk the hills in my bare feet. You will come with me."

She didn't answer. He must leave, she thought, but must I?

◆ ◆ ◆

Coming down the mountains into Ensenada, Luis turned off the highway and onto Calle Segunda. They would check the hotels and Hussong's.

"We used to stop at Hussong's," he said. "Dad wanted a beer and I went in with him to read the papers. They have all the papers, including the *Times*. Very big cantina for gringos."

She pointed across the street. "Let's start with that real estate place."

Saturnino Gomez, proprietor of *Inmuebles y Propiedades*, had finished lunch and returned to his agency for a nap. At four o'clock, he reopened and was settling in for one more quiet afternoon. Business was not good. The Depression was bad for everyone. There were days when the only people to cross his threshold were Calle Segunda neighbors. He looked up when the young couple walked in, clearly gringos—at least *la rubia*. "Good afternoon."

Lizzie smiled, happy to hear English. "Maybe you can help us." She took a photo of Willie from her folder. "Have you seen this man?"

"Ah, *el pastor*. Very big story. No, I have not seen him. Good face. I would remember. But try Hussong's. They all stop at Hussong's."

"This woman," said Lizzie, "I don't suppose you've seen her either."

He looked closely at the publicity photo of Sister Angie in white robes, hands clasped behind her head, long sleeves billowing out like wings, halo over the head, an angel.

He chuckled. "Oh, no, Señorita, I would remember something like that."

"Well, thank you anyway," she said, turning to go, then turning back to hand him twenty dollars. "Take this is for your help."

He was rubbing his chin. "Thank you, Señorita, but . . . I don't know." He hesitated. "Something there. Do you have another photo of the girl—you know, more natural?"

She took out a newspaper clipping, a photo of Angie without wings and halo.

He studied it for some time. "Could be. Very close. She came in alone, spoke Spanish, said her *marido* was shopping.

Rented a house off a dirt road a half hour south. On a hillside over the ocean. Just a month. She should be coming back soon for the deposit."

The highway was a rough asphalt road. "Someday this will go all the way to the end, to Cabo," said Luis. "I hope I am still alive." They passed a few other cars, heading north. One of them, a blue Chevy, had once been on the stage at the temple. Lizzie, who sees everything, would have noticed, but she had closed her eyes for a few moments.

The door was locked. They went around back. She picked up a woman's bathing suit draped on a chair to dry. "Still damp." She peered in the bedroom, the mattress turned down. The kitchen, everything put away.

"We missed them," she said.

"Why leave the bathing suit?

"She wouldn't need it anymore."

He was ready to leave. For three weeks he'd led a dog's life, drinking rum, visiting whores, tracked by flatfeet, back at night telling himself to move on, get his life back. He was tired of reporters. He talked to them at first, why wouldn't he? It's what happens when you cut a woman too much slack, he told them. They might never turn up. If it was him, he'd know how to disappear. There are places in the bayous where no one ever goes, places where the Cajuns have lived by themselves for two centuries and the strangers that go in after them don't come out again. Or parts of Mexico. He'd driven to the oil fields near Tampico without seeing ten people. Angie's mother was Mexican. They could go to ground in Mexico and never surface. He'd read every word printed since he hit town and no one knew a thing. Police incompetence he could understand, but neither had the newspapers picked up the scent.

Curtains drawn, lying in the dark on Angie's bed with his bottle, aroused because he could still smell her but too drunk to head for Chinatown, he decided it was time to move on. He'd thought about it, even thought he might get in on the reward. Trouble was that they'd never give him the money, not as her husband. Anyway, he'd probably kill them first.

He would wait until midnight and slip out the back. Why would the cops care where he went anyway? Maybe he'd get a job on one of the oil platforms they were building in the Gulf. He'd heard about that: platforms miles out there, people living like it was a hotel on some Caribbean island. Nobody would find him. He lay there drinking and drifting and dozing in the dark with one hand around the neck of the bottle and the other around his large warm dick. He'd finished a can of corned beef hash and bag of potato chips. He didn't want to fall asleep with the open bottle for he'd already done that and the bed stank of rum. Sneak out the back, circle around the building to escape the flatfoot, who would be asleep in his car anyway.

The coach dropped them at Fourth and Olive just after ten o'clock. They waited a moment by the depot, a stooped, bearded man in Levi's, shirt and sombrero and a young woman in a cotton dress with a Mexican *mantón* draped over her shoulders. The border buses drop off people like that at Fourth and Olive all day. Two cheap suitcases sat beside them on the sidewalk. He hoisted them, and they started up Olive. Reaching Second, they had a short wait before the Big Red Car from Alameda clanged to a stop. They walked to the rear of the near-empty car, beginning a trip that would take them onto Glendale Boulevard, past Echo Park, past the Temple of the Angels, past Sunset, past Silver Lake and over the dry bed of the Los Angeles River to Angie's apartment in Glendale.

"What day is it, Willie?" she asked.

They could have bought newspapers, could have bought them in Carlsbad or Oceanside or San Juan Capistrano or Newport or any of the stops along the way and read all about the frantic search. The *Times* and *Examiner* were on sale at the newsstand at the depot on Olive. They had no interest in newspapers. Willie had seen the papers at Hussong's days before, and the only thing changed was that they were back and no one knew it. Had they bought newspapers they might have learned about Gil, but maybe not. Anyway, they didn't.

"It's Wednesday," he said.

The trolley ran by Echo Lake, pretty little lake that first caught his eye when he was looking for a site. The park was dark, just a few couples strolling, and men with dogs, people bundled up against the night chill in the air. He sat quietly, Angie at his side, both staring out the window, thinking of the past, thinking of the future, listening to the whirr of metal wheels on the tracks and the swoosh of the trolley doors as they opened and closed, a few people in and out, not many for it was late. Past Park Avenue, the conductor clanged a car off the tracks, out of his way. The car didn't argue.

Around a turn and there it was: The Temple of the Angels, *his* Temple of the Angels. The conductor opened the door and the car sat waiting. People coming out of the temple, coming toward the trolley. Over the temple doors a large banner announced: "Rev. Willie, Sister Angie: Candlelight Vigil Tonight 8:30."

"An hour earlier and we could have attended the vigil for us," she said.

He looked straight ahead, straight into the eyes of the boarding passengers, defying them to recognize him. Filing in, pushing and chattering, most didn't notice the shabby pair at the rear. One or two who caught his eye looked quickly away, embarrassed.

The car started up again, trundling on, over Sunset, along Silver Lake. They both stared hard at Tony's ice cream shop, where it all started. They clanged across the dry riverbed and over the little cross streets, stopping to let passengers out, mostly Soldiers picked up at the temple. How well they both knew this route, how many times each had taken it—though, oddly, never before together. It was midweek and except for the temple vigil no reason for people to be out. Day workers were already home, night and swing shifters already at work.

The building would be watched, but there was a back alley. They spotted the stakeout, a dark sedan with a man inside. Getting off past the building, they circled the block to approach from the rear, checking for a rear lookout, seeing no one, slipping separately down the alley, past the car stalls, past the garbage cans, a cat darting out, into the rear entrance. Angie went first, waiting inside until Willie was safely in. They had five flights to climb up the service stairs, and Willie, with the suitcases, took them slowly.

Breathing heavily, he set the bags down outside the door and leaned against the wall. Angie had the keys out but hesitated, waiting for him to catch his breath, understanding the effort he'd made. They listened to the quiet building, people already retired, the clang of another trolley somewhere far off. Neither had given any thought to the apartment. Why would they after a month? The important thing was to get in without being seen.

She turned the key, opened the door, switched on the light and screamed. Willie came in quickly behind her and shut the door, afraid the scream would bring people into the hallway. They stood against the door, looking out over a living room littered with newspapers and trash. They instantly understood that he had been there, living there. The curtains were closed, and she had not drawn them. To their left, the kitchen alcove and table looked a mess as well, and the shades to the street were down, something she never did. To their right, the door to the bedroom was open.

"I don't want to stay here," said Willie.

"It's been a month," said Angie. "He's cleared out."

"He has a key."

"Put the chain on, Willie."

"We could go to my place."

"Walk by your front desk and it will be on the front page tomorrow. No, I'll change the sheets and we'll deal with the mess tomorrow. I want sleep."

In the bedroom, Gil lay quiet as a mouse, barely breathing, listening. He capped the bottle and came up on his elbows. Good thing he'd turned out the lights. He got up silently in the dark, catching the bottle before it thumped to the carpet. Moving quietly in his boots, he slipped behind the bedroom door. Through the crack he saw a bearded old man put the chain on the door. He saw her start toward the kitchen and stop, turning instead toward the bedroom. They'd thought he was gone but now weren't sure. She turned toward the bedroom but couldn't see because of the darkness. Couldn't make up her mind, took a step back toward the chained door, then spun around and started toward the bedroom. He held his breath and didn't twitch a muscle.

She flipped the switch.

"*Gotcha*," he cried, jumping out and grabbing her wrist.

Her scream was deafening. "*Wil-l-i-eee!*"

He punched her hard in the gut to shut her up. She collapsed.

"*This* is the guy," Gil shouted, pointing at Willie. "*This* . . . !"

Staggering to her feet, Angie moved toward the closed window that gave onto Glendale Boulevard, but Gil grabbed her and knocked her back.

Willie hesitated, turned and ran for the living room windows, tripping on a rug and nearly falling. The detective was just across the street. Surely, he would be listening and looking up. That's why he was there. Open the curtains, he told himself.

Grabbing Angie's wrists in a gnarly hand and slapping her hard with his free hand when she tried to kick him, he dragged her screaming into the living room. He had to silence her quick and smashed her mouth. With a heel she got him in the shin. "Whore," he shouted, smashing her again, throwing her to the floor, standing over his prey, kicking her in the ribs and stomach, hurting her really bad, turning screams into soft sick moans.

Willie ran at him, knocking him from the back, putting him to his knees. Willie was a big man, but not a strong one and his only chance was to delay him long enough to get to the window and signal the cop. He dashed back to the windows, tangling in falling curtains when he couldn't find the draw cord. The venetian blinds were drawn. Angie tried to get up and Gil kicked her in the face, the side of his big hard roughneck's boot catching her in the mouth, teeth against soft lips, explosion of blood.

Wrapped in curtains like a statue before unveiling, Willie tried to scream, but had no voice. An arm pulled tight around his throat, closing it so he couldn't breathe. He heard banging from the next apartment or maybe the floor below. *Why didn't they come?* He kicked out, trying to loosen the arm that grew tighter until he blacked out. His trachea was crushed, his blood was stopped, his voyage was over.

Sobbing, delirious, her dress up around her waist, Angie lay still on the carpet.

"And now you," he said, picking her up, wiping blood from her bleeding face with his sleeve and carrying her into the bedroom. "You be good to me now, just like in the old days."

Hours later, with Gil drunk and spent on stained, bloody foul-smelling sheets, she finally reached the window and screamed to the cop outside, who had awakened. She could hardly open her mouth and when she tried, the wounds that had sought to close while she was being raped reopened and blood gushed again. The cop came quickly but not quickly enough to catch Gil, who gave her a final belt and was out the door and down the back stairway.

A large man, unkept, unshaven, physically depleted, hungover, covered in blood and well known to the police, he was caught the next day at a trolley stop.

CHAPTER 19

They gave her blood, stitched her shattered face, which had turned black; set her broken jaw and right arm, bandaged her broken nose, covered her eyes swollen shut from the stitching, taped her fractured ribs, swabbed and bandaged cuts and contusions everywhere on her body, tended scratches on her thighs and around the vagina. They treated for concussion and probed for organ damage and internal bleeding. They stitched and bandaged the gashes on her legs. Capping her broken front teeth would have to wait until they unwired her jaw. She lay semiconscious for days, unable to see, held immobile by cords, drugged on antibiotics and analgesics, fed intravenously and denied all visitors. A police guard stood round-the-clock outside her room, and reporters from newspapers across the nation were kept away, though an enterprising one made it as far as the guard outside her room.

Her mind awakened at some point, telling her she was dead. She could not see or feel, had no sense of time, space or body. What is that, if not death? Her mind alone told her she was not dead, or that if she was dead that her soul had survived in some strange invisible dead place. "If a man keep my saying he shall never see death," and she had kept His saying. She had the feeling of being lost in deep, black space, some kind of heaven without light. At some point—hours, days, weeks, she didn't know—dim light seeped in, she was aware of it though she could not see. She heard distant voices. Her mind told her she was alive. The Lord's design, His trial by fire, a voice said, and she had answered. Jesus was not done with her.

Gradually she became aware of the coming and going of doctors and nurses, of people talking, changing her bandages, manipulating her body, which she had begun to feel again, at least parts of it. At some point one eye partially opened and she saw shadows in the light that with time turned into people. The people were all in white, but one day she saw dark suits, and they tried to talk to her. She began to think more lucidly and to move. Her eyes opened, both of them, and she could hear, but her lips were sewn shut.

The dark suits came again and again. She understood them, but had no desire to answer because she could not speak and could not write because she could not move. She was plastered and wired and tubed, immobilized like a ship in dry dock. Cal came to tell her about Willie's quiet burial at Forest Lawn Cemetery, but she could not cry. He told her of plans for a memorial service, plans that the Soldiers, led by Henry Callender, insisted must await her recovery. He was sitting in a chair by the window and then came over to the side of the bed and told her not to worry, that they would wait. The Soldiers wanted her, no one else. She wondered how she looked. Others had flinched at the sight. Cal did not.

She had not seen her face, had no desire to see it until the final surgery was done and time had passed and the scars healed. How many months or years would it take? Martyrdom is never pretty. Cal told her that DA Barton Pitts had abandoned his plan to prosecute her and Willie for "outrage to public morals and illegal flight." Only Gil was to be prosecuted. Cal was not sure she understood anything. There had always been two Angies for him, and he wondered if both would survive this ordeal.

Had she lain there for a week, a month, a year? Time had no meaning. One day, someone was waiting when her eyes opened.

Pitts had considered sending young Asa Aldridge, who he knew was friendly with Lizzie Mull, but changed his mind. Pitts was always careful with the Mulls, culling advantages from overlooking Eddie's operations and ignoring complaints, including from the archdiocese and the Rev. Bob Shoemaker, about Willie and Sister Angie's "healing." The murder and coming trial would test his indulgence, already stretched by the continued presence of the *Providence* in Santa Monica Bay, which he knew belonged to Eddie.

It was the morning of the twenty-fourth day (though she had no way of knowing), and the person waiting was a large man sitting sloppily with his legs spread, glancing at her from time to time while writing or doodling on a legal pad propped on his stomach. She closed her eyes, hoping he would be gone when she opened them. Who was he? How long had he been watching her? Why had they let him in? The visitor noticed the eye movement.

"Peter Federmeister," he announced, standing and approaching the bed. "Assistant district attorney." He held his business card for her to see and placed it on the bedside table. "I know you're not well. I'll be brief and to the point."

He pulled the chair closer and sat down. He was heavyset, middle-aged, with a square chin beginning to accumulate several satellites. His head was mostly bald with a few crisscrossing strands and he wore a rumpled brown suit and vest. His hat lay on the windowsill. He had nervous hands that wrote or doodled constantly, sign of a man who needed a smoke but knew he could not in a hospital room.

"Your husband has pleaded not guilty to murder charges," he said. "He is plea-bargaining with us. We'd like a first-degree conviction, intent to kill, but he is holding out for second degree, maybe even manslaughter." He looked to see if she understood, but she made no sign. "My point is this: I see your pain and suffering plainly before me. But without your help, the man who did this to you could get manslaughter or even go free."

With her face stitched, she could make sounds, but not words. She did not like to make sounds because they were inhuman. She was ugly and pitiful and hated it. For the last two days she had been able to scrawl words left-handed, and they had brought her pad and pencil.

"We are looking for a way to show that your husband's attack on you and Reverend Mull was premeditated. Can you help us with that? Letters, phone-calls, threats, things like that?"

"WAITING BEHIND DOOR!!!" she scribbled slowly in barely legible script.

He read and looked up at her. "Yes, but apparently he was getting ready to leave. If you'd returned later, maybe only minutes, you know what I mean. Fate. That's bad luck, crime of passion, not premeditation. Now if there was a threat of some kind . . ."

"*urder!*" she grunted, the "m" impossible.

"Unfortunately, we can't be sure the jury will agree."

Badly wanting to fly back to the silent comfort of her blackness, she shook her head. "Rafe," she whispered.

"What?"

She wrote again: "RAPE!!!"

Uncomprehending, he stared blankly. "*Rape?* But the man is your husband."

And the tears finally came. Her poor swollen eyes overflowed with all the built-up grief and pain and fear and frustration and anger from being dead and coming back to life and lying in bed for so long and being such a mess and now being subjected to interrogation by a man who was clearly a fool. How, when nothing else on her face worked, could tears fall? Would no one ever know the truth? No, clearly not, for she could never repeat what happened to her that night. How it felt to be pinned on the cross. Her Calvary. The doctors could tell from her battered body. No one else would ever know.

Disoriented by the tears, Federmeister fell silent.

"TRIED TO KILL ME!" she scrawled in capitals, which were easier to form.

"The man is your husband. He caught you with another man. He was aggrieved."

◆ ◆ ◆

Barton Pitts had no doubt that it would be the biggest trial of his career, the biggest in the city since the McNamara brothers were tried for bombing the *Times* building, with Clarence Darrow for the defense. Never had city newspapers, mainly Hearst and Chandler, sold more papers or made more money than since Willie and Angie went missing, and they went on milking the story for everything it was worth. Sex, religion, and murder—it didn't get any better than that. As much as Pitts longed to bring Angie to court for the showdown with her husband, the newspapers privately urged him to take his time.

If Pitts had followed his instincts things might have gone better. Gil l'Amoureux was as perfect a villain as Hollywood could produce, and Pitts wanted to get on with it. But Angie was still in and out of surgery. She was to be the star witness against her husband, waiving her right of spousal privilege. Without her testimony, Gil had a good chance of getting away with murder. The newspapers were on her side for she helped them sell papers, but the airwaves were hostile. For the Rev.

Bob Shoemaker, the most influential pastor in town with Willie gone, Angie was a Jezebel and, worse, had made Los Angeles a national laughingstock.

"Here in Los Angeles we take our religion seriously," he broadcast. "Remember the Ten Commandments, which come directly from God: Adultery is as great a sin as murder."

Pitts first learned of Angie's plans to leave the hospital in a *Times* story about the coming memorial service for Willie Mull. With thousands of Soldiers arriving, they'd moved the service from the temple to the baseball park at Wrigley Field on Avalon Boulevard, a few blocks from Exposition Park where the Soldiers would set up their campground. Pitts met with Superior Court Judge Herman Anzug, and they agreed that with Sister Angie leaving the hospital they could now proceed. The trial of Gil l'Amoureux was docketed for Nov. 14.

By then, spring had come and gone, and it had not been a good one. Willie Mull was murdered on May 3, 1940, one week before Hitler invaded France and two weeks before Capt. Arnaud Ricot de Scitivaux was shot down over Sedan. Maggie's letter informing them of Arnaud's death arrived two weeks later, and the family penned a joint letter of sympathy urging her to come home before it was too late. Willie's death also changed things for his son, who had been planning to leave the temple to begin study for law school. Cal decided to stay on to prepare the memorial service and make sure the temple passed into the right hands.

The Soldiers arrived from across the country, thousands of them, from as far as the KWEM antennas could reach. They came to honor the man who for years had been a part of their lives, a fixture on their radio dial, a voice in their homes as familiar as that of Henry Aldrich or the Great Gildersleeve. When the day arrived, twenty thousand of them marched down

Santa Barbara Avenue and filed into the ballpark as the choir sang the familiar funeral hymns—"Oh Day of Rest and Gladness" and "Cast Thy Burden Upon the Lord." They'd known death and had sung those songs before. Seated, they watched as the young woman dressed in black and wearing a black veil was helped across the grass and up to her place on the dais.

Reporting the story the next day, the *Times* wrote:

Not even a cough could be heard as the battered young woman whose lifted veil revealed her terrible scars came to the words of the eulogy that everyone was waiting for. This was the service for the Rev. Willie Mull, and surely she must say something about his adultery. What would scripture answer to a man of the cloth murdered by a husband who caught him with his wife? Scripture must deal with it today, the mourners knew; tomorrow the law would have its turn.

Speaking slowly, as though each word was excruciating, she did not flinch: "To those who say Willie Mull committed adultery, I say this: He did not know! I am the sinner."

With this, many in the crowd leapt to their feet shouting, "no, no!"

"Yes," she continued. "Willie Mull did not violate the Lord's commandment. I did! I loved him so. I loved him so much that I hid the truth, fearful he could not love me as I loved him. Cast your stones at me, not at Willie. The man's heart burst with love . . . with love for you . . . with love for me . . . with love for Jesus. He did not know! He did not know!

"And when I told him—yes, as the end approached, I told him the truth, that I was married to a monster.

What was he to do? Cast me over? Send me back? No. He comforted me. And he knew; yes, he knew what was coming, and still he loved me and he comforted me. Can one go upon hot coals and his feet not be burned? He knew, and we wept together."

Cries of sympathy and support—amens and hal-lelujahs—rang from one side of the field to the other. Toward the end, with not a dry eye left in the stadium, she closed with two lines from scripture:

"Thou shalt not harden thine heart, nor shut thine hand from thy poor brother."

When she added "or sister," the crowd roared its approval. She ended, quoting from John: "This is my commandment: That ye love one another, as I have loved you."

They had forgiven her.

Good God, thought Barton Pitts, reading the story the next day. Do they really want this woman, an admitted adulteress, to take over the temple? What has this city come to?

CHAPTER 20

McManus always said he would have hired Lizzie anyway. He knew there would be conflicts of interest and did his best to keep her out of them, but in the end there were simply too many. She was too good to keep on the sidelines just because another story touched her family in some way. He blamed himself for not putting her on her uncle's trail sooner, for she would have found him and the whole thing might have been avoided. She talked him into sending her to Union Station to interview her sister returning from Europe. He drew the line, however, at the trial of Gil l'Amoureux. He assigned a veteran *Times* court reporter. Lizzie could attend to gather information for a book if she wanted, but not to write for the *Times*.

Maggie's last letter home from Paris was dated May 20, 1940, three days after Arnaud was killed. He had pressed her to return home since war was declared the previous September, but it was a strange kind of war in the West, dubbed the "phony war" because for eight months nothing happened. There was nothing phony about it in the East and North, for Poland, Finland, Denmark, and Norway, but France and Britain spent the winter on the sidelines, preparing for the war that would start at Hitler's convenience, which turned out to be May 10. If the date was hardly a surprise, the complete collapse of the French and British armies was a shock for everyone. For Capt. Arnaud Ricot de Scitivaux the war lasted a week. For France, a month.

When the news came about Arnaud (a knock on the door from a corporal at the Ministère de la Défense), Maggie grieved alone in their little apartment on the rue de Vaugirard. Every moment of those terrible lonely days was etched into her mind. Hopelessness and helplessness. She paced in the darkened apartment, never went outside, hardly ate, turned to Arnaud's little tome of Baudelaire to share her grief: *"The abyss, the abyss, I fear sleep as one fears a great hole."* No one from the family called on her. Except for Arnaud, no one considered her part of the family. When the day of the funeral came, she draped herself in black and walked alone to Sainte-Clotilde for the service, which was brief for the church had several others to follow. There was no burial for there was no body. Still a stranger in Paris and now a widow, she attended the family *veillée* on the rue las Cases and returned home to sit alone and cry in the dark, listening to the big German guns in the distance.

With Arnaud gone, she had no ties to France, certainly none to his family, which had no use for her now. The Germans were coming fast, pushing the Allies into the sea at Dunkirk, and it was only a matter of days until they reached Paris, a city rapidly emptying as its people and government fled southward in a terrible time of death, destruction, and humiliation. Paris had known other terrible times as well, but these were the worst.

She was desperate to help, to do something, to do her part, but the armistice was signed before she had a chance. With the Germans arriving from north, west and east the only exit was to the south, which was complete chaos, thousands fleeing and, with the armistice, other thousands trying to get back to Paris. Refugees from every country, pushed south by the advancing German army, filled the roads in the direction of Bordeaux where they might find a ship bound for America or at least escape to Portugal. She made it to Bordeaux and caught the first ship she could get for the States, one fortunate enough to cross without being torpedoed.

♦ ♦ ♦

They were five at dinner in Bel Air the night she arrived home. Lizzie met her at Union Station and drove her home before returning downtown to write her story. Along with other refugees, Maggie had been interviewed in New York when their ship docked, but no one in Los Angeles saw the New York papers. Hollywood had been filling up with prominent European refugees since Hitler came to power, but Maggie was the first local girl to return home since the war in the West broke out. She held a little press conference in a quiet corner of Union Station. All the papers were represented, but the *Times* was the only one represented by her sister.

They found her more beautiful than ever, character and suffering showing in a face that had always been sans souci. The old vigor was not dissipated, but there was a new composure. "I could never have made it without the plane Arnaud gave me," she told them at dinner. "Cars, horses, carts, animals, every manner of contraption loaded till the axles broke. A few miles a day—if that. Only one highway south to Bordeaux. The side roads all go the wrong way. I found my little MS 315 sitting under a copse at Villacoublay. Amazing. I took on a French pilot who needed to get south, fueled up and off we went. In Bordeaux, I gave him the plane."

"Such a sad story," said Nelly. "Your young man died before we could meet him." She dabbed at her eyes with a napkin. She'd been in a fluster trying to decide what to have for Maggie's first night home in two years. Lizzie solved it by telling her to stop by Castillo's.

There was a sense of unreality around the table as they ate their enchiladas, a moment of family normality squeezed into the tumult of death, destruction, and disappearance they read about every day. Only Eddie seemed to take it all in stride.

"Glad to have you back, Mag," he said, raising his glass. "'Course, I never wanted you to go in the first place. America needs gals like you at home."

"Hear, hear," said Cal, raising his as the others did. "And let's drink to Arnaud, a good man. His family must be devastated."

"It is the story of France," said Maggie. "Retold for the hundredth time. There are two more pilots in that family still alive, at least last I heard. The plane Arnaud flew was not much different from the one I flew. Against Messerschmitts—no chance. They have some new Dewoitines coming out now. I flew a prototype."

"Lot of good they'll do now," said Eddie.

"Not for the French," she said. "The Germans will get them."

"If fly you must, you can fly here," Nelly said. "But it will have to be without a war. They fight all the time, those Europeans. Their quarrels are not ours."

"Hear, hear," said Eddie, lifting his glass again. "Here's to peace in our time."

Maggie froze, and only Nelly drank with him. Eddie did not notice.

She looked across at her father. "Speaking of prototypes, what do you know about Howard Hughes? I hear he's working on some new planes, making movies about planes."

"Hughes makes movies about girls, not planes," said Nelly.

"He makes both," said Eddie.

"You wouldn't happen to know him would you, Dad? Doesn't he have an airfield out near your Venice oil wells?"

"I do know Howard. Sold him that land. More like Playa del Rey than Venice."

"What's he like?"

"Never met him. Everything done on the phone. Very mysterious guy."

After dinner they drove down the hill to the girls' apartment in Westwood. Maggie was moving back into the bedroom on Tiverton she'd vacated two years before. Cal had moved from Westwood into an Echo Park stucco.

"As if nothing happened," Maggie said as they opened beers and settled down to talk. "Strange to come back as if I'd just stepped out for cigarettes. How come you're in Echo Park? What about Uncle Willie's place on Sunset?"

"I haven't set foot in it."

"Ghosts. You want me to go with you?"

"Would you?"

"I have some time on my hands."

"What's this about Howard Hughes?"

"Just an idea. Have to start somewhere."

"So where do *we* start?" said Lizzie.

"How about with Asa Aldridge?" said Maggie.

"You'll meet him soon enough."

"And . . . ?"

"Doesn't seem like a good time to get married."

"That's what Cal told me in Paris," said Maggie.

"And was I right?"

"No, Cal. You weren't," she snapped. "Changing the subject: Tell me about Sister Angie."

He looked closely, wondering what Lizzie might have said in her letters. "She's still recovering, trying to prepare for a nasty trial—if that's what you mean."

"What I meant was—how could Uncle Willie have done it, run off with a girl like that, put his career at risk, his life? It doesn't make any sense."

"Didn't you do something like that?"

"Oh, come on, Cal."

"And it's not fair to say 'a girl like that.'"

"Ah, well then, a girl like what?"

"I told you two years ago, right here in this apartment. I think they were in love."

"I think I was asking about you," said Maggie.

"Well, stop it, please."

It was getting prickly, and they exchanged long looks, looks of people who need each other too much to go to the mat. "Do you think she'll take his place?" she said at length.

"It depends on the congregation. And on Eddie, who is on the board."

"And on the trial," added Lizzie.

"The trial, of course."

"Do you miss Willie?" Maggie asked Cal.

"Of course, I miss him," he said, surprised at the question. "We went through a lot together. Won't you miss Eddie when he's gone?"

She thought a moment. "I don't know. Maybe I won't. The brothers were both so—so, how to say it, wrapped up in their own lives. Not fathers in the usual sense. I can't ever remember doing anything with Dad."

"They had their own lives," said Lizzie. "But how could you not miss Dad? He's part of you, just like he's part of me. Of course you'll miss him."

"What strikes me," said Maggie, who had lit up, smoking more than ever since returning, "is how different we are from our parents. Did you hear Dad at dinner with 'peace in our time?' How can anyone say something like that with what's happening in Europe? That's why he hates the president, because Roosevelt wants to do something about Hitler. With Dad and Mother, it's all bank accounts and charge accounts. What's in it for me? They never ask—what's the right thing to do?"

"Why should we be like them?" said Lizzie.

"Some children take after their parents," said Cal.

"Sure," said Maggie. "If you admire them, why not? Uncle Willie would have loved to see you come into the church. Dad has always wanted to take you into his businesses. You could be a bootlegger, own a gambling ship in the bay, live in a big house in Bel Air. Or Lizzie or I could do it. None of us ever showed the slightest interest."

"Because?" said Cal.

"Because we all want to do something of value. At least to try."

"I think Dad tried to do something of value," said Cal, uncomfortable.

"A lot of good it got him," said Lizzie.

"And your children," he said. "How do you know they'll take after you?"

"Why wouldn't they?" Maggie said.

"Because maybe they'll want charge accounts and a big house in Bel Air."

"Not if we raise them right, teach them right."

"It doesn't always work like that. Children react—just like we did."

"Do it their own way," said Lizzie.

"Or leapfrogging," said Cal, "to take after their grandparents."

"Heaven forbid," the women said together, laughing, ending the tension.

CHAPTER 21

The trial began November 14, six months after the murder. The Superior Court of Los Angeles held that there was no reason to move it out of the city because there wasn't a city in the state or the country that didn't know all the details. The newspapers took full advantage of the delay, and Herman Anzug, the judge unfortunate enough to be assigned to the case, knew the chance of finding jurors who didn't know the story were about as good as finding someone in Hollywood who didn't know that Clark Gable had married Carole Lombard. But knowing the story didn't mean they had made up their minds, and Anzug, who'd used every means he knew to get off the case, had no doubt he could empanel a jury.

"You're finished as a judge and maybe as a husband if you go through with this," his wife Hilda told him. "If you're not careful you'll have every woman in the county against you in the next election."

Anzug knew—or at least Hilda knew—that murder charges were only part of the trial, and the easy part at that. Sister Angie had not been idle. As "acting" pastor at the temple, she'd used her time in recuperation to meet with the Soldiers. The temple directors, led by Eddie Mull, did not want her named to succeed Willie, but were finding it hard to stop her. Willie's memorial service had sent her star soaring. Where the directors saw ambition and sin, the Soldiers saw love and penance. They also liked the idea of a woman in the pulpit. Cal stayed on to help her. Willie would have wanted it, and he wanted it himself. Keeping her on helped keep his father alive. That was part of it.

She filled the temple just as Willie had done—the difference being the presence of more women, especially single women. Never had the temple had more contributions or KWEM more listeners or advertisers. Letters poured in from women across the nation. The memorial service had done it. Angie was the martyr risen from the ashes, the standard-bearer for women everywhere. Her message was clear: women could no longer be abused with impunity. The "message of Wrigley Field," she called it.

Beyond sympathy for the battered woman who had survived by the grace of God, there was curiosity. Could she preach like Willie, bring the sick and lame down the aisles to be healed and reborn? Henry Callender, identified in newspapers as Willie's closest friend and collaborator, compared her to Mary Magdalene, purified and reborn. Skeptics attacked her more ferociously than they had Willie—for how much easier it is to abuse a woman than a man—but amid all the attacks, the Soldiers never wavered. War was on—in more ways than one.

Preparing for the trial, she refused to yield an inch. Yes, her husband must be punished for Willie Mull's murder, but he must also pay for what he'd done to her. To ignore that, she told Federmeister, who Pitts sent again to "talk sense" to her, was to treat women as second-class citizens. Frustrated, Pitts invited Angie and her lawyer to the hall of justice for a parley.

"We're on the same side, you know," he said. "Adding rape to murder and attempted murder will confuse the jury and jeopardize conviction. The man is your husband."

"Am I to understand that the district attorney condones spousal rape?" she asked.

"*What is spousal rape?*" he bellowed at her.

Up for re-election the following year, Pitts complained to Judge Anzug, who summoned them all to his chambers. Anzug had had a complete search done. Not only did California have no law against anything called spousal or marital rape, but neither was such a law to be found in US or English Common Law. "However strongly we might feel about it, spousal rape is not a crime. Plus the fact that it makes people uncomfortable."

Hilda would have gasped.

"Uncomfortable?" Angie began.

Pitts cut her off. "I agree with Judge Anzug. Attempted murder, yes. Rape, no."

"Rape may be uncomfortable to the court and to the district attorney . . ."

"Irrelevant, is what I meant," sputtered the judge. "Rape is irrelevant to this trial."

"But it is not irrelevant to me," she said, "or to the thousands of women raped and abused by husbands and frightened out of bringing charges by cowardly courts and district attorneys. Either you allow the rape charges to go forward or I will take it to the newspapers and have it tried in the court of public opinion. Let me ask you both this—what do you think the nation will think of court officers who refuse to prosecute the man who abandoned his wife, then returned and raped and tried to murder her? Do you want me to lift my skirts in court, show the jury the scars that are still there? Is that what you want?"

At home that night, Hilda, who had a good legal mind (better than her husband, some said), suggested a solution. It was not a particularly good solution, but would have to do.

♦ ♦ ♦

November of 1940 was unusually harsh for Los Angeles, and the people who waited in line the night before the trial were cold and miserable, though not enough to give up their places. Local newspapers planned extra street editions throughout the trial. Editorials, never losing sight of their owners' primary goal, which is to make money, watched closely to see how the wind was blowing. Defenders of tradition, they could not afford to offend the mainstream churches that despised Willie Mull's evangelism and recoiled at the idea of anointing an adulteress as his successor. But neither could they ignore the "message of Wrigley Field" nor the feminist wave washing across the country since Amelia Earhart took her place beside Eleanor Roosevelt as the world's most acclaimed champion of women's rights. Earhart was gone but not the cause she championed, a cause in search of a new torchbearer.

There are seventeen courtrooms scattered over the fourteen floors of the Los Angeles Hall of Justice, and for the *State of California vs. Gil l'Amoureux* the largest was chosen, seating two hundred people. That left thousands of clamoring, mostly angry women in and around the streets, steps, lobbies, corridors, and elevators who would have to stand in line another night if they wanted to see anything. It took half an hour to get the lucky two hundred into the courtroom, seated and quieted. The Hall of Justice is a massive, classic, Beaux-Arts building whose exterior is constructed primarily of marble and granite. It is stately, solid and normally quiet as any office building except for the top two floors, where the jails are housed. Yet even in his chambers many floors and corridors from the courtroom, Judge Herman Anzug could not escape the din.

Evidence on murder and attempted murder was heard first. Anzug's initial instinct had been to exclude all testimony on spousal rape, but Sister Angie's threat to try her case in the newspapers and make a mockery of his trial presented him with a dilemma: He could not try a man for a crime that did not

legally exist yet could not deny that the woman had been vio-
lently, sexually assaulted, brutalized far outside any acceptable
definition of matrimony. Happily, Hilda had shown him the
way out.

The defendant's lawyer was a shifty veteran public defender
named Albie Goodman, known to many Hall of Justice denizens, but not to Judge Anzug. Judges have their reputations
and rankings, and Anzug, unlike Goodman, was at the top,
never assigned to the kind of divorce, bunko, hustle, traffic trials where Goodman made his living. In the five miles of Hall of
Justice corridors, never once had their paths crossed. Goodman was as surprised to find himself at the center of a national
murder trial as Anzug was to find him in his courtroom. Along
with District Attorney Pitts, the judge summoned the defense
attorney to his chambers early the first morning to inform them
of part of what he (and Hilda) had decided.

"After we empanel, we will hear the murder and attempted
murder charges. When that phase is completed, we will hear the
plea for spousal rape brought by the plaintiff. I do not expect
the second phase to last long, but I've decided it's better to hear
what the plaintiff has to say inside the courtroom than outside.
Any questions?" Pitts could not move the judge to change his
mind. Goodman said nothing. He'd waited for something like
this all his legal life.

Empaneling took a full day. Pitts wanted women, and
Goodman men, and that it ended up six to six was no surprise.
The murder phase lasted three days, and arguments could not
have been simpler: For the state it was premeditated murder.
The man lay in wait for his prey, fell on them, murdered the
Rev. Mull and attempted to murder Sister Angie l'Amoureux,
who miraculously survived. For the defense it was justifiable
homicide. Gil l'Amoureux, in an understandable fit of passion,

killed the man who had stolen his wife. Goodman put to the jury the question he had rehearsed in front of the mirror in his office, posing as he rehearsed, preparing for the newspapers:

"Which one of us, confronting our wife's ravisher, would do any less?"

Blessed with a weekend for research and Sunday newspapers that titillated the public with a preview of what was coming, Goodman was fully prepared for the next phase of the trial. Sitting beside the accused, who was clothed, shaven and combed to look better than he ever had or would, he counseled his client to sit quietly, hands in his lap, with an expressionless face glued on the witnesses—not on his wife. Above all, he ordered, "do not smirk." The jurors, mesmerized by the gruesome acts and injuries described by police, doctors and nurses, never let their eyes stray far from the defendant as they listened to the witnesses.

When Angie, pretty, petite, fragile, dressed entirely in white, took the stand, Gil began to fidget, nervous hands starting to tap the table. There were gasps and groans in the courtroom as Angie described each kick and punch. She had never lost consciousness, remembered every minute of every horrible hour. She described him carrying her limp and bloody into the bedroom. "My Calvary," she said, invoking the image of Jesus. "This man tried to destroy my body and my soul. He sought to torture and kill me. I prayed to die." She turned to the jury. "Look at him sitting there content with himself." Then softly: "Use your imagination."

The defense called no witnesses. After Angie stepped down, Goodman took a book from the table in front of him and walked to the jury box. "There is no such crime as spousal rape," he said, flatly. "This trial should be over, but since the judge is allowing testimony on this business, I have brought this book to show you." He held it up "Do you know this book? Of course you do. It is The Book of Common Prayer, one of the foundations of our society, of our religion, of our law, called the Common Law."

He turned to show the book to the judge and audience. Taking his time, commanding the stage as he hoped to be doing many times after this, he thumbed the book, coming to his page. "Our wedding vows come from the Book of Common Prayer, do you know that? Let me read from them in case you've forgotten." By now, some in the audience knew what was coming, and murmuring was heard. "The woman's vow is familiar to us all," he said, "and I will read the last words of it to you. Yes, here it is. The bride promises at the altar—and I quote—'to love, cherish and obey my husband till death us do part.'"

Murmuring broke into shouting, and the judge gaveled for silence.

"Yes, ladies and gentlemen, the word 'obey' is in the vows, and I have circled it here in red. And that is why there is no such crime as spousal rape. It simply does not exist—anywhere, in any law book, in any jurisdiction, in any land. It is a complete fiction and a waste of our time here in court. The fact of the matter is this: it is the woman's duty to obey her husband."

At this, dozens of women sprang to their feet, shouting, gesturing, refusing to be silenced by Anzug's vigorous banging and repeated warnings that he would clear the courtroom. The judge had suspected something like this from Goodman and berated himself for not warning him in advance, as Hilda had suggested. He hated courtroom theatrics. With order finally restored, he glared his message at the public defender.

Ignoring the judge, Goodman continued: "Is it the prosecution's position that legions of women with chronic 'headaches' can now come traipsing through this courtroom accusing their husbands of rape for the simple assertion of their conjugal rights?"

Outrage, sheer provocation, beyond the pale, violation of every rule of decency and courtroom decorum. Half the audience, mainly women, was on its feet while Anzug pounded away. What was he to do: clear the courtroom of women? Legal suicide, Hilda would have said. Meanwhile, Goodman returned to his table for another book, this one more familiar, the Bible.

"Leviticus," he shouted over the din, "20:10. 'If a man commits adultery with another man's wife, both the adulterer and the adulteress shall be put to death.'" His shrill voice rose over everything. "The defense charges that the wrong person is on trial in this courtroom." Swinging around to point at Angie, he shouted: "There is the person who belongs in the dock."

Pandemonium, this time bringing the judge to his feet. Through it all, Sister Angie sat quietly watching, hands in her lap, her stitched, scarred face never changing expression. The din subsided, she shook her head at her lawyer and quietly asked the judge: "May I respond to the defense attorney's outrageous accusation? I will be brief." Since they were arguing the points of a crime that did not exist, how could he refuse? Sighing, he nodded.

Back on the stand, stiff, leaning forward, long white dress covering her shoes, Angie let her eyes sweep the courtroom and rest a moment on Gil and his attorney. Her face showed no expression. When she turned to face the jury she was as composed as in any pulpit. She was fully prepared. The courtroom was deathly quiet.

"Counselor quotes from the wedding vows, which speak of the women's duty to 'love, cherish and obey' her husband. Why didn't counselor read the rest of the vows?" Her voice was rising. "Why didn't he read of the husband's duty to 'love, comfort, honor and be faithful' to his wife?" She was on the edge of the seat now. "But that would not help his argument would it? Counselor quotes from Leviticus, but I go directly to the words of Jesus to rebut him, Matthew 19:9: 'Whosoever shall put away his wife, except for fornication, causes her to commit adultery.'" Around the courtroom women were coming to their feet, first a few, then whole rows, then the men began to stand as well.

"Yes!" Angie went on, loudly now—"*causes* her to commit adultery; those are the very words of Jesus Christ." She pointed directly at Gil. "That man abandoned me, alone and penniless, while he ran off with other women. *What was I to do?*"

Wild cheering as Angie stepped down, and again Anzug had to use his gavel. Order restored, his face flushed, his patience run out, he wearily turned to instruct the jury that its time had come to retire and consider the evidence against the defendant on charges of murder and attempted murder. They were not to consider the charge of spousal rape against the defendant because there was no such crime on the books—any of the books.

Booing broke out, and the judge had to ruthlessly gavel again for silence.

"However," he began, speaking slowly, intoning each word, his eyes on the rows of newspaper reporters, "just because such a crime is not on the books does not mean that it should not be. The law must constantly grow and evolve if it is to stay in touch with the people. But that is not the job of this court or any court. It is the job of the legislatures. It is the opinion of this court that the elected lawmakers of this state and this nation should move quickly to address what this trial has shown to be a most serious lacuna in our laws."

The boos had turned to cheers, and this time Anzug was slower to pick up his gavel. Hilda Anzug, watching from the audience, smiled.

At sentencing, Gil l'Amoureux got twelve to fifteen years for aggravated assault and voluntary manslaughter. He left the courtroom shaking his fist and vowing revenge. What Angie lost in court, she won in the courtroom of public opinion, which soon made her, next to Mrs. Roosevelt, the most celebrated woman in America, a heroine to women of every age. Newspapers that dared editorialize on the subject of spousal rape defended her, demanding that legislatures get to work to change the laws. She stepped into Willie's shoes at the temple and didn't take them off until the day she died—a day, unfortunately, not as far off as the Soldiers might have liked.

CHAPTER 22

Maggie never used her married name again. She came home from France as Margaret Sinclair Mull, just as she'd left, her passport unchanged. She moved on, coming to regard her eighteen-month marriage to Arnaud and her time in France as belonging to another person. She had loved as well as any twenty-three-year old girl can love, but when she thought back it was more about war than marriage. There was repression there, and she would talk about it if asked, though hated the word "widow," which she associated with mauve gowns and long strings of pearls. Years later, twice a widow though without mauve gowns and long strings of pearls, she would give her Paris interlude a luster and romance she'd once denied it.

Howard Hughes hired her shortly after Pearl Harbor, though she was certain he wouldn't. The interview had gone badly. Hughes could not have been more irritating or sexist, though as the perfect man she figured he believed he had that right. She had been prickly in return. He was so damn cocksure of himself and adamant that women couldn't fly. He didn't even spare Amelia Earhart, the first woman to fly solo across the Atlantic, whom he blamed for mistakes that led to her airplane's disappearance over the Pacific. He referred to her speed records as "women's records," as if speed had a gender. Maggie mentioned the planes she'd flown in Europe, and Hughes's only interest was in the new Dewoitines when she said they could compete with Messerschmitts.

"Neither one could maneuver with my D-2s," he said.

"I'm not sure about that," she said, and that was the end of the interview.

He called her back a few weeks later, early in the new year when the nation was struggling to get its footing. Any male who could fly a plane was disappearing fast into the army air force, and Hughes needed replacements. When she arrived at Hughes Aircraft, a stone's throw from her old stables, he started pumping her about engines—priming engines, regulating fuel pumps, adjusting throttles and props, giving her a verbal diagnostic test. She longed for him to ask something about flying itself, but it was all about maintenance.

"I don't have any female pilots at Hughes," he said. "But I try to keep an open mind about things. Might be a need coming up. All my fliers start in maintenance. That suit you?"

She was annoyed but could hardly refuse. Men were being called up every day and she had no other offers. She was also intrigued by this cocky, clever, ambitious man whose name was in the news as much for his personal life as anything professional. He was called the richest man in the world and the most desirable, his name linked to one Hollywood actress or another. He was constantly being summoned to Washington to testify on defense contracts and always flew his own planes. He'd made a series of movies, some, like *Hell's Angels*, mediocre, some, like *The Front Page*, prize-winners. He was tall, dark and handsome, with a wicked smile under a mustache he'd grown to cover up scars from various crashes. He had a little boy's sense of humor. He was exciting. She understood his appeal to women. He appealed to her.

His sexism infuriated her. He insisted that women were too impulsive to be good pilots, too emotional, couldn't keep their minds steady enough to grasp all the variables of flying. Earhart's navigational mistakes would never have been made by a man. "How do you know that?" she demanded. "Nobody knows what happened to that plane. Anyway, the navigator was a man." ·

He laughed when she said that. He dropped by the hangers from time to time to check on work on his planes, mainly the D-2 fighter he was developing for the army air force. Her supervisor apparently gave her good reports for Hughes invited her to a little maintenance get-together at his house in Hancock Park a few weeks later.

She'd been in maintenance more than a year when they rolled out the D-2 twin-engine prototype for him to take up one day. He waved to her across the hangar and invited her to come up with him. She was thrilled. By that time, she knew the plane inside and out, better than Hughes himself. She was ready to fly again.

They flew out over the Ballona Channel and banked southwest toward Catalina. Even on a routine cruise she could see he was a brilliant pilot, a man with true air instincts. Kilgore Street with its deep descent toward the cliffs was easy to spot over Playa del Rey, and she thought a moment about poor Billy Todd, who would have taken over his father's dental practice by now. She expected Howard to invite her to take the controls, but he did not. The plane started shaking when they'd been in the air less than twenty minutes, barely half the way to the island, and they turned back with a stabilizer problem that needed fixing.

Reading her disappointment, he smiled his wicked smile. "Come see me in my office when we're back."

She was still in overalls. Hughes never wore overalls. Coffee was served and he explained how Lockheed had stolen the design for its twin boom P-38 from the D-2, which would prove to be the far better plane, match up better with the Jap Zeros.

For the first time the conversation turned personal. He asked about her past, her time in Europe, what she had seen, whom she had seen. There was nothing improper about it; he asked nothing about her romantic life, and she offered nothing. She was struck by that. Most men are curious about a woman's romantic past, want to know all the details, however intimate. Not Howard. It didn't matter what she had done or with whom, but what she could do for him. She enjoyed the conversation until near the end. The offer was camouflaged but unmistakable: If she slept with him he might change his mind about letting her fly. He liked to get to know his pilots.

She'd bit her tongue and not reacted, not asked if he also slept with his male pilots to get to know them. But she was furious, and that night called Lizzie to talk about options, which came down to walking out, giving in, or putting up with ground maintenance forever. None of that was her way. Besides, there was a war on. She might be the only female pilot at Hughes Aircraft, one temporarily grounded, but she'd heard of others scattered around the country. Lizzie gave her the idea of getting in touch with the others, organizing them into a collective female unit, but they had no idea how to do it. The army air force was complaining to Congress of a serious shortage of pilots. Why shouldn't female pilots be able to serve?

Hughes laughed in her face when she mentioned it.

◆ ◆ ◆

She met Lizzie for lunch at the Brown Derby on Wilshire, a favorite place for the Hollywood crowd. Maggie had to call her at the *Times* to make the date. They had different schedules and seldom ran into each other at their Westwood apartment.

"It's like you've moved out," Maggie said.

"I suppose I have."

"Asa?"

"He's been pestering me since his overseas orders came. Looks like the Pacific. I suppose we'll get married before he leaves."

"Seldom have I heard such enthusiasm."

"All these guys disappearing—apparently more marriages being performed than ever before. How can I turn him down?"

"Easy—just say no."

"Did you say no to Arnaud?"

"We were in love. Are you?"

"I'm not the family romantic."

"Ah. So suppose you get pregnant and he gets killed."

"Did you get pregnant?"

"No, I did not. But I probably know more about that sort of thing."

Lizzie reddened. Maggie was right but didn't need to say it. "Anyway, we're not here to discuss me, are we?"

"In a way, yes we are." Maggie motioned to the waitress. "I told you something about my idea on the phone."

"You want women in the army air force?"

"If we can fly as well as men, why not? We're at war."

They ordered sandwiches and iced tea and looked around for famous faces. Neither woman recognized anyone.

"You're talking about noncombat flying?"

"As a start."

"They'll never let you fly in war."

"One step at a time."

"And you think I can help in some mysterious way? That's why we're having this lunch."

"Exactly."

Lizzie gave her a soft smile.

Despite the differences, you could tell they were sisters, something in how they walked and talked, even sat. Maggie moved her hands more, likely from her time in France, and with her darker complexion and athletic figure would always turn more heads. But Lizzie's sandy hair and easy way of smiling and inviting you to tell her everything about yourself had its own appeal. Looking at the rows of pictures as they'd entered, they spied Sister Angie in white gown smiling out between Eve Arden and Bette Davis. Uncle Willie's photo was still there.

Maggie sat back to observe her sister, who was dressed in a plain gray flannel skirt and beige sweater, the same style—maybe even the same clothes—she'd worn at UCLA. Her method was to use her anonymity to get what she wanted. No one ever mistook her for a hard-charging newspaper reporter. People felt sorry for the cute young thing in bangs and flats who didn't seem to know what to ask. They'd start blabbing to cover the awkwardness. She had a good memory, a mnemonic camera that recorded everything but didn't work when she was talking. So she didn't talk. She smiled and nodded and poked here and there and remembered. She'll marry Asa without telling a soul, Maggie thought, record it in her diary and tell us about it afterward. She'd always been like that. Little mouse sitting quietly in its corner, nose twitching, seeing everything, missing nothing.

"Howard Hughes," Maggie began as lunch arrived, "is an impossible man—sexist, stubborn, prejudiced, just plain weird."

Lizzie sipped iced tea.

"He is also extremely attractive."

Lizzie arched an eyebrow.

"For all you read about him—the planes, the dames, the movies, everything sleek, fast-moving, nonstop—he is the most old-fashioned man I've ever met.

"Old-fashioned?"

"As in neat, picky, finicky, fastidious, everything in its place, antimacassars, lace doilies on the chairs, lace pillowcases."

"Lace pillowcases?"

She smiled. "Yes, I was in the bedroom."

Lizzie's bright eyes asked the obvious question.

"No," said Maggie. "It was a party. It's where the coats were. Anyway, my point is that Howard thinks women belong in the bedroom, not in the cockpit. In Europe, I flew planes he's never even heard of, and he still won't let me fly."

Lizzie chewed, drank, smiled at the passing waitress, waited. Maggie was prouder of her little sister than she ever let on, only four years out of college and already a familiar by-line for legions of newspaper readers. Who had changed more in those four years, she wondered: she herself, who'd lived in Europe, flown everything, witnessed war, married, seen her husband killed and made it home across an ocean infested with German submarines? Or the little mouse who hadn't stirred out of Los Angeles yet somehow attained a level of stoical sophistication Maggie knew she would never have. It wasn't jealousy. She loved her sister too much for that, and how could she be jealous of someone who'd always been in her shadow? But Lizzie had changed in those years, cloaked herself in a mystifying emanation that caused you to look past her, then quickly back again, certain you'd missed something. Maggie still remembered Santa Monica Hospital with doctors and police and parents all swirling around her bed and Lizzie sitting invisibly somewhere writing it all down. When would *that* appear in a book? Lizzie no longer lived in anyone's shadow.

"Sleeping with him would make him even more stubborn," Maggie went on. "He's one of those men who gives nothing in return so what's the point."

The waitress brought coffee, watery and tasteless in two beige crockery cups. You didn't come to the Brown Derby for the coffee. They fell silent, each woman lost in her thoughts. Lizzie still had no idea the purpose behind this lunch other than that they never saw each other anymore. Maggie hadn't said a word about why she wanted to talk and obviously didn't care whether she married Asa Aldridge or not. Lizzie would wait.

"So here's my idea, Liz," she blurted suddenly, "since I know you'll never ask." She smiled nicely. "What if I could get Howard Hughes into an air race with me, one on one? He loves competition, you know. He says women can't fly, so what if I got him in a race and what if I beat him? What if the race was covered by the newspapers and followed all across the country, including in Washington? It could change everything. How could they then say that women can't fly in this war?"

"Assuming you won, of course."

"Oh, I can beat him all right. But say he fixes the thing some way so he wins—which I wouldn't put past him—what would it matter? The race is the thing, isn't it? The fact that he agrees to race a woman, one on one, that he recognizes our equality in the air."

"If not on the ground."

Maggie laughed. "That's funny."

"So how do you get him into a race like that?"

"That's where you come in."

CHAPTER 23

The five-star item appeared in Jack Smith's *Times* gossip column.

> ***** Seems that Howard Hughes, known far and wide as a man with an eye for a sleek chassis of any kind and one who never refuses a challenge, is refusing a big one. The man who has set more air speed records than any other person alive or dead has declined a challenge to race around Catalina Island in his own planes, the H-1, planes built right here in Los Angeles and used to set most of his records. And who is the temerarious man who would challenge the champ? Why it is not a man at all. It is a woman, Margaret Mull of the well-known local Mull family. Miss Mull, a Hughes employee and well-known pilot in her own right, accuses her boss of under-valuing female pilots at a time the country needs pilots more than ever. So how about this, Mr. Hughes: accept Miss Mull's challenge, invite the public to attend the race and dedicate the proceeds to the purchase of US War Bonds. The public wins—even if you don't.

Hughes strong baritone was known to everyone at the plant and boomed out over loud speakers into every corner of the airfield and beyond to the marshes of Ballona.

"Will Margaret Mull please come to my office? ASAP."

It was not repeated.

She was in greasy beige overalls, standing on a platform, her soft-helmeted head inside the motor of the F-11, a reconnaissance version of the D-2 ordered by the USAAF. Even so, she heard the announcement. All eyes immediately went to the only female in the hangar. Some of the guys shouted at her as she climbed down, her helmet muting their words, which was just as well. Ignoring them, she pushed the platform away from the plane, stowed her helmet, left the hangar, and started across the field toward the offices. She felt it like a summons to the vice principal's office, of which she'd had a few. The men turned to watch. They liked to watch her walk, even in overalls. The summons was what she'd been waiting for.

He was standing with his back to the door, staring out the window to the airfield when she entered. He'd seen her coming, watched every step for a hundred yards, though she could not see him behind the tinted windows. He was dressed in a dark business suit. He didn't turn around to see who'd come in. Melvin Cobb, his lead flack, was in a chair. They exchanged glances. She liked Mel. He liked her.

She waited for him to turn but was darned if she'd stand like some poor army lieutenant waiting for the colonel to acknowledge his existence. She sat down next to Cobb, who was natty in herringbone. It wouldn't be the first pair of greasy overalls on Hughes' snazzy furniture. He had it scrubbed down with saddle soap each night. He was a fiend for cleanliness, a fierce enemy of germs, paranoid on the subject. She wondered how he could make love like that.

"You might have talked to me before you planted this."

Still he hadn't turned.

His office looked out on the airfield he'd carved from the fields between Playa del Rey and Culver City. She was not two miles from the horses that had given her as a girl the taste for something faster. Looking northwest, beyond the runway, toward the wetlands and Eddie's oil derricks, she spied a flock of something (whimbrels, godwits?) sweep through the air in perfect formation, like a squadron of fighters. Her eyes followed the curves of Culver Boulevard over the marshes and came to rest on the spot where Billy Todd was killed in a field of lettuce. Not the worst place to die.

"And you would have laughed me out of the office—as you did last time."

Finally, he turned, wearing the sardonic smile that wasn't a smile so much as simply the way his mouth shut because of the scars. She loved the way he looked—tall, ruggedly handsome, with the self-assurance of a man who accepted no limits.

He'd been in crashes and walked away each time, which some said explained his erratic behavior. He spoke loudly, and she was increasingly aware that he was hard of hearing. His outbursts with men who challenged him were legendary. He was known to be ruthless with men and courteous with women— with whom he didn't have to be ruthless because they surrendered so easily. He was vain about his appearance and kept a large staff of lawyers and publicists to look after his image and interests. His troubles with movie censors, the notorious Hays' Office, over *The Outlaw*, the movie he'd just completed, had been in the news for months. Featuring Jane Russell in a special Hughes-designed uplift bra, the film had been banned, and Hughes set his PR department to work on public opinion to win its release.

"This is betrayal, Miss Mull, which in the Hughes bible is a mortal sin. I can't keep you on after this you must know."

She came to the edge of her chair.

"*Betrayal?* I challenge you to a race, fair and square, and you call it betrayal? What kind of a man does that?"

She thought he suppressed a smile but he turned away so she couldn't be sure.

"You went behind my back. Your sister is on the *Times*, isn't she?"

"What does that have to do with anything?"

"Maybe nothing—I'll find out."

"And I'm sure the next item in the *Times,*" she said with calculated anger, "or maybe it will be a full story this time, will be how the brave Howard Hughes dodged a challenge he knew he would lose."

He turned back, and this time it was not a smile and was not suppressed. It was a horse laugh. "Lose to *you*?"

"You won't be the only one to lose—everybody loses."

She stood to go.

Melvin Cobb was shaking his head. "Mr. Hughes, you can't do this."

"Why can't I do it, Melvin?"

Cobb spoke the words slowly, accenting each one. "Because you will look stupid and weak, Mr. Hughes."

She was walking toward the door.

"*Wait!*" he called. "Why Catalina?"

She turned. "I thought it would have more appeal."

"To . . .?"

"To everyone—to the press, to the public, to you."

She watched him sizing things up, wondering how much of the look was about the race and how much about how she would look in the Russell bra.

"Sit down, Maggie."

She came back and sat down, glancing at Cobb, whose look somehow suggested that the whole scene was arranged—Hughes the movie director at work. How else could Cobb, a factotum if ever there was one, have had the temerity to challenge his boss.

Hughes sat down behind his desk. "You think you can fly my H-1 Racer?"

"With a little practice."

"I set world speed records in that plane, you know."

"I do know that, Howard."

"And you?"

"I flew a Dewoitine 520."

"Not a bad plane. Handles like a Spitfire, wouldn't you say?"

"I've heard it said. I've never flown a Spitfire."

"You'll only embarrass yourself, you know."

Maggie's smile was so incandescent that both Hughes and Cobb broke out in laughter. "My embarrassment will be nothing like yours when I win."

Again, the men erupted in laughter. This time Maggie joined in.

◆ ◆ ◆

The race was set for eleven o'clock on a hot, bright Saturday morning with the winds strong off the ocean making the women spectators hold down their skirts and the men onto their hats. It was to start from the Hughes test site adjacent to the bean and beet fields of Santa Ana. Ten thousand gawkers and a few dozen concessionaires came ready for a fair, ready for a summer carnival, ready for an event to lift spirits. The war news was looking brighter with both the German advance in Russia and the Japanese advance in the Pacific stalling, and what better way to celebrate than an air race to Catalina?

Basking in the free publicity, Hughes gave Maggie time to practice in his H-1 racer, the plane he'd used to set his speed records. She needed it. The H-1, made of wood and aluminum and built for speed and maneuvering, bore no resemblance to the heavy steel planes, some with armor plating, she'd flown in Europe. "Take all the time you need," Hughes told her condescendingly. "I don't want any excuses afterward." He knew she would lose, but wanted a good showing by both planes, which could lead to more contracts for Hughes Aircraft, especially the D-2, the interceptor he was trying to sell to the army air force.

They brought Jack Smith down from the *Times* to act as official starter and flip the coin to see who flew which plane. Looking for idiosyncrasies, Maggie had flown both during her practice runs, finding nothing to separate them. They weighed the same, maneuvered the same and both speeds topped out near 350 mph, far faster than anything she'd ever flown. She'd been over the course four times, twice in each plane. With the planes equal, the pilot would determine victory, like the better jockey on horses of equal speed, the one who knows the animal, knows the track, knows the turns, knows the opposition, and, in the case of planes, knows the winds. Hughes had the advantage in knowing the planes, but as far as she knew had never flown the course—the attitude of someone who didn't need to practice.

They'd picked mid-July when school was out and children could be brought to the field by moms whose husbands were away at war. Flags flew, hawkers hawked, spectators crammed the ropes around the bumpy grass runway, the press kept cameras snapping and rolling and microphones stuck in the face of anyone with an opinion on female pilots. Dressed in soft helmets, dark flight suits and boots, the fliers resembled each other except for their heights.

Maggie looked closely for Movietone News, which made the newsreels shown between features of movie houses across the nation. For two months she'd lost no opportunity to remind people that this was a race to show that women could fly planes as well as any man, including the great Howard Hughes.

"How can you beat the man who holds all the speed records?" a reporter asked her.

"It's one thing to race against a clock, another to face an opponent."

"Even when the opponent is a woman?" said the reporter.

She stifled a rude reply. Hughes claimed women were too emotional to make good pilots. She wanted these reporters on her side. As they prepared to climb aboard, she noticed the windsock pointing southeast, hard off the ocean, a headwind of thirty knots, stronger than during any of her trials. It would be slow going out but coming back they would shoot through the sky like missiles.

They took off in tandem, dead into the wind, flying low, moving up for less resistance. Altitude was important but they'd agreed to stay under two thousand feet so spectators on land and water could follow the race. They flew side by side to the coast, veering southwest toward the island, wings never more than fifty yards apart, Hughes waving and smiling from his cockpit, Maggie ignoring him. Below, the seas were choppy with winds filling the sails of yachts put out to follow the race. The course was set for Seal Rocks on the southern tip of Catalina, where they would clear the first race marker, and Land's End in the north and the second marker. After that, it would be the race of the swift back to the mainland. The final marker was at Turtle Rock southeast of Santa Ana, where they would turn back into the wind for landing.

Five miles out, Hughes took his plane to two thousand feet and pulled ahead. She moved up with him, and he came down, luring her into his wake. Higher altitude meant less resistance, but also meant using more time to climb and descend. It was a matter of geometry and wind resistance, but also of intuition.

She tried to put his plane out of her consciousness and fly by what she remembered and felt in her hands, but he was always there in her peripheral vision, like an annoying wasp that would not leave her alone.

Catalina was in view from the beginning, a large aircraft carrier of an island, getting bigger each minute, its distinctive marks—Avalon Bay with the casino, the sands of strange Isthmus Cove, rocky Mount Orizaba at two thousand feet and Silver Peak in the north—slowly coming into focus. Turning northwest at Seal Rocks she lost him briefly, hoping he was behind, suspecting he'd gone higher, not sure where he was. At Land's End, turning dead east, he was suddenly on her tail like an enemy fighter, higher, faster, coming straight at her and with machine guns would have had her, but she shot up into lighter air and suddenly was ahead.

Not for long. As they made the turn around the island and caught the tailwinds that would carry them back to the mainland, he'd gone higher again and had a half mile on her. She had no idea what he'd done, somehow found the air currents. They were two-thirds of the way and flying like the wind and though he was higher and had to come down farther, she knew at that moment that she would not catch him.

Keep it close, keep it close, she told herself, pushing the plane to 360 with the tailwinds and feeling a thrill of flying like she'd never felt before.

When they passed the final marker at Turtle Rock and began to turn back into the wind she'd closed to a quarter mile. She'd outflown him on the return! They both landed under thirty minutes for the run with spectators cheering and cameras rolling as they climbed from the cockpits and shook hands. He pulled her into an embrace. Never had she felt such exhilaration! At that moment she was in love.

She had won by losing.

The following week she found a letter in her box at Hughes Aircraft, unusual because she received little mail at work, intriguing because the envelope was blank except for the address and the stamp "official" where the return address should be. The little she knew about official mail was that it usually had the address of the sending organization clearly marked in the upper left-hand corner. This one did not. She took it with her into the canteen, poured a cup of coffee and sat down to read.

Dear Miss Mull,

Fresh from seeing the newsreel of your marvelous race with Mr. Hughes and reading your interview sent out by the wire services, I am writing to say that I am thrilled beyond words at your accomplishment and wholeheartedly agree with your comments on the role women pilots can play in the war. At a moment we are experiencing a serious shortage of pilots it is quite wrong to exclude qualified women from the USAAF. In Great Britain, as I'm sure you know, women have been flying for the Air Transport Auxiliary since the war began, thus it can hardly be a question of a lack of female aptitude or competence. It seems to me that the attention you've brought to the subject can be used effectively to argue for creation in this country of something similar to the British ATA.

I suggest you write to Lt. Col. Robert Olds in care of the War Department to make the points you made in your interview. Col. Olds is in close contact with General

Arnold, commander of the Army Air Corps. I've taken the liberty of sending your interview to both men in case they missed it, which I doubt, along with a note that someone should be sent to England to learn more about the ATA. I have also sent the interview and note to my husband.

I think you should be part of any mission to England. It seems to me that the first step is to make an assessment of how many experienced female pilots we have in the United States. Perhaps that could be an assignment for you. You might want to bring the matter up with Colonel Olds or General Arnold.

It is a capital idea you have proposed, and one I fully support.

Yours sincerely,
Eleanor Roosevelt

It was typed on White House stationery and signed simply, Eleanor Roosevelt, in large, bold, slightly masculine script.

CHAPTER 24

Henry Callender had no one to play chess with. Cal had played with him for a while but then went off to war with all the other young men. His coworkers at the temple didn't play chess, and even Nyx had lost interest. Nothing was the same anymore, although he gave Angie credit for how she'd stepped in for Willie. The temple was full, the shows, in part because of the war, were more popular than ever and, yes, he had to admit it, Angie had taken the truth of Jesus and hoisted it as high as Willie ever had. Coast to coast, thanks to KWEM radio, she was acclaimed, proof for women everywhere that they could do jobs once done by men only.

But how he missed Willie! A day didn't pass that he didn't think of him, the man to whom he owed so much. Nor did a day pass that he didn't think of Willie's brother, the man who had cheated everyone.

He still played chess on Willie's board, the board that once belonged to Grandpa Otto Herzog of Monterey, the board Cal gave to him when he left and that now sat on the coffee table between his sofa and Nyx's chair. Nyx still occupied the chair, though he mostly slept now, and Henry got no more advice from him. He still played Willie, and Willie sometimes won. He'd played Willie enough to know his thinking and know his moves, and he made them as faithfully as he remembered. But Willie had improvised, too, as any good chess player does, and Henry could not improvise for him. He could improvise for himself, and that gave him the edge, except when improvisation led to disaster and loss, as it sometimes did.

He talked to Nyx more than ever and always on the same subject: There was something wrong in a world where a good man like Willie Mull was murdered and his evil twin thrived, growing ever richer, making a mockery of justice. The Lord has His ways, and that those ways are unfathomable to mortals remained as true as ever. But while accepting the mystery, Henry Callender never had been one to stand by and just let things happen. He'd gotten where he was by doing what had to be done. It had been that way on the trail. Nothing had changed.

Months of brooding weighed heavily on him. In his long life, he reproached himself only one thing: that he had never settled up with Eddie Mull for having robbed him of what was rightfully his. He couldn't do it when Willie was alive, or rather for Willie's sake he wouldn't do it. But Willie was gone, and Henry blamed Eddie for his death.

Callender knew about the *Providence*, knew about the money that came from the ship, the alms money, gambling money, tainted money, money stolen from people who'd done honest work to earn it. When they prayed together, he'd heard Willie asking the Lord for forgiveness. "Penance, penance," he would say, words telling Henry he was carrying a heavy burden, the burden of his brother, the man who'd made his fortune through every form of cheating, conniving, stealing, and transgressing and was passing the filthy lucre to his brother as payment for his silence. How could a sinner like Eddie Mull thrive while everyone connected with him was destroyed? What kind of terrible swift justice was that?

One evening, he returned to his duplex, alone as usual, switching on the light, looking to the chessboard, smiling at Nyx. The cat did not move, did not even open his eyes. He was an old cat and mostly slept, but always opened his eyes when Henry came in, always acknowledged him in some catlike way even if he did not come over and rub up against him as in the old days. He was on his side as he liked to be when sleeping, head gently resting on his cushion. But he did not move. Henry bent down to stroke him, and still he did not move. He sat down, took Nyx in his lap and began to cry. Why did things have to be like that? He held him and stroked him and thought about the fragility of life, always hanging by a thread. It wasn't right. The good die, and the bad go on living. There must be retribution. He'd talked to Nyx about retribution for so long, for so many years without doing anything, that the cat had died of frustration.

He buried Nyx at the back of the duplex in the dirt area by the fence that separated his house from the yard behind. Afterward, he went into the bedroom and took down a shoebox from the closet. He sat on his bed, opened the box and took the Remington Derringer from the oilcloth in which it had lain wrapped since he'd taken it from his backpack years before. He took out a box of .41 shorts and carried pistol and ammunition into the kitchen. He fired the gun a few times, watching the firing pin move between the twin barrels at each pull of the trigger.

The firing made a pure, clean sound, one he hadn't heard in years, the sound of perfect engineering, of metal turned to the highest precision. He'd used the pistol before, but never to kill. He put a round in each barrel and aimed at the window. The half-moon handle felt natural in his gnarled hand. He took the rounds out, laid them on the table and pulled the trigger a few more times, getting used to the feel again and to the sound of metal on metal. It was an old gun, he doubted that they even made them anymore, but it was the only revolver he'd ever owned. He oiled it, wiped it clean with a rag and put it back in the shoebox in the closet.

He'd never driven a car, never learned, never cared to. In

the mountains and deserts you used horses or mules or walked, and in town you used buses and trolleys. Los Angeles had a good trolley system, the Red Cars and the Yellow Cars, and where one wouldn't take you the other would. Callender loved trolleys, rode them everywhere, rode some of them to places like Redondo Beach that didn't have many people. Los Angeles was a smart city, running lines to places it wanted people to live and bringing them along afterward. That's how the San Fernando Valley was built, first the trolleys, then the people. Next they ran lines to the beaches so the people could get away from the growing mess that was downtown.

His favorite line was the Pacific Electric car west to Culver City, on to Playa del Rey and south along the beaches to Manhattan, Hermosa and Redondo. It was his favorite Sunday after-church excursion, less than an hour from the temple to the pier in Redondo with only two changes and the whole thing for half a dollar. He'd get a good seat by the window and watch the city clang by—downtown, west on the avenues, past MGM Studios, through the beanfields to the coast. He'd slow his mind and just observe. From years of prospecting, he'd learned not to think, to empty the mind, just be. At Redondo, he'd walk out on the pier and drink a beer, eat a sandwich and watch the men with their lines in the water. The women would come out, too, pushing prams and spinning parasols, enjoying the bracing ocean air. Life as it should be.

He never took the Venice line anymore, the Short Line they called it. Once it had been his favorite, especially Sundays when he had time before the evening show at the temple, and he'd catch it downtown, get off at Windward Avenue in Venice and stroll the strand with other Sunday flâneurs to Ocean Park. But Venice changed after it was annexed by Los Angeles and got a Sunday "sin" exemption, allowing Eddie and his crowd to turn the strand into a tawdry place of hawkers and hucksters and women who didn't bother to hide what they had and what they were. Henry had worked with Willie to clean up Venice, to close up the dancehalls and brothels, but they'd lost that fight, lost it to Eddie, and Henry didn't go to Venice anymore.

But today he was. Dressing, he'd surprised himself by taking out his old clothes, not the new ones he'd worn since coming to the temple. Maybe that was the trouble: he'd shed his old skin, which was his real skin. That had been Willie's problem too. The old clothes had been hanging for a while. The Stetson was up there, and he gave it a few swipes with a brush. The boots needed polishing, but he didn't bother. He took the Remington Derringer out of the shoebox, loaded it and put it on safety. He walked into the kitchen and suddenly had a thirst, squeezing a couple of blood oranges and downing the pulpy red juice in a few gulps, feeling it hit bottom. A small, light gun, the Derringer bulged no more in his jacket pocket than a good wad would do if he'd had one. He combed out his mustache and set out for the Short Line.

He caught the trolley at the Hill Street station and rode it past Venice to Ocean Park where he'd first met Eddie at the beauty contest and stayed on to the end of the line at Santa Monica City Hall. From city hall it was but a short walk down Olympic to the Santa Monica pier. He wasn't expected at work until four o'clock to get ready for the evening show, but he wasn't worrying about being late. Not on this day. Not ever again.

He'd already been to the *Providence,* discreetly gone out twice to check on Eddie's routine, to reconnoiter. Eddie was always out there Sundays—why wouldn't he be since he never set foot in church? He went to pick up the proceeds from Friday and Saturday and stayed until late afternoon, usually having a few drinks with customers. Eddie knew time was running out on the *Providence*. Legally, the ship was beyond the three-mile state jurisdiction and untouchable, but with the war the nation was discovering virtue again. Even someone as crooked as District Attorney Barton Pitts couldn't hold out forever against public disgust.

Arriving at the pier, Henry kept on walking, past the fishmongers and restaurants, past the Sunday fishermen with their lines in the water. Santa Monica Pier was like Redondo, a quiet sea promenade of line-fishers and strollers, not at all like the noisy carnival piers of Venice and Ocean Park. Henry enjoyed the clear day and fine-looking people, some looking like they'd come straight from church. A few of them nodded politely, which pleased him. He'd long observed that Sundays did that to people. He watched a fisherman haul in what looked like a bass. Henry's mind was on the fine day and his good mood. He was not thinking at all about the task at hand. At the sign marked "PROVIDENCE," he slipped quietly into the line for tickets.

Dressed in his trail clothes he stood out but didn't mind the stares. On the trail no one dares stare, and city stares didn't mean a thing to him. The people in the line were different from those walking the pier—noisier, edgier, no prams, no children, more men than women, though mostly older men like him. It took a few minutes to get down to the ticket office. The girl stared a moment but said nothing. She'd learned that cheap clothes didn't always mean empty pockets. He slid her a quarter, the cost of the launch. A gangway rocking gently with the waves led to the launch at the bottom.

Leaving a nice wake behind, the boat did three miles in under ten minutes, and people poured quickly out of it, up the gangway and onto the ship like rushing for seats at a football game. Boarding, you heard the clanging of slots and calls from the tables. It was early afternoon, and those looking for fortification pushed their way toward the bar and dining room on the first deck. Better to dine and drink while you still had money to do it. In the old days, he would have gone to the bar himself, but Henry was sober.

Glancing around the crowded main salon, checking the closed door to Eddie's office beyond the gaming area, he planted himself in a chair on the opposite side of the room, near a cashier's booth, where he had a view across the room to Eddie's office. There weren't many chairs because you didn't come to the gambling salons to sit unless there was a game in front of you. Beside him was a table with a box on it. He read the inscription on the brass plaque: "JUST A FEW DOLLARS OF YOUR WINNINGS WILL FEED AND HOUSE A POOR FAMILY FOR A WEEK."

He knew that box. It was the evil box, the snake box, the cursed box that had sent Willie to his knees in the chapel crying "penance, penance," the box that held the filthy lucre that ate at Willie's conscience, that bribed him to silence, that drove him away and got him killed.

Henry sat by the box and watched the people, his eyes never straying far from the door across the room. At some point, Eddie would come out with his bodyguard, cross the room toward the cashier's office with the intent of carrying the alms box into the room behind the cashier, collecting the money, filling his bags, and making his way down to the launch and back to Santa Monica to get ready for Monday deposits at his bank.

It was the routine Henry had observed on his previous visits to the *Providence*, though never from this chair where Eddie would have spotted him. He didn't mind being spotted today. Every step was clear in his mind. Eddie would cross the room greeting people, would not see Henry until he was upon him, and Henry would kill him. He would not kill the bodyguard. The bodyguard would kill him. It was clear in his mind, the way it had to be. He watched people come and go to the cashier, a few of them dropping something in the alms box. Some glanced or nodded, but most didn't even notice him, just part of the décor. The ones coming to the cashier were mostly in a good mood. The ones in a bad mood didn't need a cashier.

The day grew later, and still Eddie did not appear. Henry patted his coat pocket and ran his hand over the smooth Remington Derringer, the twin barrels loaded, the safety catch on. It was a deadly pistol, but only at close range. Shoot someone in the heart from five feet and they were dead before they hit the ground. Shoot them in the hand, and they would never use that hand again. Two bullets would do the job. He'd brought no extras.

Time passed slowly. He checked his watch, which said three o'clock. He'd been on the ship nearly two hours. If Eddie was on the ship, there would be some sign of him by now. Henry hadn't been thinking about the temple. Why would he in the circumstances? But if Eddie wasn't coming it was a different story. It took time to get to Echo Park from Santa Monica, even on the Short Line. He was suddenly discouraged. He'd planned it perfectly and said his prayers. He'd written a note and left it on the Nyx's chair, where the police would find it, by the half-finished chess match, where Willie was up a bishop and likely to win. He'd steeled for what had to be done, and now it was off. He sat thinking about it a while before getting up. He perked himself up. There would be other Sundays.

He walked out to the deck and sighted the launch speeding across open water toward him, spreading its foamy wake behind like a peacock spreading its tail. He looked toward Catalina Island and brought his eyes back over Palos Verdes Peninsula down the coast to Santa Monica. The launch was still a mile off, and he walked aft a few steps to gaze up the coast toward Point Dume. There were days when fog lay so low you couldn't see your feet, others when smog hovered and your eyes burned so you had to step inside. This was not one of them. It was a beautiful day, the sky and ocean blue, the winds calm, and you could see forever.

He came back as the launch pulled up. Lines were thrown, the gangway lowered and a new group of gamblers started up. Henry was at the front of those waiting behind the rope for the boat to empty so they could board for the trip back. He watched stylish men and beautiful women coming up, people clapping to the sound of the music from the restaurant, bubbling in anticipation of good times. On the Sabbath! He turned around to look at the people behind him, mostly silent, not so much bubbling. If there were winners among them, they weren't showing it. Act like it's not the first time. Losers, too, tried not to show it.

And then there he was.

Eddie Mull, the man who had broken every law and stolen everything—the oil, the temple, Willie's life, Henry's life and now from honest working people. Murderer? Something Willie once said about their mother's death. Fatter now, always gross-mannered, the Mull good looks turned to sallow corruption. He was shaking hands with the launch captain and starting up the gangway, the last man off. He had no bodyguard. The bodyguard was on the ship ready to escort him back. Henry moved under the rope and started down.

"Hey you, there!" a deckhand shouted, pointing at him. "No boarding until everyone has left the launch!"

Eddie was halfway up and looked up and saw Henry blocking his way. He was not five feet away, and Henry held the Remington Derringer aimed straight at his heart.

"Henry, for God's sake . . ."

"I wish I had a gun to give you, Eddie; make this fair and square. But when did you ever play fair and square?"

Two barrels right into the heart. Eddie Mull fell at his feet.

With a boot that needed polishing, Henry pushed the body under the ropes, kicked it into the sea.

"Think of the water, Eddie," the voice outside Security Trust had told him years before. The water brought Eddie to Los Angeles, and the water carried him away.

Part Three

CHAPTER 25

There was no better place in the world than postwar Los Angeles. Water had brought the first wave of people, and the Depression brought the second. The third wave was made up of hundreds of thousands of troops who'd passed through on their way to the Pacific, liked what they saw and decided that if they made it back, home would be Los Angeles. Maybe life wasn't all that bad in the Eastern cities where they were brought up, at least not compared to what they had seen overseas, and it had been good enough on the farms of the Midwest, but there was nothing like Los Angeles. Once you saw it you wouldn't settle for anything else, and the G.I. Bill made everything possible.

A county of one million people in 1920 would have four million by 1950, totally unanticipated growth for a dusty bowl cut off from civilization by desert, mountains, and ocean, without enough indigenous water to support robust life. During those thirty years, as the Klan advertised, Los Angeles was a "white" city, an "Anglo" city. However, if the Klan had looked deeper it would have noticed that not all immigration was "Anglo." The Asians, the blacks, the Mexicans, the Jews, came quietly and settled into their enclaves without fuss. Charlie Watts gave his name to a handsome ranchland south of downtown where tens of thousands of blacks escaping Southern segregation settled. At some point, they would outgrow Charlie Watts's ranchland and want out, though that was still a few years away.

Postwar Los Angeles had everything: industry, agriculture, water, mountains, beaches, a climate that meant no more freezing in winter and slushing in spring. Postwar Detroit hadn't yet started to make cars again, but Los Angeles had a transportation system called the best in the world, a modern trolley network spidering the city from San Pedro to San Fernando, from the beaches of Redondo and Santa Monica to the mansions of Pasadena and San Marino. And let's not forget Hollywood, which cast its glamorous aura over everything. The movie industry settled in Los Angeles for the land and the weather. So did millions of postwar Americans.

If there was plenty for the citizenry to like, so was it for newspapers, which hit their stride as millions of new readers arrived in town. Like movies, newspapers need action and excitement to thrive. Unlike movies, they don't make it up, but depend on the city to provide its own, preferably daily. Newspapers come in sections so there is something at breakfast for everyone. Page one is for the important news, stories about wars, catastrophes, murders. violence—things involving death. Over the years, District Attorney Barton Pitts had been a reliable source for page one stories, but Pitts had gone to prison. Elected with financial support from people he'd helped get rich, including people at the *Times*, Pitts's corruption was revealed in a series of front-page stories that won Pat Murphy a Pulitzer Prize.

And got him killed.

"The police don't find him because the police don't *want* to find him," McManus croaked in a voice scratchier than his usual baritone because he was smoking more and sleeping less. "They don't find him because they're in on it somehow—*as you all know*." The city editor paused to look around the table.

"*How* they're in on it, I don't know and neither do you, and I pay you to know. Either someone in this room finds Pat Murphy's murderer or he will go on hoisting cold ones at the Canton Bazaar until another reporter is knocked off." Another pause. "And it could be any one of you."

The conference room fell silent. Outside the *Times* third-floor windows, the First Street traffic made its usual din, muffled by double windows installed so people could talk to each other without shouting—though not all the shouting could be blamed on the traffic. Listening to the city editor, eight reporters and editors gazed out the windows to the soothing sight of palms and plants and happy people sunning themselves on the grass around city hall, where they could not hear Larry McManus.

Lizzie was fidgeting because they'd been over all this before and had gotten nowhere. They had no leads. The pressure on McManus was building inside the newspaper and out. She was ready to ask him to take her off the metro desk and have a crack at it, but wanted him to ask first. The public had no confidence in city hall. The *Times* had already hinted that the police were in on it. If the *Times* didn't catch the killer of its own reporter, who would?

McManus looked around at the faces focused on him, not one of them showing any sign of speaking. "What I'm going to do," he said, exasperation finally breaking through, "is start a running story, a daily front page notebook on the Murphy case. The notebook's success will depend on what you bring me each day. Feed me and we will look good. Starve me and we will look stupid—a notebook with no notes."

He paused for a last drag on his cigarette before stubbing it out in the overflowing ashtray. Looking up, his eyes came to rest on Lizzie, and she wondered if they were thinking the same thing. "The point is," he said, "I don't want anyone in the city to start thinking—particularly in the police department—that we're going to let this thing die. And God help us all if the *Examiner* or *Daily News* scoops us on the murder of our own Pat Murphy!"

Afterward, she phoned Asa, and they agreed to meet for lunch at the bazaar. She walked over from the newspaper to find him waiting, punctual despite everything. He looked good, she thought, sharp in pinstripes and a natty red silk tie tied in a neat Windsor, better than in the dingy old days at the DA's office. After the war he'd joined a private law office. She hadn't seen that much of him since the divorce and her remarriage. Her view was that the divorce had been good for both of them, which wasn't necessarily his view.

"I worry about Larry," she said after they were seated. "He smokes too much and worries too much. His is face redder than that tie you're wearing. Murphy's killer will have a second victim at this rate."

He was wondering why she'd called and why he'd accepted, though he had nothing else scheduled. Seeing her always hurt. "What am I supposed to do about it?"

It was not the friendliest of openings. "I'm going to ask him to put me on it. I need some names from you."

They'd ordered pot stickers and chicken with broccoli and noodles and watched as the waiter poured green tea. The Canton Bazaar on Temple was more like a two-story Chinese cafeteria than a bazaar. It was a hangout for anyone who had anything to do with city hall, the hall of justice, the courts or the *Times*. If you wanted to be seen, you stayed downstairs. If you wanted privacy, you came early and slipped upstairs. There were things going on in the back that were illegal, but nobody bothered.

"My advice is to stay away. Anyway, I don't know anyone up there anymore. The war, a new mayor, new DA, me a new job."

"Who owed Pitts, owed him enough to blow up Pat Murphy?"

The waiter brought lunch and left quickly, as they are trained to do at the bazaar.

"There has to be a secretary or paralegal or someone who's been around forever and knows everything," she said. "Just give me a name or two, somewhere to start."

"I'm sure your reporters have been through the staff."

She slurped up a noodle trying to escape. "Maybe they have."

"I thought you were happy on the metro desk, thought you liked the hours."

Which showed how out of touch they still were. They said war changed you, but how had it changed Asa Aldridge, a USC Law School, JAG Corps guy who'd spent his career handling AWOLs and Article 32s and never made it west of Honolulu? He was the same guy she'd married five years before and was sent away. They weren't the only couple to marry in the great surge of Pearl Harbor patriotism and later discover they had nothing in common.

Maggie had warned her about Asa. "Arnaud and I were already sleeping together," she said. "Are you and Asa sleeping together? No, don't answer that because it's obvious you're not." The "obvious" had irked Lizzie. *How can sleeping together be obvious?* she wrote in her diary that night. "What will you do until he's back?" asked Maggie, convinced her sister was under-sexed, whereas the truth was that she was simply more private. Why should she have told her about the affair with Joe Morton? She doubted she knew everything about Maggie's affairs either, while conceding there was more to know.

She stopped woolgathering and smiled for Asa. *"You* liked the metro desk hours more than I did."

"I thought more regular hours might help us—well, you know."

Her back stiffened. "I don't think it was my work hours that kept me from getting pregnant."

"What do you mean by that?"

She wished she hadn't said it but didn't like Asa passing the buck. With Joe, who'd left the *Times* to become a screenwriter for the studios and now was her husband, she'd had no trouble becoming pregnant. Asa knew it and resented it.

"If you'll allow me to go back to the previous question— what are *you* supposed to do about it?" She had trouble concentrating on Asa, always had. "I worked for Pat Murphy, you worked for Pitts. Murph never let me go near Pitts. The Pitts file was his alone. Even McManus didn't know what Pat had. He would have had to tell management."

Asa was still sore. "And you want me to . . .?"

She looked around, recognizing some *Times* people and a couple from the hall. She'd been out of the flow too long. At some table would be someone who worked for Fritz Singer, the new DA, maybe someone who had worked for Pitts, maybe even someone who knew who killed Pat Murphy. Everything flowed through the bazaar, the aorta of city hall life. She looked at her ex and tried a smile again. She'd hurt him and hadn't meant to. He wasn't going to help. He resented her, particularly resented Maggie who he knew had opposed the marriage.

"Who owed Pitts?" she repeated. "Who killed Pat Murphy for him?"

"It's been years since I've been up there, Liz. Before the war."

"I'm going to do it, you know, with your help or without."

"If Pitts got Murphy he's going to get any reporter who comes after him."

"Pitts is in Folsom."

"He still has friends down here."

"Oh? How about naming a few."

"Why doesn't McManus put some fearless young go-getter on it?"

She leveled hard hazel eyes on him. He'd never understood newspapers—or liked them for that matter. He'd been Pitts's lead guy on the search for Uncle Willie, but never gave her anything. She'd found Uncle Willie on her own, though too late. She and Luis Ortega, killed snapping pictures on Saipan.

"They've been on it."

"Pitts remembers you, you know. You covered his trial."

"Three to five for corruption. If we can tie him to Murphy, he'll get the chamber."

Asa finished his tea and paid the bill. Old habits. "Say hello to your sister for me. And to Cal. He still seeing that preacher?"

"I'm not sure I'd call it 'seeing her.' They go back, you know."

"Unlike your sister, Cal seemed to like me. What's he doing these days?"

"Lawyer for Pacific Electric."

"You coming?"

She kissed him on the cheek. "You go on ahead. I see someone I know."

"Don't get involved, Liz, not good for your health."

"Thank you for your concern."

McManus was downstairs with the publisher when she returned from lunch. She left a message with Rosa, his secretary, that she'd like to see him. She walked to her place at the metro desk and sat down to go through the afternoon schedule. Most of her reporters were already out on assignments, a few already writing at their desks. She went quickly through the day's line-up so far: warehouse fire on Figueroa, ten-car crash on Sepulveda, body parts dug up in Griffith Park that could be human, hold-up at a jeweler's in Beverly Hills, naked man running through the streets in Pasadena, chased by a woman. The usual stuff, nothing for the front page except possibly the naked man. It was a hot day and she felt a little sweaty under her flowered silk blouse. Her bra pinched. Lunch with Asa was still annoying her.

She surveyed the vast room that had been her home for close to ten years. She saw Miss Adelaide Nevin looking her way and waved, though Miss Adelaide, who hated wearing her glasses, didn't wave back. She had great affection for that woman, as good an editor as she'd ever known, maybe even as good as McManus but destined by her sex to stay on the society pages. It had gotten better for women during the war, but newspapers were back to being a man's world. McManus had given her a break in hiring her, taken a risk in assigning her to Murphy and a bigger risk in making her metro editor, even during the war when men were scarce. She'd turned him down at first, insisting she was a writer, not an editor, but Miss Adelaide changed her mind. "It's a step forward, Lizzie, and I don't mean just for you."

She took it and now was going to end it. Rosa was waving across the room.

He was smoking, collar unbuttoned, tie loosened (though he'd buttoned up to go downstairs), sweating, the creases running from his cheekbones down past the mouth darker than ever, shirt in need of changing though he was not even half-way through his day. He was too thin, probably from drinking more than he ate and smoking more than he drank. He wasn't sallow, just dark, Indian red dark, though certainly not from the sun. He didn't say a word when she entered, just watched her closely, as he always did. Nobody knew much about Larry McManus: came out from Detroit sometime in the twenties, married, divorced, had a son who disappeared. He'd been hired by Harry Chandler himself, the prince, which still meant something on the *Times*, especially to Harry's son, Norman, who now ran things.

As far as anyone knew, newspapers in general and the *Times* in particular were the only things that Larry McManus cared about. He knew the city inside out, had been city editor forever and didn't aspire to anything higher. He handed out awards to the staff when there were any and joined them at the bazaar to hoist a few when there was something to celebrate. He tried to be convivial, though it didn't come naturally, laughed at the jokes and sometimes even tried one of his own. Afterward, he went his way. She'd heard he lived near Echo Park somewhere. If anyone ever inquired about his personal life, he never did it again.

She sat down without being invited, and they stared at each other a moment. Lizzie was never sure why, but there was something about McManus that always made her want to cry, something in the look—caring, trusting, longing, personal— something she'd never seen in the eyes of any other man except Joe, which was why she married him. With Larry it had always been there for her, more pronounced after her uncle's murder, indelible after her father's.

"I know why you're here," he said, exhaling as he spoke.

She crossed her legs and waited.

"I don't know, Lizzie, I really don't. You have a child now."

"Robby adores his Daddy, who works at home."

He nodded. "Joe's a good man, hated to lose him."

"Thank you."

"I like you on the metro desk—where I can keep an eye on you."

He was fighting it out with himself, and she had no intention of interrupting.

"On the other hand . . ."

"The front-page notebook."

"Right. The notebook. We're in a spot . . ."

He swiveled to look out the windows, a habit he had, do his thinking without being observed.

At length, he turned back. "Can I put someone with you?"

She shook her head. "Too soon."

He fumbled with a pencil and stubbed out his cigarette. Then he actually smiled. Maggie, who'd never met him, called him a *faux dur*.

"Okay, so let's get on it. Send Teddy in here. He can run metro while you're away."

CHAPTER 26

Cal phoned Lizzie from his downtown office after taking the call from Sammy Milstein, Henry Callender's lawyer. Callender was in Folsom Prison for Eddie Mull's murder, and Milstein's call came out of the blue. "He has some interesting news," Cal said, refusing to say anything more on the phone. He was taking Nelly to dinner the following night, and they agreed to meet afterward at Lizzie's house in Brentwood. Joe was in New York trying to raise money for a movie, but Maggie would be there "with news of her own," Lizzie informed him. He took Nelly to Jack's at the Beach on the pier in Ocean Park, her favorite place, a stone's throw from where she'd met Eddie in her bathing suit in the story they all knew by heart. She wouldn't let him pay for dinner. "I can't spend it all on dance lessons," she said. Though Eddie's estate was still in probate—he hadn't counted on dying and left no will—Nelly had already slipped comfortably into the part of the wealthy widow.

The Mortons owned a bougainvillea-covered Spanish stucco on South Barrington, halfway between Sunset and San Vicente. He saw Maggie's red Ford coupé in the driveway as he pulled in, the first time he'd been back to Brentwood since soon after the wedding. Lizzie hadn't told anyone, just slipped off to a chapel in Westwood so Miss Adelaide wouldn't find out. Ten years older than his wife, Joe Morton had spent the thirties covering Europe for UPI, mostly in Germany, coming home after Pearl Harbor and missing the draft by a year—though his eyes would have kept him out if his age hadn't. He'd worked for the *Times* until selling his first movie script, a B thriller filmed in the sewers of Los Angeles. He was pudgy and balding and couldn't see his feet without his glasses but was as passionate about writing as was Lizzie and just as passionate about her. He liked to cook and didn't mind babysitting while Lizzie was at work. The baby, Robby, was Cal's godson.

Lizzie wore glasses now, had the perfect face for them, Cal thought, the dark hornrims accenting her light skin and inquisitive bright eyes. A good marriage had helped her, so had success, so had motherhood. His girls had become success-ful women. They looked on him as a brother, but he'd been more like a father, six years older than one, seven more than the other. He'd had been there when Eddie was not, which was most of the time. Maggie had needed him more, the rotor of her gyroscope. Lizzie had her own rotor.

"Callender?" she asked, handing him a beer.

"Milstein asked if I remembered the trial. Of course, I did, I said. I was in the Pacific, but you're talking about my uncle. I read the trial transcript. He said his client might have some information for the Reverend Willie Mull's son. That's exactly how he put it—'for the Reverend Willie Mull's son.' Odd, no?"

"I remember Milstein," she said. "I didn't cover the trial, but I was there every day. Callender was acting crazy, talking about Willie and chess and cats and the law of the trail, things no one understood. Milstein didn't want him declared incom-petent, said he was just a little 'teched' from a long, hard life. The jury was not impressed."

"He wouldn't be angling for a new trial, would he?" said Maggie, lighting a cigarette.

She looked smart, he thought. Back to the days at the sta-bles she'd worn Levi's and now wore beige slacks, though there was nothing slack about how they fit her. She had on a long-sleeved white silk blouse with gold chains. She wore her dark hair shorter than before, better to fit into flight helmets, he supposed. Since helping to found the Women Airforce Service Pilots (WASPs) during the war she'd become famous. There'd been talk of a fling with Howard Hughes, but her steady was a Hughes pilot named Terry Heyward, an air ace who'd somehow survived the war in the Pacific. Cal met him at Robby's christening. He liked him.

"No chance," said Lizzie. "He's up there for good."

"Might want to get his sentence cut," he said.

"How?"

"That's for us to find out."

"Come on, Cal, give! You're holding something back."

"Milstein wouldn't say exactly—not on the telephone. Just hints. Callender wants to meet me face-to-face. I gathered it has something to do with Pat Murphy and Barton Pitts."

She sat up so fast she nearly spilt her beer. *"What?* What does Henry Callender have to do with Pat Murphy and Barton Pitts?"

"I believe Pitts and Callender are residents of the same hotel—the Folsom Arms."

"I don't believe this," she said. "That awful little man who killed Dad is claiming to know something about the Murphy case? That is preposterous! Pitts may be evil. He's not dumb. Why would he talk to Callender? Pitts sent Callender to Folsom!"

He wasn't going to argue, wasn't going say that Callender was as close to a friend as Willie ever had and had been his friend as well. "Things leak in prison," he said. "I thought you might be interested. You're working on the Murphy case, aren't you?

"Going to Folsom on a wild goose chase, you mean?"

"We can drive up together."

She didn't answer. He glanced at Maggie, who was smoking and watching the little sister who usually did the watching. Lizzie curled her fingers around the stem of the beer bottle, turning it, squeezing it, signs of conflict. "That man murdered our father," she said at length. "I thought we were done with him."

Dead silence. He listened for sounds. Brentwood was quieter than Bel Air because it wasn't up in the hills where the air is thinner. He wondered about Robby, two years old now, his godson, wondered if he ever cried in the night.

"And you *would* be done with him, except he says he has information about Pat Murphy. Your call."

"He won't mind me there?"

"Why would he?"

She fell silent for a while. Then: "Okay, why not?"

He glanced at Maggie, silent, restless, drawing on her cigarette, wanting to move on. "Are you two done?" she asked.

He knew what was coming, at least thought he did. Nelly had hinted at it over dinner. "Not if it's to talk about Uncle Eddie's estate. I want no part of it, and no, I'm not being coy. I have a good job at Pacific Electric. Eddie's estate goes to you three."

"And what are we to do with it?" said Lizzie. "None of us needs that kind of money. Mother wants to buy her dance studio when it's probated. Imagine."

"As to what you should do with it, that's another matter," he said. "I have some ideas on that. No use giving it all to the bankers."

Maggie nodded at her sister, stood up, walked around behind the chair where Lizzie sat. Lizzie was smiling. Something was afoot. Maggie leaned over the chair toward him, silk blouse falling slightly open, gold chains dangling, cigarette between her long, slender fingers, looking like Lauren Bacall leaning over Hoagy Carmichael's piano. "Speaking of the estate, dear cousin, is not exactly what I had in mind."

Lizzie was giggling.

"Oh?"

"How would you like to give me away again?"

"*No!*"

She laughed. "Is that a 'no' of surprise or rejection? Terry and I are getting hitched, and you are the last Mull male left standing."

He stood to hug her. "This is getting to be a habit."

"Last time, I promise. Next time is your turn."

"No comment."

"We're thinking soon," said Maggie, sitting down again.

"Where?"

"Nothing like in Paris. Simple. Maybe the Lutheran Church on Wilshire."

"Is Terry Lutheran?"

"He thinks he had a grandmother who was Lutheran."

"Ah." He took another gulp from his beer when the thought struck him head on, attached itself in his brain and dug in. Willie would love it. And if Terry didn't care . . .

"I think you should be married at the temple."

Silence. Then Lizzie: "Surely, you're joking."

Maggie simply stared. "I will not be married in that coliseum."

"No, no, not the amphitheater," he said. "In the chapel—quiet, intimate, quite beautiful. You'd love it. So would Terry."

"So would *you*," said Lizzie. "What makes you even think . . ."

"Because the temple is—I have to say it—part of the family."

"You can't be serious."

"Angie would be thrilled."

Maggie continued to stare. When had she ever been conventional?

"Do you know," she said at length, "that I've never met Sister Angie, never even seen her. I'd never heard of her until the night—what, ten years ago?—when you two were sitting there on Tiverton talking about Uncle Willie's new girlfriend—sexier than Lizzie, if I remember."

Lizzie again: "Can you honestly be thinking of . . ."

"I'd like to meet her, really I would. Women love her, I hear."

"I'll see what I can do."

"Mother will be furious," said Lizzie.

Maggie laughed. "She can bring her dance instructors."

CHAPTER 27

An eight-hour drive on Highway 99 took them through the Central Valley toward Sacramento, where they would spend Saturday night at the Senator Hotel, next to the Capitol. The meeting with Callender was set for the next day, Sunday, visiting day at Folsom. Like other Americans, Cal was stuck with a prewar car until Detroit could switch its assembly lines from tanks back to passenger cars again. He'd bought a '41 Buick convertible from a Santa Monica woman who'd garaged it during the war waiting for her husband to come back. He didn't, and she sold the car with only twenty-five hundred miles on it. The trip up and back to Folsom would add another thousand.

They had a good palaver on the way up, their first in years. Cal found Lizzie more engaging than she'd once been, more willing to stop asking questions and taking notes and talk about her own life. She was clearly happy with Joe, happy to be a mother, though she said Joe seemed to get along better with their son than she did. "When I'm through with this Murphy thing I'm going to take leave to write a book about it and get to know my son."

"Doesn't writing a book about it depend on finding the killer?"

"Oh, I'll find him."

Cal looked over. She meant it.

They'd come up through the Grapevine pass over the Tehachapi Mountains not far from where the aqueduct passed on its way to Los Angeles. North of Bakersfield, the clean, fresh grassy smell of the alfalfa fields filled the air and Lizzie asked him to put the top down, He pulled to the side of the road and opened the car to the sun. The convertible roof mechanism still worked like new, sign of a car kept unexposed to Santa Monica salt air.

"Now tell me about you," the old Lizzie said when they were going again. "Why are you working for Pacific Electric?"

He laughed. "They needed a lawyer."

"Lots of companies need lawyers."

"Public transportation has interested me, back to the days when I used to take you to the stables on the trolley. I had a professor, one Wesley Pegrum by name, who knew everything about it. Told me to check out the European cities, which I did, with your sister."

"I thought it was more fun when you got your own car."

"We won't talk about when Maggie got *her* own car."

"Seriously. You could have gone to work for anyone. Why a trolley company?"

"Biggest employer in the county, running ten thousand trains daily, which happens to be a world record. P.E. is definitely more than a trolley company."

"Doesn't sound very exciting."

"Pegrum liked to say Los Angeles had a chance that most cities never get: to do its planning *before* the people arrived. Here was this dry empty plain that overnight gets enough water to become a metropolis—the exact opposite of most cities, always trying to catch up with growth. And the secret of it all was transportation. You lay out your grids *before* the people come so you don't have to destroy neighborhoods and dig up roads to lay lines and all that. You put down your tracks where you want the people to live. Pacific Electric did it the right way. You can call Harriman and Huntington and the whole crowd of them robber barons, but they gave the city the best transportation system in the world."

She didn't respond, and he fell quiet, too, keeping the car at a steady 65 miles an hour on a highway with few other cars. The time had come to tell her what was bothering him, but he hesitated. He still wasn't sure. He trusted her, but she was a reporter and could hardly be expected to keep quiet about it. But did he want her to keep quiet about it? Wasn't it time for people to know? He had to set conditions.

They stopped for lunch at a Basque restaurant in Fresno where he listened to Lizzie talk about Joe's new collaboration with Bertolt Brecht, the German playwright he'd met in Berlin in the thirties. Brecht had escaped Hitler to find refuge, along with a few dozen other German literati, in Santa Monica. "They're collaborating on a play, or maybe I should say Joe's helping Brecht put his play into English. We've had him over a few times, a nervous, chain-smoking little man even more near-sighted than Joe. His English isn't bad, but he writes only in German. Joe's German is apparently flawless."

"Isn't Brecht a Communist?"

She laughed. "Isn't Joe a Communist?"

They drove in silence through the long fertile plain bordered on the west by the coastal ranges and on the east by the Sierra. Grasslands that once stretched from Sacramento to Bakersfield were slowly being replaced by crops that one day would feed the nation.

"You have something on your mind, don't you?"

"Perceptive as always."

"We go back a long way, Cal."

"To the beginning."

"So?"

"Story's not ready yet. I'm still working on it. What I tell you is off-the-record. If you agree, then when it's ready it's all yours."

"Fair enough."

"Pacific Electric is being sold. We're not sure why."

She turned to face him, putting on the bland reporter's face he knew without looking. "Why is that news? Companies are sold all the time."

"First of all, companies sold all the time are usually not this big. Second, it so happens that the outfit buying us—something called National City Lines—doesn't have any lines and doesn't have any money. It is a front."

"For . . ?"

"General Motors mainly. And a few others."

"General Motors is going into the trolley business?"

"General Motors wants to destroy the trolley business."

Without turning he could feel her eyes boring into him. He stayed silent. Let her ask the questions. Gauge her interest.

"So why would the city do something like that?"

"Not sure."

"A few others?"

"Standard Oil, Mack Trucks, Greyhound, Firestone Tires."

"In other words . . ."

You can imagine how much money a consortium like that has to offer councilmen to junk electric trains and buy their gas engines."

Still she stared. "That sounds like a hell of a story, Cal."

"That's all I can tell you for now."

She smiled. "Fortunately, I have this other story for the moment."

◆ ◆ ◆

Folsom is not the world's ugliest prison, though some inmates might not agree. Built on the banks of the American River rushing down from the Sierra and still carrying flecks left over from gold rush days, Folsom had its share of hangings until the "invention" of the gas chamber moved executions to San Quentin, allowing Folsom to acquire a gentler reputation. Photos taken at certain angles, with the river in the foreground and the walls and buildings nestled in the shrubbery and fields behind, hardly show it as a prison at all. On a picture postcard, with its turreted cupola rising over granite walls, it has the aspect of a medieval castle, perhaps in the Rhine Valley or along the Loire, ramparts gazing down on the sweet-flowing river below. Other angles, those with guard towers and electrified fences, show it for what it is.

They were identified at the main gate, searched and admitted. Lawyer Milstein was waiting at the gate, and they were escorted across the yard to the visitors' waiting room. It was hotter inside than out, and a guard suggested they wait outside in the visitors' patio area.

Several broad canopies had been set up, each covering a table and two benches. A handful of prisoners in blue strolled the yard with visitors. People sat under the canopies or in the shade of the main building, talking, holding hands, nervous, saying what they could in the time they had, afraid they would forget something. Visitors were dressed casually, though here and there men in lawyers' uniforms—dark suits, ties and fedoras—were spotted. Lizzie found herself looking for Barton Pitts but knew Milstein would have arranged to have him kept far away. Gil l'Amoureux was at Folsom, too, a popular place. She hadn't thought of Gil since his trial. Twelve to fifteen, she recalled. She wondered when he'd be getting out and what Angie thought about that, made a mental note to ask her at the wedding.

"Not bad as prisons go," said the lawyer as they waited, "and I've seen 'em all—at least in California." Lizzie remembered Milstein's baggy eyes and lisp from the trial. She'd said nothing about the coming meeting to Cal on the drive up—uncomfortable about seeing Callender again and convinced they were on a wild goose chase. She'd come because curiosity got the better of her, as it usually did.

They sat at a table under a canopy that stopped the sun but not the heat, their eyes fixed on the door leading to the visitor's room inside the main building. Time crawled as the sun rose higher, beating down ever stronger on the canopy. At length, Callender emerged from the building and stood a moment outside shielding his eyes, accustoming them in the bright sun. He nodded to a guard posted by the door and started across the grounds alone.

She watched him coming: the man who'd been cheated by her father and killed him in revenge. Cal knew him; she didn't. She'd seen him at the trial. McManus wouldn't let her cover it, but she'd been there. What she remembered, what she would never forget, was what he did after the shooting. Pitts, still the lead prosecutor in those days, kept emphasizing it, making sure the scene was indelible in the jurors' minds. "You shot Eddie Mull, Mr. Callender, but why did you kick his body into the ocean, why did you have to do that?" Watching Callender coming toward the tent, she didn't want to look at his face. She made herself do it.

Milstein went out to shake his client's hand. "Why don't we all sit down," he said. No other hands were offered, though Lizzie saw Callender start to offer Cal his hand, then stop. The man's blue eyes had lost none of their intensity, she noted, and he stared hard at her as introductions were made. The mustache was gone. He and Milstein sat down on one side of the table, leaving Lizzie and Cal to slide in on the bench across from them. Everyone but Callender, who looked serene and cool, was dripping in the heat. She felt her blouse soaked through.

Callender was the first to speak. "Calvin Mull," he said, chagrin in the voice, "I understand that you would not want to shake hands with me, though in other times we were friends, just as I was a friend of your father, may his soul rest in peace. I have his chess set here with me, at Folsom, the set you gave me, the one he had from his grandpa. Willie and I still play, do you know that?" His face brightened. "Sometimes he wins."

Cal smiled, and Callender looked to Lizzie, who'd not spoken a word. "I am happy that you are here, young lady. I did you a terrible grievance and for that I am sorry, but it could not be otherwise. I will share your pain if you will share mine. You lost your father, and I lost my savior and mentor, the Reverend Willie Mull, the man I loved more than any other in the world, the godly man who led me back to Jesus Christ, the father of this fine young man who sits beside you. When that beautiful man was taken away, the goodness went out of me, the goodness Willie Mull had taught me to keep in my heart, the goodness that drove away the rancor that had lodged there since the day I was cheated.

"When Willie was gone, I determined to settle the score, as I would have done sooner except for Willie, as I had always done out on the trail. Nothing could dissuade me, and I was full ready to accept the consequences. I embraced the jury's verdict and even wished for the death penalty so I could join Willie in heaven. Do you know that when he went we were in the middle of a chess game? We always kept a game going at the temple. Cal knows that. I finished that game in my home, with Nyx, my cat, who is gone now, too. Do you know that the Reverend Willie won that game?"

His bright eyes fixed steadily on Lizzie. Finally, he dropped them to stare at his gnarled hands. "Through me, he was making the moves from heaven."

No one said a word. Milstein opened his mouth to say something and quickly closed it again. Callender was not done.

"I do not seek to atone. A man cannot atone for a mortal sin, though it be an eye for an eye. I feel no guilt, for what I did was in the situation." He paused for some time, and still no one thought to intercede. Eventually, he raised his eyes to Lizzie again. "I do not seek to atone, but think maybe I can help you. I know what you are doing, Miss Mull. I know about the murder of Pat Murphy. Folsom has a good library and I read the *Times* every day. I follow the story in the front-page notebook. I believe I have learned something that can help you. I want to help you. I believe I can give you the name of the man you are looking for."

Lizzie went suddenly stiff. Her mouth was the only dry part of her. She'd thought this man might be crazy, but there was nothing crazy in his words or his demeanor. She believed everything he said, just as she had in the courtroom. It would all be in her book.

Milstein laid his hand on Callender's arm. "First there must be an understanding," the lawyer said. "My client has a record of good behavior at Folsom. If he helps you solve the vicious murder of Pat Murphy, it must be recognized."

"No, no," cried Callender, loud enough to attract attention of the guards circulating in the yard. "A thousand times, no! I seek no favor, no deal. I do what any righteous citizen would do. The Reverend Willie Mull expects no less."

CHAPTER 28

A string quartet played Bach. A pretty cellist in white satin, golden locks cascading down over bare shoulders and soft undulating breasts, lost herself in the arco movement of the bow. She'd played wedding receptions before, though never in the Embassy Ballroom of the Ambassador Hotel, sometime home to Freddy Martin's orchestra, which most evenings played down the hallway in the Coconut Grove. Howard Hughes had come and brought some aircraft friends and a few more from Hollywood. Since Sister Angie was officiating, Miss Adelaide Nevin had led her Sunday column with the wedding, and Angie's presence at the reception meant that the broad lawns reaching to Wilshire Boulevard would be teeming with Soldiers for God, though only a select few had any chance of making it to the ballroom. The chapel wedding had been intimate, but 225 invitations went out for the Ambassador reception, which meant twice that many would show up. Freddy Martin didn't do weddings anymore, but the string quartet would be replaced by Lester Lanin for dancing. Forty tables surrounded the dance floor, the main tables with name cards carefully placed by Maggie herself.

The ceremony had been perfect, though through it all she found herself thinking of her first one. Was it Paris, or do all brides do that the second time? She thanked Cal once again for walking beside her. She seated him next to Angie at the main table. She didn't know much about them, Cal was too much the gentleman for that, but knew there was something. She saw it in his eyes. Angie had taken his hand at the chapel and held onto it. How odd it must be, she thought, with the ghost of Willie hovering. The main table also included her and Terry, her new husband; Nelly and a samba specialist named Marco; Howard and a ravishing Latin thing named Gabriela who smelled of coconuts and wore pink plumeria in her hair. The fifth couple was Lizzie and Joe.

Cal had been initially puzzled by Maggie's interest in Terry Heyward, an amiable, red-haired flier in the Hughes mold who at first seemed totally outclassed by his bride. Thinking more on it, he realized that all the men in Maggie's life, at least the ones he'd known, had been similar types: dashing, dominant, high-risk fliers. Maggie was cut from the same mold, though softened by her femininity and sad first marriage. Hughes was the most interesting of her beaux, but she'd been smart enough to end their wartime affair. Paired, type A's reduce their chances of survival exponentially, something to do with the multiplication theorem of probability. Terry would be smart to stay out of planes with her. You could see the respect Howard had for him. Howard held all the speed records, but had never shot down a Jap Zero.

Cal had not seen Angie for a while, had not desired to return to the temple. She was in the news more than ever, adding to her notoriety by taking the Church of the New Gospel on the road each year. She'd played the Cow Palace in San Francisco and gone into the Central Valley to preach to farm immigrants who didn't have a radio to hear her and wouldn't have understood if they had. She moved from place to place with truckloads of equipment, setting up her tent like a traveling circus. In Salinas the tent went up in the Spreckels' fields, which once had been Tesoro. The New York Times put her on page one when she preached at Madison Square Garden during the war. She'd met Eleanor Roosevelt on that trip.

Before the wedding, Angie took him on a tour of the temple, which was showing some wear since his days on the second floor. She was also showing some wear, but it only added to her allure. She could have had the facial scars removed, but preferred wearing them as her badge of honor, as a duelist wears his. She'd kept her figure, as he saw when she emerged from the vestry after changing from white robes into in a clingy black frock for the reception. He remembered their first time alone together, at the Brown Derby, when he realized there were two Angies. He wondered if there were men in her life, which would not be easy given her celebrity. She was never far from his mind, but was he ready to compete with Jesus? Or with his father? They'd chatted on the ride over. She lived in Los Feliz, in the foothills above Sunset, invited him to come over some time. He told her about visiting Folsom. Gil had come up once for parole, and she'd written to oppose it, reminding the board of his courtroom threats.

In setting up the main table, Maggie consulted no one. Of course, she included Howard, not thinking that he and Joe Morton might already be acquainted. Hughes's Hollywood career was long on big hits and big flops, but two constants were his insistence on total control of his movies and his rejection of anything left wing. He would not employ union workers, which was a problem because postwar Hollywood was heavily unionized. For his part, Joe had marched in a few picket lines and never crossed one. His sympathies were hard to miss in his latest film, *The Brotherhood of Man*, panned by critics as socialist propaganda. He'd had trouble raising money in Hollywood for his next script, a collaboration with Bertolt Brecht, but found backers in New York, where money was more familiar with Brecht and less afraid of his politics.

Lizzie didn't mind Joe's politics. Her view was that writers ought to be nonconformists, and she was happy to be free of her first husband's sniffy conventionality. Her Westwood wedding to Joe had had nothing in common with her sister's temple event except being the second for each. Miss Adelaide didn't mention it. Joe had worked for the *Times*, and Lizzie still worked there, which created a newspaper conflict. Joe was controversial in Hollywood, but had the good taste to put his politics into his writing, not his conversation.

The reception started at five, and sharply at seven Bach gave way to Cole Porter. The genius of Lester Lanin is that his music brings onto the dance floor people who normally would never leave their seats. The Lanin two-step is a little like a march, but happier because the champagne is flowing and the men are holding onto something softer than a rifle. Part of his genius is that Lanin can put almost any music into a two-step. There is never any excuse, aside from exhaustion or too much champagne, not to be dancing.

Morton was tickled about getting Terry Heyward as a brother-in-law. The two had nothing in common except being generally good-natured guys. They'd bonded on their first meeting, when Maggie brought Terry to dinner at Brentwood. They were smart enough to talk about things they had in common, not things they didn't. As a dancer, Joe was more enthusiastic than talented, and as the evening wore on danced with every woman at the table but the one smelling of coconuts and wearing plumeria. He detested champagne, which he regarded as something for christening ships, but found the Ambassador's bourbon acceptable. He'd had a few drinks, but held his liquor well, always had. He'd found over the years that liquor stimulated his creativity, as if he needed an excuse.

When the orchestra launched into a Jerome Kern medley he found himself awkwardly alone at the table with Howard, who did not dance anymore, and Gabriela, who did. Glancing at her, he wondered what was in it for the girls—sex, publicity, a mention by Miss Adelaide, a role in his next movie? Who'd ever heard of Jane Russell before *The Outlaw*? He considered that he might have had Howard instead of Terry for a brother-in-law, sharing holiday turkeys with him at Nelly's place in Bel Air. Not that Howard was unattractive, but he was not convivial, not at all like Terry. What would they talk about? Certainly not movies. Not much of a drinker, not much of a dancer, not much fun. Plus he was deaf. Did all his business on the telephone because it was the only place he could hear. One thing they had in common was draft deferments: one who couldn't hear, one who couldn't see. After a moment, Joe switched his musings from Howard to Gabriella and smiled across the table. She smiled back. He took a swig, rose and circled the table; it seemed the gentlemanly thing to do. Appropriately, the orchestra was playing "I Won't Dance."

"Sit down, Joe," commanded Howard as Joe inclined himself toward the lady.

Gabriela was half out of her seat, but sat back down. Joe sat beside her. "How are you doing, Howard?"

"I hear you're having trouble raising money."

Hughes was not good at small talk. "Who isn't?"

"You're a good writer, Joe, just write the wrong stuff."

"And what would you say is the right stuff?"

"What's that?"

Joe leaned across Gabriela, which was not unpleasant, and repeated the question.

"It's not the moment for your peace drivel," Howard responded. "The Bolshies are in Poland, Czechoslovakia, Hungary. Do they have to take Paris before you wake up?"

"I am awake, Howard. I rarely sleep."

"I hear you're working with Brecht, something about teaming up on an allegory."

"All good writing is allegorical."

"How's that again?"

A dialogue with Hughes was essentially a monologue: He heard only his own voice.

He leaned across Gabriela again. "I said: ALL GOOD WRITING IS ALLEGORICAL."

Hughes retreated. "What kind of allegory?"

"You interested in seeing the script?"

"Brecht's a Bolshie."

Morton looked up into his eyes, strangely luminescent and opaque at the same time, too many crashes, probably. He had a strange ostrich-like head, a neck too long for it. Deafness isolates people, especially those too arrogant to get a hearing aid.

"Brecht is brilliant, Howard. It is an honor to work with him."

"Going to be subpoenaed just like you."

"I expect you to be back there, too, Howard."

Hughes hesitated. He was reading lips.

"Oh, I'll be there—but it won't be under subpoena."

"Maybe we can discuss this another time."

The music stopped, the players went on break and the dancers returned, Maggie with Terry, Nelly with Marco, Lizzie dropped off by a *Times* colleague, Cal with Angie.

"If Terry doesn't stop stepping on my feet," said Maggie, reaching for a shoe.

"Light, light," said Marco, holding Nelly's hand and executing a mincing little *pas*. "As if you are floating. Maggie you must bring Terry to the studio."

"What are you three talking about?" said Lizzie, looking suspiciously at Howard and Joe crushing in on poor Gabriela.

"Waiting for you to come back," said Howard. "I'm ready for a talk."

Finally, it was quiet, which might have had something to do with Hughes's previous reticence. Terry went off to the buffet to bring back plates of food. The cake had been cut long ago, and the toasts were over but no one seemed to have left the party. A waiter passed to refill flutes and spike Joe's bourbon. Angie left to greet some Soldiers.

"What's on your mind, Howard?" said Maggie.

"Those Venice oil wells."

"What here . . . on the dance floor . . . you want to talk business?"

When he smiled, which wasn't often anymore, you could see traces of the boyish charm, the impishness that once radiated. "Why not? I want to make an offer."

"For the Venice oil wells?" said Lizzie.

"I remember Maggie telling me once that she hated them. Right, Mag?"

"What are you after, Howard?" said Maggie, slipping her shoe back on, wobbling from dance and drink and sitting down beside Joe. "You're always after something."

"Look, we have to leave, but I want to talk about it some time. Eddie sold me the land for the airfield. I should have bought more at the time."

"Since when are you in the oil business, Howard?" said Cal.

Cal was the only member of the family that Hughes had not met before. "I have always been in the oil business, son," he said, too abruptly. "And so was my daddy."

"Eddie Mull couldn't have sold you more land," said Cal, undeterred. "He didn't own the land between the airfield and the oil wells. It is undeveloped county marshland."

"What about my stables?" muttered Maggie. "You leave my

stables alone, Howard. I'm trying to get Lizzie to go back with me. She won't go near horses anymore."

"Never was my thing," said Lizzie.

"Remember Billy?" said Maggie.

Lizzie shot a glance at her sister, who was tighter than she thought.

"That land's too good for stables," said Hughes.

"No, it's not," said Cal, loud enough to be sure Howard heard him. "It's good for horses and a hundred other species. The oil wells are an abomination. They're coming down."

"So I'm right," said Hughes, standing, "you want to sell."

"Don't be too sure, Howard," said Maggie.

Terry returned, leading a waiter with a tray of plates.

"We are discussing the disposition of your oil fields," Howard said to Terry, "for I take it that they are yours, too, now, my friend and associate, as part of the common property." He turned to Nelly. "Though perhaps I should be talking to this fine lady as well."

"It's the girls' business—the girls and Cal." She smiled at Marco. "Just leave me enough for my friends." Marco stood as the musicians returned, announcing an Irving Berlin medley.

"Irving Berlin is my speed," said Joe, looking at Gabriela.

"No," said Hughes, standing, "we are leaving."

Angie returned, and Hughes took her by the hand. "We didn't have time to talk today, but I thought it was a fine wedding. My first time at the temple, Angie. I make movies, you know. Would you allow me to call you sometime?"

"I would love to see you again, Howard," she said.

Annoyed, Cal watched them together, noticing the facial scars in common, which they both refused to have removed.

"Howard, you stop doing business at my wedding," said

Maggie, standing and hugging him. Terry stood as well. "But thank you for coming." She kissed Gabriela.

"I wouldn't have missed it," he said, shaking Terry's hand. "Terry is a fortunate man. Since Maggie accuses me of doing business, let me say that I am dead serious about that land. And I will give you a guarantee: sell to me and the wells come out and the stables stay. You won't find another buyer to make that promise."

CHAPTER 29

Chili was the name Callender heard.

He heard it in the Folsom game room, heard it during a chess game, heard it in the same sentence that he heard the name Murphy, and that's what struck him, that the two names were used together, Chili and Murphy, two things that didn't go together, like frijoles and Irish stew. After he thought about it a while and thought about whom Pitts had been playing chess with, he decided he might have something. That's when he called Sammy Milstein who called Cal Mull at Pacific Electric.

The game room at Folsom is arranged in rows. The most popular games are dominoes and checkers, followed by chess and backgammon, and finally the Chinese game, Go. The prison provides lockers so the games can be put away at night if not finished. The game tables and card tables occupy half the long, rectangular room, with ping-pong tables at the opposite end. Inmates can check out games or bring their own, and most evenings all the tables are filled.

Bob Jones was Pitts's chess partner that day, and they were playing two tables down from Callender and his partner. Most of the chess players knew each other, or at least knew of each other, which is to say knew why they found themselves at Folsom. The beauty of chess is that it doesn't matter what you do, or did, away from the table. To have a murderer and a corrupt prosecutor playing is no stranger than to find a bank embezzler squaring off with a penny-ante grifter. Pitts and Callender would never choose to play each other, but could not avoid occasionally finding themselves at the tables at the same time.

Chess players don't talk much, but the evening in question Pitts was muttering in a low voice and Jones was listening and Callender caught those two names, Murphy and Chili, and knew they weren't talking about food. Callender knew about Jones, an ex-LAPD cop hired by the L.A. city council and sent to jail for taking money from people he was supposed to be investigating. Callender kept up with the news and wondered why Pitts would be talking to a crooked ex-L.A. cop about Pat Murphy.

Pitts had the perfect alibi for the murder: he was in Folsom. But if he didn't have opportunity, he had motive, and no one else did. Murphy had worked the Hall of Justice forever, but was more of a police crony than an investigative reporter. The only person Murphy ever really went after was Pitts, most likely because after all those years he'd had a bellyful. Or maybe his daughter the nun pushed him. The archdiocese had never agreed with Pitts's high threshold of tolerance for corruption. It had the makings of the perfect crime. Pitts could not be accused unless a tie between him and the killer could be shown. Lizzie understood from the beginning that her job was to find the link, the *means* by which Pitts could execute the crime, which is why she kept badgering people with the question: "Who owed Pitts?"

Lots of people owed Pitts. The question was, who owed him enough to kill Pat Murphy?

While at Folsom to see Callender, she'd checked the records on Pitts's prison visitors. Nothing stood out. Records of phone calls were not kept. Her assumption was that he'd not had time to set up the hit before arriving at Folsom. She came back from Folsom with the possibility that a man named Chili might be the link, but who was he—the mob, a hired gun, a cop, an ex-cop? Why was Pitts talking to ex-cop Jones about him?

Days, even weeks, of combing through back editions of the

Times and directories of L.A. police officers would be fruitless if Chili was a nickname, as she supposed it was. The faster way was to check with the *Times* police reporters, though that came with risk of leaks if the person assigned to the Murphy case, namely herself, did it. After hashing it over with Joe, who hated everything about the assignment, she came up with the idea of having Teddy Lubrano, her replacement on the metro desk, have discreet inquiries made at the Hall of Justice about someone called Chili.

It didn't take long. One of Teddy's metro reporters knew of a downtown beat cop named Carlos Chaidez, aka Chili. Locating the name in the police directory, Lizzie started through old *Times* files to see if Officer Chaidez had ever made the newspapers, discovering his name in more stories than a good police officer would want. He'd killed three people in fifteen years and been cleared each time by police boards of using unnecessary force. The first was during a holdup in the jewelry district. The issue was that the robber's rod was rubber, but how was Office Chaidez to know that? The second time came during a confrontation in New Chinatown. The board faulted Officer Chaidez again for being too quick on the trigger, but surprisingly recommended no penalty for a second citizen killed.

The third death was the most intriguing. A building maintenance contractor named Jerry Korngold fell from his eighth-floor apartment on South Grand when Chili and his partner arrived to question him about a complaint Korngold had filed at the police department. The officers testified that Korngold had not answered their knock, and that they broke the door down after hearing him scream, the scream he made as he jumped, they said.

The *Times* treated the story as routine filler, the miscellaneous stuff reporters copy from the daily police docket that ends up at the bottom of an inside local page. The story said nothing about the nature of Korngold's complaint or why the police considered it important enough to call at his residence. Did building maintenance contracting have something to do with it, have something to do with Pitts, who had his fingers in many pockets around the city? No reporter had gone beyond the perfunctory docket report. But what if the scream had come after the police broke down his door? Why had no neighbors been interviewed? When Lizzie attempted to find out more, she found that the police had no record of Korngold's complaint. She showed them the *Times* clipping. They shook their heads. The only thing of value in the brief *Times* account was that Officer Chaidez's partner was Officer Bob Jones.

Pitts to Jones to Chili to Murphy—is that how it was done? She needed more before going to McManus. The evidence was circumstantial, but because there'd been a witness to the murder it was a start. Pat Murphy was blown up leaving his South Pasadena residence to drive to work. The witness, an elderly neighbor, had pored over dozens of police mug shots in hopes of making an identity, but the photos were of known criminals, not members of the LAPD. She wasn't sleeping well that night and got up to rock in the chair by the window, finding that a few minutes of gentle rocking helped her get back to sleep. Staring out the window she'd noticed a shaft of light moving under the car parked across the street. It didn't make sense so she put her glasses on and saw a man crawl out from under the car, Murphy's car. For a moment the flashlight illuminated his face. The car blew up when Murphy started it up that morning, sending parts of the reporter and his car flying into her yard.

"Hard on herself for not understanding what the guy was doing," Lizzie told McManus.

"And you say the guy is Chili."

"Pitts was apparently Chili's good fairy. Saw they kept him on the force despite his horrible record. Chili owed Pitts. Honor among thieves sort of thing."

"What about Jones? How did he end up at Folsom if Chili didn't?"

"Don't know. Maybe he got sent up after Pitts was gone."

"We can't ask for a lineup with Chili in it. They'd laugh in our faces."

"How about we get his photo and show it to her?"

"Would she recognize him from a photo? Would she testify? She'd be testifying against the LAPD. So would we."

She knew what he meant. The *Times* and the LAPD were not exactly friends, but it is one thing to be uncooperative and another to be public enemies. Mutual enmity had gotten Pat Murphy killed, and Lizzie knew how much time McManus had spent downstairs with the publisher after the murder. He didn't want her to be next. Readers and advertisers like to think that newspapers and law enforcement are on the same side.

"She would testify. She's that sort of woman. Reminds me of my sister. Doesn't flinch."

He leaned back, shaking his head, exhaling a cloud of smoke toward the ceiling. "What you're telling me is that the former L.A. district attorney, a man elected twice—no three times—to enforce the laws of the county, a man whose election this newspaper supported, is responsible for two murders, Murphy and Korngold."

"At least two."

"There are more?"

"With a guy like Pitts, who knows?"

He looked her straight in the eyes. "You don't think I'm thinking about that?"

McManus was surprised by what she'd found out, but not

too much. He'd arrived in L.A. when Charlie Crawford, a colleague of Eddie Mull's, ran the Prohibition mob, and no police-
man ever touched Crawford. The mayor at the time, George
Cryer, went through six chiefs of police during his tenure, each
worse than the other. They couldn't get Charlie because Charlie
paid everyone off. Everyone but assistant DA Dave Clark, who
went to Charlie's office one day and shot him dead, along with
a reporter who'd picked the wrong time to visit Charlie.

McManus covered the trial. Clark claimed he'd done his
civic duty to rid the city of a scoundrel when no one else would.
The reporter was just a case of bad luck. He was acquitted.
"Would Clark have done his civic duty if he'd been in on the
payoffs?" reporter McManus wrote. They cut it out of the story.

"You expect the police to do a line-up with Chili in it?" he
asked Lizzie.

"If Fritz Singer orders it."

"Why would the DA turn against his mentor?"

"Because I'm going to write the story and make him.

The day she wrote the story that brought Pitts down from
Folsom to stand trial for the murder of Pat Murphy was the
day Lizzie had her first row with her husband. Certain she was
putting her life in danger and maybe their son's as well, Joe
Morton hated everything about the Pitts assignment. He'd told
her that at the beginning, easing off only when she told him
she'd take six months off after the story ran. They'd go traveling
and let things blow over.

The row came when she told him she couldn't keep her
promise.

They were in the living room after dinner. Joe had had his
usual two drinks before dinner and glass of cabernet at the
table. He was almost ready to go into his study and start working when she told him.

"No," he said, quickly. "You can't renege. Too dangerous. Plus, you promised."

"Something has come up."

"Doesn't matter."

"Don't you want to know what it is?"

"Don't they have other reporters at that newspaper?"

"Not for something like this."

Annoyed, angry even, he went to the sideboard for a snifter of Courvoisier to calm down. He didn't care what had come up. Another murder? Something worse? She'd do it anyway. He was intensely proud of his wife, but he just didn't always respect her judgment. That was the trouble with being the best. They want you, only you, no one else will do. He'd been there, covering the rise of the Nazis in the thirties. He knew that the best stories involve the best reporters and the biggest risks because the stakes are highest. Every reporter knows it and lusts for it. No one declines the assignment.

"So tell me," he said, sitting down again, calmer.

"It's Cal's story, and he won't give it to anyone else. The head of the L.A. public utilities board, a guy named Fred Barrett, resigned. It wasn't much of a story because who's ever heard of Fred Barrett or the public utilities board? He resigned because the city council overruled his board to approve the sale of Pacific Electric and Los Angeles Railway to something called National City Lines."

"That is a story?"

"It gets better. National City doesn't have any lines and doesn't have any money. It is a front for a consortium led by General Motors, which wants to junk the city's railways and replace them with buses. Barrett calls it an illegal conspiracy and says he informed the council in closed session and had assurances the sale would be disapproved. He also informed the US Department of Justice. Nobody wants more gasoline engines in this city with the smog we already have. Barrett says he has proof that at least three council members were paid off by the consortium to change their votes. We're about to lose the world's best transportation system."

CHAPTER 30

When Eddie Mull's estate was probated, the bankers at Security Trust invited the widow and her daughters to bank headquarters on Hollywood Boulevard for discussions. Joe Sartori, Security's founder and Eddie's friend, had passed on by then, but the founder's successors were determined to hold on to the widow's jointure, valued at some $90 million. If Eddie was not quite in the league with Ed Doheny, whose oil fortune had had a few years more to grow, it was still a handsome sum, nicely up from the $107,650 he'd started with. Lending banks like Security Trust needed all the deposits they could get to keep up with demand from young war veterans settling in Los Angeles and seeking loans for new homes and cars.

The bankers were businesslike and the meeting was expeditious. After deducting taxes, the probate court had passed the Mull estate entirely to the widow, who informed the bankers that she wished to share it equally with her daughters. Cal Mull had already declined to share in any part of the assets. The daughters considered liquidating, but Cal urged them to hang on. In the postwar housing boom and with Detroit starting to produce passenger cars again, prices of land and oil would only rise. He had some ideas.

After meeting the bankers, Nelly took her daughters to lunch at Chasen's, a Beverly Hills restaurant not convenient for either working daughter but their mother's favorite because of its proximity to her dance studio, which she now owned. Her dance instructors, all young, athletic, attractive and hoping to be discovered, preferred Romanoff's to Chasen's because it was brighter inside and easier to be seen, but Nelly liked Chasen's for lunch. It was closer and quieter. She rarely saw her daughters together and she wanted to talk. She ordered chardonnay. The girls chose iced tea.

"Wasn't Uncle Willie's first church around here somewhere?" asked Maggie after the drinks arrived. Marriage to an easy-going flyer seemed to her mother to have been quite the right medicine for her test pilot daughter, brought her down to earth, so to speak. She'd been happily surprised when Maggie showed up at the bank in a skirt instead of her usual pants.

"Farther down, almost to Hancock Park. And it was his second church. The first was a little place just off Wilshire. Eddie used to call it a grocery store with a steeple."

Chasen's was a comfortable, red-leather booth and wood-panel place that became boisterous at night with the movie crowd and gossip columnists and sometimes a brawl or two. At night, the bar was three or four thick with heavy drinkers and you never got your table on time, which was the point. Maggie had been there once before with Howard, who lived nearby and always got his tables on time. Lizzie had never been there.

"I wish Cal would change his mind," said Lizzie.

"Why?" said Nelly, quickly. "No one adores Cal Mull more than I do, but he has less need of money than you do. Just be thankful to your father."

"And to you too, Mother dear," said Maggie, patting Nelly's hand.

She was a handsome woman, as vain about her appearance as the day Eddie first spotted her on the boardwalk at Lick Pier. She'd kept her Iowa body, which is to say it was more farm solid than city slender, but still well maintained as she advanced through middle age. She'd never had surgery, though lately had begun to wonder. She'd had enough money to purchase the dance studio and with probate was ready to bring it up to the standards of her Beverly Hills clientele. Widowhood, in her daughters' view, was engendering extravagance. She wore too much make-up, dyed her hair too light and wore clothes with too much red. She seldom appeared with a man who was less than thirty years her junior. But if she had no great virtues, neither were her vices worse than those of any other Bel Air matron. The girls admired how quickly she'd rebounded from tragedy, but worried about her running around so much. She wouldn't talk to them about any of it.

Maggie smiled at her sister. It was the signal.

"Mother," she said. "First chance to tell you. I'm five months pregnant."

Nelly smiled and reached for her hand. "I thought I saw a little tummy but wanted to let you tell me." She looked to Lizzie. "You knew, of course, you who know everything. It's your turn next, you know, one child's not enough, at least two in each family, that's what Granny Sinclair used to say. Of course your father wanted to have more, but it wasn't meant to be."

"Why at least two?" asked Lizzie.

"On the farm you want as many as possible, but at least two, because that way the family doesn't shrink, generation to generation." She looked back to Maggie. "By the way, I hope you don't do any flying while you're pregnant."

"Why not?"

"You might crash and kill the baby."

Maggie laughed, couldn't help herself.

"I'm certainly not going to have another," said Lizzie.

"I think I might like it," said Maggie.

"You like everything," said Nelly. "Maybe too much." She sipped her wine and looked for something else to say. It was never easy with the girls, always easier with Cal. "I trust you're not involved with this monster plane I keep reading about."

Maggie laughed. "The Spruce Goose? Howard hates the name. Plane's not even spruce, it's birch. To him it's the H-4 Hercules, and he keeps it surrounded in the hangar like it was radioactive. I'm testing the F-11, different program."

"Why don't you want to be pregnant again, Lizzie?" Nelly asked, switching back. "Robby needs a sibling. He's an aggressive little thing, don't you think?"

The problem was that Nelly didn't like Joe. Or maybe it was that she'd liked Asa better even though it was Joe who provided her first grandchild. She rarely had them over because Joe didn't fit in with her friends. At her last Christmas party, an annual thing she'd had for twenty-five years, there'd been a bad moment when a tipsy Freddie Gibson from the Bel Air Club staggered over and asked Joe why he wasn't in jail. Along with some other Hollywood types he'd been called back to Washington by the House Un-American Activities Committee and convicted for holding views unpopular with Congress. Joe, who was appealing the conviction, turned his back and walked away. Nelly thought he should have defended himself.

Lizzie ignored the second question and answered the first. "We don't have the time."

"It doesn't take long."

It was their mother's humor. They smiled.

"It's not making them," Lizzie said. "It's everything else."

"Is Joe too old? He must be nearly my age."

Lizzie frowned. "We can't all find men thirty years younger."

Nelly smiled. "My boys aren't for making babies, dear."

◆ ◆ ◆

Deirdre Mull Heyward, called Didi, was born the summer of 1948. Even in the basinet she was an intense, restless child. It was a good year to be born in Los Angeles, off to a perfect start. The Rose Parade had never been more glorious. Whatever miseries affected the rest of the world, Los Angeles, cut off by its deserts, mountains, and ocean, remained apart. It still took three days to arrive by train from the East, just a little less than to cross the Atlantic. Hollywood quickly adapted to the postwar era. Gone was the slapstick of the twenties, the shootouts of Prohibition, the frothy romances of the late thirties and battle triumphs of the war years. Westerns were more popular than ever—the lonesome sheriff standing up to the gang was the perfect metaphor for America in a nasty world. If some didn't agree, the House Un-American Activities Committee and Sen. Joe McCarthy were there to persuade them.

Cal was Didi's godfather, just as he was godfather to her cousin Robby. Maggie had considered asking Joe, but Joe was in jail and would have his hands full when he got out with Robby, who made it clear from the first that he didn't like having a new cousin. With Joe gone, Lizzie hired a UCLA co-ed as nanny in exchange for room and board. Terry questioned if Didi really needed a godfather, but the Mulls, on both sides, Catholic and Presbyterian, had always had them. Godparents are there when the birth parents aren't. So once again, for the hundredth time in her life, she turned to Cal, deprived of a godfather himself for having been born in China and still without wife or children of his own.

Maggie and Terry lived in a brown, two-story wood shingle house on Montreal Street in Playa del Rey, up the hill from the stables and looking out across Santa Monica Bay. Hughes Airfield was ten minutes away, and either of them taking off flew directly over the house just before reaching the ocean. Nelly was right: Terry was good for Maggie. Love, no. Arnaud was for love. Five years older, Terry was a good guy and lucky or skilled enough to have survived a war of island-hopping in P-38s. He was a bachelor and intended to remain one until he met Maggie. He'd paid $15,500 for his house and spent most of his spare time just down the hill at the Westport Beach Club. Maggie had been the boss's girl, but when she wasn't seeing the boss anymore Terry invited her to Westport for dinner and before long she was sleeping over. Maggie regarded herself as equal to any male pilot, but Terry had thirty-two known kills in the war and been shot down and fished out only once, and no one could match that. He was slow and easy and loved her madly, the opposite of Hughes, who was a dervish of motion and constant agitated calculation and didn't offer love as much as he took it.

With no churches in Playa del Rey, the christening on a hot summer Sunday afternoon was at St. Michael's in El Segundo. Afterward, they returned to the bar at Westport, a potted-palm, beachy room with the usual netting, cork, and seashells. An upright piano with stains telling many tales stood on one side ready for the piano player if he showed up or anyone else if he didn't. The dozen bamboo tables between piano and bar would be full by then. They ordered rum drinks and whiskey for Joe, who was just back from prison, and the children stayed until they got noisy and were driven up the hill by their grandmother. A sitter had been arranged, and Nelly would come back for dinner and dancing. Claude, her latest dance beau, would join them.

Playa del Rey was a special place for the Heywards, a sleepy little village surrounded by Ballona marshlands, beach, and ocean. The village consisted of grocery store, drugstore, a couple of burger joints and a gas station. The trolley tracks from downtown to Redondo Beach were still there behind the paddle tennis courts, though the trains weren't running anymore. The Westport was the center of activity, but was a monastery compared with the snazzy beach clubs up the way in Santa Monica and Malibu. The village was Maggie's favorite place back to her stable days. The crash with Billy Todd might have rubbed some of the magic away but hadn't. She joked with Terry that it was as much the village as the man that had seduced her.

Aside from the christening, the occasion was to welcome Joe back. His appeal denied, he'd served nine months in a Tennessee prison with some of his friends and returned to a Hollywood that wanted no part of him. Prison had not changed him. The nanny was gone, and Joe was babysitting again, writing and giving Lizzie more time downtown, which she needed. The second Pitts trial had resettled the former district attorney at San Quentin, and she had moved on to investigating why the Los Angeles City Council had allowed the world's greatest transportation system to be sold to a shell company serving as front for General Motors.

Cal passed a letter from Howard Hughes around as their drinks arrived. "This came last week. He wants to meet to discuss the land. It's up to you all, of course. I'm just your lawyer. Just tell me how to answer him."

"How about lawyer and adviser," said Maggie.

"And negotiator," said Lizzie.

"I heard you hung up your shingle," said Joe.

"In Echo Park," said Maggie, smiling. "He just can't break away."

"From . . . ?"

"From the past—what else?"

"It's where the memories, reside, my dear," said Joe. "We are all prisoners."

"Howard wants to speculate on the land," said Cal, trying

to get back on subject. "I can't see any other reason he'd be interested. He's certainly not going to expand his airfield with L.A. International so close. He knows he'll have to shut it down one of these days."

"One of these days will be when jet planes arrive," said Terry. "No way the FAA allows two airfields so close with jets buzzing around."

"So why sell?" said Maggie. "We can speculate as well as Howard can."

"Keep those awful wells?" said Lizzie. "Howard promised to pull them out."

"And keep the stables," said Maggie, sipping her Daiquiri.

"I'm glad Nelly's not here," said Cal. "She loves the wells and hates the stables."

"For Howard, it's always money," said Maggie.

"The wells are coming out sooner or later for the marina," said Cal. "My guess is that Howard thinks he can make money by holding the land for a few years and selling to the county, and that you'll sell now because you want out of the oil business."

"So do we meet with him?"

"Of course," said Cal. "Find out what he's up to."

"You just told us," said Maggie.

"There could be more to it. He might have his eye on the land between the wells and the airfield, the wetlands of Ballona. But why? We won't know until we sit down with him."

"Include me out," said Joe. "Howard and I don't mix now that I'm a criminal."

"I think you should come," said Lizzie. "Howard Hughes is a feast for writers."

Joe smiled and patted his wife's hand. "Right as always."

"I'm out," said Terry. "This is for the girls."

"You're coming," said Maggie. "You're the only one Howard likes."

♦ ♦ ♦

He'd put it off but could not put her out of his mind. She had asked him to drop over some time, but did she mean it? He decided to write rather than call, and he put it in a short note. After a few days the answer came: Come for a drink at seven the following Tuesday. Tuesdays were a slow day for preachers. It had been the same for Willie. He caught the Big Red Car direction Burbank and got off at Los Feliz. He walked across the Los Angeles River to Lambeth Street and up the hill. The house, a villa really, was set back from the street and hidden by palms, deodars and junipers running up toward Griffith Park in the San Gabriel foothills. Built with small windows in the Spanish style, the house was meant to be cool in summer and warm in winter. He stood a moment in the front courtyard under a tall rubber tree wondering what he was doing. He felt tense.

Dressed in flared pants and a loose cotton sweater, with a dangling pendant that looked to be a tiny elephant with ruby eyes, she answered the door herself. They embraced, and she led him by the hand into the cool salon overlooking a rear patio. The house was not small, surely she had servants, but none were visible. In the rear, behind another patio, a cottage in the same Spanish style was partly hidden by cedars and ficus trees, possibly a servants' quarters. He saw a fountain burbling. The living room had tall ceilings supported by heavy oak beams. A gallery walkway ran around the second floor. The staircase was at the front of the living room, just off the hallway.

She had chardonnay cooling on the bar and poured two glasses. She pulled her legs up as they sat together on the couch, exactly as she'd done the first time on Willie's couch on Sunset. He still remembered what she was wearing that night: the red and blue checkered cotton blouse and swishy skirt. Her legs were bare. He'd been overpowered by her, by the pull of her sensuality. It seemed like a lifetime ago, but was hardly more than a decade. She'd kept her youthful figure. He remembered that she'd worn no make-up that night. She wore more now but not a lot more, and it was not to hide the scars. The scars were to remind people of the wars she'd been through. Been through and won. Her hair was exactly the same: fluffed, tossed over an eye. A little lighter, maybe some gray in there somewhere, he wasn't sure about that.

"Silent Cal," she said, smiling.

"You can't imagine what I'm thinking."

She laughed. "I'm thinking the same thing."

He joined her. "You two chased me out."

"Better that way, don't you think?"

They sipped their wine and talked, never about Willie and never about Jesus. He'd always liked that about her. When she was with him she was a different person, not a famous preacher, but an interesting, alluring woman. She could be funny, something she never was on stage. After another glass they walked down the hill to Los Feliz and ate steaks and salad in a local restaurant. She was incognito in her own neighborhood. Walking back up she asked if he had a car, and he said he had one but mostly took the trolley. She offered to drive him back home. When he didn't answer, she slipped her hand into his. He knew.

Hungry, insatiable, relentless, these words would come to him later. A caged animal who had been let out. The other Angie had been repressed for so long that when it was freed it could not hide its joy and exultation. They said very little, but he understood. She was trapped, as Willie had been trapped, into a personage that only represented half of what she was. The other half had to be suppressed, buried, there was no other way. He understood what she meant without being told. She was not safe, could not trust any man but him. It was that simple. It had been the same for Willie. She wrapped her naked brown body around his and would not let go. He refused to let his mind wander, would not let it go where it might have gone. That was then. This was now.

In the morning he slipped out as he had come, took the trolley home. She was awake when he left. Neither said a word. Time would do its work.

CHAPTER 31

Joe Morton worked in the study of his Brentwood house, a room that gave onto the backyard where Lizzie had planted flowers and vegetables. He liked looking into the garden as he wrote, taking inspiration from plants that grew a little each day, just like his scripts, even if they didn't sell anymore. Even in winter he kept his eye on the ground, knowing the roots were down there gathering strength, waiting for spring to struggle up again, just like his scripts would one day see daylight again. Among the flowers, he liked lilacs best, seeing them shoot forth each spring in colors unlike any others, watching them reign over everything before their brief moment was gone. Writing was like that: short fertile days, long fallow ones.

During the day he took care of Robby. The boy's full name was Robinson Adams Morton, the first two names taken from Joe's mother's side. Lizzie was up each morning to dress Robby and give him his breakfast, make coffee and leave for downtown. When she'd left, Joe read the paper until Robby was finished eating and shitting. Afterward they headed into the study. Robby had no trouble amusing himself while his father tapped out strange rhythms on the black machine. He liked the racket, and Joe didn't mind the racket made in turn by his son, which got closer to language each day. Occasionally he glanced over into the boy's deep blue eyes, a genetic anomaly, and wondered what he was thinking. When he looked into Robby's eyes, Robby always stopped what he was doing to look back. His gaze never wavered. Even in the crib he understood a contest.

That was their routine during the early years, with time

out when Joe went to prison. Nine to eleven in the study and then into the garden. Robby liked to toddle over to the Seville orange tree and prop himself up against the trunk like Ferdinand the bull against the cork tree. One day Joe watched his son pick an orange off the ground and bite into it. Why warn him, Joe thought, let him find out for himself about bitter oranges, sourer than lemons. Instead of spitting it out, Robby smiled across at him and took another bite. Another challenge met. After lunch he would put his son to bed, sometimes to sleep, and return to the study for two more hours of work. At four, they went walking to the stores on Montana or sometimes down to San Vicente, father pushing son in his pram, enjoying sunshine and exercise.

When Lizzie took on the new assignment instead of book leave, Joe discovered he didn't really mind. He and Robby had their routine, and where would she have worked at home? The spare room was Robby's, and the study wasn't big enough for two people, for two desks. Could he work with someone in the room tapping out rhythms in a different key? He had his quirks. He read out loud. He talked out loud. He paced. He argued and fought with himself, sometimes acting out scripts in different voices. Robby enjoyed it, thought it was normal adult behavior, but it wouldn't have worked with Lizzie there. They would have had to move into something bigger, and he didn't want to move. He was writing again, that was the important thing. He liked the study, liked the house, liked the orange tree. Where else could he find another orange tree bitter enough to keep his son happy?

With time, they found a preschool at a neighborhood co-op on Montana across from the Wadsworth Veterans Home on Sawtelle. It was only fifteen minutes away, and Joe and son would walk together. If they were running late, they hopped the trolley at Barrington to the Veterans Home. Joe was back to fetch him when school let out at three. On the way home they would stop at the stores and be home by four, in time for the afternoon *goûter*. Robby had cookies and milk like a normal child, and Joe would have a beer or a scotch, depending on his mood and the weather and how writing had gone that day. From his college days at NYU, he'd always enjoyed his drinks. As husband, father, ex-con, and unemployed middle-aged writer, he'd tapered off, usually making it to teatime before his first drink. He hated tea.

The result of their long routine was that Robby knew his father far better than he knew his mother. As an infant he'd hungered for his mother but by age five had fully adjusted to masculine life. To his parents he seemed normal enough, though his teachers said he didn't bond well and was on the bossy side. He had an edge, but why wouldn't he be?—an only child being raised by an edgy father and a missing mother.

Fathers, if they have a mind to, can do all the basic stuff mothers do: they can change diapers, empty potties, walk children to school, go shopping on the way home, read to them, sit with them for the afternoon *goûter*. They can do a lot but they aren't mothers. They don't touch as much, hug as much, smile as much, aren't as unconditional. They tend to ignore children and go off in their own worlds, no one more than writers. Robby knew more about his father than about his mother, but more important, knew more about his father than his father knew about him: he knew his tics, his tastes, his moods, his habits, what tickled him, what angered him.

One thing he didn't know was why he spent so much time pounding on the noisy black machine producing reams of paper that often ended up in the wastebasket.

♦ ♦ ♦

"Okay, Joe, ten minutes, no more. Come on back."

He'd tried for months to make an appointment with Buddy Fix at RKO, finally deciding the hell with phone calls and planting himself at reception outside Fix's office. He'd skipped lunch and already been there an hour, but had two more before it was time to pick up Robby. Ten minutes was a start. He'd had no trouble getting through the front gate. They'd taken away his studio pass when he went to prison, but the guards all knew Joe Morton. He'd stood with them on the picket lines.

"What can I do for you, Joe?" said Fix, swinging his ample bottom around the desk and planting it on the cushioned swivel chair. Joe heard a fart slip out. Buddy had not skipped lunch. Joe sat down without being invited.

"Got a helluva script, Buddy. Think you'll love it."

Fix loved steaks and beer and French bread slathered in butter and his beefy body paid the price. The hair on his face grew faster than the hair on his head, and he gave off a sweetish odor no matter how many times a day he changed his shirt. They'd been friends of a sort in the old days, or at least colleagues, and Joe's scripts had made the studio some money. Joe had never ranked Buddy up with the really bad guys, the high and mighty studio schmucks who couldn't do a deal without diddling everyone.

Fix leaned back and clasped his hands in the prayerful manner. "And so say I love it, Joe, like I probably will, like I usually do with you. What then? You're untouchable. You know who owns this studio now."

"Yeah, I know who owns it and I know how much he loves money. Just read it, Buddy. That's all I ask."

Fix checked his watch. Eight more minutes to go.

"What's the story?"

"Sheriff sends up some bad guys and they're released from prison. Send him a message they're coming back. Warn him to clear out. He won't go."

"Done and redone. Man against the mob. What's new about that?"

"What's new is that he'd rid the town of this bunch. If the town stands with him the gang has no chance."

"And?"

"Town turns its back on him. Leave, say the elders. We want no more trouble."

"And?"

"Now he has the gang *and* the town against him."

Fix smiled. "You've been working with Brecht too long, Joe. So the town is the Germans, who instead of standing up to Hitler embrace him. No more trouble."

"It's all in the writing, Buddy, the telling, you know that, classic tale with a new twist. Put Gary Cooper in it."

"I saw *Galileo*, you know," he said, referring to Brecht's play. "Dreck. Why did he make him snivel like that?"

Morton had worked on the revision of *Galileo* before going to jail for refusing to talk to Congress about people like Brecht. Brecht had written his first draft while on the run from the Nazis, making the Italian astronomer a hero who stands up to the Inquisition, a metaphor for the Nazis. In Santa Monica he realized he'd written a lie. No one stood up to the Nazis.

"To show the monster he was up against."

Fix sighed and stood up, hands on hips. "Can't do your story, Joe. Gary Cooper is the last guy who'd do a script with your name on it. Not to mention Howard Hughes, who's the boss now. Howard's talking about Cooper for *The Fountainhead*. Ayn Rand."

"So forget Cooper. Hughes will love my script. Just get him to read it."

"Nobody will do a film with your name on it."

Joe didn't move. "How do you know?"

"How do I know? Because it's my business to know, goddam it, because I'm paid to know what the American people will like and to help them like it. Because people think you're a goddam Commie, Joe; because Congress cited you along with the others like your pal Brecht, who left the country for East Germany just in time. Because you just got out of jail."

"With my name on it, eh?"

Fix started to say something and stopped. "Hey, you write something I like, give me another name to put on it and we can do business. Hey, I've got a still better idea: we'll put your wife's name on it. Why not? She's a helluva writer."

"*What*? Me ghost for Lizzie?"

"Ghost, schmost. Get her to write it."

"What—my sheriff story?"

"No, not your goddam sheriff story. Morality doesn't sell anymore. What sells today is strength—Superman, good against evil, John Wayne against the Indians and Gary Cooper against the bureaucrats. They want Galileo standing up to the bad guys, not going all blubbery. Look, Joe, I'm trying to help. Get Lizzie to write up the whole Pitts-Murphy-Chili business. Helluva a story. Make a classic noir."

"I'm not here to shill for my wife. I've got my own story. Why don't you take a look? What do you have to lose?"

"Time, dammit, time, which is what I'm losing now. I can't touch you, Joe. Read the Waldorf agreement. My hands are tied. Your time is up."

Joe hadn't risen. "The Waldorf agreement! I saw your name

on that screed. The others I can understand: Goldwyn, Mayer, Harry Cohn—Galileos all. I didn't expect to see Buddy Fix on that reactionary list of infamy."

"Infamy? We told it like it is, Joe. We're businessmen, not moralists."

"That's what the Krupps told Hitler."

The intercom on the desk sounded. Fix ignored it and turned to watch a great truckload of maple trees chug by toward the Brooklyn street at the rear of the lot.

"Here's how it is, Joe, just as real as those maple trees out there: Anything with your name on it is poison, end of story. Your pal Brecht is the toast of East Berlin—the man who came back when everyone else was getting the hell out."

"Brecht was anti-fascist, anti-war, anti-Hitler long before we lifted a finger. So he's a leftist now. So were a lot of people who fought against Hitler."

"C'mon. You were with the Bolshies before the war. Admit it."

"So I admit it. The Crash made a lot of people ask questions. Then came the Depression. What about you, Buddy, weren't you asking questions?"

He was leaning on the desk. "Never. I've always been a true-blue Ayn Rand capitalist."

"And your father . . . ?"

Fix froze, pudgy fingers pressing white-tipped into the desk, tie dangling, beady eyes squinting. Joe watched his expression change from anger to surprise to curiosity.

"What the hell do you know about my father?"

"I ran into him on a picket line once."

Fix grimaced, then burst out laughing. "Yeah, right, well, we all make mistakes, don't we? At least he didn't go to jail. Now get out of here."

"What about my script?"

"So leave your fucking script," he shouted. "And get yourself a nom de plume or whatever the fuck they call it!"

CHAPTER 32

"Los Angeles has, young lady, the most perfect transportation system in the world."

The man leaned forward in the redwood chair and jabbed his finger toward the blazing fireplace to make the point. "I bet you didn't know that. Most people don't. They get up and hop a trolley that covers eleven hundred miles of track for a quarter—that's more than half the distance to Chicago—and they take it for granted. Dumb clucks don't even know what they've got." He sighed and sank back into the canvas cushions. From the kitchen the coffee gurgled. "Well, they'll know when it's gone."

Fred Barrett had not been that easy to find. An angular, bearded, ageless man on the wrong side of fifty, maybe sixty, he'd quit his job on the Los Angeles Utilities Board and gone to ground. It took her two weeks to locate him at Lake Arrowhead, where he'd built a cabin. "Sick of the whole thing," he told colleagues before he disappeared. People knew he lived in Venice, but he was gone when Lizzie found the house. "Up in the mountains" was all he'd ever said about his cabin. After knocking on a few Venice doors Lizzie found a neighbor who knew it was Lake Arrowhead. Some mountain sleuthing led her to his cabin on a snowy winter day.

"I had to get out of that place before it ruined my health," he said, staring back into the fire. "I couldn't stand to see what they were doing. People are going to go to jail. They damn well better. Trouble is it'll be too late." She'd taken out pad and pencil, but after listening for a few minutes put them back in her purse and flipped on the tape recorder. Fred Barrett liked to talk. At his office, they'd told her he knew every mile of every line in the city and could tell a story about all of them. She'd come to listen.

The *Times* had taken its time getting into it because few people grasped what was happening. Reports came in of tracks being pulled up here and there around the city, but other tracks were being laid. It didn't seem different from what had been going on for years as Los Angeles grew and spread and redistributed itself. The Pacific Electric Company of Henry Huntington was a business, and it was natural that unprofitable lines would be replaced by profitable ones. All this was overseen by the utilities commission because trolleys were public transportation, monopolies to be regulated in the public interest. Some of the construction had been spectacular, like the grading through the Cahuenga Pass that took trains over the Hollywood Hills to Studio City and Sherman Oaks.

"They do it in the dark of night," said Barrett. "People wake up and where there'd been a train that took them to work they find a hole in the road."

Cal's tip put her onto the story, but it took time because she'd been wrapped up in the second Pitts trial and because beyond the sale of Pacific Electric to National City Lines it wasn't clear what the story was. It wasn't until more tracks started to disappear that she knew she had something. And when she went looking for National City Lines, she couldn't find it. How could that be? Pacific Electric was the largest employer in the city, running lines into every corner of the county, carrying over a hundred million passengers annually. The Sawtelle trolley downtown to the *Times* was an easy ten-minute walk from their Barrington house.

How could the new owner of such a leviathan be invisible?

And if they were pulling up old tracks why weren't new ones being laid?

When Fred Barrett unwound his gangly frame from the redwood chair to head into the kitchen, she had a chance to look around. He'd built the house himself, he said, over countless weekends, countless years. It was his therapy. The house was built in the shape of a tower, or maybe pagoda, at the end of a dirt road winding up from the lake, which was frozen solid as she drove by. It seemed all one room, though the kitchen had its own round corner behind a partition, and a spiral wooden stairway led to a loft bedroom under the exposed beams of the roof. Like the man, the house was sparse and neat. The fireplace kept it warm though it couldn't be much above twenty-five degrees outside. Through skylights on either side of the loft she saw falling snow. She'd had to wait at the *Times* while they put chains on the company car, "just in case." It was snowing by the time she hit San Bernardino, and Highway 18 up to Crestline was impassible without chains. The *Times* stringer at Lake Arrowhead found Barrett's address at the post office and told her how to find the house. It was mid-afternoon by the time she arrived. Despite his surprise, Barrett welcomed her warmly.

"It's accumulating, darling," he shouted from the kitchen. "You better drink your coffee down and get out of here or you'll be snowed in."

"I didn't come all this way just to go back. I don't suppose you have a phone."

"No phones up here. That's why we come. Tell you something else. People come up here because they're afraid of the 'Big One'—you know, the earthquake that's supposed to level the city one day." She heard a guffaw. "What they don't know is that the San Andreas Fault runs right under Lake Arrowhead. When the Big One comes we'll be at ground zero."

He had a good fire going, and when he returned with a coffee tray and biscuits she was not sure she wanted to leave. He put a new log on the fire.

"Any place to stay in Arrowhead?"

"You don't want to stay up here. Never know when you'll get back down."

She took a sip of the strongest coffee she'd ever tasted.

"Better pour some milk in that," he said, settling into his chair. "Tell me, how did you get onto this?"

"I have a friend who worked at Pacific Electric."

"And what did he tell you?"

"Just that the P.E. was being sold and nobody knew the buyer."

"Best kept secret since the Manhattan Project."

"But how can that be? The city council was involved. The public utilities commission was involved. The state railroad commission had to know something."

"I'll tell you how it happened," he said, putting his feet up on a wooden stool. "If you're not going back then you've got some time and might as well get comfortable. We can drive into town in a bit and check out the Village Inn. They'll have something for you. Now, turn that machine of yours on and we'll get going."

He drank his coffee half down. "I assume you know that National City Lines is a front. If you didn't know that you wouldn't be here. Guy named Roy E. Fitzgerald runs it, or maybe that's E. Roy, never was sure about that. Signs his name both ways. He's as much of a ghost as his company. Got started in a town called Galesburg, near Chicago, with money from General Motors to buy the town's railway system and junk it. GM promised Galesburg buses to replace it—you know, those yellow things they make. Worked so well that GM kept on giving and E. Roy kept on pulling up tracks in little towns all around Illinois. Nobody complained—too much money being sloshed around. Pretty soon GM had partners named Standard Oil, Mack, Firestone, Greyhound, and they started eyeing bigger fish. Took their act to Tulsa, Montgomery, St. Louis. Tracks come out, buses go in. By the time the public knows what's going on it's too late. But none of these towns is anything compared to Los Angeles. They were fishing for minnows and then went for the whale. Best transit system in the world, I tell you."

"And that's what you told the city council?"

"That's what the public utilities board told the council. And we told the council what these guys were doing back east. I went back myself to see and wrote it all up for the council."

"So it's all part of the record."

"It's all in there." He paused. "But try and find it."

He crunched on a biscuit. "Where you from?"

"Born right here in Los Angeles," she said.

He smiled. "One of the few. I got my start in New York, little town called Syosset. I worked on the Long Island Railroad. Went right through Syosset. After the war—the First World War, that is—I came out here. Docs said I needed a dryer climate. Went to work for the P.E. and watched our train system grow up and surpass the Long Island. We laid half again as much track as the Long Island. Now can you imagine New York without the Long Island Railroad? You cannot. New York would not function without the Long Island Railroad. Where would the people live? Now don't you imagine that General Motors and Standard Oil and the rest of them would love to pull up seven hundred miles of Long Island track and replace it with cars and buses? You bet they would. And any New York city councilman or Long Island town supervisor who let that happen would be up at Sing Sing the next day."

He finished his coffee and glanced up at the skylights, now

dark with snow. "I tell you, darling, the day will come in Los Angeles—don't know when it will be, maybe twenty-five, fifty years out, who knows?—when the city is so inundated with cars and smog and bumper-to-bumper traffic and general misery and frustration that it will look back at what it had in the thirties and forties and wonder how in hell people could have been so stupid. Mark my words, there will be a highway from downtown to the beach that will follow the exact path of the Venice Short Line, only instead of a half-hour ride while you read your newspaper you'll be shut in your car barely moving and breathing the exhausts of the cars all around you. It will take four times as long and you'll arrive four times as frazzled—and then try to find a place to park.

He stood up. "And you know what they'll do? One day, after wringing their hands and pulling their hair for years, they will start to rebuild what they destroyed. They will pull up the roads and scrap the buses and lay down track—maybe subways, maybe elevated, who knows what they'll have by then—and those tracks will go exactly where Pacific Electric had laid them. I'm telling you, they will follow the exact same routes. How much will the new system cost? It will cost a thousand times what it cost to build the system we have today. Hah! And they say that the human species is getting smarter."

He stopped talking and walked to the front door for a peek outside. A gust whooshed in that made her shiver. "Getting pretty heavy. The 18 will be closed by now. Tell you what. I'll drive to the Village Inn. You follow me in. They'll have a room. Better for you than stuck out here. We'll get some dinner and talk. Time this story gets the attention it deserves."

She'd brought only a purse, but the village shops would get her through the night—or maybe a few nights. Her main problem was shoes, so after checking in at the hotel and leaving Fred Barrett at the bar she went searching for boots and heavy socks. In another shop she found pajamas and a woolen cap and then it was back into the snow to the local drugstore for toiletries. At least she'd had the foresight to bring her good woolen coat. Back at the inn, she had her things sent up, went into the ladies' room to freshen and then off to find Barrett. As a rule, she didn't drink in the daytime, but it didn't seem like daytime anymore and she was cold enough that she would have broken her rule anyway. Barrett was seated at a table in the bar reading the *Times,* and they ordered hot rum grogs.

"First time at Arrowhead?"

There was a fire going. She'd kept her boots on and with new socks could finally feel her toes again. "First time," she said, keeping her hands wrapped around the warm mug. "Beautiful place, though I'm not used to the snow. We live in Brentwood."

"Brentwood? Santa-Monica-Sawtelle Line—runs from downtown right out to the Veterans Hospital. Say, your name's Mull. You by any chance related to the late Willie Mull?"

"Willie Mull was my uncle."

"Well, darling, you have my deepest sympathies. That was one sad story. I've never been to the temple, but been by it enough times, right smack on the Glendale-Burbank Line, one of the finest lines of all, private right of way, no cars to slow us down."

"But you were a commissioner, not a trainman . . ."

"I was a trainman before I was a commissioner. I've been on every line in the city, dear, know 'em all, ask me anything."

She turned her tape recorder back on. She still had no feeling for this story, for how to approach it, for where its center was. Usually she knew from the beginning what she had and what she didn't and whom she needed to see to fit everything together. This story was too amorphous. She needed to pull back to view it better, go up on a hill like the generals do to look down and see the big picture. The heart of the story—that some mysterious Roy E. or E. Roy comes to town and takes over its transportation network without anybody noticing—was simply too preposterous. Takes it over and takes it apart. Cities have utilities boards and city councils and mayors and newspapers to prevent things like that. How could this have slipped under the radar? That was the guts of this story—that the whole thing was done in secret. Why didn't Fred Barrett blow the whistle instead of disappearing up into the mountains? Or did he?

"Say, come to think of it, Eddie Mull was Willie's brother. Are you . . ."

"Eddie Mull was my father."

He stared at her for some seconds before dropping his eyes. "That's a load of grief that you've had, young lady. More than enough for one family, I'd say."

"Thank you."

He held up his mug. "You use another?"

"I think I could."

He ordered, and they fell silent for a while, both facing the fire, both lost in their thoughts. When the new drinks arrived, she took a big swallow, and when the grog had run down deep enough to warm her toes a little more, she checked her recorder and turned back to face him. "Okay, Fred, now you're going to tell me what you plan to do about this."

"Well, you remember back at the house when I said the story was part of the record?"

"Try to find it," you said.

"Well, darlin' you've come to the only man who knows where to find it."

CHAPTER 33

Playa del Rey wasn't much, which was its charm to the few hundred souls who lived there. A sandy hill and beach on a trolley line to Culver City and downtown, with a spur to Venice, it had no schools, no local government, no police, only a volunteer fire department and irregular trash collection—people mostly burning trash on the sand, providing occasional work for the firemen. It had one grocery store, Charlie's Market; one drugstore, Doc Dolson's; a malt shop, gas station and burger joint called the Dutch Village. The only institution of any class was the Westport Beach Club, which was too costly for most of the denizens, who weren't clubby sorts anyway. Officially part of Los Angeles, Playa del Rey was ignored by the city, which was fine with everyone. When people from downtown went to the beach they went to Venice, Ocean Park or Santa Monica, glitzy places with piers, shooting galleries and beauty contests.

The only school for Didi Heyward was Florence Nightingale Elementary in Venice, which meant that Maggie or Terry had to drop her off on their way to Hughes Aircraft, which wasn't on their way, but no school buses ran to Playa del Rey, and they'd recently pulled up the tracks for the spur to Venice. School was reached by driving down Pacific Avenue through the oil derricks, which intrigued Didi as much as they once had her mother. Maggie explained that they'd been built by Grandpa Eddie and now belonged to her and Aunt Lizzie, who didn't know what to do with them.

Didi didn't like Nightingale, didn't like the teachers, didn't like the other children, many of whom were children of oil roughnecks and beach drifters. Didi, in fact, did not like any-thing about Playa del Rey or the beach. She was a fastidious lit-tle thing who from the beginning disliked dirt, sand or anything gritty, reminding Maggie of her mother. On weekends, when she and Terry took her to the beach club, she'd spend the day alone in a chair in the sitting room with a book. She always wore a dress and would not go near a pool, beach or grill. She hated sand in her pumps and refused to go barefoot. She insisted on having egg salad or chicken salad sandwiches (no tuna, please!) sent to her in the sitting room, crusts removed and cut into four neat little squares with not too much filling to squish out the sides. That was how Granny served sandwiches in Bel Air and the only way Didi would eat them.

She liked collecting things, especially expensive things. When Granny gave her an antique doll (the very doll she'd kept in a trunk for years after discovery that Maggie hated dolls and Lizzie wasn't interested) Didi wanted more of them. It was a rare German bisque doll from 1900 and hard to find another like it. Nelly, who finally had a girl she could spoil, found a French bisque doll on Rodeo Drive with the same embroidered costume, swivel head, glass eyes and pretty little booties. It cost four hundred dollars but Didi had to have it. Nelly loved tak-ing her meticulous little granddaughter shopping with her. The shop owners loved to see them coming.

After school was a problem until Maggie found an older woman, Mrs. Gertz from up on Rees Street, to stay with her. Didi didn't like Mrs. Gertz, and the feeling was mutual. Soon Mrs. Gertz decamped and the teenage niece of a friend at the club came by after school, but that didn't last either. Maggie often flew until dark, which in the summer was eight o'clock, and Terry spent so much time with Howard flying back and forth to the new Hughes missile plant in Tucson that he often didn't come home at all. Lizzie had found a UCLA co-ed for Robby when Joe was in jail, but Playa del Rey was not Brentwood, and no co-eds were available.

"Can't go on like this," Terry said one evening when they were having drinks on the patio and watching the sun sink into the Pacific. Soon the nightly marine layer would be forming, when the coolness of the water mixes with the warmth of air off the land. "She hates school, hates the club, hates the people who stay with her, has no friends and as far as I can see has no fun in life at all."

"Didi's her own person," said Maggie. "Nothing wrong with that."

"But she's so different."

"From . . .?"

"From everything—from other children. From you, from me."

"So she's different. Weren't you different? I know I was."

Maggie had tried everything with her, but Didi was a drudge. At the club, she refused swimming lessons. Throw her in the pool to sink or swim which was how she'd learned herself, but Didi would probably have let herself drown. When they went to the stables, Didi would not get on the pony, would not get on the horse with her mother, would not touch the reins, hated the dirt and dust and shit as much as Nelly did. Sometimes you force your children to do something, thinking it's for their own good and knowing one day they'll thank you for it, but Didi knew her own good better than anyone.

Maggie had had the discussion with Terry before, and defended her daughter every time. But the truth was she'd reached the end of her tether, driven to tears sometimes by anger and frustration with Didi's obstinacy, her refusal to do anything her parents might have liked, that might have given them even a hint of the joys of parenthood. Maggie began to wonder if it wasn't calculated: selfishness used as a means of punishment. But why? She had no idea how to deal with something like that.

"I wasn't *that* different," Terry said. "Can't figure it. She has everything."

"Doesn't like it here."

"Doesn't like the beach."

The thought hit them simultaneously as they sat sipping rum in the ocean breezes. Sailboats from Santa Monica Pier tacked a few miles off Venice.

"Nelly adores her. Remember last Christmas in Bel Air? We couldn't separate them."

"Maybe that's it," he said.

It was too obvious. She called her mother that night.

They brought her over in Terry's station wagon. Three suitcases of clothes and belongings were left in the hall while Didi walked around deciding which bedroom she wanted. Thinking she would want her mother's old room, Nelly had installed bright yellow curtains and a new pale blue bedspread set, but Didi didn't want her mother's room and hated yellow; she wanted Aunt Lizzie's room, farther down the hall from the master bedroom. Nelly looked to Maggie, who smiled as if to say get used to it. Terry carried the bags to the bedroom, and four of them sat down to lunch. Iris, who'd been with Nelly since Lupe left after Eddie was killed, poured the chablis and brought in a fresh tomato salad from the garden followed by chicken croquettes in béarnaise and squash from the garden. Didi was delighted to have a real lunch served by a real maid. She liked maids.

"Tomorrow Ralph will drive us down to Westlake," Nelly

told her granddaughter. "Miss Pierce, the vice principal, will show us around so you can get a feel for the school. Some of the girls are already there, I understand, for summer activities."

Didi was eight, tall for her age, happy that her legs nearly reached the floor at Granny's dining room table. She was a pretty girl, solid, not delicate, with her mother's dark Latin hair and not a touch of her father's Welsh red. Nelly thought she took more after Lizzie than Maggie for she tended to observe rather than talk. She was polite to a fault, and from what Nelly had heard from friends, would fit in perfectly at Westlake, where they had classes on etiquette. She was stuffy, no question, but Nelly liked that. No more Maggies, please! She was aware of everything around her, her reticence growing not from shyness or lack of observation but from withholding judgment. Above all things, Didi hated making mistakes. She was a cautious creature, circumspect to a fault, mortified by failure. The saying is that the girl is the mother of the woman, but in Didi's case, for reasons no one ever understood, the saying would not hold.

"What kind of summer activities, Granny?"

Nelly sipped her wine. She'd seen her granddaughter carefully pose her fork before she asked the question.

"Well, I'm sure I don't know. We'll find out tomorrow."

"Summer sports, probably," said Maggie. "Girls' sports, like field hockey."

Terry smiled at his wife. "Somehow I can't see you in knickers playing field hockey with the other girls."

"I never did," said Maggie. "I played with the boys."

"You know I don't like sports, Mother," said Didi.

Terry took a sip of wine and smiled at his daughter. He would never admit he wouldn't miss her, but it was the truth. He couldn't warm to her, and it wasn't for not trying. With a son he would have known how to break through the shell or with a cuddly girl or even with a tomboy like Maggie. A little thing like Didi who shunned physical contact and liked sitting by herself was a mystery to him. He had an image of Alice McKee, his friend Tom McKee's little girl, jumping into her daddy's arms by the club pool, a little monkey in a wet bathing suit, wrapping her skinny arms and legs around Daddy and screaming with joy as they jumped in the water locked together. Terry would have loved it. Didi would have died of shame.

She fit right in at Bel Air, where the crusts were always removed, the sandwiches never squishy and tuna never served. For her part, Nelly was thrilled. She was starting over again, a second chance. She knew Didi would love Westlake, an exclusive girls' school where the girls would be just as stuffy and fussy as she was. It meant a half-hour drive each day, each way, but Nelly had Ralph. Many of the girls at Westlake had chauffeurs like Ralph.

Nelly bonded with Didi in a way she never had with her daughters. With the girls, there'd always been a gap, based on what, Nelly was not sure but sensed that the girls never looked up to her. She hadn't been able to guide them the way other mothers guided their daughters. It was like she did not have a single quality or idea her girls admired. She was proud of what she'd done with her life: from the farm to Woolworth's to Mull Gardens to Bel Air; Iowa to the Blue Book and Junior League. She'd tried all the things the other Bel Air moms tried, but her girls weren't interested. With Didi it would be different. They were birds of a feather.

Looking back, she decided she'd never had any fun with her girls, never got to do the things the other moms did. Most Bel Air girls went to Westlake and Marlborough, but private school wasn't for Maggie or Lizzie, little public-school democrats from the start. She'd talked to Eddie about it, but Eddie didn't care. With a son he might have felt differently, but she couldn't give Eddie the son he wanted, and Cal and Eddie were never close. Cal wasn't that close to his own father, and it hurt Willie, she knew it did.

Such thoughts bothered her more now than they had at the time. At the time, she'd had no problem turning the girls over to Cal so she could spend her afternoons shopping and playing bridge. She'd gotten used to wine spritzers in the afternoon and sometimes even martinis. Thinking back on it, she would have loved to do what the other moms did, take her girls to birthday parties and sleepovers and dances. She could easily have given up a shopping day or even bridge to take the girls to the club for tennis or golf or to the Wilshire Ebell for dance lessons. It wasn't her. It was the girls who wouldn't go!

Worst of all, neither girl would attend the coming-out ball at the country club where the Bel Air debutantes always got a mention by Miss Adelaide Nevin. For moms, debutante balls are the sublime reward for seventeen years of work and worry. Their darlings are officially presented to society and can find husbands who, with any luck, one day will have their own homes in Bel Air. Two Junes in a row Nelly had opened the newspaper to Miss Adelaide Nevin's column and found all the Bel Air girls mentioned but her own. She still felt the pain and embarrassment. This time would be different. With Didi, she was starting over. Didi had loved Bel Air from the moment she'd set her little baby booties in it.

Neither of her girls had made what Nelly would call a good marriage—a good *second* marriage. Nor had either one shown any inclination to move up in status and give their children what they'd had themselves. A stucco in Brentwood and a wood shingle in Playa del Rey waiting for a cigarette to drop was all they could show for the millions they'd inherited from Eddie. Nelly had never approved of Maggie's running around, from poor Billy Todd to Howard Hughes. As for Lizzie, Nelly had liked Asa of the Aldridge Furniture Store family well enough, but not Joe Morton, who was now an official criminal.

Didi was her chance to make amends. Nelly had read an article in the *Woman's Home Companion* called "Skipping Steps" about how children often reject parents and bond with grandparents because grandparents are more indulgent and more tolerant of their imperfections. The bond is just as strong in the opposite direction, according to the author, because grandparents have learned from their earlier mistakes and now have more time and affection—and money—to spend on children.

Exactly!

CHAPTER 34

Calvin Mull, discharged with hundreds of others from Pacific Electric, the world's most extensive interurban railway system, opened the Sierra Club's first Los Angeles office downtown in the Richfield Tower, the tallest structure in the city thanks to a 130-foot tower in the shape of an oil derrick on the roof. The Richfield was a glorious amalgam of New York's Rockefeller Center and Chrysler Buildings and an historic landmark from the day it opened in a city with few of them. For the Sierra Club, an oil building made a strange headquarters, but Cal liked the irony. From Richfield's observation deck he could see oil wells pumping in every direction—Signal Hill, Santa Fe Springs, La Brea, Beverly Hills, Baldwin Hills and, of course, Venice. Los Angeles had become one gigantic oil field.

Howard Hughes had long coveted Eddie Mull's Venice fields. Rumors of a vast marina to be built in the Ballona wetlands had circulated for years, and in 1949 the Army Corps of Engineers completed a study showing that a harbor for eight thousand yachts and small boats could be dredged for $25 million. The marina would replace the oil fields. Study in hand, Los Angeles County obtained a loan from the state, which appealed to Washington to make Marina del Rey a federal project. The people of Los Angeles deserved more than just highways. Hughes flatly refused to come to Richfield Tower, which he regarded as enemy territory. Cal was not surprised by the refusal. He had no role in his cousins' decision, other than acting as their legal advisor. It was agreed to hold the meeting in the offices of Hughes Aircraft, looking out over the marshes, dunes, and oil wells that Hughes was determined to claim as his own.

Maggie brought Terry for moral support. Lizzie was accompanied by Joe Morton, whose primary interest in the negotiation was literary: It was easier to write about tough guys like Hughes if you observed them in action. Cal arrived with a mind full of questions. Hughes knew the Corps of Engineers' study as well as he did. The county would seek to buy the land from whomever owned it. If a fair price could not be agreed upon, the power of eminent domain would be invoked. What made Hughes think the Mulls would sell him the land so he could flip it at a higher price? What did he have up his sleeve?

Cal had something up his sleeve as well, something he'd not yet vetted with anyone, including his cousins, the landowners.

Hughes's private office was more fitting for an aircraft man than a movie or oil man, though it served all his business interests one way or another. From the top floor of the administration building, broad picture windows looked out over the nation's longest privately owned runway toward Ballona Creek and the marshes, with the Mull oil derricks in the distance. Beyond that, invisible from the office, was the Pacific Ocean. The stables where Maggie and Lizzie had learned to ride were barely visible. Models of Hughes's planes and photos of him with planes and trophies ringed the room. Maggie was disappointed he'd never hung a photo of the Catalina race, which had changed her life. A giant blow-up of the Spruce Goose hung on a side wall. The Goose, amphibious, would never use the runway.

Hughes led them not to the chairs by his desk but into a semi-circle by the windows overlooking the runway. It was an odd seating arrangement, the chairs set close to each other, with Hughes's chair, higher than the others and facing them, in the center. It looked like a setting for a group therapy session, but in fact was an arrangement for a man hard of hearing. Behind them, facing Hughes, sat chief factotum Melvin Cobb, taking notes.

Coffee and rolls were offered. Hughes was in business clothes—gray slacks, a brown sports jacket, and blue silk tie with red polka dots. He didn't own a lot of clothes, and Maggie recognized the jacket, recognized the button she'd once sewn on it. She found the clothes oddly baggy, noticing that he had grown thinner. She'd heard the rumors. "Howard would fuck a tree if he could get it in bed," Joan Crawford had said in words that made the rounds. But you don't get syphilis from a tree. Degradation was setting in, physical, mental, she didn't know. She looked on him with affection, everything a man should be, right down to his weaknesses. It wasn't nice seeing a man like that disintegrate. Rumors were that he was making a mess of RKO, driving Robert Mitchum during the shooting of *His Kind of Woman* to break up a set.

"There it is," he said, commandingly, waving his arm across the windows, an amiable smile on his face. The guests had seated themselves, but still he stood. "That's where the marina goes—right after Eddie's wells come out."

"We know that, Howard," said Cal, after a moment, breaking the mood of edgy camaraderie. "What we don't know is why you want the land."

Hughes sat down at the center of the semi-circle. Maggie, Terry, and Cal were on one side, Lizzie and Joe on the other. Lizzie brought out a pad and pen, not risking the tape recorder. She'd been to Hughes Aircraft once before, for a story on the Spruce Goose shortly before its one and only flight. Since then, Hughes kept it locked up.

Either he hadn't heard Cal or chose to ignore him. No sign

of a hearing aid. "You're looking at an oil man who is going to bring down derricks and plug up wells." Again he smiled. "You don't find that every day."

"Don't forget the stables," said Maggie.

He was staring at Lizzie. "You're not writing about this for the *Times,* are you? You're invited here as a principal, not as a reporter."

"I am not writing about this for the *Times*, Howard."

"It's a habit with her," said Maggie. "Some people fidget, Lizzie writes."

"I have your word?"

"You have my word."

He looked over them to Cobb, making sure he got that down.

"Good. Well, as we all know, Los Angeles County, with backing from the federal government, wants to build a marina out there, maybe ten thousand yachts, bigger than anything south of San Francisco. You own the property and the government wants to buy it. How does Howard Hughes fit in, you ask?" He turned to look around, eyebrows arched high over expressive blue eyes. "Hi Joe," he said with a smile, and winked at Maggie. "Easy: With me involved you make more money. Simple as that. You get richer. Up to you. End of pitch."

Maggie felt a tingle. Hughes had always dazzled her. For a while she'd wondered if they would marry, but she knew better. Arnaud was dashing and handsome, but Arnaud had no surprises. Howard, dashing and handsome, was shrouded in a mystery no one had ever broken: wealth, genius, passion, courage, deafness, charm, humor, obsessiveness, paranoia, his contradictions made him unique. Irresistible.

She'd gone to work for him soon after he'd broken up with Kate Hepburn. He'd grown a scraggily mustache to hide the scars from too many crashes, but she'd rather liked it. Their first dates were not in Los Angeles but in Washington where she was based, thanks to Mrs. Roosevelt, to help set up the Women's Airforce Service Pilots, the World War II WASPs. Hughes was often in Washington to meet with the War Department and testify to Congress on the constant cost overruns and delays on his planes. He needed a place to stay, so he stayed with her. The affair lasted on and off for two years. When she returned to Hughes Aircraft after the war it was as employee. She had no complaints.

"How do we make more money, Howard?" asked Joe.

Hughes looked benignly at him. He'd heard about a script for a Western being read at RKO. Something about a pseudonym. He made a mental note to call Buddy Fix. "Because the government will screw you, Joe, but it won't screw me. We know each other too well. In short, you will make more money, much more money, selling the land to me and letting me negotiate with people I've been negotiating with for years."

You had to admire his balls, thought Cal. The argument was preposterous: that somehow they could do better with Hughes getting a cut of the proceeds than without him. Having worked with city government, Cal knew the weaknesses of civil servants, but why should they overpay just because they were negotiating with Howard Hughes? Buying property just to flip, wasn't that a kind of flimflam? What about government auditors? What about the press? Would Lizzie be able to keep from writing about something as fishy as a huge land flip?

"What guarantee can you give, Howard?" asked Cal.

"Guarantee? There are no guarantees in business negotiations, son. Call it experience against inexperience."

"Howard was good with Congress," said Maggie. "I've seen him perform."

Hughes turned to her. "Perform is not the word I would have chosen."

She smiled. "Okay, negotiate."

"I'm willing to go as high as $50 million."

"Because you think you can get $100 million from the government," said Cal. "You'll have do better than that."

"Can't do it. Bankers won't let me."

It was time for Cal's surprise.

"You want our land, Howard. What about your land?"

"*What*?"

"What about the land we're sitting on right now?"

Hughes leaned closer. Did he miss something? "What about it?"

"Let's assume the marina is built. Now look a few years down the road, a decade or two. Say the marina has ten thousand yachts by then—a huge man-made harbor surrounded by dry docks, shops, apartments, yacht clubs, restaurants—a seaside community unto itself."

They'd all turned toward him.

"What are you saying?" said Hughes.

"Do you intend to hold on to an empty airfield during all this?"

"What do you mean empty airfield? This is Hughes Aircraft."

"Which can be moved anywhere—Lancaster, Ontario, Riverside, the middle of the desert for that matter, where you do most of your testing. You'll want to move by then, Howard, and the question is, what happens to this land we're sitting on?"

Hughes face was blank. If the future of his airfield was something he'd never thought about, he wasn't going to show it. Cal's guess was that the idea was new to him. A man of action, a dealmaker and egotist focused on whether he could fly the fastest airplane, run the best studio, own the most successful airline and screw the sexiest actress, why would he think about the future? He was buying new land, not selling what he had. Who cares about two decades out? We'll all be gone.

"This land stays an airfield."

"It can't for long," said Terry, speaking for the first time. "Not with the expansion of L.A. International two miles away. Not with jet airliners on their way."

Hughes stared at his pilot, having trouble remembering why he was there.

"All this land belongs to Ballona," said Cal, sweeping his arm across the window. "Maggie, Lizzie, and I have been coming here since we were children, long before you came to town, Howard. All of it—from the airfield, across the wetlands, beyond the stables to the beach, down Ballona Creek and across to the oil fields and the Venice canals—becomes more vital as the city grows. A marina is good land use, but what will surround it? Hughes Aircraft will have to move. Are you going to sell to developers who put up high-rises right down to the ocean? How is that better than oil wells? How do the stables survive, as you promised?"

Hughes had been leaning forward to make sure he heard every word. Now he sat back. One could almost see the wheels of his mind spinning.

"What exactly are you asking for?"

"A stipulation concerning the future use of your airfield."

"You're crazy."

"No, not crazy. Looking to the future."

"You want a land swap?"

"Of course not."

"So what is it?"

"Do you have a will?"

A smile inched slowly across his rugged face and he looked around at the others. "I believe that he wants the Sierra Club to be in my will. No sir, I have no will. Why would I have a will? I am a healthy man. Ask Maggie. I have no heirs and don't intend to have any. Anyone who claims to be my heir is an impostor."

Cal looked closely at him. A little gaunt maybe, but still impressive. He thought of the pretty girl in pink plumeria at Maggie's wedding. But there were the plane crashes, the loss of hearing, the rumors. You can't always tell by looking at a person.

"What about a statement of intent? Would you sign a statement with Mull Oil that Hughes Aircraft land is protected and cannot be used for future commercial development?'

Hughes looked over them to Cobb.

"No such statement would be legally binding," said the factotum.

"Of course not," said Cal. "So Howard would have no problem signing it.'

Hughes's mind was processing. "How would such a statement influence the present negotiations?" he asked at length.

"Maybe it wouldn't. I haven't discussed this yet with my cousins, who look as surprised as you do. On the other hand, maybe it would."

"An interesting idea," said Lizzie.

"We need to talk," said Maggie.

Hughes stood up. "When you're ready, call me."

CHAPTER 35

The fifties were the golden age of Los Angeles, when a perfect balance was achieved between man, his resources, and his ambitions: Human life was good. Population went on growing, but was no longer doubling every decade. Governments were progressive, but not too. The Cold War continued, but in Los Angeles that meant jobs at companies like Hughes, Douglas, and Lockheed. Dwight Eisenhower, a moderate Republican, was elected in two landslides, winning California and Los Angeles both times and presiding over a booming national economy that paid record high income taxes no one seemed to mind. Public education was free and was good. Tuition at USC, a private university, cost eight hundred dollars a year. Across town at UCLA, tuition was free and accessible to anyone with a B average from public high school.

The oil wells on the beaches came down. The movie industry had never been stronger, and the mob decamped from Los Angeles to Las Vegas (where air-conditioning had arrived) for legalized gambling and off-track betting. Palm Springs was a pleasant two-hour drive away where a few thousand dollars would buy you a stucco and a date ranch. A federal highway bill passed that would make a mess of the city, but that was still a few years out. The interurban rail system that once was the envy of the nation was demolished, but Eisenhower was promising to bring the demolishers to justice. The water arriving from the Owens and Colorado Rivers, the water that built Los Angeles, was no longer sufficient but a state water project would be passed to bring water from Northern California, where the water was, to Southern California, where the people were.

It was a period of stability and equilibrium. It would have taken a person of diabolical imagination to foresee the chaos that was coming: the smog, traffic, trash, crime, riots, drugs, viruses, and homelessness; the building frenzy that would destroy hillsides and mountains and guarantee the revenge of summer fires and winter floods; the Big One that finally struck—but was it really the Big One when the epicenter was in the Valley and only fifty-seven people died? In the fifties, people didn't know about any of that. They didn't make much money, but nothing cost much either. Doctors and dentists made no more than anyone else, hamburgers were nineteen cents and gasoline twenty-nine cents a gallon. Movies were a quarter. You could buy a prewar stucco in West Hollywood for fifteen thousand dollars or pay the same for a new tract house in Westchester. Free of oil wells, beaches were again for sunning and swimming. The Dodgers arrived from Brooklyn and the Rams still played in the Coliseum. The fifties in Los Angeles was as good as it gets.

Lizzie had not forgotten her inheritance. When Eddie's estate was probated, taxes paid and assets distributed, Security Bank and Trust set up a trust in her name with a value just under $20 million—not counting the Venice oil fields. What to do with it? She'd worked for the *Times* for twenty years, been reporter, editor, reporter, editor, and reporter again. She had no intention of stopping writing. She'd filled pages of private notebooks—thoughts and profiles and sketches back to her days writing for Miss Adelaide Nevin. She had material ready for a Pitts-Callender book when an idea for a novel struck her: a corporation takes over a town, destroys what has been built up over decades, ruins lives and gets away free. She showed Joe the outline and watched him take a book from the shelves, *The Octopus*, by Frank Norris. She read the book and tore up her outline. She would stick to nonfiction.

Saturday morning and they were in their garden. They had hangovers from a few too many the night before with Maggie and Terry at Lawry's on La Cienega, but coffee and Seville oranges (with sugar) in sunny chairs and the green freedom of the garden without their son was restoring them. Robby had spent the night at a friend's house and was due back anytime. They talked a while about what to do with their son. His teachers said he was two years ahead of his classmates and ready for high school—academically but not emotionally. He was twelve years old and a handful. They didn't mind at all when he slept over with friends.

"You know I didn't mean to discourage you the other day," Joe said. "Frank Norris had a good idea but was no good at characterization. The subject can be done better."

"Let's see how the Pacific Electric trial turns out first."

"Why? If it's a novel, you can make it turn out as you like. Use your imagination."

He liked the way she looked in the morning, something about her short, mussed, sandy hair being provocative. She was aging well; or maybe it was because she was a dozen years younger, and he was aging faster. He liked making love to her Saturday mornings when she wasn't rushing off to work. She'd thrown on jeans and a shirt to sit with him in the privacy of their garden, read the newspaper and talk.

"Not sure I have the imagination for novels."

"You never know till you try."

"Sure you do. You, for example, are always making things up, composing stories in your head, inventing dialogue. I just watch and listen and take notes."

They fell silent. He watched her reading the paper, thinking he loved her more than he thought he could ever love any person. But he had something else on his mind. She glanced up and saw the look that said something was coming that she didn't really want to hear.

"I've never told you this before, but as a newspaper the *Times* stinks."

She didn't say a word.

She knew it, of course, but that made it no easier to hear. She'd belonged to the *Los Angeles Times* for two decades, the only professional life she'd known. She'd given it all she had, put her life on the line and wasn't yet done. Joe's arrow hit its mark and it showed in her face and her silence. He wanted her to quit the newspaper and write books. He worried about her always being on the frontlines of stories that put her in danger.

"That doesn't mean you stink, hon," he said, trying to recover, "just that the *Times* isn't good enough for you. You deserve better. So does this city."

She levelled angry eyes at him. "This is Los Angeles, Joe, not your precious New York. We don't have six dailies. The *Times* is still the best newspaper in town. In New York, you don't like the *Trib,* you go to the *Times*; you don't like the *Times*, you go to the *Sun* or *World-Telegram* or *Post* or *Daily News* or whatever. What can I do here—work for Hearst?"

"You are at the point where you don't have to work for any newspaper."

"It's what I do, Joe, who I am. Novels—that's not me."

"So do a blow-by-blow story about Pitts-Callender. We'll put it in a script."

She tried a smile. "Maybe . . . someday."

He finished his coffee and lit up, first one of the day. "My question is simple: why isn't the *Times* better? The Chandlers own this town. They are drowning in money. What's wrong with that family? Why can't the *Los Angeles Times* be the *New York Times* of the West? Why is everything local? Give us national news, foreign news, tell us about the world. People here care about things beyond the city limits. This is a city of foreigners."

"Rich family newspaper. No real tradition. Clip coupons and bank their dividends. Big houses and cars. Why change?"

"Norman Chandler could do it. He's the boss, isn't he?"

"Norman is afraid of his family."

"What about son Otis, the golden boy—any hope there?'

"Otis comes in every day—when he's done surfing and weight lifting."

"Aren't you sick of it?"

"No."

"Try your hand at a script. Maybe Howard Hughes and RKO would like it."

"Howard Hughes doesn't like me."

"You haven't slept with him yet."

She picked up an orange to throw, but started laughing. "I never compete with Maggie."

"With the money you've got you can do anything you want."

She stopped laughing. "That money is yours, too."

"If I didn't write I would die."

She smiled. "What would Hollywood do without Memory Laine?"

"You don't like my nom de plume?"

"It's cute—just that everybody knows it's you."

"Buddy's tired of the game. He'll put my name back up one of these days."

"My point is, money doesn't change a thing, does it?"

"Why don't you do something useful with it?"

"Like give it to the Sierra Club?"

He laughed. "Cal would name a mountain after you."

"Not to change subject again," she said, "but back to Robby."

"Any ideas?"

"I keep telling myself it's a phase, but he doesn't talk to me anymore."

"Doesn't talk . . . ?"

"Not a word. Something boiling in there.

"He doesn't say much to me either."

"No," she said quickly, "it's different with you. No hostility with you."

"Hostility?"

Agitated, she was tapping on the table. "I don't know what else to call it. I guess I've never been much of a mother. Never home. Loved my work too much. He noticed."

"Nonsense."

"No, it's not. My mother was always meddling, and I figured—Maggie, too—that I'd let my kid grow up as he wanted. But that doesn't seem to work either."

"You did it the way you wanted. Robby's the same way. He'll turn out the way he wants. We all do. So what's new?"

"What do we do?"

"Send him to Bel Air?"

"He doesn't get along with Didi—or Nelly, for that matter."

"Sounds vaguely Oedipal. Anyway, Bel Air is University High. At twelve—they'd kill him."

"Private school?"

"Every decent boys' school in Los Angeles is a military school: Black Foxe, Harvard, California Military Academy. I've checked. Cold War phenomenon."

"So what about that?"

"Hey, I'm supposed to be a pacifist."

"I wonder about military school. He already seems so . . . so . . ." She had to think a minute. "Hostile is the word that keeps coming back."

"There's always boarding school back East. The British built an empire that way. Theory is that schools are better than parents at raising children. Less emotional. More professional. I'd miss the little bugger. Did some of my best writing with him banging on his crib."

She smiled. "Why did you have to make him so smart?"

"Me? He scores on math tests, not English."

"A complete genetic aberration. Two literary parents who can't balance a checkbook."

"So what do we do?"

"Send me away!"

Lizzie jumped, turned and saw him standing on the porch. He'd slipped through the house without a sound and been listening, how long they didn't know.

"Shame on you!"

"Why shouldn't I listen?"

"It's not listening, it's spying," said Joe. "You want to listen, you come to the table."

"Then you'd stop talking."

He looked twelve, with the delicate face bones and smooth, pink cheeks of pre-puberty. He was scrawny, but had the kind of frame that would fill out. The face was Lizzie's, more girlish than boyish, but with Joe's foxy eyes, watchful, myopic, a little dangerous. The nose was pug but would grow out, and the eyebrows too thick for his face. Another boy might have come bursting outside with tales from the night's sleepover, but not Robinson Morton. He didn't like showing emotion, didn't like others to know what he'd been doing and didn't like finding his parents at breakfast discussing his future without him.

"Sit down," said Lizzie, calmer now. "Did you have a good time at Tommy's?"

He didn't answer.

"You want to go to the beach today?" said Lizzie.

"Nah, stuff to do."

"Like?"

"Just stuff."

Joe stood up. He didn't like one-word conversations. "I've got stuff, too."

"Why are you talking about me?" demanded Robby.

"We have to find you a school," said Lizzie.

"Do I get a vote?"

"Of course you do," said Joe.

"It didn't sound like it."

"No," said Lizzie, "we were just thinking out loud."

"Just so it's not Uni High."

"No," she said, "not Uni High."

"Which means going away," said Joe. "Somewhere."

"Tommy's brother's at Harvard Military."

Joe and Lizzie exchanged a glance, which Robby instantly understood.

"What's wrong with military school?" he asked.

"Nothing," said Joe.

"As if I didn't know."

"There are other options," said Lizzie.

He turned to leave. "Be sure and let me know."

CHAPTER 36

They agreed to meet at Jack's at the Beach and hash it out. They'd been sitting on the estate money like Mother Goose on her precious eggs. So far, the only ones getting any use from it were Nelly and her dance studio and the bankers, whose fees kept climbing, though neither sister was clear about what they did to earn them.

The marine layer had hung around longer than usual that morning, but by the time Lizzie threw on a skirt and sweater, picked out a beige scarf and set out down Wilshire the sky was a brilliant blue. Joe was at Culver Studios for the day, Robby away at boarding school, it was her day off and she was looking forward to lunch with her sister. They talked on the phone more than they saw each other, though they tried to get together with husbands every few weeks, usually in the bar at the Westport. Despite their differences, Terry and Joe were amiable men who enjoyed each other's company. They spoke in a kind of male code that used little nods and frowns more than actual words. Joe was deeply political but kept his views in his writing. Terry was apolitical. Didn't matter that one was a war ace and the other a pacifist. So they drank and smoked and kidded each other and talked about old times and basked in the good fortune of being married to talented and attractive sisters who were suddenly rich. Life could be worse.

Lizzie was waiting when Maggie handed the keys of her silver Porsche to an eager valet at Jack's and started up the steps. Beneath them, waves sloshed against pylons sunk deep in the Ocean Park sand. Farther out on the pier, they heard the swoosh of the roller-coaster.

Lizzie watched her coming. "Silk, n'est-ce pas? You look gorgeous."

She wore a jade silk blouse over cream slacks and a Hermès scarf in turquoise and beige showing a Paris bistro. She'd let her dark hair grow out into a medium updo. No jewelry, just a Rolex. To their mother's chagrin, the sisters had never cared for jewelry. Maggie's diamond ring from Arnaud stayed in its box. Lizzie felt almost disheveled next to her elegant sister.

"You tend to overdo things when you get out of a jumpsuit."

With wrap-around windows looking out across Santa Monica Bay, Jack's was as popular for lunch as for dinner and already nearly filled. Lizzie knew a little cove above Paradise Cove beyond Malibu and searched the horizon as they were led to a window table. Joe was not a beach guy, but enjoyed the isolation of the cove. They would park a mile or so back, trek across sand and ice plant and down a steep hill to the water. They'd never run into anyone. Joe would take out his notebook while Lizzie sunned and swam. The cove was her day off.

The waiter, whose platinum blond hair and Indian skin showed he was a surfer, offered menus and filled water glasses.

"What if we ordered a half bottle of some nice little white wine," said Maggie. "I'm not flying today."

"I recommend a Sonoma Sauvignon blanc, '56, in half bottles," he said, staring at Maggie. "Slightly chilled. Perfect with the abalone, which is fresh today."

"I'll have the abalone," said Lizzie, closing the menu.

"Sautéed," he said, "fresh from Catalina. Might have caught it myself. Comes with a light oyster-ginger sauce."

"Since you caught it yourself, make it two," said Maggie, smiling nicely for the young man. "And green salads."

"And so how is everything?" Maggie asked when they were alone.

"You've heard we have a new boss."

"On the front page, how could I miss it—the golden boy, the dauphin."

"Otis has been well brought up. Extremely polite. Scared to death of his mother."

"So Mother will be running the paper."

"As if she hadn't been."

The waiter poured the wine. Maggie raised her glass. "Here's to Otis."

They clinked. Maggie smiled, happy she'd come, happy to be alone with her sister, happy to be out of overalls and jumpsuits and jeans and feeling elegant again. It didn't happen often. "I gather we're here to discuss business. So what's on your mind?"

"Money. Do you know that except for Robby's school, which the bank handles directly, we've not touched one cent of the estate. Joe thinks there's something evil about it."

Maggie smiled. "Does he know how Dad made it?"

"Do *we* know how Dad made it?"

"Oil and real estate."

She laughed. "And . . . and . . .?"

"We don't talk about the other stuff. We haven't touched it either. I wouldn't know what to do with it. Terry has no interest in money, just planes."

"Anyway, here's what I've been thinking. It's silly to leave all this money sitting in the bank. We have husbands who don't want it and children who don't need it. So what if we set up a foundation?"

"What's a foundation?"

"Like Rockefeller, Ford, Carnegie—foundations that give money for good causes."

"Oh, come on . . . Dad was never in that league."

"I wouldn't be so sure. Together, we have about $40 million—and that's before the Venice sale."

"Do foundations even exist out here?"

"In San Francisco they do, where all the gold rush money settled. People in Los Angeles like to hold on to their money. Like Dad. We might be the first."

"A foundation to do what?"

"That's what we're here to discuss."

The waiter dropped off salads and French bread. Starting away, he spun back to Maggie. "Excuse me, I have to ask: Are you a stewardess?"

Lizzie smiled. Maggie fought an impulse to tousle his pretty blond hair. "Now what makes you think that?"

"I heard you say you weren't flying today."

They burst out laughing.

The waiter's tan darkened a notch. "Did I say something funny?"

"Dear boy," said Maggie, "did anyone ever tell you that you are darling? Now bring us that abalone before I do something I shouldn't."

"You're such a flirt," Lizzie said when he was gone.

"Stewardess? Might be fun, no? Maybe Howard can get me a job at TWA, which he owns. Cute red dresses and little hats with feathers. Paris with long layovers. Pilots who look like our waiter. Anyway, back to business. You've been thinking a while about this foundation thing, haven't you?"

Lizzie was looking across the bay, letting her eyes run up into the Malibu hills. "I have a question for you: Have you ever heard of May Rindge?"

"I read your story."

"It was Joe's idea to do something on the dowager queen

of Malibu, the little lady who put up fences and hired goons on horseback to keep people off *her* beaches and out of *her* ocean. It was hers, damn it, bought by her dead husband from some Mexican back in the good old days and she wasn't going to share it. Took the US Supreme Court to stop her."

"Good story."

"Anyway, Larry had to get approval from Otis himself to run that. The Chandlers own land from here to Owens Lake and don't like the idea that some court—even a supreme one—might tell them what to do with it. Otis doesn't mind so much."

The platinum waiter returned with their main course, the strange Pacific mollusks whose fleshy feet can be pounded until tender as chicken breasts and whose taste is to chicken as caviar to carp. Fingerling potatoes and parsley were on the side, along with oyster-ginger sauce in little bowls. He smiled down on them. "You can't get abalone like this anywhere but Jack's, though I do know a special place in Avalon if you ever go over."

"Let's get the name of the place," Lizzie said when he'd left. "Might be fun to go to Catalina. I imagine Terry knows how to sail?"

"Terry can navigate anything."

"And Joe almost nothing, including cars. Took the trolley when we had one. Now walks."

"Safer."

"Still hates the *Times*. Thinks the Chandlers are part of the problem."

"And Otis?"

"Nobody knows what he'll do. He wouldn't just be taking on the establishment; he'd be taking on his own family, the family that didn't want him, that wanted Phillip, Norman's brother, the John Bircher. Mom got him the job."

"Which is why he's afraid of her."

"The only person not afraid of Buff Chandler is Miss Adelaide." She sipped her wine. "Anyway, back to May Rindge. After the Supreme Court ruling, the county started building roads over the Malibu mountains to the Valley and the state started the coast road to Ventura. Poor May became depressed and insolvent and started selling off her land."

"What does any of this have to do with a foundation?"

"Because the people buying beach land today, up and down the coast from Mexico to Monterey and farther north for all I know, are a lot of little May Rindges. They build fences and hire guards to keep people off *their* land, off *their* beaches and out of *their* ocean."

"They can do that?"

"Joe and I go up to this place past Paradise Cove, beyond Malibu. You trek over hills and down a steep drop to the beach. Golden sand, maybe twenty-five yards across, hidden on both sides by hills. The ocean laps in soft and blue and almost warm. Like a little atoll in mid-Pacific. We've never run into a soul; it's like we discovered it."

"And?"

"Should someone have the right to ride down on a horse and tell us it's theirs and we're trespassing and to get the hell off their beach and out of their ocean? That's what May Rindge's goons were doing."

They'd finished their lunch and hadn't noticed the waiter standing behind them. "Nobody asked me," he said, "but I'd say the answer is no."

"Bravo," said Lizzie. "A supporter."

"You two are sisters, aren't you?"

"You have a good eye, honey," said Maggie. "Most people don't see it."

"I do have a good eye," he said, smiling, looking from one to the other. "Now what if I bring you some dessert and coffee?"

"Just coffee," said Maggie. "No desserts. And write down the name of the special place in Avalon. We may be going over."

"Nobody can own the ocean," said Lizzie when he'd left. "And if you can't own the ocean, how can you own the beach that gives access to it?"

"But the Supreme Court *stopped* May Rindge."

"Because the state and county needed to build roads. It was a legal taking, said the court, in the public interest, fairly compensated. What's happening now is people trying to shut off public access to the beaches and ocean in their private interest. It's insane, but it's legal. My idea is to create a foundation that buys up coastal land for a public trust, like a state park. Make sure the beaches stay open to everyone, forever."

"We have enough money to do that?"

"Why wouldn't others join in? The Sierra Club, for instance. Their job is to protect natural resources. Why do you think Cal wants that letter from Hughes? To make sure the Hughes's land never turns into a slab of concrete stretching to the beaches."

"Have you talked to Cal?"

"He thinks the money could be used to sponsor a campaign for a state constitutional amendment that permanently protects the entire coastline."

"Would he be involved in the foundation?"

"He wanted to hear what you had to say first."

"I love the idea of the three of us doing something. Preserve the stables. You know, I go riding some mornings, still love the feeling of sitting on a horse, letting that big beast under me stretch out. They still have a horse called Dynamite, though it's not my Dynamite."

"Speed is your thing. Funny, isn't it? Speed makes me nauseous." She hesitated a moment. "You know, speaking of

Cousin Cal. The last time I talked to him he was meeting Sister Angie for dinner."

"For dinner . . ."

"That's what he said."

"It's the way you said it."

"I don't think it was the first time."

"You don't?"

"No, I don't."

They fell silent, both women staring out over the cobalt blue bay toward the green mountains in the distance, lost in their own thoughts.

"You know, I asked Cal once if he'd ever been in love. We were in Paris. He was trying to talk me out of marrying Arnaud."

"And . . ."

"He wouldn't answer. I wonder what he'd say now."

The waiter was back. He put down a stub of paper with an Avalon address on it. "I'm not eavesdropping, but I'll tell you this: You do what you're talking about and I'll bring a hundred friends to work with you."

Maggie pushed the paper back to him. "Write your name and number down."

Lizzie watched her sister drop the paper into her purse when he was gone. She was smiling.

Maggie looked up. "What's so funny?"

"I'm not sure I trust you with that boy's number."

CHAPTER 37

"Page Terry before you go, Clara," Maggie called out to the receptionist who was getting ready to leave. "He's probably in hangar three. Have him call me." She stood, hands on hips, looking out over the airfield toward the sinking sun over the Ballona marshes. She saw a flock of birds rise up and head off over the oil derricks toward the ocean. Godwits? No, terns. She was getting to know the birds. The office line buzzed.

"Howard just called," she told him. "He wants me ASAP. I want you to come."

"See you about what?"

"He wouldn't say. Just 'Maggie get on over here.'"

"Over where?"

"He's at the Flamingo."

"I'm supposed to be leaving for Tucson."

"Vegas is on the way. Get Dieter to bring out an Electra. You can go on to Tucson after we see what he wants."

"Vegas is north and Tucson is south."

"Right, but they're both east."

"Now?"

"You know Howard."

"We won't be in Vegas before ten o'clock."

"So. When did Howard ever keep normal hours?"

Coming in from the southwest shortly after ten, they spied the lighted Flamingo tower beyond McCarran Field. Far beyond the Flamingo, the lights of the city twinkled against a dark sky. There was not much to Las Vegas, but the gamble of opening its first resort hotel five miles from downtown had paid off for Bugsy Siegel. The Flamingo was a smash from the beginning.

"I'd hate to come in from the north in fog and run into that tower," said Terry.

"The sky is always clear in Las Vegas."

"Except for dust storms."

"They come from the north so from the south you'd be landing into them."

"Smart girl."

They left flight suits on the plane and walked through an empty airport to a waiting car. Five minutes later they were crossing the busy Flamingo lobby to the front desk.

"Mr. Hughes is expecting you," said the night manager, eying Terry, "though the reservation is for one. I guess it's okay. Suite 1400. The boy will take your bags directly to your room, room 209. Here are your keys. This gentleman will accompany you."

The gentleman, in white shirt and skinny black tie, grunted, and they followed him down long empty corridors that looked too much like the airport they'd just left.

Anointed the world's richest man by *Time* magazine, Howard Hughes lived everywhere and nowhere. He kept in touch by phone when he wanted, but don't try to call him. He hadn't been seen at Hughes Aircraft since a dispute with the IRS prompted him to split Hughes Aircraft off from Hughes Tool, the cash cow his father had left him, and form something called Howard Hughes Medical Institute. HHMI was a neat way of avoiding taxes. He didn't pay his Mormon lawyers for nothing. He liked Mormon neatness.

He'd opened a plant in Tucson, offices in Miami and flew his own Lockheed Electra everywhere he went. He kept rooms at the Flamingo and Desert Inn and when in Los Angeles rented houses in Santa Monica, Bel Air, and Beverly Hills from Hollywood friends. His latest film, *The French Line,* was universally regarded as a disaster, even by its star, Jane Russell. They said his luck in Hollywood was running out, but Hughes had other ideas.

Two more gentlemen in LDS uniform of white shirt, dark pants and skinny tie, were stationed outside Suite 1400. A knock, an opening, an identification and the chain was lifted.

"Like old speakeasy days," Maggie whispered to Terry.

"You're too young to know about that."

"Learned from my dad."

The gentleman inside the room looked more respectable, at least wore a jacket. "I'm Bill Schmidt," he said, pointing across the room toward open French doors that looked out onto lighted palms, lawn, and cactus. In the distance they heard noises from a pool. Beyond the window lurked the shadow of what would be another gentleman.

Hughes sat by the French doors in a leather Eames chair with ottoman. Approaching, she saw he wore beige slacks, an open shirt with a Billy Eckstine collar and apparently didn't shave anymore. He had his feet up and was watching a television movie with the sound off. He bore little resemblance to the man she'd dated during the war, looked changed even from the last time she'd seen him at Hughes Aircraft, whenever that was. Plane crashes, loss of hearing, acute mysophobia and advancing syphilis were taking their toll.

She noticed grotesquely long fingernails and felt a chill, as if entering some kind of quarantine sanctum. He looked up, frowned and did not stand.

"What the hell are you doing here, Terry? You're supposed to be in Tucson."

"I asked him to come, Howard."

"Well, he can just go on to Tucson. This doesn't concern him."

"What doesn't concern him?"

"Bye-bye, Terry."

"What, *now*?"

"Why not? Your Electra's equipped for night flying, isn't she? I invented that system myself. Fuel up and you'll be there in two hours. They start testing the new radar units tomorrow morning. *I want you there.* Hell, you should already be there."

Terry stared silently, then turned to Maggie. "I'll call you in the morning."

"Call me, too," said Hughes. "I want a full report."

"Jesus, Howard," she said when he was gone. "What's gotten into you? What's one more day matter? Why am I here?"

He looked to Bill Schmidt who was still standing by the door. "You want anything, Maggie? Probably haven't eaten. How about a sandwich?"

"How about a sandwich for Terry before he leaves?"

"Terry can get his own sandwich. Restaurant never closes. Sit down, Maggie, in the chair where I can see you. You look good. Terry taking good care of you?"

She was more than a little tired and vastly annoyed. She hadn't liked flying to Vegas at night and didn't like Terry flying past midnight to Tucson. The Hughes night-flying system was still new. She didn't like jumping when Howard snapped his fingers, when any man snapped his fingers. She thought he looked cadaverous and wanted to find out what he wanted and get the hell out of that room. She wondered how she was supposed to get back to Los Angeles.

"We're fine, Howard. Now what's on your mind?"

He motioned to Schmidt. "Bring the folder on my desk, Schmitty. Then you can leave. Tell the others to leave. Lock the door to the garden."

She didn't like it. She felt better with the goons hanging around.

"Maybe I will eat something. Could your friend phone for a chicken salad sandwich and a beer for room 209?"

He glanced at Hughes.

"Have it sent here, Schmitty. Wait till it comes. We're going to be here a while."

"Doing what?"

"That depends on you."

"Howard, you're crazy."

"Not entirely." He took the folder Schmidt handed him. He smiled for her. "Have a look."

There it was, the letter Cal had asked for on official stationery of the Hughes Tool Company. She read slowly, taking her time with each sentence, each paragraph. It was clear enough, though she wondered what possible legal value it would have. The places for dates and signatures were blank.

I, Howard Robard Hughes, sound of mind and body on this date as witnessed by the under-signed, do stipulate that pursuant to the contract signed between Hughes Tool Company and executors of the former Mull Oil Company, that the following is my intention:

That the land now occupied by Hughes Aircraft Company, a newly created subsidiary of the Howard Hughes Medical Institute, shall remain part of Hughes Aircraft Company in my lifetime. The land in question, located in the city of Los Angeles, is bounded by Lincoln and Jefferson Boulevards, Centinela Avenue and the Loyola bluffs.

That in the event of my death or incapacity and the

sale of the aforementioned land, the new owners will make all necessary efforts to maintain it as an airfield.

That if for some future reason an airfield is no longer practical on the designated land, that it shall be returned to its original state as part of the Ballona wetlands and so maintained.

That the land between Lincoln Boulevard and Falmouth Avenue, bounded by Culver Boulevard and the Playa del Rey bluffs, owned by Hughes Aircraft Company pursuant to the aforementioned contract with the executors of the former Mull Oil Company, land which is at this time undeveloped, shall remain in its present state.

"That good enough?" Howard asked.

"To my un-lawyerly mind it looks like what we wanted. When is it to be signed?"

"When I'm back in L.A."

"Which is when?"

"I don't know. My lawyers tell me it's not legally binding, but they still hate it." He paused a moment and looked across the room. "Don't you, Schmitty?"

Schmidt, moving silently around the room, stared back, but did not respond.

"My Mormon minders," said Hughes. "Never happy. Happiness is for the next life. They're going to get me to the next life, did I tell you? Got their own planet. Schmitty can get me there even if I don't want to go, which I don't. Baptism of the dead they call it, and you can't do a damn thing about it because you're already dead."

Maggie looked at the man she'd taken for a bodyguard. A lawyer factotum. She wondered how much Howard paid him to be humiliated. She heard a knock, and Schmidt admitted a waiter, directing him to the table by Maggie's chair. Hughes nodded and Schmidt left with the waiter. The door clicked. The French doors were closed and the shadow gone.

She began eating, uncomfortable under the scrutinizing eye of her former lover and present employer. It was a long time since they'd dated, and this was not the same man. *That* Howard had liked restaurants and company and people buzzing around and a photographer or two so he could see his picture in the papers the next day with the sexiest Hollywood girl available. He'd been with so many of them—Hepburn, Russell, Peters, Crawford, Gardner, Sheridan, Rogers, Tierney, Davis, Fontaine, her sister de Havilland. Sisters, Maggie thought, how strange. Why would sisters want to do it? Lizzie certainly wouldn't.

This was a creature she didn't know. The man she'd dated didn't need a flying squadron of Mormon lawyer/goons to protect him. That man was attractive and sexy and, yes, fun. This man was a mess. The fingernails alarmed her, and she was not easily alarmed. Why would a man as fastidious as Howard Hughes let his nails grow like that? She was aware of his stare as she wolfed down her sandwich. She hadn't realized how hungry she was. She chug-a-lugged the beer and wanted nothing more than to get up and get out.

"Don't see much of you anymore, Maggie."

"Well, drop around sometime. I work at Hughes Aircraft."

It was the same laugh, deep and genuine, a bit of a surprise to people who judged him by the slightly cynical smirk that was the natural set of his face.

"I wish I could. The TWA business is eating away at me. It's the bankers, goddamn it. *Time* calls me the world's richest man, and the goddamn bankers put a lien on my airline before they'll lend me enough to buy a few Convairs. Now why would the world's richest man need a bank loan to buy planes?"

Again he laughed.

"I have to go, Howard. It's been a long day."

"Live in the moment, my dear." He tried a smile. "Why don't you stay here tonight?"

"I am staying here tonight."

"I mean with me."

She knew it would come to that, but still it astounded her. It didn't shock her; she knew Howard too well to be shocked, but it astounded her, yes. Some things shouldn't have to be said. Terry Heyward was his friend. Moreover, what woman would get in bed with something like this? Be shredded by those claws?

"I'm married, Howard."

"What the hell does that have to do with anything?"

"Maybe nothing for you. For me, for women, it's different."

"For *women*? Christ, I haven't dated a single woman since I met you in Washington. I never heard any protests."

She wanted to say that maybe that was before he grew vampire fingernails, caught syphilis and traveled with a gang of lawyer/goons. Instead, she stood up. He stood, too, a little shakily, she thought, and came over and put his hands on her shoulders. She still wore a heavy flying shirt and so couldn't feel the fingernails, but was aware of them.

"Why don't you get into something more comfortable? Let me show you the ladies' bedroom—every kind of nightgown and robe you can imagine."

"Sorry, Howard, not tonight. I don't want to ruin the good memories."

Later, she couldn't tell what time it was. With the inch-thick black curtains, it could have been 3 a.m. or 8 a.m. or noon or anything, but she was still dead tired so too much time could not have passed. A telephone was ringing and after a while she knew it wasn't a dream and reached for it but couldn't find it, couldn't even find the lamp if there was one, had no recollection of where she was or why but the ringing kept on.

Half asleep, groping in the dark, she knocked the phone off the bedside table and couldn't get the lamp turned on and got down on her knees beside the bed and eventually located the receiver.

It was Howard.

"What the hell do you want, Howard?"

"Terry," he said.

"Terry what?"

"Terry's down. They're looking for him."

She understood immediately. Pilots don't need more than that.

"I'm sorry, Maggie, I'm truly sorry. Mount Lemmon, coming into Tucson, lost contact. No idea why he was over Mount Lemmon. Shouldn't have been. They're up there looking."

She dropped the receiver. She had no idea how long she stayed like that. On the floor, in the dark, leaning against the bed, the receiver voice squawking until a horrible buzzing started that might have been in her head. Why had she insisted that he come?

CHAPTER 38

Joe called Lizzie with the news. She was in Chicago covering the trial of "The Great Transportation Conspiracy," as the newspapers called it. The carmakers' scheme to destroy electric rail had started in Galesburg, and nearby Chicago is where the justice department chose to conduct the trial, which was already into the second month. She'd been home twice so far, catching the Super Chief each time to spend two days with Joe in the garden. She was due home again a day before the funeral, but Joe decided not to wait to inform her.

"Maggie would have called," he said, "but she's still in Tucson. She's coming back today with the remains."

Lizzie didn't answer right away. She sat with the phone in her hand thinking of her sister and how sad it was: two husbands, two airplane crashes, two deaths. She'd been blue anyway from too many days in courtrooms, nights alone in hotels, meals in diners. Terry's death stunned her.

"The remains," she whispered. "That's what we are when we're dead."

"If we're lucky."

"I'll be on the train tonight. At least it's the weekend."

"I'm glad you prefer trains. When's this trial going to be over?"

"Who knows? So many indictments, so many lawyers—GM, Firestone, Standard Oil, Greyhound, Mack, on and on, and they all have to tell the judge that they really didn't know what was going on, and anyway what's done is done, and the new buses are so nice and gasoline is cheap and so let's move on, etc., etc.

And then the lawyers from a dozen cities argue that costs run into the tens of millions and somebody is responsible and somebody has to pay and somebody has to go to jail. Thank heaven Fred Barrett's back here to keep things focused on Pacific Electric. His records are meticulous. The judge understands that the damage done to Los Angeles dwarfs everything else."

◆ ◆ ◆

The services were in the Wadsworth Chapel on the V.A. campus off Wilshire, about which Terry surely would have had mixed feelings. He was not religious but kept in touch with many of his wartime buddies through the V.A. His health was good, but he was a regular for checkups at Wadsworth and always walked the grounds looking for the few guys left who'd flown with him in the Pacific.

The chapel is a white shingle Victorian from the turn of the century, one side for Protestants, one for Catholics. Other denominations get to choose. Terry wouldn't have cared. The grounds are neat and verdant, and it's as good a place as any to spend your last hours above ground, dead or alive. Lizzie and Joe could walk over. Robby's old pre-school co-op was just over the hill. Burial was to be down Wilshire in Westwood Village Cemetery; it was pricier than the V.A., but Maggie thought Terry deserved more than a white stone.

Arriving home alone in Playa del Rey after flying in from Tucson with the casket, she'd finally let go. She'd held it in for three days, showing no weakness in public. But stepping into the house—*his* house—was too much. She mixed a drink and went out into the patio as they'd done so often. The marine layer was in early that evening, spreading sea air and stillness like a blanket over the hill. Looking out over the calm Pacific, the center of Terry's life, suddenly the tears came, psychic tears, the kind that start when the plug is finally pulled. They'd been building for days, couldn't get out, and suddenly burst the dam. They tumbled down her face onto her blouse like the horrible days in Paris. She was the crier, had always been the crier, and she'd wondered at it. Her stoical sister could get through anything with dry eyes, but Maggie held them in until she couldn't bear it anymore.

◆ ◆ ◆

He was a popular guy, and with friends from Hughes and the beach club and his V.A. war buddies they would fill the Protestant side. The pastor, the Rev. Browne, did not know Terry or Maggie, but that's the way it is at the V.A. She'd given the pastor a few pages of notes, and he had a kindly, preacherly way about him when they met that made her feel better and think maybe a little more church would do her good. She'd talk to Nelly and Didi about that. It couldn't hurt them either.

Arriving early, she walked the chapel, grateful for the solitude. The casket was closed. She knew how little was in it. She'd been with them when they reached the plane. The flowers were at least half from Hughes, who was not coming, to her great relief. Hymnals and prayer books in place, the organ ready, nothing to do, she went outside to wait. The sweet fragrance of flowers, mostly gardenias, came out the door to mix with the fresh smell of grass and touch of sea air drifting in from the bay. Cal, coming up the steps, gave her a big hug, and they stood alone for a minute, each one alone with memories. She was crying again. How many tears for how many warriors from how many battles had been shed on these chapel steps?

"Thanks for coming," she said, stupidly.

"There's Lizzie and Joe crossing the grass," he said, waving.

Surrounded by family, she felt better. "I thought you might not come alone."

"Angie?"

"You're seeing her."

"I'm staying with her for a while."

Up the hill, men were coming out of the vet's home and starting down toward the chapel. A few nurses pushing wheel-chairs were the only women in view. If the men had women they wouldn't be in the home, would they?

"Staying with her?"

"Her ex is out of prison."

Maggie stared. "And . . . ?"

"It's better this way."

"I thought they turned down his parole."

"They did. Twice. He served his full sentence."

Her mind went to Willie. "I hope you know what you're doing."

"Till it blows over."

She'd asked Nelly and Didi to come early, but saw no sign of them. Lizzie had invited her to stay with them in Brentwood, stay as long as she liked in Robby's empty room. She declined. Better at home, get over it sooner, go riding mornings, walk on the beach. She needed to be alone. Anyway, Lizzie was return-ing to Chicago the next day.

The chapel was filling when the long black sedan started slowly up the incline from Wilshire. She was annoyed. She'd specifically asked that the hearse not arrive until after the ser-vice began. She wanted a celebratory service, not a morbid one. She'd asked the pastor for uplifting passages. But it wasn't the hearse, it was Nelly's black Buick with Ralph at the wheel. She watched as the car stopped and Ralph dashed around to open the door, first for her mother, then her daughter.

They came up the path, Didi nearly as tall as her grandmother. Nelly was dressed suitably for a Santa Monica funeral, which is to say you knew they were mourning clothes but someplace else they might pass for something else, the chiffon dress not quite black enough and maybe a little too airy, a little too short. Her mother always had nice legs. Didi wore subdued gray, a clingy wool dress Maggie had not seen before. She was a pretty girl already with signs of a figure. They looked like mother and daughter, and Maggie felt a surge of affection for them both. They kissed, Maggie holding her daughter close for a moment, feeling the sprouting body before Didi pulled away. She had an odd look on her face, not so much mournful as sullen. Maggie had seen the dismay on her face when she'd told her. She'd called Nelly on the phone from Tucson, but told her not to say anything, that she'd come over to tell Didi in person. Come at teatime, said Nelly, and I'll have Iris bake a cake.

They'd sat in the living room with Didi still in her navy Westlake skirt and white polo. Tea and cake were set out on the low table by the sofa. Nelly served. Didi sensed that her mother did not have good news. It was hard. Maggie saw shock when she told her. The girl's head sagged. Was it anger? No tears, just a little choking sound, and she got up and went to her room, Lizzie's room. "Keeps things in," Nelly said. "Good student, her teachers say, but shy. Not popular, but then you weren't either, were you? Not with girls, you weren't. I don't know where it comes from, certainly not my side of the family. Dr. Lambert says she's acrophobic." Dr. Lambert went back with the family a long way, all the way to Santa Monica Hospital.

"*Acrophobic*—with two pilots as parents. Is that possible?"

"Well, where did your daredevil side come from? Certainly

not from me or your father. Or Lizzie's literary side for that matter."

Maybe it hadn't been anger on Didi's face, but blame: blaming them for flying, blaming them for leaving her alone, for sending her away.

But she'd wanted to go to Bel Air!

"Front pew right," she whispered to Nelly and turned to watch them disappear inside, walking slowly, erect, looking straight ahead. The pastor had already gone in. Lizzie, Joe, and Cal followed. She greeted one more guest, and that was it. She stood alone, looking out toward Westwood, back toward Wilshire.

How many times had they passed this place on their way to the beach? She felt the rush of life swirling past. Already past forty and yet still the girl screaming into the wind from the back seat of the Chrysler as Nelly made the turn down toward Rustic Canyon, always too slowly, always too cautiously. How can life slip away so fast while things like the chapel remain constant? As a girl she'd wondered about this building, the pretty white-clapboard chapel with steeples and cornices and balustrades, none of which fit with the rest of the grounds, like dropped into Westwood from New England by accident. So many years, so many deaths.

Lizzie was still with her, thank God, dear Lizzie, so steady, so clever. She'd been in the back seat of that Chrysler, too, observing her mad sister shouting into the wind, never joining in but never critical, quietly enjoying all that life had to give. She'd come today in a navy frock that she'd probably worn to a dozen funerals for the *Times*—go home and put it in its plastic bag until the next person died, whoever it was. Maggie watched them go down the aisle, Joe taking her arm, Joe who had so much more than he showed, keeping it in so he could pour it into his writing. Joe would miss Terry. Who would have thought Lizzie could make such a good marriage with a pudgy, bald socialist? First marriages are for glamor; second marriages are the real ones, the ones for children, however the children turn out. Behind Joe, Cal walked alone. Living with the woman whose husband killed his father.

The hearse was waiting when they came out, sinister black death vehicle followed by two V.A. buses and a few cars, Ralph's Buick at the front. Six men of varying ages and physiques carried the casket, two from Hughes, two from the beach club, two from the V.A. The gathering broke up, some people joining the cortege, some apologizing that they couldn't make the burial or the repass in Bel Air. She understood. Some of the vets could barely walk. Some couldn't walk at all. Many had sent regrets.

The Buick was specially made, heaven knows where Nelly had found it, not at all like Eddie's old Buick. It had gray velveteen seats, a roll-up window between the front and back and ample room for three in the rear. It was the first time Maggie had been in it. Nelly quickly pointed out that the window was never rolled up. Ralph was part of the family.

"What did you think of the service, honey?" Maggie asked her daughter as Ralph followed the hearse down to Wilshire. Motorcycle policemen were stationed at each end of the cortege to keep cars together. In the chapel, the casket had remained closed. He'd flown right into the mountain. The control tower said they'd lost contact; that he shouldn't have been over Mount Lemmon but coming down the Highway 10 corridor. There'd been a storm and he'd strayed off course. So much for the Hughes night flying system. She'd watched her daughter standing by the casket, her lips moving like she had things she wanted to clear up with Daddy while there was still time. Maggie felt tears, but Didi's eyes stayed dry.

"I don't want to go to any more funerals," she said as the Buick turned off Wilshire toward the cemetery.

"Ah," said Nelly, "that is a wish I share with you completely."

"The funeral is not quite over," said Maggie. "Now comes the hardest part."

"Do we have to?" asked the girl.

The thought of bringing Didi back to Playa del Rey had passed Maggie's mind, but it wouldn't happen, couldn't happen. She would remain alone. Didi was happy with Nelly, grandmother substituting for mother. Why interfere?

"Life is full of things we have to do, sweetie," said Nelly.

"Why?"

Maggie turned to look at her daughter, pretty, vulnerable, something of Terry's solid build in her, not as fragile in appearance as in character. Different from the rest of us, she thought, with an odd sort of emotional lethargy. Where did it come from? No one else in the family had anything like it.

"Duty," Maggie said.

"To whom?" asked the girl, who at least had the grammar right.

CHAPTER 39

He bought a .38 Colt Detective Special and took it to an indoor pistol range on Sixth Street to learn how to fire it. Along with most able-bodied men born in 1910, he'd been to war but never learned how to fire a pistol. A rifle, yes, the M-1 that every infantryman learned to handle, but a pistol was something new in his hand. The gun shop on Pico sold him on the Colt after asking what he wanted it for. Dangerous neighborhood, he said. The salesman, looking at the Los Feliz address on the application, knew it wasn't true but wasn't going to argue the point. He pulled out the snubby Detective Special, let Cal turn it over in his hand a few times and made the sale. No good for long range, he said, but for household protection it was the best. Up close, you can't miss. Can't miss *what* was left unsaid. It was a strange conversation, but Cal supposed not really that different from buying a car or a hat. "What are you looking for, sir?" they ask. There are different cars for cross country and tooling around town; different hats for rain, sun, snow, show; different pistols for firing ranges or shooting someone up close in the heart, as Henry Callender had done.

She'd showed him the card Gil sent to the temple from San Francisco after they released him from Folsom:

> Been thinking about you, Angie baby.
> Been thinking about you for 15 years.
> See you soon.

Of course, it was unsigned. If he violated the restraining order he'd be back in Folsom. She took it to the police who said there was nothing they could do. After that she invited Cal to move in. They were still seeing each other, so why not? She was scared to death and didn't hide it. He bought the pistol without telling her, stashed it in the closet by the back door off the kitchen and moved into the upstairs bedroom next to her master bedroom. It was a nice arrangement. They saw each other when they wanted, and went their own ways the rest of the time. She had new locks put on every door and thought of fencing the property but no fence would keep out killer or coyote that wanted in bad enough. Pines and slopes on both sides made fencing impractical. She thought of getting a dog but didn't like barking dogs.

All that was six months ago, and she'd never heard from him again, evidence perhaps that the restraining order was working despite what he'd written. Cal gave up his apartment at Echo Lake. Los Feliz was only ten minutes further from his office. The temple and the Richfield Building were on the same bus line and sometimes they rode together. The G.M. buses were a poor excuse for the Glendale-Burbank trolley with its own right-of-way—which his father had taken years before to visit the same woman—but the trolley was gone.

Angie was a phenomenon. Nothing had been certain when she took over from Willie. Her position was provisional for the board and its chairman, Eddie Mull, but not for the Soldiers, who wanted her and no one else. After Eddie was gone, the Los Angeles establishment, which hated notoriety, still opposed her for a while—just as it had opposed Willie until it saw he was good for downtown business. None of it turned out to matter. Sister Angie had become a postwar symbol for women who'd stepped into new roles during the war and had no intention of giving them up. Angie was too good a politician to hold a grudge, and with time the establishment came to accept her. Like Hollywood, the Temple of the Angels was a national institution, good for morale and good for business. Make your peace.

She left her robes at work. At home, she was all woman, barefoot on the carpet, bare legged on the couch, naked in bed. She loved quoting from the Song of Songs, that strange Old Testament book celebrating sexual love. Everything about the Song is a mystery, she told him: when it was written, where, by whom and how it ever got into the Bible. Blasphemous for Christians, it was a product of old Jerusalem, its origins closer to Egyptian love poems or Tantric sex hymns than anything in the Bible. In sermons and shows she never mentioned it, but knew it by heart and would recite it to excite him. Never did the subject of marriage come up between them. They didn't expect the arrangement to last forever. One day at a time while Gil was at large. People found out if they wanted that Calvin Mull was living with Sister Angie. It made sense if anyone thought about it: Sister Angie needed protection from a murderer who had vowed to kill her. Her protector was the son of the man he had murdered.

Gil l'Amoureux had gone to ground. After Folsom he'd gone to San Francisco for that's where he'd posted the card. From there he disappeared. Much later, in an interview with a *San Francisco Chronicle* reporter who visited him in San Quentin, he claimed he'd simply worked his way down the coast on derricks, boats and in the fields, the kind of jobs where no one asked about you or expected you to stay. If he ran out of money or slept with the wrong woman or got drunk or in fights or fired, he simply moved on down the coast a little farther, getting closer to Los Angeles as he went. He never sent another card, but as he got closer, he told the *Chronicle* man, his nose started twitching and that wasn't all. He hadn't used his real name when he got out of Folsom for it was too well known. As he got closer, he began to use it again. Let them wonder.

One evening found them, unusually, alone together in the dining room. Catalina, the Mexican housekeeper who lived in the cottage behind the rear patio, had made mole poblano and sopa de tortillas, and Cal opened a bottle of Spanish Rioja to go with it. Dinner with them was never formal, just something that happened if they both found themselves at home and Catalina had prepared something ahead of time. Cal, who now had a private law practice in addition to running the Sierra Club, often stayed out for dinner with clients, and the temple regularly scheduled evening events requiring Sister Angie's presence and kept its soup kitchen open until eight. Life on Lambeth Street was casual. The kitchen, which looked out onto the rear patio, was normally a busier place than the dining room, and it was more common to find one or the other in the kitchen munching tacos or enchiladas Catalina had stacked in the refrigerator than to find them together in the dining room with a bottle of wine.

It was a handsome room, with a lower ceiling than the salon because of the bedrooms above it. Dark heavy beams angled up to the vault at 45 degrees from both sides to connect with a longitudinal beam running the length of the room. The table, chairs, and sideboard were heavy California oak, and the floor of dark travertine tile. Leaded, arched windows gave onto the front patio. Evenings, curtains were always drawn. They never entertained together. Angie occasionally had Soldiers or benefactors for dinner, but Cal never joined them. They saw no point in advertising the arrangement.

They'd been talking about a legal case that was to take Cal into the San Bernardino Mountains the next day. Developers were seeking permits to build a ski resort near Palm Springs on Mount San Jacinto, a mountain sacred to the desert tribes, and Cal had been hired to represent the tribes in opposition to the permits. They hadn't had dinner together in a while but planned this one because it wasn't certain how long Cal was to be away.

"Three days at the most," he said. "In any case, I should be back before the weekend. Make our pleas, submit the files, see what the judge has in mind." He looked to see if she seemed at all bothered, but she was in good spirits. He would be sleeping in her bedroom that night. With time, Gil and his threats were fading. It had been more than a year since he was released. If he was coming, it figured he would have come already. The conversation was interrupted by buzzing from the kitchen intercom. Catalina was calling from the cottage, something she rarely did.

"I think I see someone in the patio looking into the kitchen," she said when he answered. "Maybe you check."

Slipping into the kitchen, he turned out the light and looked through the window. He saw nothing moving.

"What is it, Cal?" came the call from the dining room.

"Nothing," he called back. "Catalina wants something."

He took the .38 from the cabinet by the rear door, from the back of the highest shelf where neither woman could find it or reach it. He loaded it and walked out the rear door into the patio. Standing silently in the dark, he listened for sound, watched for movement. Yes, something was there. He couldn't see it, but sensed it, something pulsing, the nightlife too quiet. He stood dead still, hoping Angie would stay put so he could hear anything that moved. He spun the chamber, wanting it to be heard. Whether it was a housebreaker or a murderous ex-husband, he would be unlikely to carry a gun. Gil had needed only hands to kill Willie. He glanced up to the second floor of the cottage and saw the curtain fall back into place. Catalina had heard the gun clicking and that was enough for her. Had she really seen something? She'd said "someone," which would rule out critters, though the neighborhood was full of them, possums, skunks, raccoons, coyotes, and it was close to dinner time for night critters.

If it was a someone it was likely to be Gil. The man at the gun store was right: Los Feliz is a quiet neighborhood, nothing dangerous about it, not at all a good place for prowlers, too many dogs and children and comings and goings, patrol cars cruising Glendale and Los Feliz Boulevards. He stood motionless in the penumbra, the pistol pointed in front of him. If someone was in this patio he had to have entered from the slopes on either side of the house, not from the front, for the gates were locked. He saw Angie at the kitchen window, her silhouette clearly visible. More silence. Why no crickets? Bizarre.

Suddenly there was rustling and movement on the southern slope, twigs breaking, a shadow in the moonlight. He hadn't thought of a flashlight. He didn't move, and silence crept back in. He walked to the slope and saw footprints rising to the top. No animal. Someone was up there. More rustling and then the shadow was gone.

"I could ask for a postponement," he told her next morning as they were dressing, "ask the judge to reschedule." He'd already called the police, and they were sending a patrolman to investigate.

She finished brushing her hair. "And what would you tell him: that your girlfriend is jumpy? Is that good enough for a postponement?"

He smiled, but it wasn't funny. They were both jumpy, hadn't slept that well. "Maybe we can get them to put a watch on the house while I'm gone."

"Or I'll bring back one of the security men with me from the temple. For a couple of days, we'll manage."

"If it was Gil, he's risking a lot. They'll send him back to Folsom."

"Maybe you scared him off with your gun. At least I know where it is now. Why didn't you tell me?"

"Have you ever fired a gun?"

"What do you think?"

He went to her and took her in his arms, her small body reaching only to his shoulders. She shuddered, and he pulled her tight, kissing the top of her head. They stood for some time like that. "You won't need it. We'll get you all the protection you need. Three days at most and I'll be back." He lifted her head and kissed her.

CHAPTER 40

"Larry wants you," Phil MacPherson called across the news-room. "He's agitated. Better get in there."

She looked up and saw him waving his arms like a monkey in a glass cage, a sign that meant whomever you're talking to, hang up and get over here. Fast! As it happened, she was on the phone with someone she'd been trying to reach for days for comments about the federal court verdict in the great transpor-tation conspiracy. This better be good, she thought, hanging up, pulling down her skirt and starting toward McManus, fast but not too fast. She was in a bad mood, no question. The Chicago verdict sickened her.

He was standing. "Temple of the Angels," he said, brusquely. "Salazar is already there for photos. Verducci has gone from the hall of justice. Let them handle the details. The obituary is being updated. I want a full background story from you. Full! Get going."

"Sorry, Larry. You forgot to tell me what happened."

"I thought that's why you were on the phone. Someone got Sister Angie."

She waited for more, but that was it. She ran out, grabbed her purse and a notebook, decided a cab would be faster than a *Times* car and she wouldn't have to look for parking. She took the elevator down from the third floor, hailed a cruiser on Spring Street and told him to take the tunnel to Echo Park.

Someone got Sister Angie—what did he mean exactly?

"You don't want me to take Temple, lady, more direct?"

"Too much construction, take Second Street."

"To the park?"

"The Temple of the Angels."

"Ah."

He'd swung around and was heading west toward Second.

"You wouldn't be a reporter, would you?" He was looking at her in the rearview mirror, staring more at her than at the street. "I heard the news on the radio. Helluva thing. She was good for this town. Place will be mobbed. Might not be able to get you close."

He pushed a button, and they heard an excited voice on KHJ. Sister Angie attacked by her ex-husband, who apparently got into the building through the kitchen with vagrants having breakfast. The police had him in custody. Still no report on the condition of the victim.

Normally it was a ten-minute drive, except that with police action everything was slowed to a crawl. People in the streets. It wasn't a mob, but was getting close. Traffic barely moving. She tried to shut the KHJ reporter out and think for a minute, but was jolted back by the news flash: "KHJ has just learned that Sister Angie has been pronounced dead; I repeat: Sister Angie l'Amoureux, pastor of the Temple of the Angels, is dead."

She sank back into the worn leather seat and sighed. How ghastly. That poor woman. Why did they let him out? They knew he would try again. Suddenly she thought of Cal. Where was he? Richfield Building? Had he heard? How would he take it? No time for that now, had to focus on the task. The *Times* would run a murder story, an obituary, interviews, probably a sidebar on Gil. She was to do a full background story, which meant pulling everything into a narrative—*everything*. She'd worked for McManus long enough to know he'd expect twenty-five hundred words. She'd have to talk to Gil. Ugh. They'd have him downtown by now. No manslaughter this time; this time the gas chamber and he wouldn't even blink. She'd covered brutes like him before, men always ready to trade death for a good orgasm. She wondered how he had killed her. Strangled, like Uncle Willie? Traffic wasn't moving. At Glendale, people on the sidewalks had moved into the street and still more flowing out from the side streets as word spread around the city. She'd do better to get out and walk but decided to wait to see if traffic started moving again. She started back over events in her mind, back to the beginning:

Uncle Willie meets Angie in an ice cream parlor in Glendale. Before the war. Gil finds out so they flee to Mexico. Larry sends her and Luis to find them, but too late. Gil is waiting when they come back, kills Willie, rapes Angie. Gil threatens Angie at the trial. Angie steps in for Willie at the temple, becomes a symbol for women. Spousal rape becomes a crime, at least in California. The temple becomes bigger than ever. So does Sister Angie.

How much of it would be in the obituary? *Times* obituaries, dry, bloodless things done years in advance for important people. This is for your obituary, the reporter says, voice flat, usually on the phone. Really, am I dead? the subject asks. Ha ha. Always gets a nervous laugh. Reporter never joins in. Filed away and forgotten and pulled out when the big day comes. She'd worked on obits herself, the dead beat, it's called, though not on Angie's. She wondered why. She knew more about Angie than anyone else at the paper. Maybe that was it: they didn't think she'd be objective. Then why put her on this story? Because Larry didn't handle obituaries.

Suddenly she felt nauseous, inhaling fumes, wasting time in a taxi that wasn't moving. Momentary panic. How to do this? Why am I heading for the temple? What can I learn there? Cabbie staring at her in the rear mirror, waiting for traffic to move again, which it wasn't doing. Cal . . . the Richfield Building.

That's where I should be. She spied a phone booth, paid the driver with a nice tip, jumped out and made the call. He was watching the news, about to leave for the temple, voice shaky. Roads blocked, she said, you'll never make it. Wait for me.

"I have to get over there," were his first words when she walked into his office.

"Impossible," she said. "I already tried."

He was disheveled, jacket off, tie loosened, shirt wrinkled, pacing, restless, clearly lost. They stood a moment watching the television reporter. Cameras, reporters, police, a huge crowd pressing in on the closed-up building. They'd have to open doors before long. He turned it off and walked to the window from where he could see the antenna on top of the temple. "I failed her," he said, simply.

"You didn't fail her, Cal. You're not a bodyguard."

"Why exactly are you here," he said suddenly, anger in the voice, turning back from the window. "You're not planning on putting me in this, are you?"

"I've got until eight o'clock," she said, avoiding a direct answer, the old writers' conflict. "You knew Angie better than anyone."

"No," he said, the voice dry, empty, "I can't talk about any of that."

"No secrets, remember?"

"This is different. You're talking about publication."

"Yes."

"I can't . . ."

She headed him off.

"Because, Cal, people won't let go of a person like Sister Angie, let go as if she were, well, an ordinary person, like you or me. She left her mark. She changed things for women for-ever." She was floundering. "Help me, Cal, that's all I ask. What was it? What did she have? Where did it come from? Was it authentic?"

He stood there with his eyes closed. She was losing him.

"No secrets, you say," he said, at length, opening his eyes. "You're asking me, an agnostic, to comment on people of religion. Is that fair? Was it authentic? Are you trying to get me to tell you she was a hypocrite?"

"Cal, please!"

"Sorry, but this is hard."

Anger in the voice, so unusual. She'd never understood the relationship. Now she did.

She regrouped. "At this very moment there are thousands of people trying to get to the temple, millions watching and listening. Imagine what the funeral will be like! What was it? What was her magic? Why do they refuse to let her die? Help me."

Just get started, she thought, her mind turning, let it come out. Yes, Cal, it's hard, only don't let me down. She hadn't taken her notebook out. She didn't want him distracted. He stood framed in the window for some time, beautiful San Gabriel Mountains rising behind him, handsome face grieving, trying to hold it in. First his father, now his lover. What is he thinking? She didn't know him, not like she knew Maggie. Is that the way it has to be, women and men? Always protecting themselves. A good man, trying to do so much, maybe too much: advise his cousins, protect the environment, be a lawyer, be a godfather, good friend, always there. And love? Told Maggie he'd never been in love. But that was then. So strange. She thought of the line from *Wuthering Heights*: "Our souls are the same."

He moved away from the window and started pacing.

Now, Cal, now . . .

It came tumbling out. "She was so alive, so vibrant, someone you wanted to understand every way possible—spiritually, emotionally, physically. You wanted to draw her power into you. Do you think Dad wanted to ruin his life? He was bewitched. So were the millions who followed her when he was gone, after the trial, the thousands who came down the aisles every week to be healed, to be saved, to get down on their knees with her and pray. She changed things. Isn't that what we all try to do in our little way? She made lives better. She had the power. Don't ask me what it is or how it's done. Yes, it *was* a kind of magic. She lay near death for months—and then the message of Wrigley Field, and the trial where everyone opposed her—the law, the newspapers, the public, everyone but the Soldiers. And to turn it all around and become a national hero. The courage, the phenomenal courage!"

And you, she kept thinking. *And you?*

Gesturing as he walked, the words came flowing out non-stop, seeking to articulate something he'd never expressed before. It was coming too fast, and she took out her notebook. He didn't even notice.

"It worked on me like it worked on Dad, like it worked on everyone."

"Aren't you describing love?"

He stopped pacing and stared. A cloud passed, and it dawned on him he was talking of her in the past tense. Circuits in his mind were flashing: *Angie is dead! Angie is dead!* He turned away, back to the window, shook his head to be rid of it.

"Dad loved her. I saw the way he looked at her—and she at him. Of course it was love. A higher kind of love, physical, yes, but mixed with something most of us don't have. Mixed with God." Her eyebrows might have raised, but he was not looking. "People like that are believers. They attract other believers. They attracted each other. That's when their love began."

"Did *you* love her?"

She had to ask it. Another reporter might not have, but Cal was her brother.

He spun back to face her. "Love her! *Of course I did."* And then: "But not like Willie. That was impossible."

He stopped, trying to gather his thoughts.

"There was a physicality to her. There has to be, you know. Have you ever looked closely at religious figures, the ones we see in paintings and icons—the Virgin Mary, Jesus, John the Baptist? These are not unattractive people. Who knows if they really looked like that, but the people who make the paintings and icons know what they're doing. A homely woman could never have accomplished what Angie did. Her appeal was in the idea that God or nature or whatever gave her something special—physically and spiritually special—and that people who believed in her could tap into it. Dad had the same thing."

He slumped down into a chair shaking his head. It was over. He'd given as much as he would. The rest she would find elsewhere. She sat quietly wondering how she was to get it into words, the right words, knowing that she would do it for the *Times* in the next few hours, but that later, on her own time, in the future, she would make it into something more, much more, something between hard covers, something that would endure as long as the temple itself. The words she would use now—*his* words—were the words she would use then.

She sat back and closed her notebook. She checked her watch. Already noon, the day slipping away, deadlines closing in. She had to be back at the office by four o'clock to start writing, which gave her four more hours for reporting. Where to start? Where to go? Whom to see? She had no time to lose.

Suddenly: "I remember that Uncle Willie met Angie in an ice cream shop in Glendale. You wouldn't happen to know where that shop is?"

The idea revived him. "Tony's? Of course I know Tony's. Let's go."

The funeral was bigger even than Willie's memorial service at Wrigley Field. Angie's body lay in state in the temple for three days. The *Times* reported forty-five thousand people filed past her bier before it was closed, many coming from outside the state. No one recorded how many of them were women, but it would easily have been two-thirds. Flowers valued at fifty-thousand dollars were contributed, and a record eight thousand worshipers attended the three-hour service, which was led by the Rev. Marcus Wynetski—two thousand obliged to listen outside to the KWEM broadcast that went out around the nation.

Afterward, mourners followed the casket to Forest Lawn Cemetery in a mile-long cortege across Griffith Park while eleven trucks transported the flowers. Twelve pallbearers struggled to transport the 1,200-pound bronze casket to a grassy spot next to Willie high in the hills, rest platforms stationed for the casket along the way. Across the nation, newspapers and magazines devoted special sections to her life and achievements, above all her work to give women equal spousal rights and to bring evangelical pentecostalism into the mainstream of American religion.

Even the Rev. Bob Shoemaker, Willie's old tormentor, who'd turned his righteous wrath on Angie after Willie's death (and after his application to succeed Willie at the temple was turned down), had something nice to say on his radio program, surely biting his teeth as he said it: "I will never understand why God used the Soldiers for God to start such a movement, but I can easily understand why He will use them to carry on. They are effective. They are more like Wesley's army than we Methodists would like to admit."

Part Four

CHAPTER 41

"Didn't they teach you to at least try to see the other person's point of view?"

Robby frowned. "That from you, Dad, the former communist? I am amazed."

"Things were different before the war. Everyone but the plutocrats was on the left." He was on a glass of cabernet after two Jim Beams. "You'd have been there, too. There were no jobs. Today, jobs for everyone!"

Robinson Adams Morton—Ram, to his friends (only the immediate family was allowed to call him Robby)—was home. Four years at Phillips Exeter, followed by six years at Stanford, where he'd earned an undergraduate engineering degree and graduate law degree, had opened all the doors. There was the little problem of Vietnam, but he was working on it. Exeter was a prep school for the Ivy League, but after four years he'd had enough of the New England ladder: Exeter-Choate–Harvard-Yale=Wall Street. He'd visited enough of his Eastern classmates' homes to know he didn't want to end up like their fathers.

From his grandmother, he knew all about Grandpa Eddie. He knew about the murder, of course, but what mainly interested him was how Eddie had ruled Los Angeles for a while, which one man couldn't do in New York or Boston, which is why he had come back. On grad day at Stanford Law, Robby had interviewed with every law firm and corporation headquartered in Los Angeles. An Exeter-Stanford connection didn't mean much in the East, but in Los Angeles it was gold. It was only a matter of which firm to choose, and Robby was taking his time.

He glanced at his mother sitting back after dinner sipping her coffee and listening as she always did. As much as he enjoyed going toe-to-toe with his father, his mother vexed him. He blamed her, not his father, for sending him away. If she'd wanted him, she would have kept him, but she was too busy. A decade later, the pain was still there, abated only slightly by knowing how few of his Exeter classmates were close to their mothers. That was the whole point, wasn't it? The weaning that would make them men.

"Me a communist?" he said with a little smirk. "I don't think so."

"I wouldn't be one today either," Joe said. "Don't you see, that's my point: things were different in the thirties. It helps to remember that."

Nothing his father did shocked the boy, not even his ridiculous nom de plume. Letters arrived at their house addressed to Memory Laine. Some secret! It had, however, been a shock to find out what his mother was doing, she and Aunt Maggie: a shock to learn of the $50 million Mull Foundation. With money like that, why did his mother still work and his father scrounge out a living writing scripts for B movies and translating the works of communists like Bertolt Brecht? At Exeter, the headmaster called him in one day to talk about that. They weren't going to expel him, he joked; punish the son for the sins of the father was not the Exeter way, ha-ha, au contraire. But for heaven's sake, Robinson, hasn't your father heard of the Cold War?

And that was before Vietnam.

"No, Dad," he said, careful not to raise his voice. Emotion defeats reason, defeats judgment, they taught at Exeter. The greater man the greater courtesy, said Tennyson. "To say that something bad is good because of the circumstances is relativism. There are objective criteria for judging things. The communist system was as flawed then as it is today."

Joe didn't mind anyone getting onto dialectical ground. "Actions grow out of context," he said. "Take revolutions, for example. The communist system may be flawed, but the capitalist system didn't look so hot either in the thirties with half the country out of work. Then the war came along, and the communists were our allies. The enemy of your enemy, you know. What did Roosevelt say? 'In times of trouble sometimes you must walk with the devil to get to the other side of the bridge.'"

"The only trouble with the capitalist system is government interference," said Robby, avoiding the point. "That was true in the thirties as well."

"I hope you didn't learn that at Stanford."

Robby smiled. "Actually I learned it at Exeter in Professor Farnsworth's class. Our textbook was *Atlas Shrugged*."

"Good God!" laughed Joe. "Ayn Rand at Exeter? I hope it was a science-fiction course."

Lizzie always learned something in these sessions, little odds and ends, like the Roosevelt thing. Of course, Joe could have made it up, he was good at that, but it had the ring of truth. And of course Robby would check. The conversations between them were intense, but managed to stay civil. With her, things always got down to the personal level, which she hated. Robby knew his father wasn't a Mull, but Lizzie had more to answer for—like the family, like boarding school, the *Times*, the Mull Foundation. Robby hated the foundation as much as he hated the *Times*, both unfairly, she thought. The *Times* was vastly improved under Otis Chandler. Even Joe conceded the point. It had taken her some time to understand her son's resentments, which she resented herself. What right did he have to be resentful?

She'd had to endure his mockery over the outcome of the Chicago transportation trial. "I read about that," he'd said at breakfast one morning. Joe was gone early leaving her alone at the table with her son, something that rarely went well. "So you work on this story for how long, six months? And the trial lasts for two months or something? And then, mirabile dictu, you get a guilty verdict and the jury fines the guilty corporations what—the stupendous sum of five thousand dollars each. As if they cared! And you call that a victory? When will you people learn? Don't mess with the market system."

You people! he'd said. God, how she'd wished Joe had been there! She wasn't a polemicist, never had been. She'd said something pitiful about the injustice of five thousand dollar fines compared to the criminal damage done to the city, and Robby began quoting from Ayn Rand about the evils of government regulation. Afterward, she knew what she should have said: that governments are established to assure that markets work for everyone, not just for big corporations. She'd been too angry to think straight.

She told him about the foundation soon after he returned from the disastrous trip north with Cal. She'd been sitting with him in the garden and mentioned it innocently enough. He had a right to know what they were doing with the estate. His reaction astounded her. "So you and Aunt Maggie set up a foundation with your inheritance from Grandpa Eddie? Shouldn't I have something to say about that?"

She'd never discussed money with Robby. The bank handled his school expenses and provided him with a generous allowance.

And there he was challenging what she and Maggie were doing and asking if the money was his? What if I need that money to get started in business? he said. Isn't that how Grandpa Eddie got started, with money left by his mother? She'd refused to talk any more about it. Got up and walked into the house.

"By the way," said Joe, his imagination stimulated by alcohol and a good duel with his son, "I gather you haven't heard anything from our friends at the Selective Service System. Setting up a lottery system is the damndest thing I've ever heard of. Either you have a draft or you don't. Sounds too much like the Civil War when you could buy your way out of serving."

"How can you buy your way out of a lottery?" said Lizzie. "That's the whole point, isn't it? Your number comes up or it doesn't."

"My point," said Joe, "is that in a real war everybody goes."

"So Vietnam isn't a real war?" said Robby.

Joe took a sip of cabernet. "What do you think?"

Robby had thought about it all right, just as every boy of draft age in the sixties was thinking about it. You could hardly take a political course at Stanford or any university in the country where Vietnam didn't come up. Students had deferments as long as they were in school, but the war started to heat up just as Robby's class came close to graduation. Their future lives depended on the lottery.

"I guess I don't have to ask what you think, Dad."

"I asked first," said Joe, smiling. "What would John Galt do? Would he go?"

Robby's eyes widened, showing his surprise. "Don't tell me you've read it."

"Who is John Galt?" said Lizzie.

The men laughed. "A mysterious character in *Atlas Shrugged*," said Joe. "Everyone runs around asking: 'Who is John Galt?'"

"And so who is he?"

"He controls the world and has disappeared into the Rockies."

"I don't like governments telling me what to do," said Robby.

"War is different isn't it?" said Lizzie.

"Different if you're attacked. Not if you're the attacker."

"Your number will be in the lottery," said Joe. "The question is, what do you do if it comes up?"

"What business do we have keeping Vietnam from uniting?"

"You mean you wouldn't go?" said Lizzie.

Robby examined his mother. People who saw them together saw no resemblance, no more than they saw between Joe and Robby. It was as if nature took the genes of both parents, shook them up and produced a cocktail that resembled neither. Robby had his mother's thick hair, though it was darker. His eyes were blue, unlike anyone in the family but Cal, whose blue eyes came from his mother. He wished he had the Mulls' good eyesight but had his father's myopia. Both his parents were artistic, and he had none of it. He took himself for a throwback to Grandpa Eddie—smarter, shrewder, tougher.

"No. I won't go."

If Robby was looking for approval, he got none. His parents did not respond. Joe had been too old for the other war, the good one, but would have gone. A war lottery was something he couldn't understand. Lizzie didn't like the war either, but was patriotic enough to feel uncomfortable with her son's answer.

◆ ◆ ◆

With no job offer he deemed worthy and growing Vietnam uncertainty, Robby had moved back into his boyhood bedroom in Brentwood. Lizzie had hoped Cal would ask him to move in with him in Westwood, where he'd returned from Angie's house in Echo Park into the same apartment building on Tiverton she'd once shared with Maggie. But Robby and his godfather were no longer on speaking terms.

During two summers at Exeter and two more at Stanford, Robby had come home to work with Cal at the Sierra Club. He was more an intern than an employee, but earned a little money and enjoyed the work, which got him around Southern California. She'd been happy about it, happy that Robby and Cal were close. Part of it, she believed, was that Robby looked on Cal as the last male Mull, and Cal looked on Robby as the son he didn't have. With their blue eyes, they even looked a little alike. Cal took his role as godfather seriously.

Between Robby's junior and senior years at Stanford, Cal took him on a field trip to Northern California. Castle and Cooke, which owned much of Hawaii, had bought a swath of land in Sonoma County with the intention of building a residential development along ten miles of virgin coastline. At the time, only a hundred miles of California's thirteen-hundred–mile coast were still accessible to the public, and the plan to shut off access to ten more miles at a place called Sea Ranch just north of Gualala was the last straw. The Sierra Club and other environmentalists formed the Coast Alliance to oppose the project.

The Sonoma coast is an isolated and desolate place where former Indian villages like Gualala are connected only by narrow north-south Highway 1, a former Indian coastal trail. There are no east-west access roads from inland civilization over the coastal mountains to the sea. North of Sonoma is the so-called Lost Coast, where the mountains come right down to the water and there are no roads and no people.

The Sea Ranch hearings were tumultuous. Hundreds of protestors descended on Gualala, marching its narrow streets. These same people had been coming to the seashore for years, pitching tents, casting lines, some even brave enough to test the frigid waters. They would not be evicted from the coast without a fight. Neither would the Indians. So many protesters came out that the supervisors moved the hearings to Santa Rosa, the county seat. The hearings were front-page news across the state. Castle and Cooke won the battle, but lost the war. Sea Ranch launched the grass-roots movement that led to passage of the California Coastal Act, creating a public commission to take the coast out of the hands of developers and return it to the people.

It took some time for Lizzie to get the truth about the rupture. She sensed something was wrong when Robby didn't come home after the hearings. Cal dropped him off at Stanford though it was still mid-summer. When neither Cal nor Robby would tell her what happened, she called Hal Kornheiser, the *Times*'s San Francisco bureau chief, who'd covered the Santa Rosa hearings. Hal checked the transcripts: Yes, a Robinson Morton of Los Angeles had taken the microphone to speak in favor of Sea Ranch, accusing the Sierra Club and its allies of interfering with private land rights in violation of the Fifth Amendment, quoting author Ayn Rand.

The incident poisoned relations between Robby and his godfather. Nor did it improve matters between Robby and his mother, stunned that under the auspices of the Sierra Club he would have spoken out in favor of the project, an act of blatant family treachery. It didn't help that the Mull Foundation was one of the Sierra Club's and Coast Alliance's principal benefactors. If Sea Ranch was a watershed in California environmental history, it was also an aberration, for it took place along the desolate Northern California coast, where few people lived. The bloodiest battles to preserve the coastline were about to take place in Southern California, where the people lived. The primary focus of the war would be the property of Howard Hughes.

CHAPTER 42

"What the hell is the Summa Corporation?"

"If you don't know, Mr. Hughes," said Melvin Cobb into the phone, which was on loudspeaker, "you'd better find out. Summa is acting in your name and doing things you aren't going to like. I'll send you everything I have if you give me your address."

"No, goddam it! Got to keep my address private. People on my trail."

Maggie looked across to Cobb for a reaction, but he wore his usual encrypted look. Beyond him she glimpsed the Hughes runway and beyond that the cranes of the great dredging operation where the Mull oil wells had once stood, oily sand one day to become Marina del Rey, the world's largest man-made small craft harbor. Howard had done all right on that deal. So had the Mulls. Then came Summa.

She'd been sitting in Cobb's office speculating with him where Howard could possibly be when the call came. Where was he? Why was he calling? They hadn't heard from him in months. She whispered not to let him hang up, that she'd like a word with him.

No one at Hughes Aircraft or Hughes Tool or Hughes Medical Institute or TWA had any idea where to find the increasingly elusive, increasingly paranoid billionaire. He had disappeared. His wife—Jean Peters had finally married him—lived in Bel Air and thought he was at the Desert Inn in Las Vegas, which he owned along with just about every other resort hotel in the city. But calls to the Desert Inn, including hers, were not returned. Others said he was in Florida or Nicaragua or had permanently gone underground, like John Galt in *Atlas Shrugged*, because he couldn't stand dealing with the government and banks anymore, both of which he blamed for taking TWA. According to the press, both were on his trail with subpoenas.

"Maggie Heyward is here with me, Mr. Hughes. She'd like a word with you."

"Maggie—my little Maggie." Silence, then: "Heyward? Hell, that's not her name." More silence. "Hey, Cobb, do you remember that show with Gale Storm?"

"It was *My Little Margie*, Howard, *Margie*," said Maggie. "And where the hell are you? Do you know what's happening back here?"

"I'll tell you where I am but don't tell anyone, not even Cobb." (Too deaf to hear the speaker, she thought). "I'm on Paradise Island. But not for long."

She stared across at Cobb, who shook his head. "I'm sorry, Howard, I don't know where Paradise Island is."

"The Bahamas, and a hell of a lot better than Nassau. But don't tell anyone."

There was a laugh and a crack on the line. "Remind me who this is again."

"It's Maggie Heyward, Howard, damn it, Mull to you and you've got to get off your meds and get back here." She waited for a response, but none came. "Summa is selling everything out from under you. I can't stay here any longer. I'm gone unless you do something."

"Don't leave me now, Margie. You're one of the few people I trust back there, you and Cobb—Cobb, you still there?"

"I'm here, Mr. Hughes."

"And what about this so-called Howard Hughes memoir the newspapers are talking about," she said. "It's lying trash. Are you going to let that pass?"

′ "You tell them, Margie. That's why I called. You call a press conference and tell them it is fraud, beginning to end, bogus, fake, garbage. I don't know this guy Irving and never talked to him and we'll sue the shit out of him and the publisher. McGraw-Hill, isn't it? Do they think I'm so far gone I can't defend myself?"

"Cary Grant already did the press conference and told them all that, Howard, but you have to do it yourself. People are going to believe it until you denounce it yourself. Live!"

"Cary Grant, best friend I ever had. I was best man when he married Betsy in that Arizona farmhouse. Introduced me to Kate, did you know that, Cobb?"

She looked up at Cobb who was shaking his head.

"They're drugging you, aren't they, Howard?"

"It's the goddam pain," he said. "Trying to keep it down."

"People are stealing you blind, do you know that? Why did you let them sell Hughes Tool just when the Supreme Court was taking your side on TWA? Do you know how much money you lost on that sale?"

"When did the Supreme Court ever take my side?"

Cobb continued shaking his head. "He doesn't even know about it," he whispered.

"Look, the movie here's starting," he said, "The projector's loaded. Have to go. *Goldfinger*. You seen it? How the hell are you, anyway, Margie? We had some good times together, didn't we?"

"Howard. Before you go. You have to stop Summa."

"Summa . . . *Sum*-ma . . . Sum-*ma*. Never heard of it . . . what the hell is it? Cobb. You still there, Cobb? Speak up."

"I'm listening, Mr. Hughes."

"What the hell is Summa? Don't even know how to pronounce it."

"It is your company, Mr. Hughes. The board set it up. It's to be the parent of all your properties. I've seen the documents. You signed them."

"Bullshit, I never signed anything with the name Summa on it. Anything set up should be called HRH for Howard Robard Hughes—*and I have to sign off on it!* Great initials, aren't they, Cobb? Mean something else, you know." He laughed. "My Dad had that in mind, you know. I'd say I lived up to it, wouldn't you?"

Cobb dodged the question. "It looked like your signature."

"Then it was forged. Where are my lawyers, anyway, where's Schmidt, where's Gay, where's Bautzer?"

"They're the ones doing it," he whispered to Maggie. "They're not here, Mr. Hughes. If they're not with you then they're downtown."

"Romaine Street?"

"That's my guess. Hughes Productions."

"Check with them. Whatever it is, don't call it Summa. Any parent company should be the HRH Corporation. And send me the documents!"

"We don't have your address, Mr. Hughes."

Silence. Then: "I'll let you know."

"I'll do what I can, Mr. Hughes," he said, loudly. "The board, you know . . ."

"Howard, before you go," said Maggie, panicking slightly. "You are my dear friend. You hired me, you introduced me to Terry, you came to my wedding . . ."

"I remember."

"This Summa thing is bad, Howard. The land—*your* land— the land Melvin Cobb and I are sitting on right now—they're taking it. The *Times* published drawings. Playa Vista, they call it. They're acting in your name but you would hate it. Melvin can send you the drawings. Ugly gray concrete buildings running on for miles—faceless, colorless, concrete tenements! *Communist,* Howard, *communist!* Like East Berlin. They can't do that. We have a commitment from you, a contract."

She waited for an answer, but none came.

"Somebody cut the line," said Cobb. "I don't think it was Howard."

She didn't know what to make of her life anymore, but it couldn't go on like it was. When you're young, decisions make themselves. She knew it wasn't so, that like any other young woman she'd had to make decisions, but at the time they seemed inevitable, something growing naturally out of the situation: the break with Harold, the trip to Europe, Arnaud, marriage, Howard, flying, the WASPs, Terry—one thing leading naturally to another, life on autopilot. Turn fifty and no more autopilot. You're back at the controls, and God help you if you drift. Drift means spin and spin means wreck.

Howard, what an opportunity he gave her! The man was paranoid and sexist and domineering and all the things women are supposed to hate, but he was a genius and au fond, he was a dear. At least until disease got him. If you judge men by the women who love them, Howard was the top of the heap. Men feared him; women loved him. She flew with him and slept with him and left him in time. Just in time.

She'd stumbled along for a half century without a thought to what came next and now had no clue. Men? Marriage? Middle Age? Menopause? The horrible Ms. Women have a dozen things to think about before they get in bed with a man, and finally she was free of them. She'd lost an ovary because of a stupid fling with Hans, the musclebound lifeguard at the beach club she'd brought home because why not, and she was drunk from too many daiquiris and forgot she'd put in a Tampax and then Hans banging away on top of her and the next day she thought her whole insides had ruptured. The look on the doctor's face said it all.

She never flew anymore, hated her job, which was all paperwork and men in business suits. A few years back she could have gone for a commercial pilot's license. God, how she'd love to fly those new Boeing giants for TWA. Howard would have swung it for her. First woman WASP, why not the first woman airline pilot? Now she'd have to leave Hughes. How could she work for a company she was suing? Howard was no use, turned into a demented invalid, putative head of a company he'd never heard of and didn't even know how to pronounce.

Leaving Hughes Aircraft meant she'd have to leave Playa del Rey. It was too far to the foundation offices downtown. Too bad they'd scrapped the trolley. Terry's house was the one in which she'd been happiest, but she didn't need two stories and three bedrooms and three bathrooms when no one ever stayed with her except guys like Hans. Cal came down sometimes, and Lizzie and Joe stopped by on their way to Westport but never stayed. Didi wouldn't set foot in the house. The house on the hill with the view from Malibu to Catalina was the beautiful painting that no one ever saw.

The showdown with Summa was coming, coming even though nobody knew what Summa was, not even Howard. They, it, whatever it was, had taken over the building on Romaine Street and was writing letters to everyone signed by names she'd never seen before, always with the comment underneath: "(for Howard Hughes)."

It was nonsense. Summa was acting on its own to sell Hughes Aircraft and turn Playa del Rey into Karl-Marx-Allee because Howard wasn't there to stop them and no one could find him *and it wouldn't matter if they could because Howard was crazy!* Mel Cobb said Howard had become like Norma Desmond in *Sunset Boulevard*, Howard's favorite movie: Remember me for what I was, not what I am. At first he'd thought Howard loved the movie because of Bill Holden, another old pal, but it wasn't that at all. It was Norma Desmond, who was a wreck.

If all of that wasn't enough, then guilt came and took up residence.

Why should she feel guilty about her mother and daughter? Maybe she hadn't been the best daughter, but Nelly hardly noticed. As for Didi, she was unhappy so they sent her off to Bel Air and Westlake so she could be happy with bisque dolls and charge accounts and sandwiches with the crusts cut off. She, Maggie, did it. Terry didn't know what to make of this sulky little thing but would have made it work. Why did life have to be so messy? Easy to blame the parents for everything, but that only works for so long. After a while, it's on you.

But was guilt such a bad thing? Maybe guilt is like pain, a necessary warning that something is off and needs fixing. If it's your body you seek medicine; if it's your conscience, you make amends. Maybe guilt helps you back onto the right path: the oil wells destroy the coast, but lead to the Mull Foundation, which brings back the beaches. Los Angeles was even trying to make amends with Owens Valley for stealing its water. You defeat guilt by making it useful. It was too late to make it up to her mother, but maybe not too late for Didi.

There would be no guilt and no amends over Playa del Rey because Summa would not get away with it. They had not torn down the Mull oil derricks to replace them with Summa concrete. They had a letter from Howard stating his intentions, and Howard, not Summa, owned the land. Howard's signature on the contract with the Mull Foundation was his real signature, not the forged signature of those who were drugging him to death so they could take over everything he'd created when he was gone.

When he was gone . . .

She wondered: Did he have a will?

CHAPTER 43

She was neither the most popular girl at Westlake nor the most popular Tri Delt at UCLA. She was too shy and self-absorbed to make friends easily. She had a circle of girls who were more or less like her, but it was a small circle. Didi's strong suit, though not necessarily with females, was that she had become a striking young woman. Like her mother, she had dark hair and dark eyes and a perfect Garbo face. She was as tall as Maggie with a body that men liked to watch. She'd had small roles in school plays at Westlake and dreamt of playing Eliza in Shaw's *Pygmalion*, but her drama teacher never would have taken the risk. She was fine in rehearsals, but could not act in front of an audience. He'd seen other girls like that. It was a pity, for Didi was a joy to look at, but the stage is no place for anyone with a fear of failure.

Her picture dancing with Kenny van Swerigen had been prominent in the *Times* society feature on the debutante ball at the Bel Air Country Club. Didi was radiant and Kenny handsome in his white dinner jacket. Finally, Nelly had a girl at the ball. She didn't worry about Didi's shyness. With all the things happening to their bodies, teenage girls are often like that. She'd been shy herself as a girl. She couldn't have been prouder of her granddaughter, so hard to imagine this statuesque beauty as the fussy, stuffy, knobby-kneed little thing Maggie dropped off to live with her years before, whose feet didn't quite reach the floor at the dining room table. She'd been such a careful little girl, so afraid of making a mistake, of saying something dumb or wrong. Westlake had been just the thing and Delta Delta

Delta the perfect sorority at UCLA. Boys were attracted to the Tri Delt house like hummingbirds to honeysuckle.

For Didi's UCLA graduation, Nelly planned a cocktail party. There was a dance at the club on graduation night, but the following Wednesday was perfect for something more intimate. Sixty invitations was not exactly intimate, but with Didi's sorority friends and Nelly's studio crowd it was the absolute minimum. Kenny van Swerigen had to be invited, though Nelly was not keen on him. He was polite and cute in his tuxedo and at least taller than Didi, but the boy was so very bland. Kind of Iowa bland, as she remembered back, people moving around silently in the sitting room with a dull look on their face like they were still out there with the cows. Kenny came from a good family, in the country club and Blue Book and the Junior League because Bruno van Swerigen was head of psychiatry at the UCLA School of Medicine. Didi had known Kenny forever, but Nelly saw no oomph in the boy.

She hired Lester Jones whenever she entertained. Eddie had found him years ago, God knows where. He had to be fetched each time for he lived in Watts and didn't drive, but Ralph, the chauffeur, knew the way. Lester wasn't the greatest piano player, but knew everything, was accommodating to a fault, and wasn't expensive. He made enough tips in the big brandy snifter on the piano that she probably didn't need to pay him anything. Lester didn't even mind playing on her Baldwin spinet, which she always had tuned for him, though the tuner hated it. "The sea air, the sea air," he told her once. "Spinets are no good anyway the way the strings are bent around. Get yourself an upright—or a baby grand. A house like this deserves a baby grand."

Promptly at six, the first cars pulled up Roscomare Road, the long, winding street running from the club up to the reservoir.

Plenty of parking along Roscomare so Nelly never hired a valet. Ralph should have been back with Lester by six, but Wednesday rush-hour traffic can be bad. Didi was radiant and dashed out to greet the girls coming up the path, boys right behind. This wasn't just a younger crowd, it was a young and beautiful crowd with a touch of Hollywood because more than a few of the Tri Delts came from Hollywood families. Didi introduced Nelly to the Volker twins, two gorgeous redheads who'd been on the cover of *Time* magazine for their success on *Password*, a game show where they'd won for weeks, setting some kind of record. The story was that Frank Sinatra called the Tri Delt house and invited them to the Academy Awards. Both of them! Sinatra who was fifty if he was a day! Chiffon dresses, one lime, one powder blue, came just above their knees and the décolletage was maidenly modest. And such lovely pale skin! Redheads are so lucky!

And there was Maggie making a beeline for her daughter. Nelly loved seeing them together, so rare. With Howard Hughes's disappearances Maggie had taken on more duties and seldom made it to Bel Air anymore. When she came, she came alone. After two dead husbands it was like she was giving up, Nelly thought, so unlike her. The *Times* photographer started snapping pictures. Maggie towered over her mother, and Didi was a bit taller than Maggie.

"Mother, get in the middle," said Maggie.

"Never!" she said, pulling away. "I'll look like a dwarf. You two stand together."

"Would someone please hold this drink," said Didi. "I don't want to look sloshed."

"Are you getting sloshed?" asked Maggie, taking the champagne flute and handing it to Nelly. "And that dress, my goodness!"

Didi's black cocktail dress was shorter and dipped lower

than the dresses of the other Tri Delts, but had more to hold
it up. Nelly had wondered about the dress, too, which they'd
picked out together at Bullock's Westwood, but Nelly didn't
know about the call from Jonathan Schwartz, who was bringing
someone with him with movie connections to meet Didi. Jonathan was a Hollywood lawyer and man-about-town whom Nelly
knew from the dance studio. He'd been to Roscomare Road and
had met Didi. He was a hustler, but you never knew. It was time
for her granddaughter to get out in the world.

Didi leaned toward Maggie and whispered edgily, "Mother,
stop being a mother. It's a little late, don't you think?"

"There's your Aunt Liz," said Maggie, ignoring the comment and waving to the door where Liz and Joe had just come
in followed by Robby and a girl they didn't know. Cal was a few
steps behind. Nelly didn't know what to make of the quarrel
between Cal and Robby. She liked Robby well enough because
he liked to talk about Eddie, which no one else ever did. She
knew Didi couldn't stand her cousin and wondered why she'd
invited him. In any case, in any quarrel involving Cal, Nelly
would stand with Cal, always had.

"No music," said Joe. "Where's my favorite piano player?"

"I have no idea," said Nelly, who with time had accommo-
dated herself to her socialist son-in-law. "Ralph left hours ago
for Watts."

"Watts, did you say?"

"That's where Lester lives."

"Some kind of police action in Watts I heard on the radio,"
said Joe.

"Not tonight of all nights, please!" cried Nelly. "What will I
do for music?"

"Someone will play," said Joe. "Someone at these parties
always can play."

"Call for you, Miss Lizzie." It was Iris, the maid, out from the kitchen where she was supervising the catering.

"This is Dominique," said Robby, ignoring Didi and approaching his grandmother with a luscious girl on his arm.

When Didi had phoned to invite Lizzie and Joe, it was Robby who answered, Robby the vile cousin whose only virtue in her mind was that he'd gone away for so long. Lizzie wasn't home, and Robby wouldn't call Joe to the phone until she told him why she was calling so she had to invite him as well, hoping, of course, that he wouldn't come. She'd hoped that Robby's years of exile might have improved him, but, no. As children they'd hated each other, and the only improvement with age was that hatred had turned to contempt.

What Didi could never forgive—it had been chiseled into her hippocampus as an infant—was that Robby was vicious. The few horrible times they'd been put together as children, most often in the spare bedroom at Playa del Rey, Robby, two years older, would sneak over and pinch her until she started crying. By the time someone came in, he would have slipped back to bed pretending to be asleep. For years he'd found ways to torment her whenever they were together and shift the blame onto her. To her, he was mean and devious and probably a misogynist. She felt for any girl unfortunate enough to find herself with him. Robby's opinion of his cousin was hardly better: To him she was weak and stupid.

They stood waiting for Dominique's last name, but it was not offered. She looked as French as her name, but the accent was Midwestern flat. Lizzie had met her for the first time on the path outside. She hadn't spoken to their son since he moved into his own place somewhere in West Hollywood. He'd apparently found a job, but no one knew anything about it.

"We've got to go," said Lizzie, coming back from the phone

with the *Times* photographer. "Something going on in Watts. They're calling everyone in. Sammy has a car."

"What's up?" said Joe.

"Not sure. Trouble in South Central. Pulling in police from everywhere."

"Ralph is somewhere down there," said Nelly. "With my car! Lizzie, for heaven's sake. At your age. What's wrong with that newspaper!"

Lizzie ignored her mother. "Sorry Didi. Work calls. Bye everyone."

"That's my mother," said Robby, who was not smiling.

"Ah," said Nelly, reviving as other guests came in the door. "There's Jonathan Schwartz. Who's that with him?"

"I believe that would be Archie Zug," said Joe.

"Who is . . .?"

"An agent I know from Universal."

"I don't believe he's on the guest list."

"I think he's here for me, Granny," said Didi.

Joe sighed. "I certainly hope not."

Archie Zug was the Hollywood talent agent par excellence. His agency represented a good many of the top stars, but Archie was also known for developing talent, especially young female talent. Hollywood was a vortex, if not a maelstrom, for young females and had been since the movie industry arrived. Males, too, made their way west if they thought they had something, but the suck on females was greater because they had more to offer and more to gain. A young fellow off a Midwestern farm or from an Eastern blue-collar family could always step into Dad's shoes when the time came, and if he had a college education, he might set his sights on a career in business. It was different for young women. Despite the gains they'd made during the war, the business world was closed to them unless they could type or work a switchboard. The situation wasn't as bad as in places like Germany, where the tradition of *Kinder, Küche, Kirche* reached back to the Middle Ages, but it wasn't good either. Home economics was still the most popular college major for co-eds, as they were called, and for more adventurous girls there was always nursing and teaching. Hardly a wonder that if a girl was attractive enough and had a little gumption she would set out for Hollywood.

The first thing they did off the train was visit a talent agency. They didn't need an appointment. Just show up and let the agent have a good ogle from all angles. The girls generally fell into three groups. There were the ones away from home alone for the first time, and the agent's job was to be surrogate comforter and father confessor. The second group was girls who didn't need surrogates because they came equipped with mothers, who often saw beauty and talent where no one else did. For agents, mothers were something to be tolerated only if the girl had something truly special, like Judy Garland or Ginger Rogers.

Finally, there were the girls who came to the agent to escape their mothers, who had some sort of psychodynamic grudge against them for being too domineering or too successful. Think of the daughters of Mary Astor or Joan Crawford. Motherly success casts a long shadow over insecure daughters. Or maybe the case was the opposite: Mother just didn't give a damn. Sometimes mothers just can't win.

◆ ◆ ◆

Nelly never saw her black Buick again. Lester Jones never played for her again because no one dared go to Watts to fetch him. Lizzie, the *Times* metro editor, returned home Thursday morning in a taxi, caught a nap and, frazzled, sat down with Joe for coffee. Joe had read the paper while she was sleeping, and nothing surprised him. It wasn't the Marxist class struggle but the racial struggle that had gone on in America since emancipation. For decades it had been the problem of the East and the South and maybe the Midwest and Los Angeles hadn't paid much attention. When blacks discovered the West after the war, real estate covenants, known as "redlining," conveniently hid them away in their own part of town, mostly on Charlie Watts's former ranch. Los Angeles still didn't pay much attention. Watts became the city's Harlem, where you didn't go except maybe for the music, and everyone was fine with that. As the black population increased over the next two decades, Harlem West kept on growing. By 1965, with the new federal Civil Rights Act just passed, its people were sick of redlining and wanted out

"How are you doing?" he asked his wife, who didn't look too rested.

He could tell without asking, but asked anyway.

"Wait till I finish this coffee and I'll tell you."

He passed her the paper. "The whole front section is Watts."

"Those guys did a hell of a job."

"You mean *you* guys."

"Everybody, Joe. I mean we were mobilized. Every reporter, every editor, every photographer worked all night. Two special editions."

"I heard on KHJ this morning that it's getting worse. More dead, houses burning. Police chief called it a revolution. Says it's like fighting the Viet Cong."

"More like an uprising than a revolution."

He sipped his coffee. "There's a difference?"

"Uprisings fail. I'm going down to have a look."

"You!" he sputtered. "You're the general. Generals stay back at headquarters. Where it's safe. That's the point in being a general."

"I need to get the feel of it."

"Read the stories. Look at the pictures. How much of a feel do you need?"

"We don't have another edition until four. Sammy picks me up at eleven."

"That gives you five more minutes. KHJ said something about the national guard."

"Probably a good idea. Chief Parker has no credibility with those people."

"You know, there's something fraudulent about this city, something Potemkin, and I don't just mean Hollywood. How many people have even heard of Watts?"

"They've heard of it now."

They would hear of it again a quarter century later when police beat up a black man named Rodney King and were acquitted of unnecessary violence by a white jury, though a video showed the brutal beating of a man who was not resisting. The '68 Watts riots claimed thirty-four lives. The '92 riots doubled the number and burned down a good part of South Central. Both times, the US Army had to be called out when police and national guard couldn't do the job. The video of King's beating was sent to police forces around the nation as an example of what not to do. Apparently, not many watched it. Two years later, in '94, a black ex-football player named Orenthal James Simpson would get even by killing two white people, including his wife, in Brentwood. He was acquitted by a mostly black jury. The jurors said he'd been framed by the cops.

CHAPTER 44

Watts was it for Lizzie. She was still a young woman—when were your fifties ever old in California?—but she needed something new. She found it hugely depressing that a community in her city could have been smoldering away all those years and that it took an explosion and dozens of deaths to get anyone's attention. As the metro editor she held herself responsible. Why didn't she know? The *Times* had never really covered Watts, certainly not like the white areas of the city. That was her fault. Under Otis Chandler the newspaper had made huge strides, become a national newspaper right up there with the East Coast papers. After a history of ignoring world news, the *Times* had as many foreign bureaus as the *New York Times* and had opened bureaus in cities across the nation. Circulation was close to a million, advertising was never stronger, and she could easily have asked for a budget to cover Watts. The newspaper that covered the world and the nation had turned its back on its own community. She'd grown stale.

To her professional angst, she discovered that somewhere along the way she'd lost her son. Lately he'd completely dropped out of sight, but she'd lost him long before that. The funny thing was, as much as she blamed herself for her failure on Watts, she felt no guilt over Robby. She'd left him alone—Joe had, too—to become what he wanted, which he had done. As children, she, Maggie, and Cal had asked for no more than that. It was the way she believed children should be raised. Advise them, support them, encourage them and send them off. Robby and Didi had both come to see their parents as enemies. How to explain it? Were the parents not caring enough? But they *did* care. In their own way they had always cared and always acted in their children's best interest. Maybe they hadn't suffocated the children with love, but that was not their way, not the Presbyterian way, not the Mull way. Beyond that, they'd had their own careers to look after. Shouldn't mothers have careers? She and Maggie had always agreed on that point: Don't let the children get in the way. It's the same way they'd viewed things as children: Don't let the parents get in the way. Do your own thing; find your own level.

Otis wanted to give her a sendoff in the Gold Room of the Biltmore, but she wouldn't have it. She didn't have that many friends left at the newspaper. Miss Adelaide was retired and living in a home in the Valley; Larry McManus had died on the job, as expected, and was carried out. Lizzie was a decade older than Otis himself, and people had started calling her ma'am. It was time to move on. Go out on your own terms. Joe was working full time at Universal, and she could move into his study to write. Or into Robby's room, for that matter. She would write mornings and spend afternoons with Maggie in the foundation's offices down the corridor from the Sierra Club. The three of them would be together. As always.

Her first afternoon at the foundation was a shock. She'd taken two weeks off after leaving the *Times* and flown with Joe to Hawaii on the first vacation they'd ever had together. "*This* is vacation," Joe would say whenever she'd raised the subject. "People come here, to Southern California, on vacation. We don't need to go anywhere." But they'd gone to Waikiki, sailed to other islands and come home refreshed. Joe was busier than ever. Memory Laine was a distant McCarthyite memory, and Buddy Fix, who'd moved to Universal when RKO and Howard Hughes moved on, put him on the permanent writing staff.

Lizzie settled into Joe's old office looking out on the garden and got to work on the first of her books, the one Joe hoped to turn into a Los Angeles noir, *The Barton Pitts Story*. Her next book, which she would think about daily stuck in downtown traffic, would be called: *The Great Transportation Conspiracy*. She remembered Fred Barrett's prediction: the new freeway would exactly parallel the old Santa Monica trolley tracks. After that, she would tackle Willie and Sister Angie.

She arrived downtown after lunch on their second day back from the islands. She'd looked into Cal's office on the way and was surprised when he got up to accompany her down the corridor to the foundation. "Got some news for you my dear," he said. "Brace yourself."

The foundation's assets had grown nicely over the years, giving them close to $10 million annual income to spend. They had a staff of twelve, including four officers whose job was to review the dozens of proposals that came in each year. They were an important contributor to the Sierra Club and had spent heavily to assure passage of the initiative to create the California Coastal Commission. Though massively outspent by lobbyists and developers, the people's initiative won easily. Sea Ranch had done it. Playa Vista was next.

Maggie was waiting, and the sisters settled onto the couch. Cal stood by the window. Looking at him, the way the light hit his face, Lizzie saw traces of Uncle Willie she'd never noticed before. Do boys come to resemble their fathers as they age? She'd thought it was only girls and mothers. She wouldn't mind resembling Nelly at her age, before her stroke, that is. She glanced sideways at Maggie, sitting quietly, expressionless, staring straight ahead. Whatever the news was, her sister was in on it.

He laid down the manila folder he'd brought from his office and extracted a paper.

"This letter from Summa is in answer to my letter to them. You recall I sent them a copy of Howard's letter to us about disposition of his airfield after Maggie and I flew to Las Vegas to witness the signing before he disappeared. Summa's answer says about what we expected, but look at the signature."

He handed her the letter.

Under an elaborate Summa Corporation letterhead, under the text, the letter was signed:

>   Robinson A. Morton, vice president
>   (for Howard Hughes)

◆ ◆ ◆

Four of them gathered that night in Brentwood. Lizzie was still shell-shocked, but found Joe more intrigued than surprised. He had a perverse habit of always seeing the story side of events, however dire.

She, however, was angry. "It's the treachery of the thing."

"Not the first time, is it?" said Cal.

They settled in the living room with drinks before dinner.

"He's never hidden his views," said Joe.

"I could forget the treason," said Cal, "but how could he be so blind about the land?"

"Robby goes his own way," said Joe. "Think Sea Ranch."

"But *Summa*?" cried Lizzie. "Sea Ranch is one thing, but working for Summa is setting himself up directly against the foundation, against the family, against *us.*"

"Of all the companies in the world, how in God's name did he end up working for Summa?" said Maggie. "It has to be deliberate."

"We won't know until we ask him, will we?" said Lizzie.

"I have a good idea without asking him," said Joe, taking a book from the shelves. "It's called *Atlas Shrugged* and is the new bible for people like our son, superseding *The Fountainhead*, Ayn Rand's first paean to capitalism. Geniuses, we're told, are created to move the world forward, and whoever or whatever gets in their way must be destroyed."

"Robby's a genius?" asked Maggie.

"Of course," said Joe. "In his own mind."

"Robby believes in that stuff?" said Lizzie.

"Remember our little discussion about John Galt?"

"Who is John Galt?" asked Maggie.

Joe explained.

"So Robby believes he's John Galt?"

"Something like that. Remember the name of Robby's girlfriend? Dominque is the name of the protagonist in *The Fountainhead*."

"Oh come on, Joe," said Maggie. "You don't date someone because of their name."

"If you're Robby, maybe you do."

"Rand's writing is lunacy," said Lizzie.

"She's no lunatic," said Joe. "She's a smart Russian Jew getting even with the Bolsheviks. She has a talent for turning pulp fiction into pseudo philosophy."

"I tried once to read *The Fountainhead*," said Lizzie. "Couldn't get past the sex scenes. It's comic opera."

"Then try *Atlas Shrugged*," said Joe. "Rand's women enjoy being raped, use rape to control men, very liberating."

"So Robby's letter from Summa means we now go to court," said Maggie.

"Can you get a letter from Hughes disowning Summa?" asked Joe.

"Howard hates Summa," said Maggie. "But where is he?"

"I've been trying to track him down," said Cal. "After Las Vegas, he went to the Bahamas, to Nicaragua, which he left after the earthquake, back to Las Vegas, back to the Bahamas, and at last report he was in Acapulco. I've made some calls. He's at the Princess Hotel, has the entire top floor, but no one ever sees him. Doctors come and go. He's either dead or dying. Surely drugged. His minders, whoever they are, have total control of him and his assets."

"Poor Howard," said Maggie.

"Does he have a will?" asked Lizzie.

"No one knows but the minders," said Maggie.

"Summa," said Cal. "Which probably wrote it."

They adjourned to the dining room where Lizzie laid out a Mexican spread. Joe opened a bottle of Almaden rosé. "I don't see exactly how this plays out," he said. "I mean, not in real life. In my writer's imagination I see a hell of a family story: the Barrymores, John and Lionel, *Arsène Lupin*, remember that one? Or maybe a courtroom scene, son against uncle, Lionel in his wheelchair against alcoholic John. One of those family love-hate things—rejection, insecurity, jealousy, all the things psychiatrists make their livings on."

"Joe," said Lizzie, "this is serious."

"You know what Summa will say about the Hughes letter," said Cal. "That it was written by a man losing his faculties."

"But he wasn't!" said Maggie, louder than she meant to. "When I picked it up at the Flamingo, Howard was fine."

"That's not what you told me," said Lizzie.

"Physically, he was a mess. Those fingernails, ugh! But mentally he seemed all right, OK enough to make a pass at me."

"But it had already started, hadn't it," said Cal. "I saw it at the signing."

"You're saying the letter is worthless?"

"I'm saying that its potential is more moral than legal. Since no one knows the relationship between Hughes and Summa, any court will want to know Hughes's intentions. Especially if he dies intestate."

"Whatever Robinson A. Morton may have to say about it," said Lizzie.

"*For* Howard Hughes, of course . . ."

"There's my story," said Joe.

"No, Joe. Before we get too deep into this family fight, I want to talk to him."

Joe stared for some time at his wife. "We're too far into it now, Liz."

"He's my son. I want to do it."

"You want me?"

She shook her head. "Let me try first."

Joe finished pouring out the wine and the table fell silent for a moment. Then: "Speaking of our children," said Lizzie, looking at her sister, "what's the latest on Didi?"

"Ralph drove Mother up in the Hollywood Hills before her stroke. Directions were vague. He got lost and couldn't find it."

"Couldn't find what?" said Cal.

"She's living with that guy. Didi told me to butt out when I called. He gave her a screen test, which she failed. I could have saved him the trouble, but they take one look at her and say, my god, another Jane Russell. Then she gets in front of a camera."

"Jane Russell's talent was all in her blouse," said Joe.

"Living with him on Angelo Drive. Drugs and sex. Mother had no business going up. I went up and found it. Wish I hadn't."

"Living with whom?" said Joe.

"The guy at Didi's party—you remember."

"Remind me."

"Zug."

"Good God."

"Means train in German," said Cal.

"Archie Zug, human locomotive," said Joe. "Some leave off the motive and just call him loco. Hollywood comer. Works with Trevor Bonfeld who left United Artists and is about to open his own studio, something called Wonderworld."

"Wonderworld?"

"Supposed to be the next big thing—space aliens, high-tech animation, Disney for the twenty-first century. Who needs actors?"

"Angelo Drive is Benedict Canyon," said Lizzie. "Not far from the old Polanski place."

"There'd been a party," said Maggie. "Maid was cleaning up, everything quiet, everyone still in bed. A few splashes from a pool somewhere. Stank of drugs and booze and other things. Maid just stared at me. I didn't wake them."

"They go their own way, don't they?" said Cal.

"Well, didn't we?" said Lizzie.

"Oh, come on, Liz," said Cal, "not at all the same."

"You do what you can," said Maggie. "Didi hated everything we did so we took her to Bel Air where she got everything she wanted. Story should have a happy ending."

"In Hollywood, happy endings are only on the screen," said Joe.

"Not in the stuff you write," said Lizzie.

"I do real life."

CHAPTER 45

Didi's eyes were glued shut. She felt across the bed to see if anyone was there. She remembered going to bed with Archie, but then someone else came. Was it Kurt? She thought it was Kurt, and whoever it was had fucked her all night. Archie wouldn't like that but maybe she wouldn't tell him. She rubbed her eyes and they came open and she looked to make sure, but no one was there. She wouldn't mind if it was Kurt because he was to die for, but whoever it was kept waking her, and she lost count and might have stopped coming to him, but she didn't really mind. She thought it was Kurt but it might have been Vern, her shrink, but he'd come with the braless blonde in the baggy green sweater. Each time she went right back to sleep and didn't know if it was the sex or the pills. Her brain was dead. What were they taking last night, Nembutals or Seconals, reds or yellows or maybe both? She didn't remember. She just kept popping them down with the screwdrivers.

She was trying to decide how she felt. You couldn't really tell until you stood up, but sort of could tell by how much desire you had to get up. She wondered what time it was. She listened. Often she could tell by the sounds, but there aren't many sounds up in the hills. You'd think there might be roosters or dogs, but people who live in the hills and stay up late don't like morning noises. Sometimes she could tell by the angle the light entered the room, but not if there were clouds. Today there were no clouds. She guessed it was after eleven. She heard birds, but no house sounds. Splashing from the pool. Someone trying to drown a hangover.

She wondered if Kurt would come back. She didn't think Vern had stayed, but you never knew in this house. She wouldn't mind seeing Kurt again. It might help her decide to get up. If she laid there much longer she'd fall back asleep. She wouldn't mind that either. She wondered what she would see when she looked in the mirror. She felt around her body for bruises. The nipples hurt. Nothing else until she felt bruises on her neck. That was not good. Easier to hide breasts than necks. Especially by the pool.

A mob of people had come up, some she'd never seen. You were only supposed to come if Archie invited you, but word got around about Angelo Drive and friends brought friends and then it was out of hand. The Sharon Tate lure. Archie supplied the booze, but people brought their own stuff and sharing and mixing started and people started to go down, sometimes on the floor or the lawn, and some of them even made it upstairs until they were thrown out by whoever's room it was. She was sure it was Archie who she started out with, but afterward was a blur. Whoever it was never gave up. Or maybe it wasn't the same guy. She didn't think Archie would allow that, but Archie might have gone down the hill. Or to someone else's room. He keeps saying no more parties, but he loves them too much, loves the action.

She liked Archie and knew he liked her. Archie saw her potential. Job is to figure out what keeps her from realizing it, he said. She'd stick it out. Archie was Hollywood's future. Archie and Trevor Bonfeld. Archie sent her to Vern, the psychologist, who said there was some kind of block. Paying was no problem with the trust Granny had set up for her. The thought of Granny gave her a pang. She'd called Granny, and Iris said she was at UCLA Med Center for tests. She'd tried to find Angelo Drive a few days before, Iris said, come up with Ralph to tell her how everyone missed her, how Kenny Van S. kept stopping by and how Kenny was such a swell boy. Didi smiled. The same Kenny that Granny used to tell her to ditch. Ha!

The windows were brightening. Sounds from the kitchen. Had to be way past eleven. Begonia, the Basque maid, would have cleaned up by now, and people would be making their way to the kitchen. *Kenny.* Down deep she missed him and the good old days, maybe because they went so far back, back to dances at the country club. He was a good dancer and a nice boy and so fucking loyal. But such a nebbish. She liked that word, "nebbish," a Hollywood word, Archie said, because there were so damn many of them around.

She'd wanted to do it with Kenny that first time and maybe if she had things would be different, but it wasn't her fault. Other girls were doing it and talking about it and telling her about diaphragms, and with Kenny it would be safe and secret and so she got the diaphragm and one night when she was home for the weekend, and Iris was off and Granny out with her gigolos she invited him over and put Sinatra on the phonograph and got him on the couch. They'd hardly kissed when he exploded and excused himself and when he came back from the bathroom was so embarrassed he left. *Comme ça.* Imagine having that for a boyfriend!

Lizzie wanted to drive. As the crow flies, Angelo Drive isn't all that far from Sunset, but crows don't follow mountain roads. Angelo is technically Beverly Hills, but not the part people know about. You've got to find the right canyon and then the right road, only three of which make it all the way over the mountains. The others go in circles or lead to dead ends. Lizzie knew the way because she'd been part of the *Times* team that covered the Manson murders on Cielo Drive, which is even harder to find than Angelo. Manson knew the house. You don't find Cielo Drive by accident.

Lizzie insisted on taking her Ford rather than Maggie's Porsche. Angelo is winding and endless and dangerous with steep drops, and Lizzie knew how Maggie drove. So did Billy Todd. They came to the black mailbox with the name Zug and turned off onto a pocked asphalt road leading up a steep hill. The road was cut through jagged stone that sprouted scrub grass and some chaparral stalks through the cracks. Above the cut for the road, scrawny brown pines lusting for sunlight leaned south.

"Not the most inviting driveway I've ever seen," Lizzie said.

"Discourages drop-ins."

"Imagine going back down that canyon at night after a few drinks."

"Drinks or something worse."

The Zug house was a sprawling, two-story, Spanish-style hacienda with white stucco walls and towers on each end and a red tile roof and tiled eve overhang running the length of the facade. Despite its stylistic lavishness, there was something fake about it. In front, five cars, all foreign, all expensive, were parked around a grassy, well-tended roundabout. The scent of jasmine and gardenias rose from bushes, and bright red Bougainvillea climbed along both sides of blue and yellow ceramic steps wending up to the front door, which was open behind a screen. From somewhere they heard cries and splashes. Ascending, they heard voices inside and saw the screen door slowly pushed open. Didi had seen them coming.

"My goodness, a family delegation, mothers, aunts, could a cousin be lurking around somewhere? And a Ford—Mother, how shameful! Where is your Porsche?"

Maggie tried a hug, but it didn't work.

Didi wore a wrinkled purple muumuu and her feet were bare. Her dark hair was brushed after a fashion, but it was too early for make-up, which wouldn't have helped much with the circles under her eyes and bruises on her neck. Her skin was tight and sallow and a little bit twitchy and she held the railing by the door for support. Bad hangover. Maggie looked at her once beautiful daughter, and the word "slovenly" passed her mind.

"How did you find me? Granny told you, didn't she?"

"Granny couldn't find this place. Are you going to invite us in?"

"Just a minute," she said, retreating inside and closing the screen. They heard voices, muttering, doors slamming before she returned. "Some of my friends weren't, shall we say, dressed for the occasion. They've gone out to the pool."

"I would like to meet your friends," said Maggie.

Didi smiled. "They were—well, never mind. They felt like a swim."

The furniture was Spanish oak, large and clunky and made semicomfortable with enormous bulky cushions. The living room was long and, in the Spanish style, dark. They sat down, and Maggie caught a fleeting glimpse of the maid she'd seen on her first visit. The house seemed clean enough, but it was surface clean. Under shaggy rugs and thick cushions and heavy furniture was stuff accumulating faster than any maid could get it out. The smell was the kind you only got out with something that smelled worse. It was a luxury house on a handsome estate high in the hills and icy as an igloo. Two giant sofas faced each other across a well-stained oak coffee table. Didi took one of the sofas, leaving her mother and aunt on the other, a more adversarial positioning than Maggie would have preferred. She was happy to have Lizzie there. Her sister's presence always helped.

"I suspect this delegation has come to take me home," said Didi with a tight little smile. "Wherever home might be."

Maggie looked across at this disheveled, dissipated and dispirited presence. She observed the neck bruises. Not a doubt what they were from. The image of the fastidious little girl at the beach club sitting alone eating egg salad sandwiches with the crusts cut off passed her mind. How could it be? "Your home is in Bel Air, I believe."

"I'm not going back there. What's happened to Granny, anyway?"

"Your grandmother has had a stroke," said Lizzie. "She'd like to see you."

"Probably wouldn't even recognize me."

"Who does?" said Maggie. It slipped out. She tried recuperating. "You could always come live with me."

The arrow had hit its mark, and the girl reddened. "I don't even know where you live, Mother. You never bothered to tell me."

"Because I couldn't find you. Anyway, I'm back in Westwood."

"Either of you have a cigarette by any chance?"

Maggie took out her Tareytons and Zippo. She stood and shook one out for Didi, snapped the lighter and held the high flame toward her daughter, whose hand shook so badly she had to grasp her mother's hand to steady it. Didi's hand was ice-cold.

Maggie lit her own and switched couches, sitting down beside her daughter.

"I live on Tiverton, one floor down from your godfather."

Didi inhaled deeply, and they could almost see the smoke hit her bloodstream and begin mixing with the other poisons. She gave a little shudder. "You three really stick together, don't you?" she said with a massive exhale. "Always have—the Mull musketeers. All for one, and one for all. Ever make room for anyone else in your neat little group?"

"The answer is, yes," said Lizzie, seeing her sister stiffen and cutting in before she could reply. "You want to join, there's plenty of room."

"Sorry, it's a little late."

"You could come stay with Joe and me for a while," said Lizzie.

Didi stared fixedly at her aunt. "Aunt Liz," she said, taking another huge swallow of smoke and hesitating until her lungs fully injected the nicotine into her bloodstream, "do you happen to know how much your son and I hate each other and always have?"

"Robby's gone."

"Why all this venom?" said Maggie suddenly. "Where does it come from?"

Wherever it came from they saw it in her eyes, dark, anxious, lost, distrust mixed with envy and regret. Was there a way out of this, the eyes asked? No, too late, a voice replied. Down deep, maybe, there was a way out, but to get there you had to strip away layers of resentment and remorse and hostility and other stuff, and no one could dig that deep. It couldn't be erased anyway, etched into hippocampus as into granite. The sisters had come to help, and that made it worse. Pity mixed with solicitude makes a sour brew.

Her face still red, she turned to face her mother. "My shrink says everything I do is in reaction to you. My vertigo comes as a reaction to your flying. My fear comes from your fearlessness. He says I have built up antibodies to protect myself against you. That letting you back into my life could kill me."

Maggie's cigarette tasted foul, and when Didi put hers out

on the tile floor, crushing the butt with the sole of her bare foot, Maggie put hers out as well, grinding down harder than she meant to do. Give the maid some work. She was angry; whatever guilt she'd felt over her daughter's disappearance exorcised under the deluge of accusations. We become what we choose. We alone are responsible.

"Had we known this was how things would turn out, we'd never have sent you to Granny's. We thought it was the right thing. Obviously, we were wrong."

"You said, *we*, but it was *you*. You alone." From behind the house somewhere they heard splashing and shouting.

"Not exactly," said Maggie. "Anyway, isn't it what you wanted?"

"What I wanted? How old was I, eight? Why wouldn't I want to go to Granny's when I never saw either parent and spent all my time in that awful public school and with that witchlike old woman with her hairnet and cigarettes and she smelled, smelled—did you ever get a whiff of Mrs. Crotch? I hated her. Of course, I went to Granny's."

"She asks for you," said Lizzie.

"Oh, nice, Aunt Lizzie. A little guilt trip? Well maybe I'll go see her. Or maybe I won't. Maybe I'll just telephone."

"She can't talk on the telephone anymore."

"That's my fault, too, isn't it?"

Lizzie was staggered. Was it something about these hills? The thin air, maybe? She could not come up here without thinking of the Manson murderers, of those girls running around stabbing to death people they didn't even know, butchering poor Sharon Tate who pleaded to let her unborn baby live, zombies stalking the night with their knives, ghoulishly drenching themselves in blood on Manson's orders. She had covered every major story in this city for three decades, yet nothing came close to Manson. Every other calamity lent itself to some sort of explanation. Manson alone was inexplicable horror, the sort of thing we thrill to in movies because it is so obviously bogus. Looking into the dead eyes of her niece, she understood the Manson girls. Killing ourselves or killing others: programed to a hatred of life, life of hatred.

She had to try. "Why are you trying to be so tough, Didi, tough and mean? Forget what your shrink tells you. Granny wants to see you, and you want to see her. We wouldn't mind seeing more of you either. Why not drive down? I'll take you myself if you don't mind my Ford."

"What, tear yourself away from the *Times*?"

"I've left the *Times*."

"God, all this family news I'm missing! No more work, no more prizes. Just you and Uncle Joe in Brentwood."

"We have the foundation. Do you know about the foundation? I'd love to show you around sometime."

Maggie wasn't going to interfere. If Lizzie thought she could break through impregnable barriers of disgust and self-loathing, let her try.

"Do-gooders, that's what you are. That's what Archie calls you: do gooders. Where would the world be without the Mulls?"

"Archie?" said Lizzie.

"Archie Zug, the man in whose house you are sitting. Archie is my director, among other things. Vern is my counselor, also among other things." She was holding nothing back.

"Archie is Wonderworld, isn't he?" said Lizzie.

"That's Trevor. Archie works with Trevor. They're going to build their own studio just as soon as they find the land."

"Tell me, Didi," said Lizzie, fighting against an instinct that wanted to bolt from this noxious presence and these murderous hills, "what's wrong with doing good? Isn't that what life is all about? Isn't that everyone's duty."

"*Duty*? God, wait until I tell Vern that one! My only duty is to myself. Fortunately, Granny gave me some money to do it with—the only Mull who ever gave me anything. I'm in her will, you know. *The only one!*"

"And what will you do with all this money?"

"Why, *spend* it, of course, just like Granny taught me."

They were quiet most of the way down. Too many curves, too many cliffs, too many thoughts. Maggie finally spoke: "So where did we go wrong?"

Lizzie glanced over. "You don't believe that, do you?"

"Of course not."

She fell silent a moment. "My turn next. It took a while to find him. He lives in West Hollywood with his girlfriend. Not far from Uncle Willie's first church."

"Second church."

Lizzie laughed. "That's what I meant, of course."

"Of course."

They were almost down, almost to Sunset. "Here's what Miss Adelaide told me once. She had this big garden up in these hills someplace. She brings home two identical plants from the nursery, plants them in the same sun, feeds them the same, waters them the same: one grows, one withers. What's the answer?"

"It's their nature."

CHAPTER 46

They met in a former wholesale bakery on Romaine Street, a dingy neighborhood in West Hollywood that Howard Hughes had once used as headquarters for Hughes Productions. Robby would not come to the Richfield Building and would not agree to meet on any neutral ground. Even to see him on Romaine Street took a series of phone calls over several weeks. It was not normal behavior for lawyers representing adversarial clients, but they carried more baggage than just lawyers' briefs.

If feud it was, then Romaine Street was a good place for the shootout. The building was two stories of dun-colored stucco with bunker-sized slit windows perfect for Springfields but in fact designed to defeat gawkers and germs in a semi-industrial area you didn't visit unless you had good reason or were lost. Vacant lots filled with debris and stripped-down car carcasses were flanked by metal grinding shops and car painters. Over time it had evolved into Summa's corporate command center, uninviting to the curious, which is what Summa liked about it. Howard Hughes hadn't set foot on Romaine Street in years.

He parked down the street and walked around the block looking for an entrance. It was as welcoming as a castle with the drawbridge up. Various entrances from bakery days had been cemented up so he circled to the rear, finding an alley with a dock area where the bakery trucks once picked up their daily bread. He ascended a ramp and tried a rear door that didn't open. He rang and the door was opened by a young man in LDS uniform, crewcut, white shirt, dark trousers and skinny black tie. He led him inside to a desk and picked up the phone. "Right, sir," he said before hanging up.

"Follow me."

Down a long corridor, Cal heard voices behind closed doors but saw no people. Numbers, not names, on doors, something grim and penitentiary-like about the place. The corridor must have been fifty yards, though hard to judge precisely without windows and in dim light. They took a left turn at the end and came to a glassed-in, heavily lighted switchboard area fitting for a hotel. Manned day and night, the young man said, connected to Summa's worldwide network. Continuing, they turned into another long corridor heading back the original way. He understood he was being taken on a tour. "All these rooms were once used for filmmaking," his guide said. "Developing, cutting, editing, splicing, exhibiting. This one," he opened a door, "was where Mr. Hughes lived for days viewing films and entertaining actors—and actresses, of course," he added, smiling.

He pointed down the corridor. "Those are vaults used to store Mr. Hughes's memorabilia—trophies, awards, clothes, films, photographs, relics from every stage of his legendary life. Only Mr. Hughes and Mr. Gay are allowed to enter the vaults. I'll take you upstairs now for your appointment with Mr. Morton. Perhaps he'll show you the rest of our complex."

Already he hated coming. The tour was to impress him with the power of an institution so secret even its founder had never heard of it. If this was Robby's way of softening him up on the disposition of the Hughes Aircraft properties, he had miscalculated. It was the classic tactic of bullies: flaunt power in expectation you'll back down before the contest even begins. Tactically, it is both clever and risky—clever if it works, risky if it fails and raises the stakes. Eddie Mull had been the master of it, but how would Robby know?

He remembered talking once—only once—with his father about Uncle Eddie, always a taboo subject. He'd wandered down the second floor at the temple to schmooze with Miss Shields, and Willie asked him to come in. He'd been working on a sermon that wasn't coming and needed a break. "Like the Buddha," he said. "You search and search and don't find so you stop. And the answer comes by itself." He'd told Cal what Eddie said about Grandma Eva's death. "Eddie called it a sad event that turned out well for everyone," Willie said. "I didn't respond. How could I? It was his confession. I forgave him."

Cal had steeled himself for this meeting, telling himself it was just one more lawyers' conference. The problem was he couldn't think about Robby Morton without visceral pain. Most people he knew, certainly everyone in the family, had a constancy about them. The more you knew them, the more you got into them, the more you understood. Even truly exotic people like Howard Hughes, ones who operated in the alternative universes of Hollywood and government, had characters that could be pegged. Robby Morton was the one person who did not add up. The adult person he'd become bore no resemblance to the boy Cal had known. He'd asked Joe about it once, Joe who knew his son better than anyone. "Robby is as authentic as any of us," he said. "The problem is that he is authentically duplicitous."

The office was halfway down the drab second-floor corridor. His escort buzzed and the door opened electronically. Inside was a different world from the prisonlike corridors, elegant, obtrusively expensive. It was like the sultans who disguised the entrances to the harems: the pleasures inside are for only the initiated. The reception room was furnished in leafy plants and designer furniture. Oils in the Flemish style and sumi-e black ink drawings were hung. Two young male secretaries in white shirts looked up, one of them nodding and announcing his arrival over the intercom to the room behind, which was shut off by two closed mahogany doors alongside a large, easily visible brass plate with the words:

ROBINSON A. MORTON
Vice President

The door opened electronically, and for the first time since entering the building Cal saw sunlight, though filtered through darkened windows. Behind an impressive desk, mahogany like the doors, his godson greeted him and bid him be seated. He did not rise. There would be no forced bonhomie.

Neither man was given to chitchat, so they simply stared. Though he did not regard himself as a supplicant, there was no doubt about who would be first to speak in this silent duel. "How is Dominique?" Cal tried as opener.

"She is well. Thank you for your interest."

"Your letter came as a shock."

"The letter or the signature?"

"The signature, of course. How did it happen?"

"An opportunity to run one of the most powerful corporations in the world—how could I say, no?"

"With Howard Hughes still alive?"

"Is he?"

"You mean . . .?"

"Think of John Galt."

Silly, sophomoric, maddening, but he'd not come for a discussion of Randian dystopia. "The Sierra Club is not in the same league with Summa," he began, "nor is the Mull Foundation. Our interest is the land. If Summa is now the legal owner of the land, what we'd like is recognition that Summa will respect its founder's wishes as expressed in the letter."

Robby smiled. "What makes you think that Howard Hughes is Summa's founder?"

"*What?*"

"We accept the letter as authentic. The problem is that it is also irrelevant."

Already Cal had learned more than he expected. If Hughes was dead, certainly the news would have come out, even if his minders sought to suppress it. That meant he was alive and quite possibly in disaccord with Summa.

"That will be for a court to decide if we go to trial. I'm hoping to settle this out of court."

"Settle what? You have no standing. We own the land. Hughes is out of the picture."

"Is he dead?"

"That's for you to find out."

Cal had not expected it to be easy. "No court will allow you to build that monstrosity on protected land. So why get the courts involved at all? We can settle this between us."

"*What?* A little side deal? If that's all you've come for, you're wasting my time."

"You *want* to go to court?"

"There are important principles in play here, my friend. We're lawyers, aren't we? That's what we do."

"Principles such as . . . ?"

"Such as preventing outside interference with a property owner's disposition of his land—known, legally, as I'm sure you know, as a taking."

"Oh come off it, Robby, you know perfectly well you can't do whatever you want with that land. I've seen the drawings. You don't have a chance in hell of winning approval for that."

"*Approval.* What are you talking about? *It is our land!*"

A calm man, Cal's temperature was rising. It was not like he was arguing lawyer to lawyer, that had never been hard. But this was Lizzie's son, his own godson. He'd been there at the christening. What could motivate him to set himself up against his own family? It had to be more than just thralldom of a passing pseudo-philosophy. We all grow out of our sophomoric impulses. There was something personal in it. But why?

"Sorry, it's not so simple. You thought you won at Sea Ranch, didn't you? You won the case and the result was that the people passed the California Coastal Act. There will be no Sea Ranches in Playa del Rey. I guarantee it. You are setting yourself against federal, state, and local law—and against the will of the people."

Robby stood up. "I don't have time to argue these pathetic points with you. It is our land. End of story. We have a vision for it. We will find a judge who agrees with us. You mention the people. We intend to build a city on our property—a people's city, just like Sea Ranch is a people's community. The architect is Fred Goering, the best in the world after the Finn, who is dead, and the Chinaman, whom we couldn't get. Goering did the Revlin in Madrid and the Bonhoeffer in Berlin, near the old Bauhaus. No one is going to tamper with his inspiration."

Cal laughed. "Howard Roark. My way or I'll blow it up."

"Cal, I am impressed. You've read *The Fountainhead*!"

"Maggie says the drawings look like East Berlin."

Robby laughed. "I admire Aunt Maggie. Howard Hughes admires her as well, I hear. Tell me, what did she do for Howard at the Flamingo to get that letter you keep bringing up? Or had she done it before? You wouldn't want that to come out in court, would you?"

Cal stood up to face him. "Good God, Robby, what has happened to you?"

"Don't lose it, Cal. You're a better lawyer than that. I'm giving you a taste of what will come out if you try to stop us. Playa Vista will spread to Playa del Rey, right down to the beaches. That is Fred's vision. The ocean must be part of it."

He had to get out, had to breathe again. "Summa doesn't own that land. What exactly do you have against preserving a piece of pristine coastal land in this cemented-over city? You want everything to look like Romaine Street? You don't think people are going to need open spaces more than ever in the future, access to beaches and the ocean, a chance to wander in the wetlands to get away from life on the freeways? You think preserving that is somehow an interference with your private property rights? And you expect some judge to agree?"

"Let's put it this way: Summa doesn't own that land *yet*. We're working on it."

"You'll never get it."

He smiled. "I'll let you in on a little secret. Do you know who has signed on to be the anchor at Playa Vista, to be the industrial hub of our new community? You've heard of Wonderworld? Trevor Bonfeld, founder of Wonderworld, the boy genius of Hollywood, has joined us. We're planning a press conference in a few days. Imagine that. Wonderworld will be the centerpiece of our new city. Just like Hollywood was the centerpiece of old Los Angeles. Get out of the way, Cal, before you are run over."

CHAPTER 47

It wasn't easy to find him. He'd vacated the house in Brentwood without a word and without a forwarding address. Lizzie had come home from work one evening, and Joe announced, "he's gone, packed his suitcase and decamped." They assumed he'd moved in with Dominique, and if they didn't know a thing about Dominique, including her last name, it wasn't for lack of trying. He'd been as mysterious about her as about the job he'd taken. They'd seen Dominique exactly once, at Didi's graduation party, and Cal was the only one who'd had a chance to talk to her. The only communication they'd had from Robby since his departure was the letter from Summa, purportedly written by Howard Hughes.

Lizzie hadn't worked at the *Times* for three decades without knowing her way around the city. She wouldn't go through Summa, so she went through the post office. Robby had filed a forwarding address from Brentwood, and after a few calls she had it. Curiously, his house was not only close to Uncle Willie's second church on Beverly, it was also just off San Vicente—the Los Angeles San Vicente, not the Brentwood one—the house itself on a street called Dorrington, a name not that different from Brentwood's Barrington. Funny coincidences that she was sure didn't mean a thing. Aside from his curiosity about Eddie Mull and his estate, Robby had never shown the slightest interest in family history.

Unannounced, she arrived early on a Wednesday evening. Robby was a creature of routine, and there was a good chance of finding him home. It was a pretty little street of Spanish stuccos not that far off the Strip but quiet and neighborly under spreading Ficus trees. She parked in front, walked up and rang. She'd hoped that Dominique would be out, but it was Dominique who opened the door. Surprised, she stood a moment speechless, then smiled and welcomed her. "Mrs. Morton, it's been so long."

Lizzie put her hand out. "Hello, Dominique. And please call me Lizzie. I was hoping Robby might be home."

A screen door at the rear opened, and she saw him looking in. He stood at the door a moment, advanced, blinking behind his horn-rims. "Mother, anything wrong?"

They stood there like adversaries, across the room at ten paces, Dominique looking on. In the brief moment Lizzie had with her before the screen door opened, she'd looked closely, remembering back to the one time she'd seen the girl at Bel Air, just before being called away for the horrible week in Watts. Even in simple skirt and sweater, she was stunning, with long dark hair put up in back and a figure that reminded her of Maggie. She had a reserve about her, a vulnerability that Lizzie suspected appealed to Robby as much as her appearance.

"Nothing wrong, Robby. I was hoping we might find a few moments to talk."

He hesitated, then said, "Sure, come out into the yard."

"Would you like something to drink Mrs. Morton"

Lizzie touched the girl's arm. "I'm fine, honey, thank you."

She crossed to the screen door, which Robby held open, and they went into the garden. Dominique did not follow.

She'd been into dozens of houses like this over the years, houses she'd come to think of as old Los Angeles, though few went back further than the twenties. They lined both sides of streets like Dorrington with their white stucco facades and red tile roofs, all one-story, usually with two windows onto the street. There'd be a postage-stamp lawn and sometimes a hedge or picket fence in front for those who liked privacy. The back yards were never much, big enough to toss a ball around and hang the laundry. Rear hedges or wooden fences separated one row of houses from houses the next street over. Robby's back-yard consisted of untended grass and a fruitless apricot tree that needed trimming. A redwood table and chairs where he'd been working sat in the mottled shade of the tree. The house was clearly rented.

"Have a seat, Mother. What's this all about?"

The Mulls were never big on outward displays of affection. Maggie had come back from France kissing people on both cheeks, but it hadn't lasted. Lizzie always assumed it was the Presbyterian way, something careful about it, unsure, never demonstrative, even in church. Even Uncle Willie, despite his preacherly gifts, had not been a kisser. An occasional hug, yes, when they were children, but that was it.

"It's about us," she said.

She waited a moment, watching him shift in his chair, obviously uncomfortable. Late twenties, hair receding slightly, Joe's myopic look behind horn-rims, physically unexceptional, socially difficult but mentally at the top of every class. She won-dered why she felt so awkward in his company. The grass under-foot wasn't all that different from the grass in Brentwood where she'd crawled around with him when he was a toddler. Those were good times. She remembered him sitting under the bitter orange tree, sucking on that sour sap. He would make faces but go right on eating, unphased. She didn't see enough of him then, she understood that now, but had loved him as much as if she had. It went by so fast. And they sent him off to school as parents have been doing forever. What was so wrong with any of that?

"Dominique is lovely," she said, drifting. "I'd forgotten."

He took off his glasses, and she recognized Joe's myopic look. "You didn't come here to talk about Dominique. How did you find me, anyway?"

She ignored the question. "Robby, we don't want this quarrel to end up in court. We don't want to be suing each other. You don't want that either, do you?"

"That's the same thing Cal said. You didn't come barging in down here just to repeat what he said, I hope. Waste of time."

She ignored the barging in. "I didn't know you'd seen Cal."

"He came to Romaine Street. Don't you two talk?"

"All right," she said, straightening up. "We won't talk about that. Let's talk about us."

"Nothing to say."

"But there is, you know. This wall of hostility you've put up against everyone: Can't we do something about it?"

He started to respond and stopped. He turned to look around the yard, and she wondered if he had the same thoughts she'd had earlier about Brentwood. Probably not. He'd never been nostalgic as a child.

"You're wrong," he said. "The only hostility I feel is—toward you."

It stung, but didn't surprise. She felt the same way toward him and wondered about it—which is why she'd come: to see if there was a way out.

"Why?"

A little laugh escaped him, and he fidgeted in the chair. "Do we really want to go there?"

"You're going to say I wasn't a very good mother."

"Oh, come on," he snarled. "We're beyond that. Maybe I wasn't a very good son. Who knows? Who cares? Look, let's lay our cards on the table. You remember that day in Brentwood when you told me what you and Aunt Maggie were doing with

Grandpa Eddie's estate? I asked if I shouldn't have something to say about it, and you brushed me off. Got up and walked in the house. Do you remember that? I wonder if you do." He leaned closer to her across the table.

"Did you really expect that after that things could be normal between us? How much are we talking about—forty, fifty million, and it's none of my business? I don't think so."

She stared in disbelief. In all her self-reproach over countless missteps as a mother over countless years, never had she considered that money might be the root of the problem. Love, affection, involvement, those were the things she had thought about. Never her father's estate. How naïve she'd been, how stupid! She sat stunned, embarrassed for him, angry at the venality of it, as if she was staring at the reincarnation of her father. She didn't want to blurt out something she would regret, but wanted to set the record straight. "We are doing good things with that estate, Robby. Without your help."

"You have no right," he said, the voice louder now. "It's not just yours. I am family, too. Do you know what Eddie Mull would say about what you're doing with his money—he would say you're dishonoring his memory, spitting on his grave. That's why I asked you about it back then. At least I could have used the estate in a way that honored him."

He stood up quickly, flushed, angry, staring hard at her. "And what about Grandma Nelly's estate. She's not going to leave anything to that stupid Didi, is she? That would be another insult to Eddie's memory. I hear she's had a stroke. Incompetent. You're not manipulating her, I hope. I could sue over that, you know."

Awful. She got up to go. There was no salvaging this. If she'd known money was behind it she never would have come, never would have wasted so much emotion feeling guilty. He had freed her, expiated the guilt. She just hoped she could get away without exploding. She saw Dominique watching from inside. She eyed a path along the side of the house. She did not want to have to go back inside. "I'm sorry. I'm leaving. This hasn't worked."

Scowling, he came up close to her. The vision of the little boy with the sour orange in his mouth came back to her. "Why did you come?" he demanded.

Her chest felt tight. She caught her breath. "Do you know, I had a dream that one day you would take over the foundation. Help us do all the good things we're doing, atone for some of the evil done by my father."

"The first thing I would do at the foundation is liquidate it. You are the enemy, Mother, and the sad thing is you don't even know it. You and your little old ladies in tennis shoes and purple hair are standing in the way of progress. Your father would be ashamed of you."

She shuddered, looked him in his blue eyes and hated what she saw. Could babies have gotten mixed up, switched at birth? No, he was too much like Eddie. He had become exactly what he wanted, free of inhibition, free of constraint, free of conscience, free to do what he wanted regardless of consequences. He hadn't needed her help.

"I was wrong to think you would help," she said. "You're worse than he was."

He slapped her face. "Eddie Mull was the only one of you worth anything."

She felt the sting, felt the tears, tears of pain, not emotion, she wasn't a crier. She'd never been slapped before. She held her ground, stunned, infuriated, repressing an instinct to slap back, something she'd never done.

The screen door to the house slammed, and Dominique ran out, shouting.

CHAPTER 48

"Rosie Roberts is here for your eleven o'clock," said the voice on the intercom.

Maggie went to the door to meet her visitor. Rosie Roberts had called reception a few days earlier with a message that she had information that would interest the Mull Foundation. She wouldn't say more than that. She identified herself as president of something called the Ballona Club and, no, they were not seeking a grant.

"You don't remember me, do you?" said the attractive fiftyish woman holding out her hand. She had thick, short, straw-colored hair and wore a mint silk blouse over beige flare pants. A gold wedding band was her only jewelry. Her skin was delicate white with tiny freckles. Simple and stylish, something un-Californian about her. Also something familiar. Maggie stared, searching her memory.

"Charlie's Market," said Rosie. "I saw you there a few times when you lived in Playa del Rey. I knew who you were, always have." She smiled. "Or at least since the war."

"I do remember seeing you. You should have said something."

"Too shy to accost a lady doing her shopping."

She didn't seem shy at all. "Come sit down. How are things in Playa del Rey?"

"Funny thing is that we were neighbors. You lived in the corner house on Montreal, and I lived just down Fowling Street with a view straight out over Ballona. Used to walk my dog by your house, hoping we'd meet, but the only place I ever saw you was Charlie's."

"I tended to get up early and come home late."

"And now?"

"I'm back in Westwood. It's a shorter drive."

Yes, Maggie remembered this woman, remembered catching sight of her in the little market at the foot of the hill where everyone shopped, remembered thinking that she was too elegant for the beach, too pale, though it would be natural with hair and skin like hers to stay out of the sun. She did nothing to hide her age—no makeup, no lifts, no makeovers, a woman content with what nature had given her.

"How is Charlie's?"

"Same place. Charlie died. Owned by Koreans now."

"Tell me about the Ballona Club."

She'd come to talk about the Summa hearings. An hour later they decided to continue the discussion at the Sixth Street Grill, where the hamburgers were good.

Like countless others, Rosie Travers had come west because she thought she was attractive and talented enough to land a job in Hollywood. The stories of those who never quite make it are the stuff of films usually better than those for the ones who do make it, but Rosie had no regrets. She met Bruce Roberts, who worked for a local television station, a man who loved the outdoors as much she did. She'd been brought up on Long Island, near the Seatuck Wildlife Refuge. Her father, Ed, had a twenty-foot ketch, and by the time Rosie was a teenager he'd taken her into every cove and inlet between Great Cove and Nicoll Bay. Their favorite cruise was south to the little islands north of Fire Island, dots in the Great South Bay. They went with poles, buckets, backpacks, cameras and boots. Ed had filled a dozen scrapbooks with photos of their excursions by the time Rosie left home.

"Playa del Rey was natural for us," she said, biting into a

juicy burger. "Bruce was raised in Newark—California's Newark, that is, on San Francisco Bay. He grew up with boats and tides and marshes just like I did. We actually met on an outing. He kept a rowboat in Ballona Creek, not far from the old UCLA boathouse." She laughed. "Our first date was in his rowboat if you can believe it. He kept an inflatable raft in the rowboat, one of those one-man army surplus things . He would paddle around the marshes and do a little fishing. He tried to get me into that thing once, but there's no room for two—which he knew."

Rosie was entertaining, but her serious side kept breaking through. "Those Ballona marshes, by the way, with rowboats and rafts, are part of the area that Summa claims is not wet enough to be classified as wetlands. Now you tell me how you can row a boat and fish on ground that isn't wet. I doubt anyone from Summa has ever set eyes on Ballona, which, if you think about it, is actually a mini Everglades. The name wetlands does not fit a place where you can push out in a rowboat and drop your line six feet in the water."

As much as Rosie talked, Maggie had the feeling she was holding something back, something to do with the real reason she'd come to the foundation. She mentioned trips to Sacramento but offered nothing about why she'd gone, even when Maggie asked. "One more trip to make first," was all she would say. The Ballona Club had grown from five members to more than a hundred, growth spurting on news of Howard Hughes's death, which people in Playa del Rey understood was going to change things permanently for the place they called home.

In Salt Lake City, Bill Gay announced that a search was underway for a Hughes will, which would clarify any questions about disposition of the Hughes land. In Los Angeles, "Ram" Morton, with Trevor Bonfeld by his side, held a press conference to proclaim that Summa was going ahead with Fred Goering's plan to create a unique "city within a city" called Playa Vista that encompassed land from Hughes airfield to the Pacific Ocean. Howard Hughes, said Morton, had signed off on the design before his death.

Maggie's second meeting with Rosie came a month later in the Sierra Club's offices in what was now called the ARCO Building, with Cal and Lizzie also present. This time Rosie came with a thick, heavily tabbed notebook and was finally ready to talk about Sacramento, whence she'd just returned. Since Hughes's death, she had visited every state agency that had any responsibility for land management, wildlife or the coast. She'd met with staffs and directors and spent time in their archives and libraries, making notes and taking photos with a mini archival camera.

"It looks like someone in the governor's office has been bought," she said, turning to a tab at the back of the notebook and producing several photos. "These survey documents from the Department of Land Management classify one-half of the Ballona land, or roughly sixteen hundred acres out of thirty-two hundred, as wetlands protected from development under the Coastal Act. That would protect everything between the Hughes airfield and the new marina and west to Playa del Rey." She passed the documents around. "However, in its official filing, the governor's office stated that the Ballona wetlands consisted of only five hundred acres, not sixteen hundred, which is ridiculous."

"How could they do that?" asked Lizzie.

"Summa got to somebody. I had the feeling that Land Management wanted their report to be made public, that they don't agree at all with the governor's office. They are as interested in stopping Summa as we are."

"I smell a story," said Lizzie

"But you're not a reporter anymore," said Cal. "You run a foundation."

"Why would the governor be cheating on official survey documents?" asked Maggie.

"I doubt it got to the governor," said Rosie. "More likely someone in his office is on Summa's payroll."

"The Coastal Commission will have to rule on this," Cal said. "Trouble is that commissioners are politicians, too. What if Summa gets to them?"

"So we go to the people again," said Rosie. "As I've told Maggie, that's why I came to the foundation."

"So you *do* want money."

"No! This will be your campaign."

"Do you have any idea how much it costs to run a referendum campaign? Against Summa, with its billions?"

"We'll have the *Times* on our side," said Lizzie.

"Isn't Dorothy Chandler fundraising for a huge arts pavilion across First Street from the *Times*?" asked Rosie.

"I believe so," said Lizzie.

"And isn't the pavilion architect Playa Vista's own Fred Goering?"

"Otis won't sell out because of his mother's arts pavilion, will he?" said Maggie.

"You've never met the mother," said Lizzie.

Cal threw up his hands. "How do you do battle with something like Summa?"

"Resistance starts with a few brave souls meeting over coffee and cookies," said Rosie, "and grows and grows. On Long Island, nearly the whole south coast is a national wildlife refuge thanks to a group of ordinary New Yorkers influencing one man." She smiled. "Of course that one man was Theodore

Roosevelt. Interesting to think that Roosevelt's main legacy today, the thing that put him on Mount Rushmore with the three greats—the only thing in my opinion—is his conservation legacy, the national parks. Everything else is forgotten."

"If we pull this off, we'll get someone to carve Eddie's head into the Hollywood Hills," said Cal.

"Who's Eddie?" said Rosie.

"Eddie Mull was my father," said Maggie, looking at Lizzie, "our father. He made his fortune on oil and land, which is the money we used to start the foundation. He doesn't deserve his head on the Hollywood Hills. He would not be with us today."

"But his money is," said Lizzie to Rosie, "and that's what matters. They were twin brothers, Eddie and Willie Mull. Willie was Cal's father. Eddie was our father. They arrived in Los Angeles with the water."

"I want to make another point," said Rosie. "Actually it is my main point. Our view at the Ballona Club is that we can't stop Playa Vista from developing the airfield—hence, we shouldn't even try. The airfield is already zoned for industry and has to go anyway because of its proximity to L.A. International. Our goal should be to protect everything west of that."

"I agree absolutely," said Cal. "Everything west of that is the land Mull Oil sold to Hughes, half of which went to the county for the marina. The other half, south of the marina and west of the airfield is the land we want to protect. If we achieve that, we win."

"And, finally, we atone," said Lizzie. "The oil wells are gone and the land restored."

Rosie went back to her notebook and extracted a letter. "Do you know anything about this fellow Morton?" she asked, passing the letter around. "That's the signature on this letter from Summa requesting—actually ordering—us to stop our campaign to preserve Ballona. Morton claims Hughes supported Summa's plans."

"Howard hated Summa," said Maggie.

"That's not what they say," said Rosie. "They think his will makes clear his agreement with Summa on Playa Vista."

"If they find a will that supports Summa," said Maggie, "it is a forgery. I can testify to that. Howard had never even heard of Summa. I was the one who told him."

"Morton is lying," said Lizzie, softly.

"Who is he?" said Rosie.

"You don't know?" asked Cal.

"How would she?" said Lizzie. "I don't use the name Morton." She looked to Rosie.

"This whole story is a family story. Eddie Mull, our father, owned the land we're talking about—all the land except Hughes Aircraft. When he died, it passed to Maggie and me and we sold it to Howard Hughes who gave us a letter stipulating that the land remain protected."

Lizzie stopped long enough to look at all of them, one by one, remembering the sting from her son's slap, feeling her face reddening again. Was that possible?

"Robinson Morton is my son, who now works for Summa. We don't agree on this. Or on anything else to be honest."

CHAPTER 49

"A Miss Dominique Martin on the line. Says it's personal. Will you take it?"

"Dominique Martin?" he said over the intercom. "I don't know any—ah, yes, as a matter of fact, I do know a Dominique. Or did. Put her on."

"I'm not sure you remember me, Mr. Mull," sounded a hesitant voice when he picked up. We met at Didi Heyward's graduation party a few years ago, back when—well, you know, back then."

"I do, remember, Dominique, of course I do. You're Robby's friend."

"Robby, yes, Ram, I am Robby's friend . . . at least . . . anyway, that's what I'm calling about."

"Ah."

The line went silent.

"Dominique?"

"I wonder if I could talk to you."

"Of course. What's on your mind?"

"It's just that, well, it's rather personal. I wondered if we could meet."

What could possibly prompt Robby's girlfriend to call him on a personal matter, he asked himself. Robby was devious, but probably not to that point. On the other hand, better not invite his girlfriend to his office with the Summa hearings coming up.

"Where are you, Dominique?"

"I'm at Union Station."

Union Station? How strange, he thought. He checked his

watch. He had no lunch plans. "Are you going or coming?"

Long hesitation. "I'm not sure."

Trouble in the voice. Should he do this? Family. No choice.

"Do you know la Golondrina on Olvera Street?

"I can find it."

"Just cross Alameda Street in front of the station, turn right at the plaza and follow Olvera to the restaurant. If you get lost, just ask. Everyone knows La Golondrina. It's been there forever. I'll meet you in half an hour."

"I'll be there."

She was as gorgeous as he remembered, though not quite so blooming. Her dark eyes fixed on you with a startling openness. An alluring girl, not joyful but easy to like, probably easy to love, serious, fragile, not someone to be frivolous with. She wore a gray worsted suit, of all things, well-tailored, far too proper for lunch on Olvera Street. Travel clothes. White blouse with a simple gold chain around her neck. No rings. Carried a small black purse. Feminine though not stylish. Dark hair pulled up in back. People watched her as she stood alone outside the restaurant. She looked exhausted but put on a pretty smile for him. They shook hands. He was moved by her without knowing why. Something in her of Angie, the young Angie, courage and vulnerability. What was this fragile flower doing with the brute who called himself Ram?

The waiter led them to a table. He thought briefly of margaritas, but they ordered iced tea and a fajitas plate for two. The waiter put down salsa and a basket of chips. Still quiet, no mariachis in sight, thank heaven. She'd thanked him outside for coming, but hadn't said much else. He smiled. He didn't know what else to do. Despite seeing Robby professionally, he knew nothing of his private life. Robby was a mystery. So was Dominique.

"Union Station?" he said. Again the shy, silent smile.
"Checked your bags?"

"Bag." The iced tea came. She took a long sip, glancing at
him over the rim. For some reason he was starving. They took
their time at Golondrina, thus the chips and salsa. "The train's
not until two-thirty."

"Where are you going?"

"I don't know."

How could she know when the train was leaving if she
didn't know where she was going? Something strange going on,
but not coming out. Maybe the fajitas would help. He ate some
chips and salsa, wondered again about margaritas. He didn't
want the iced tea. She was eating, too. Good sign, he thought.
Hot salsa to burn out the truth.

"I wonder if I should be doing this," she said, hesitantly. "I
was staring at the departure board, asking myself what train to
take, and it struck me how silly it was to come to Union Station
and not know where you're going. I looked around at people
dashing in every direction, everyone with a destination—north,
south, east." She tried a little smile. "Obviously you can't go far
west. I needed someone to talk to. I thought of you. Just looked
up the Sierra Club in the book and here we are."

Lovely smile, but so sad. Odder and odder, he thought.
Why couldn't she talk to Robby? Or friends or relatives? How
long had they been together? And no one to call but me who
she's met once in her life and that time at a party years ago. He
decided not to bother her with questions. Let her tell it her own
way. There was something moving in her sad manner.

"Why you, you're wondering, but who else? I couldn't call
Ram's mother, not on something like this."

Like *what*, he wondered.

"They don't talk anyway. In fact . . ."

She started a thought and abandoned it, taking a sip of iced tea instead. He waited.

"Then I remembered how nice you were to me at Didi's party. So sad about her, isn't it? And then there's the fact that you and Ram have been in contact, that you have influence with him. He doesn't talk to his mother or dad anymore, but still talks to you."

He didn't bother to say that the only reason Robby still talked to him was that they were antagonists in a long and difficult legal proceeding. As for influence, not a chance. She probably knew that anyway. Or did she? Did they talk to each other? He had no idea of her relationship to Robby. Apparently, they were still together. How long had it been? Surely someone would have heard if Robby had married. And there would be a ring, wouldn't there?

The fajitas came, a big plate of carne asada with vegetables and frijoles and side dishes of peppers and cheese and a smaller plate of tortillas covered in a linen napkin.

"You first," he said and watched her start filling and wrapping the tortilla. He could see she was hungry. When she'd finished, he started on his own plate.

"It's hard, Mr. Mull, hard for me to do this."

The eyes were brimmed, but tears were not yet falling.

"It might be easier if you'd call me Cal."

She nodded. "You're Ram's kin, but also a stranger to me. It's just that I had to tell someone. I couldn't just get onto a train to nowhere without at least trying to talk to someone in the family."

Train to nowhere?

"You were absolutely right, Dominique."

"You've probably guessed by now that I'm pregnant."

He looked quickly up. No, he hadn't guessed, not at all,

the thought never having crossed his mind. A woman might have guessed. He hadn't. Pregnancy would explain the suit and jacket, but so would the train. It certainly didn't show. The changes he'd noticed were in her face and demeanor, not her figure.

She took a bite. He did the same. Golondrina supplied knives and forks but you don't eat fajitas with knives and forks.

"I guess that's why I'm so hungry."

Silence fell as they ate. He had no idea what to say, the things coming to mind all ringing false. He obviously couldn't tell her that everyone in the family was sick about Robby, that no one trusted him, not even his father, who'd made excuses for him until running out of excuses. She clearly had a reason for calling him beyond commiseration. Hungry or not, she ate delicately, carefully taking little bites, dabbing at her mouth. He remembered how Robby ate, ravenously, sloppily. What did she see in him? She looked up from time to time with her little smile, sad maybe, but there was determination in there, too. He liked that. After a while she stopped eating, wiped her hands gently and took a long drink of iced tea.

"Ram offered me money for an abortion," she said, staring hard, unblinking, "but I wouldn't take it. I don't want an abortion. As crazy as that sounds for a single girl like me, I don't want an abortion. I don't know how I could possibly earn a living with a child, but I don't want an abortion. It's nothing religious or anything like that, just instinctive. Ram threw me out, said how could he be sure the child was his—which is absolutely untrue and unfair." This time the tears fell. "Who else's could it be?"

He took the handkerchief from his breast pocket and passed it to her, holding her hand briefly. Warm hand. She tried smiling again, but her heart wasn't in it.

"I thought of you because you could talk to Ram's mother. I thought—she's lost her son, but might like to have a grandchild. She seemed like such a nice person, though we only met that one time at Didi's party, the same time I met you. Actually, I saw her once after that, which put the thought in my mind." She handed the damp hanky back to him. "Stupid of me, isn't it, giving a baby away that isn't even born, but I wouldn't be giving it away, would I? Not really. I could still be there. It might work out for everyone. Just like Didi's baby."

She'd packed a lot into those sentences.

"You know about Didi's baby?" he said, at length.

"I do know. I know that Eric—that's his name, isn't it?— is being raised by his grandparents after Didi's death; that he apparently shows no signs of being a drug baby. How very, very hard it must be for Didi's mother. I can't imagine something like that. I don't think Ram liked Didi, but she was so beautiful. I met her just that once at her grandmother's party, and I did like her. Ram didn't want to go to the funeral."

He'd stopped eating, unable to take his eyes off her, so gentle, so vulnerable. "The arrangement with the van Swerigens has worked out well." he said. "Kenny sees Eric when he can. Kenny's at UCLA Medical School, you know. Didi's grandma would have approved of the arrangement. Do you remember Nelly Mull from the party?"

"I do remember her."

"A lovely woman, like a mother to me. She was very fond of Kenny. Nelly passed away you might know. Another funeral Robby missed."

"No, I didn't know."

"Didi was clean when she married Kenny. We don't know what happened, why she went back to using."

"Ram said the baby wasn't Kenny's."

Cal froze, his eyes boring into the girl. "He is lying."

She dropped her eyes. "I'm sorry. I shouldn't have said that."

He struggled not to say more, not to say everything he knew about the man she was living with. Maybe she knew already.

She fixed him in the eyes but did not dispute him. They sat in silence, picking at their plates. He was mad. Rarely did he lose his temper, but he could not let pass such calumny. He needed to calm down.

"You know, Dominique, in this state a woman has rights. You have lived with Robby and become pregnant by him. Any court will see that you obtain a decent settlement. Perhaps you could afford to keep the child. Robby is a wealthy man."

"No," she said. "No, I couldn't accept money from him now. That's why I thought of Ram's mother. If Kenny's parents are raising Eric, Ram's parents might want to raise my baby."

He wondered about her own parents. From the Midwest somewhere, wasn't she? If she was breaking up with Robby why wouldn't she think of her own parents instead of Robby's? Why didn't she know what train she was catching? And to where? The Super Chief to Chicago? Leaves every day at four.

"And your own parents?"

Slowly, she shook her head. She said nothing, but it was not hard to imagine: One more pretty girl breaking with her family, coming to Hollywood and getting lost. She went back to eating, her body demanding nourishment. He wondered how far along she was. Maybe it did show under the jacket. How different it was to be a woman! A woman obsesses about it, and a man doesn't even notice. He thought of Angie, the young Angie in the swishy skirt and tight sweater. Angie always knew what she was doing. He was not so sure about Dominique.

"I'm going to order a margarita," he said. "Would you like one?"

She shook her head. He ordered just as the mariachis came in from Olvera Street, strumming their way across the floor toward them in their gaudy charro outfits. A few other inside tables were occupied, but why wouldn't musicians head for the table with the pretty girl? The lead guitar said something and they began singing "La Llorona." Had they seen her tears? He wondered if she understood the song of the woman crying over her lost lover.

She caught his eye, trying to be brave, trying to let the music comfort her. Even when sad, mariachis never depress, always manage to convey something infinitely human in their laments. What kind of man abandons a woman like this; any woman in such a situation? He would not think about that; he would throw himself into his work in hopes of making a better world for the little ones hiding in the wombs of girls like Dominique. He wished she'd called Lizzie rather than him, but understood. He didn't know how Lizzie would react to raising a grandchild, to skipping steps, as Nelly called it. No, of course she would agree. Joe, now in his eighties, would become a new daddy.

He had his own situation to think about. One way or another Robby would hear of this meeting, and how would that affect the hearings? Tampering? He was not tampering; he was a family member whose advice had been solicited on a delicate matter that had nothing to do with their legal dispute. He'd wondered at first if Robby might have had something to do with this meeting, but it was impossible. The girl was guileless.

His drink came. The cool tequila felt good in his veins. The mariachis were on to "La Norteña," a happier piece. He lifted his glass. "Here's to you and your baby, Dominique."

She smiled gently, a ray of happiness in there somewhere.

CHAPTER 50

April 29, 1986. Lizzie stood alone in the center of the children's room in the Los Angeles Central Library. For *Barton Pitts*, she'd given her reading in the library's main room, beneath the rotunda, under the sweeping Cornwell murals depicting California's history, a spectacular setting but she might as well have been in the Hollywood Bowl for all the intimacy. For *Transportation Conspiracy* and *Sister Angie*, she'd chosen the children's room, long and narrow, crammed with books and tables under exposed beams and leaded windows and a dozen tall reading lamps; large enough to seat two hundred yet intimate like a comfy den or the corner of an old bookstore. For her fourth book, she was back again.

"Why did you write this book, Ms. Mull?" asked a prim, middle-aged lady probably more comfortable with Austen or Trollope than with contemporary memoirs. "It is so personal, so—so *intimate*. Your son can't be too happy. Didn't you feel you should hold something back?"

Laughing would have been rude. She'd finished her reading, now the readers got their turn. "You tell what you know. I wanted a story about my city in my century. The Mull family tells that story, from the aqueduct to Playa Vista. It's all in there, the good and the bad. Any memoir that holds back or embellishes is a lie. My son can write his own book."

She'd aged well, some said better than her sister, but then she was a year younger and her life had been less turbulent—at least in the beginning. Her thick flaxen hair had turned gray and grown thinner, which she didn't mind. In her seventieth year, her weight hadn't changed more than a few pounds, nor had anything given out on her yet. Her eyesight wasn't what it was, but she remained healthy and active and walked constantly around Brentwood, even more now that Joe was gone. It was a good neighborhood for walking. She greeted neighbors she'd known for years.

With Joe, they would write mornings and walk in the afternoon. She set up her desk in Robby's old bedroom, leaving Joe alone to work in his study. After work, they'd take a light lunch, putter around in the garden, pick some oranges off the Sevilla for orangeade (sweetened, of course) and do a little more work before heading down San Vicente to Thirty-One Flavors for coffee and ice cream. Sometimes they walked up to Sunset. There was more traffic than there once was, but they'd scrapped the trolleys hadn't they? The traffic was no better anywhere else, so they stayed put. They'd grown used to Brentwood.

When Joe died and they buried him next to Terry in Westwood—just down the path from Baby Snooks—she'd thought of moving into something smaller but as things turned out was glad she didn't. Little Maggie moved into Robby's old room when she arrived, and Lizzie moved her work into Joe's study, redecorating to not drown in nostalgia. Before long, she was walking Maggie to school, the same walk Joe once made with Robby, and home again to make coffee and eat the bagel picked up at the bakery on San Vicente. She'd be showered and at her desk by ten and sometimes go straight through to mid-afternoon when school was out. Twice a week she spent the day in research at the central library. She was as busy as ever.

"What's your sister think about you revealing all her secrets?" asked a neat little Miss Marple type in rimless spectacles and a gray chignon. She sat next to the Austen lady.

"Maggie's sitting behind you. You can ask her at the signing. I didn't reveal all her secrets because I don't think I know them all—thank heaven."

She laughed with the audience.

"Oh, I *will* ask her," said the lady, turning around to look. "I want to know all about Howard Hughes." More laughter.

Following the question period, the audience would queue up at the table next to the podium for the signing. One of the librarians was there to help. A young girl roamed the room with a microphone. Always happier asking than answering, writing than speaking, Lizzie had learned to endure these sessions. Readers generally were fans, though not always. She'd been threatened over the Pitts book and sued over the transportation conspiracy. She'd learned to scrutinize her audiences and decided this one was fine except for the blond boy who kept moving around in the back, in and out, never sitting, something on his mind.

"Are you worried about libel suits?" asked a knife-faced man in a baggy brown suit and wearing an ugly purple and gold tie. A reporter? "The Chandlers can't be too happy."

"Newspaper people don't sue each other," she answered. "We don't want readers to get any ideas."

It was a large, mostly friendly crowd. Library people, she'd discovered over the years, were different from bookstore people. She'd done readings at Campbell's in Westwood and Vroman's in Pasadena, pleasant enough places, but her favorite site was the central library. Something about a library, especially one as grand as the central, commanded a reverence you didn't always find in bookstores. The silence? Or to be surrounded by the prophets of the ages staring down on you from the heaven of their high shelves. Be in awe. Be respectful. Check bad thoughts at the door. She looked out on an audience of maybe a hundred and fifty, smiled toward Maggie and Cal, still there for her, as always.

Someone with a camera made her think of Luis Ortega and their trip to Baja in search of Uncle Willie. The *Times* had a plaque for Luis in its rotunda, as it did for all its people killed in action. There might be a *Times* reporter here as well, though she'd scheduled an interview later in the week. She scarcely recognized the *Times* anymore, which had returned to the bad old days. She still had some friends there, but rarely saw them. Poor Otis turned into a recluse grinding his teeth up the coast at Ojai. The revenge of the family coupon-clippers. He'd put it to them for a while, cut into their dividends and interest to build a newspaper worthy of the city.

"What makes your family different from any other?" a man asked. "Lots of families arrived with the aqueduct. That's why they built it."

Long mustache and longer bolo tie, made her think of Henry Callender. No aggression in the question, just curiosity. She didn't see a book in his hand. Potential customer. Be nice. He was seated near Rosie and friends from her Ballona group. "That is for you to judge, sir. You're here for a reason. Must be something about the Mulls that interests you."

"Yes, there is," he said, quickly, before the girl could get the microphone back. "The Reverend Willie Mull. Goodness gracious, could we use him today in this godless place!" Some embarrassed tittering, but clapping as well, the god-fearing against the godless. "He wasn't your pa, that would be Eddie, but maybe you could tell me this: Why did he do it, Ms. Mull? Why did he run off to Mexico with that little tramp?"

He sat down amid a few hisses. Don't speak ill of the dead, she thought, especially when she's been murdered. Cal would hate that. She glanced toward him. Cal and Angie. He just couldn't do it, not after his father, though who knows what might have happened had she lived. More people remembered Angie these days than Willie. The strange young blond man with long hair appeared in the door and was gone again. Like he was reconnoitering.

"Last time I heard, the Temple of the Angels was filled every Sunday and still doing its broadcasts," she said. "People remember the good that Sister Angie did for Los Angeles and for its people."

A man stood up who bore every mark of a reporter except the fedora with a press pass in the brim. Couldn't be the *Times*. Maybe the *Herald-Examiner*. He held up a copy of the book.

"You've made enemies with this book, ma'am, just like you did with the Pitts book. You must know that. Trevor Bonfeld: he's big in Hollywood. Kids love his movies. Provides lots of jobs. Fred Goering is one of our foremost architects. You dismiss them as misguided narcissists. Are you being fair to them?"

He sat down, and she stared at him for some time. Doing his job, she supposed, just as she'd done in her time. No, not just as she'd done. This man's snarky comments were not meant to elicit information but to provoke her into saying things she'd regret, make her sound like she was settling scores rather than laying out a well-documented history of events.

"Am I being fair? Once you've seen Playa Vista it's pretty hard to be fair. The studios own the mountains all around Hollywood. Plenty of room up there. No lagoons and wildlife to destroy in the mountains. Up there they like things like that, which make movies more authentic. I used to go up there on shoots with my husband." She paused to put on her reading glasses and glance through the book's index, finding what she wanted and turning to the page. "You want to know Bonfeld's attitude toward nature? This is what he said at the Wonder-world press conference with Summa. She read from the book:

> "'All those people worried about the frogs at Playa Vista can rest easy. I'll put frogs in my movies.'"

She looked up and saw heads shaking.

"No other single comment, in my opinion, played a greater role in Summa's defeat than that one. It was so . . . so arrogant, so incredibly supercilious. My hope is that Bonfeld withdraws from this project before he does himself more damage."

The reporter wasn't done. "And Fred Goering?"

The blond with long hair was back. What was he up to? She'd lost her thread. Fred Goering, yes. The architect. She was no public speaker, but the reporter had challenged her.

"Let me tell you about the ordeal we went through—the ordeal of taking on the rich and powerful in this city—and we took them all on, developers, lobbyists, Hollywood, everyone who saw in the beauty of Ballona personal fortunes to be made. All through this battle, which we were given no chance of winning, the one name I kept hearing was Ayn Rand—Ayn Rand the patron saint of capitalism, Ayn Rand the sworn enemy of government, Ayn Rand the purist who prefers death to compromise. In one of her novels, Rand's protagonist is an architect named Howard Roark. When Roark's drawings are altered, Roark dynamites the buildings." She paused to look out at the audience. Rand's reputation had faded badly in recent years except among fanatics, but these library people would remember. "Like Roark, Goering thought he could do it his way. He was wrong. He lost. We won. We used no dynamite."

Some in the audience started to clap, but she held up her hand. "We proved that the people, not money, still rule this country. The Coastal Commission, established by the people of this state, was crucial in stopping Summa. This building we sit in today, this beautiful library, was built and paid for by the people of this city, not by some corporation selling shares, acting in its own interest. It is up to us to be stewards of what we've inherited—both of natural treasures like the lands of Ballona, and manmade ones, like this library."

The blond boy had stopped to listen and was grinning. He was carrying something. Then he was gone again. A young woman in the audience had the microphone.

"Your niece, Didi Heyward, was my sorority sister at UCLA. We were Tri Delts. I came to the graduation party your mother gave for her in Bel Air. Such a sad story, so tragic, such a beautiful girl. Do you blame Archie Zug for what happened to Didi?"

Blame? She glanced toward Maggie. She wouldn't get into that. "We tried to help Didi. Maybe none of us tried hard enough but there's a limit to what you can do when someone is self-destructive. It's up to them. Didi left behind a beautiful boy, Eric Van Swerigen, being raised by her husband Kenny and his parents. Eric has a bright future."

A trim young man in crimson sweater with gold USC letters took the microphone. He cleared his throat and fiddled with the microphone until it cracked and the library girl told him to stop. Self-conscious but determined.

"I wanted to ask about your father, Ms. Mull, a man who's long interested me. I've done some research on Eddie Mull for my thesis." He paused. "I'm not sure how to put this: Your life, and your sister's life, were so different from his, so strangely different, almost like you set out to undo what he did; or do the opposite, yin and yang. Am I right about that? What's your view of your father a half century later?"

She smiled, brushed back a strand of hair, closed the book on the stand in front of her so she could see only the cover, a brilliant gold, green and blue panorama of the city of the angels nestled in the valley under the beautiful mountains. She read the title:

THE MULLS:

A 20th Century history of Los Angeles.

She ran her hand over the smooth dust jacket. "Eddie Mull was a character right out of Ayn Rand: He succeeded, and it cost him his life, a life that had been, let's be honest, ruthless and selfish, just as Rand likes it. He had few friends and mostly ignored his family. He ran roughshod over people. When he died, he left a fortune, which the Mull Foundation is now using for many good causes, none better than to defeat Summa, a company now run, in an ugly twist of fate, by Eddie's grandson."

"But *did* you defeat Summa?" cried a man in the front row. "I've been down there. I've seen Playa Vista."

"Playa Vista is an abomination," she said, "full of darkness and gloom. This is not the sunny place of mountains and beaches and marshes where I grew up. Howard Hughes would be appalled to see what they did to his land. I suspect Playa Vista will be torn down some day and the earth restored, like San Francisco did with the Embarcadero Freeway. Playa Vista will be recognized as a dreadful mistake, like my father's oil wells."

She drank thirstily. Her eyes had begun to hurt. Something in the air.

"But here's the thing: Playa Vista got the Hughes airfield, but that's all it got. Loyola Marymount University has the misfortune to look down on Playa Vista under its cliffs, but if it lifts its eyes just a bit it sees beyond to the marshes and the wildlife, to the beach and the ocean, all as they should be, all as nature made them, free of oil derricks. And it sees Marina del Rey, which shows how man can imitate nature when he tries, instead of destroying it. Eddie Mull did one good thing: He left enough money so his family could undo all the bad he had done. We balanced the ledger."

At the side, she saw Kenny slip into the room, *Doctor* Kenny, the gentle English major Nelly thought was not quite good enough for Didi, had arrived from the hospital. Beside him was Dominique, each holding a child by the hand, Kenny with Eric, Dominique with little Maggie. The children waved, and she smiled back.

"Did we defeat Summa? It is a fair question. Yes, they got the airfield, but they owned property down to the beach and north to Ballona. That's why they called it Playa Vista, which means 'view of the beach.' But they have no view of the beach and never will have. That was our victory."

"How is Los Angeles better today from what it would have been without the Mulls?" asked an elderly gentleman with wispy white hair. "Can you sum the story up in a few words? We're not here just for the wine and cheese, you know."

She took a deep breath while people chuckled and glanced toward the wine and the cheese tables. "A few words, you say. How about this? It is a story of water, oil, land, money, religion, newspapers, aviation, movies, construction, destruction, corruption, murder, birth, death, love, defeat, and victory." She found herself laughing and coughing. "Everything but an earthquake. What else can possibly happen? Surely, there's nothing left."

But there was. The air was growing heavier, and she noticed people with their hands up suddenly bringing them down and nervously looking around. Handkerchiefs were coming out. Suddenly, the shrill sound of an alarm brought people to their feet.

"That's the fire system," announced the librarian calmly into the microphone. "I'm afraid we'll have to leave the building. Nothing serious, I hope. Please take your belongings and follow me out through the rotunda and down the stairs."

Lizzie waved toward Maggie, Cal, and the others as she grabbed the phone from the desk near the podium. The air was smoky. She would call the newspaper and report a fire. Instincts die hard.

"Who is this calling please?" said a voice on Metro desk.

"My name is Elizabeth Mull. I'm at the central library and I want to report a fire. I don't know how serious it is," she paused to listen, "but I can already hear the trucks. Maybe you hear them, too."

"Hold on, please . . . "

"Hold on . . . ? But there's a fire here!"

"Lizzie, is that you? Teddy Lubrano here."

"Teddy, my goodness. It's been so long. Yes, it is me, at the central library, which is on fire. I think it's arson, and I think I saw the boy who set it."

"I've got people on the way. *Times* car. Give them everything you have. Wait outside on Fifth Street. You stay there, Lizzie, don't you move."

They followed the others out of the children's room, people moving steadily but nervously across the main room and down the stairs, bumping a little more than they meant to do, in a hurry but not a panic, handkerchiefs still out as breathing was hard in the acrid air. Kenny was carrying Eric, Cal, little Maggie.

The shrill scream of the fire alarm merged with the sirens of the fire engines as they reached the ground floor, were swept out the door by twos and onto the sidewalk. They crossed the street while Lizzie searched for the *Times*'s car. Lots of smoke but no flames—fire still trapped inside, feeding on books from across the ages, seeking nourishment to break out. The crowd stood stunned, quiet, awed by the uncontrolled brutality of fire, listening, watching, glass shattering, wood cracking, timbers falling, sirens, smoke pouring out, fire finally making it through broken windows, flames licking out, desperate for oxygen.

They stood together, holding hands. Three women, two men, two children, one extended family.

Cal put his arms around the sisters, who each held a child by the hand. "Fitting end to the Mull story," he said, softly. Dominique watched him, wondering.

Lizzie turned to him. "Meaning?"

"Starts in water . . . ends in fire."

She looked down at the children, smiling at little Maggie and squeezing her hand.

"Ends? Won't that depend on what these two have to say about it?"

CODA

They caught the blond man, a compulsive liar and exhibitionist named Harry Peak. He was arrested, but never charged, though there wasn't much doubt that he did it. He'd told friends about it. Lizzie could not identify him. The boy she'd seen had long hair. Harry had short hair. Detectives found his barber. Only one other person had noticed him that day, and she wasn't sure either. It was mere coincidence that Harry picked the day of her reading to set the fire. Nothing personal. Didn't know a thing about the Mulls.

Harry sued the city for $15 million for false arrest. The city counter-sued for $23 million, the estimated value of the lost property. He was paid $35,000 in a settlement. More than a million books were consumed, priceless ancient monographs to contemporary pulp. Fire didn't know the difference. The library stayed closed for seven years. Harry didn't have time to enjoy his money. He died of AIDs. Life returned to Los Angeles normal.

Westport Beach Club, 1938, looking north toward Venice oil fields.

ACKNOWLEDGMENTS

I will start with my parents, who had the good sense in 1945 to head west. We'd been an eastern family up to then. I was eight years old and about to discover the greatest place in the world. We lived at the beach. There was only one freeway, the Pasadena. I rode the trolley downtown and to Venice and Ocean Park. I fell in love with Los Angeles.

As for writing, the first tip of the hat would be to Charles McCabe of the *San Francisco Chronicle*, the "Fearless Spectator," who helped me land my first newspaper job in that once great newspaper city, although I was completely unqualified. Next would be Sandy Zalburg, city editor at the *Honolulu Advertiser*, who taught me how to write. Years after I left Honolulu in a huff, Zalburg, spying an article of mine in the *New York Times Magazine*, wrote to me as follows: "Enfin, I said to myself, the twit is learning how to write tersely. Mazel tov." Other fine editors along the way who helped: Henry Bradshaw and Larry McManus in San Francisco, Buddy Weiss and George Bates in Paris, James Chace in New York. A writer's education never stops.

The road from newspapers to fiction is a bumpy one. After years of suppressing opinion and imagination—just the facts, ma'am—you suddenly face blank pages demanding opinion and imagination. You meet new kinds of editors, ones less concerned with writing tersely than with telling a good story. I was fortunate to find editors like George Walsh at Macmillan, Sheryl and Harold Maguire at the Local History Company, David Wilk at Prospecta Press, and literary agents like Tom Wallace.

Beyond editors, acknowledgment is owed to colleagues, mentors, supporters, people who helped smooth the path. I would single out Bill Bundy at *Foreign Affairs*, Flora Lewis at the *New York Times*, Tom Hughes at the Carnegie Endowment, Don Cook and Chuck Champlin at the *Los Angeles Times*, Neil Morgan at the *San Diego Tribune*, people willing to take a certain risk, believing it would all work out in the end.

They were right. This story, my story, the story of twentieth century Los Angeles, owes something to all of them. As for relatives and friends, I would single out my sister, Carol, who had to take three buses to Marlborough School after they junked the trolleys; my brother, Bill, who was only two years old when we hit the coast and thus regards himself as a true native; and Bobby Taylor, who first showed me how to explore the Ballona wetlands in a raft.